Steve Perry

D0027913

BANTAM BOOKS
New York   Toronto   London   Sydney   Auckland

This edition contains the complete text of the original hardcover edition. NOT ONE WORD HAS BEEN OMITTED.

STAR WARS: SHADOWS OF THE EMPIRE
A Bantam Spectra Book

PUBLISHING HISTORY
Bantam hardcover edition published May 1996
Bantam mass market edition / April 1997

ISBN 0-553-57413-2

Published simultaneously in the United States and Canada

PRINTED IN THE UNITED STATES OF AMERICA

OPM 10 9 8 7 6 5 4 3 2 1

Rave reviews for previous
Star Wars® adventures:

HEIR TO THE EMPIRE
by Timothy Zahn

"CHOCK FULL OF ALL THE GOOD STUFF YOU'VE COME TO EXPECT FROM A BATTLE OF GOOD AGAINST EVIL."
—*Daily News,* New York

"MOVES WITH A SPEED-OF-LIGHT PACE THAT CAPTURES THE SPIRIT OF THE MOVIE TRILOGY SO WELL, YOU CAN ALMOST HEAR JOHN WILLIAMS'S SOUNDTRACK."
—*The Providence Sunday Journal*

DARK FORCE RISING
by Timothy Zahn

"CONTINUES [ZAHN'S] REMARKABLE EXTRAPOLATION FROM GEORGE LUCAS'S TRILOGY."
—*Chicago Sun-Times*

"ZAHN HAS PERFECTLY CAPTURED THE PACE AND FLAVOR OF THE *STAR WARS* MOVIES. THIS IS SPACE OPERA AT ITS BEST."
—*The Sunday Oklahoman*

THE JEDI ACADEMY TRILOGY
by Kevin J. Anderson

"ANDERSON HAS ALL BUT ASSUMED THE TITLE OF CHANCELLOR OF *STAR WARS* UNIVERSITY."
—*Starlog*

"DEFTLY PUTS THE *STAR WARS* CHARACTERS THROUGH THEIR PACES WITH NEVER A SLIP, AND WITH NEVER A DULL MOMENT."
—*The Sunday Oregonian,* Portland

Other books in the *Star Wars*® series:

X-WING by Michael A. Stackpole
Book 1: *Rogue Squadron*
Book 2: *Wedge's Gamble*
Book 3: *The Krytos Trap*
Book 4: *The Bacta War*

THE BLACK FLEET CRISIS by
Michael P. Kube-McDowell
Book 1: *Before the Storm*
Book 2: *Shield of Lies*
Book 3: *Tyrant's Test*

The Truce at Bakura by Kathy Tyers
Tales from the Mos Eisley Cantina edited by
Kevin J. Anderson
Tales from Jabba's Palace edited by Kevin J. Anderson
Children of the Jedi by Barbara Hambly
Darksaber by Kevin J. Anderson

And in hardcover:
The New Rebellion by Kristine Kathryn Rusch
The Illustrated Star Wars *Universe* by Ralph McQuarrie
and Kevin J. Anderson

For DIANNE;
and for
Tom "Mississippi" Dupree,
who put me in the rotation and
thus let me get a chance to bat.

Acknowledgments

I could not have written a book set in such a wonderfully rich and complex universe as this all by myself. I had help, lots of it, and I owe thanks to many people. You should know who they are. My apologies to any I might have missed, and the usual caveat applies: If I screwed up their input, it is my fault and not theirs. If you are a fan of the books, comics, games, or movies, you'll probably recognize some of these names.

My gratitude goes to: Tom Dupree; Howard Roffman, Lucy Wilson, Sue Rostoni, and Allan Kausch; Jon Knoles, Steve Dauterman, and Larry Holland; Bill Slavicsek; Bill Smith; Mike Richardson, Ryder Windham, Kilian Plunkett, and John Wagner; Timothy Zahn, Kevin J. Anderson, and Rebecca Moesta; Jean Naggar; Dianne, Danelle, and Dal Perry; Cady Jo Ivy and Roxanne de Bergerac. I'd also like to thank the fans in the Star Wars Forum on America Online—I got some great ideas as I lurked and listened there. And last but certainly not least, thanks to the man who dreamed up, then built this absolutely terrific toy in the first place: George Lucas.

Appreciate it, gang. Really.

"Face it, if crime did not pay,
there would be very few criminals."

LAUGHTON LEWIS BURDOCK

Prologue

He looks like a walking corpse, Xizor thought. *Like a mummified body dead a thousand years. Amazing he is still alive, much less the most powerful man in the galaxy. He isn't even that old; it is more as if something is slowly eating him.*

Xizor stood four meters away from the Emperor, watching as the man who had long ago been Senator Palpatine moved to stand in the holocam field. He imagined he could smell the decay in the Emperor's worn body. Likely that was just some trick of the recycled air, run through dozens of filters to ensure that there was no chance of any poison gas being introduced into it. Filtered the life out of it, perhaps, giving it that dead smell.

The viewer on the other end of the holo-link would see a close-up of the Emperor's head and shoulders, of an age-ravaged face shrouded in the cowl of his dark zeyd-cloth robe. The man on the other end of the transmission, light-years away, would not see Xizor, though

Xizor would be able to see him. It was a measure of the Emperor's trust that Xizor was allowed to be here while the conversation took place.

The man on the other end of the transmission—if he could still be called that—

The air swirled inside the Imperial chamber in front of the Emperor, coalesced, and blossomed into the image of a figure down on one knee. A caped humanoid biped dressed in jet black, face hidden under a full helmet and breathing mask:

Darth Vader.

Vader spoke: "What is thy bidding, my master?"

If Xizor could have hurled a power bolt through time and space to strike Vader dead, he would have done it without blinking. Wishful thinking: Vader was too powerful to attack directly.

"There is a great disturbance in the Force," the Emperor said.

"I have felt it," Vader said.

"We have a new enemy. Luke Skywalker."

Skywalker? That had been Vader's name, a long time ago. Who was this person with the same name, someone so powerful as to be worth a conversation between the Emperor and his most loathsome creation? More importantly, why had Xizor's agents not uncovered this before now? Xizor's ire was instant—but cold. No sign of his surprise or anger would show on his imperturbable features. The Falleen did not allow their emotions to burst forth as did many of the inferior species; no, the Falleen ancestry was not fur but scales, not mammalian but reptilian. Not wild but coolly calculating. Such was much better. Much safer.

"Yes, my master," Vader continued.

"He could destroy us," the Emperor said.

Xizor's attention was riveted upon the Emperor and the holographic image of Vader kneeling on the deck of a ship far away. Here was interesting news indeed.

Something the Emperor perceived as a danger to himself? Something the Emperor feared?

"He's just a boy," Vader said, "Obi-Wan can no longer help him."

Obi-Wan. That name Xizor knew. He was among the last of the Jedi Knights, a general. But he'd been dead for decades, hadn't he?

Apparently Xizor's information was wrong if Obi-Wan had been helping someone who was still a boy. His agents were going to be sorry.

Even as Xizor took in the distant image of Vader and the nearness of the Emperor, even as he was aware of the luxury of the Emperor's private and protected chamber at the core of the giant pyramidal palace, he was also able to make a mental note to himself: Somebody's head would roll for the failure to make him aware of all this. Knowledge was power; lack of knowledge was weakness. This was something he could not permit.

The Emperor continued. "The Force is strong with him. The son of Skywalker must not become a Jedi."

Son of Skywalker?

Vader's son! Amazing!

"If he could be turned he would become a powerful ally," Vader said.

There was something in Vader's voice when he said this, something Xizor could not quite put his finger on. Longing? Worry?

Hope?

"Yes . . . yes. He would be a great asset," the Emperor said. "Can it be done?"

There was the briefest of pauses. "He will join us or die, Master."

Xizor felt the smile, though he did not allow it to show any more than he had allowed his anger play. Ah. Vader wanted Skywalker alive, *that* was what had been in his tone. Yes, he had said that the boy would join them or die, but this latter part was obviously meant only to placate the Emperor. Vader had no intention of killing Skywalker, his own son; that was obvious to one as skilled in reading voices as was Xizor. He had not gotten to be the Dark Prince, Underlord of Black Sun, the largest criminal organization in the galaxy, merely on his formidable good looks. Xizor didn't truly understand the Force that sustained the Emperor and made him and Vader so powerful, save to know that it certainly worked somehow. But he did know that it was something the extinct Jedi had supposedly mastered. And now, apparently, this new player had tapped into it. Vader wanted Skywalker alive, had practically promised the Emperor that he would deliver him alive—and converted.

This was most interesting.

Most interesting indeed.

The Emperor finished his communication and turned back to face him. "Now, where were we, Prince Xizor?"

The Dark Prince smiled. He would attend to the business at hand, but he would not forget the name of Luke Skywalker.

1

Chewbacca roared his rage. A stormtrooper grabbed at him and he knocked the man flying, armor clattering as he fell into the pit. Two more guards came in, and the Wookiee battered them both aside as if they were nothing, a child tossing dolls around—

In another second one of Vader's troops would shoot Chewie. He was big and strong, but he couldn't win; they'd cut him down—

Han started yelling at the Wookiee, calming him.

Leia stared, unable to move, unable to believe this was happening.

Han kept talking: "Chewie, there'll be another time! The princess, you have to take care of her. D'you hear me? Huh?"

They were in a dank chamber in the bowels of Cloud City on Bespin, where Han's so-called friend Lando Calrissian had betrayed them to Darth Vader. The scene was bathed in a buttery golden light that made it seem even more surreal. Chewbacca blinked at

Han, the half-assembled droid Threepio jutting from a sack on the Wookiee's back. The traitor Calrissian stood off to one side like some feral creature. There were more guards, techs, bounty hunters. Vader and the stink of liquid carbonite permeated the air around them all, a smell of morgues and graves combined.

More guards moved in, to put cuffs on Chewie. The Wookiee nodded, calmer. Yes, he understood Han. He didn't like it, but he understood. He allowed the guards to cuff him—

Han and Leia looked at each other. *This can't be happening*, she thought. *Not now*.

The emotion took them; neither could resist it. They came together like magnets, held each other. They embraced, kissed, full of fire and hope—full of ashes and despair—

Two stormtroopers jerked Han away, backed him onto the liftplate over the makeshift freezing chamber.

The words erupted from Leia unbidden, uncontrollable, lava blasted from a volcanic explosion: "I love you!"

And Han, brave, strong Han, nodded at her. "I know."

The Ugnaught techs, not much more than half Han's height, moved in, unbound his hands, stepped away.

Han looked at the techs, then at Leia again. The liftplate sank, lowered him into the pit. He locked his gaze with Leia's, held it, held it . . . until the cloud of freezing vapor boiled up and blocked their view—

Chewie yelled; Leia didn't understand his speech, but she understood his rage, his grief, his feeling of helplessness.

Han!

Stinking, acrid gas spewed up and rolled over them, an icy fog, a roiling soul-chilling smoke through which Leia saw Vader watching it all under his inscrutable mask. She heard Threepio sputter, "What—What's going on? Turn 'round! Chewbacca, I can't *see*!"

Han!
Oh, Han!

Leia sat up abruptly, her pulse racing. The sheets were sweaty and wadded around her, her night garment damp. She sighed, swung her legs over the side of the bed, and sat staring at the wall. The chronometer inset showed her it was three hours past midnight. The air in the room smelled stale. Outside, she knew, the Tatooine night would be chilly, and she considered opening a vent to allow some of that coolness inside. At the moment, it seemed too much effort to bother.

A bad dream, she thought. *That's all it was.*

But—no. She couldn't pretend it had been only a nightmare. It had been more than that. It was a memory. It had happened. The man she loved was embedded in a block of carbonite, had been hauled away like a crate of cargo by a bounty hunter. Lost to her, somewhere in the vastness of the galaxy.

She felt the emotions well, felt them threaten to spill out in tears, but she fought it. She was Leia Organa, Princess of the Royal Family of Alderaan, elected to the Imperial Senate, a worker in the Alliance to Restore the Republic. Alderaan was gone, destroyed by Vader and the Death Star; the Imperial Senate was disbanded; the Alliance was outmanned and outgunned ten thousand to one, but she was who she was. She would not cry.

She would not cry.

She would get even.

Three hours past midnight, and half the planet slept.

Luke Skywalker stood barefoot on the steelcrete platform sixty meters above the sand, looking at the taut wire. He wore plain black pants and shirt and a black leather belt. He no longer had a lightsaber, though he'd started constructing another one, using the plans he'd found in an old leather-bound book at Ben Kenobi's. It was a traditional exercise for a Jedi, so he'd been told. It had given him something to do while his new hand had finished final bonding to his arm. It had kept him from thinking too much.

The lights under the canopy were dim; he could barely see the stranded-steel line. The carnival was done for the night, the acrobats and dewbacks and jesters long asleep. The crowds had gone home, and he was alone; alone here with the tightrope. It was quiet, the only sound the creak of the syn tent fabric as it cooled in the arms of the Tatooine summer night. The hot desert day gave up its heat quickly, and it was cold enough outside the tent to need a jacket. The smell of the dewbacks drifted up to where he perched, and mingled with that of his own sweat.

A guard whose mind had accepted Luke's mental command to allow him inside the giant tent stood watch at the entrance, blind now to his presence. A Jedi skill, that kind of control, but another one he had only begun to learn.

Luke took a deep breath, let it out slowly. There was no net below, and a fall from this height would surely be fatal. He didn't have to do this. Nobody was going to make him take the walk.

Nobody but himself.

He calmed his breathing, his heartbeat, and, as much as possible, his mind, using the method he had learned. First Ben, then Master Yoda had taught him the ancient arts. Yoda's exercises had been the more rigorous and exhausting, but unfortunately, Luke had not finished his schooling. There really hadn't been any choice at the time. Han and Leia had been in deadly danger, and he'd had to go to them. Because he had gone, they were alive, but . . .

That hadn't turned out well.

No. Not at all.

And there had been the meeting with Vader . . .

He felt his face tighten, his jaw muscles dance, and he fought the anger that surged up in him like a hormonal tide as black as the clothes he wore. His wrist ached suddenly where Vader's lightsaber had sliced through it. The new hand was as good as the old, better, maybe, but sometimes when he thought about Vader, it throbbed. Phantom limb pain, the medics had said. Not real.

"I'm your father."

No! That couldn't be real, either! His father had been Anakin Skywalker, a Jedi.

If only he could talk to Ben. Or to Yoda. They would confirm it. They would tell him the truth. Vader had tried to manipulate him, had tried to throw him off balance, that was all.

But—what if it was true . . . ?

No. Leave it. It wouldn't help to dwell on that now. He wasn't going to be able to do anybody any good unless he mastered his Jedi skills. He had to trust in the Force and move on. No matter what lies Vader had spewed. There was a war on, much to do, and while he was a good pilot, he was supposed to have more to offer to the Alliance.

It wasn't easy, and it didn't seem to be *getting* any easier. He wished he felt sure of himself, but the fact was, he didn't. He felt as if a weight were riding on him, more than he'd ever thought possible. A few years ago, he'd been a farm boy, working with Uncle Owen, going nowhere. Now there was Han, the Empire, the Alliance, Vader—

No. Not now. That's in the past and in the future, this wire *is the* now. *Concentrate or you're going to fall off it.*

He reached for the energy, felt the flux begin to flow. It was bright and warm and life-giving, and he called it to himself, sought to wrap it around his form like a suit of armor.

The Force: Once again, it was there for him. Yes . . .

But there was something else there, too. In a place that was removed but somehow right next to him, he felt that pull he had been told about. A hard, powerful coldness, the opposite of what his teachers had presented to him. The antithesis of light. That which Vader embraced.

The dark side.

No! He pushed it away. Refused to look at it. Took another deep breath. Felt the Force permeate him, felt it attune itself to him. Or maybe it was the other way around. It didn't matter.

When they were *one,* he started to walk.

The high wire suddenly seemed as wide as a public sidewalk. It was natural, the Force, but this part always felt like magic, as if he could do miracles using it. He'd seen Yoda raise the X-wing from the swamp using his mind. It was possible to do things that might look like miracles.

As he lifted his foot to take another step, he remembered other things about his time on Dagobah.

Under the soft, damp ground, in the cave . . .

Darth Vader came toward him.

Vader! Here! How could that be?

Luke pulled his lightsaber, lit it, brought it up. The gleaming blue white of his blade met Vader's reddish beam as they crossed in on-guard salute. The power hum and energy crackle grew louder.

Suddenly Vader swung, a powerful cut at Luke's left side—

Luke jerked his blade up and over, dropped the point, blocked the slash; it hit so hard it vibrated him, nearly tore his lightsaber from his grip—

He smelled the mold around him, heard the power hum of the lightsabers, saw Vader with a crystal clarity. All his senses came to life, as sharp as they'd ever been, sharp as a warehouse full of vibro-shivs—

Vader cut again, now at Luke's head, and Luke's panicked overhead block barely stopped it, barely—he was so strong!

Again Vader chopped at him, a blow that would have cut Luke in half had he not jammed his own weapon out, just in time!

Vader was too strong for him, Luke knew. Only his anger could save him from being killed. He remembered Ben, remembered Vader hacking him down—

Unthinking rage drove him. Luke whipped his blade around backhanded, all of his arm and shoulder and wrists behind it, and—

The cut took Vader's head off.

Time seemed to drag like some heavy anchor. He stared. Vader's body dropped, oh-so-slowly . . . and the severed head fell to the ground and rolled.

Rolled. Then stopped. There was no blood—

There came a bright flash, a sudden blast of light and purple smoke, and the mask covering Vader's face shattered, shattered and vanished, revealing, revealing—

The face of Luke Skywalker.

No!

The insurgent memory had flashed by much faster than the events had actually taken. He had moved but a single step in reality. Amazing what one's mind could do. Even so, he nearly fell from the wire as he lost contact with the Force.

Stop this! he told himself.

He took a deep breath, balanced uneasily, reached for the Force again.

There, he had it. He steadied, started walking, one with the Force again, flowing.

Halfway across the wire, he started to run. He told himself it was part of the test. He told himself that the Force was with him and he could live up to his name without fear, that anything was possible to one trained as a Jedi Knight. It was what he had been taught. He wanted to believe it.

He didn't want to believe that he ran because he could feel the dark side walking the wire behind him, catfooted and evil, following him. Following like the memory of his face on Vader's severed head, following and—

—and gaining . . .

Xizor leaned back in his form-chair. The chair, which had a bad circuit he kept meaning to have repaired, took this move as an inquiry. Its voxchip said, "What is your wish, Prince Sheeezor?" It slurred his name, dragging out the first syllable. He shook his head. "Nothing save that you be silent," he said.

The chair's vox shut up. The machineries within the cloned leather seat hummed and adjusted the support to Xizor's new position. He sighed. He was rich beyond the income of many entire planets, and he had a malfunctioning form-chair that couldn't even pronounce his name correctly. He made a note to have it replaced, now, today, immediately, as soon as he was finished with his business here this morning.

He looked at the one-sixth-scale holoproj frozen in front of him, then up at the woman standing across the desk. She was as beautiful, if not as ethnic, as the two Epicanthix women fighters in the holograph between them. But her beauty was of a different order. She had long and silky blond hair, pale and clear blue eyes, an exquisite figure. Normal human males would find her attractive. There were no flaws in Guri's face or form, but there was a coolness about her, and that was easily explained if you knew the reason: Guri was an HRD, a human replica droid, and unique. She could visually pass for a woman anywhere in the galaxy, could eat, drink, and perform all of the more personal functions of a woman without anybody the wiser. And she was the only one of her kind programmed to be an assassin. She could kill without raising her ersatz heartbeat, never a qualm of conscience.

She'd cost him nine million credits.

Xizor steepled his fingers and raised an eyebrow at Guri.

"The Pike sisters," Guri said, glancing at the holo. "Genetic twins, not clones. The one on the right is Zan, the other is Zu. Zan has green eyes, Zu has one green and one blue eye, the only noticeable difference. They are masters of *teräs käsi*, the Bunduki art called 'steel hands.' Twenty-six standard years old, no political affiliations, no criminal records in any of the major systems, and, as far as we are able to determine, completely amoral. They are for hire to the highest bidder, and they have never worked for Black Sun. They have also never been defeated in open combat. This"— she nodded at the unmoving holoproj image again—"is what they do for fun when they aren't working." Guri's voice was, in contrast to her appearance, warm, inviting, a rich alto. She activated the hologram.

Xizor smiled, revealing his own perfect teeth. The holo had shown the two women mopping the floor with eight Imperial stormtroopers in some rat's nest of a spaceport bar. The soldiers had been big, strong, well trained, and armed. The women weren't even breathing hard when they finished. "They'll do," he said. "Make it happen."

Guri nodded once, turned, and left. She looked as good from behind as she did from the front.

Nine million and worth every decicred. He wished he had a dozen more like her. Unfortunately, her creator was no longer among the living. A pity.

So. Two more handpicked assassins now under his command. Assassins with no ties to Black Sun, not before and, with Guri's expert manipulation, not ever.

Xizor glanced up at the ceiling. He'd had the pattern of the galaxy installed into the glowtiles. When the lights were dim—and they usually were—he had an edge-on view of the home galaxy floating holographically there, with more than a million individual glowing dust-small stars hand-drawn in it. It had taken the artist three months and had cost a warlord's ransom, but the Dark Prince could not spend what he already had even if he tried hard, and more than that kept flowing in all the time. Credits were nothing; he had billions. A way of keeping score, that was all. Not important.

He looked at the holograph again. Beautiful and deadly, these two, a combination he enjoyed. He himself was of the Falleen, a species whose distant ancestors had been reptilian, and who had evolved into what was generally considered the most beautiful of all humanoid species. He was over a hundred years old, but he looked thirty. He was tall, had a topknot ponytail jutting up from his otherwise bald head and a hard body crafted by stim units. He also exuded natural pheromones that made most of the human-stock species feel instantly attracted to him, and his skin color, normally a dusky green, changed with the rise of those pheromones, shading from the cool into the warm spectrum. His handsomeness and appeal were tools, nothing more. He was the Dark Prince, Underlord of Black Sun, one of the three most powerful men in the galaxy. He could also kick a sunfruit off the top of a tall humanoid's head without a warm-up stretch, and he could lift twice his own weight over his head using only his own muscles. He could claim a sound—if admittedly devious—mind in a sound body.

His galactic influence was surpassed only by the Emperor and the Dark Lord of the Sith, Darth Vader.

He smiled at the image before him again. Third—but about to become second, if his plans went as intended. It had been months since he'd overheard the Emperor and Vader talking of a threat they'd perceived, months, and now the preliminaries were done. Xizor was ready to move in earnest.

"Time?" he said.

His room computer answered and gave it to him.

Ah. Only an hour remained before his meeting. It was but a short walk through the protected corridors to Vader's, not much beyond where the Emperor's massive gray-green stone and mirror-crystal palace thrust itself up into the high atmosphere. A few kilometers, no more; a brisk stroll would put him there in a few minutes. No hurry. He did not want to arrive early.

A chime announced a visitor.

"Enter," Xizor said. His bodyguards were not here, but there was no need for them in his sanctum—no one could penetrate its defenses. And only a few of his underlings had the right to visit him here, all of them loyal. As loyal as fear could make them.

One of his sublieutenants, Mayth Duvel, came in and bowed low. "My prince Xizor."

"Yes?"

"I have a petition from the Nezriti Organization. They wish an alliance with Black Sun."

Xizor gave Duvel a measured smile. "I'm sure they do."

Duvel produced a small package. "They offer a token of their esteem."

Xizor took the package, thumbed it open. Inside was a gem. It was an oval-cut, bloodred Tumanian pressure-ruby, a very rare stone, apparently flawless, and easily worth several million credits. The Dark Prince held it up, turned it in his fingers, nodded. Then he tossed it onto his desktop. It bounced once, slid to a stop next to his drinking cup. If it had fallen onto the floor, he would not have bent to retrieve it, and if the cleaning droid came in later and sucked it up, well, so what? "Tell them we'll consider it."

Duvel bowed and backed away.

When he was gone, Xizor stood, stretched his neck

and back. The evolved reptilian ridge over his spine elevated slightly, felt sharp against his fingertips as he rubbed it. There were other applicants waiting to see him, and ordinarily he would sit and attend to their petitions, but not today. Now it was time to go and see Vader. By going there instead of insisting that Vader come here, he was giving away an advantage, appearing to be himself a supplicant. No matter. That was part of it; there must not seem to be any contention between them. No one must suspect that he felt anything but the greatest respect for the Dark Lord of the Sith, not if his plans were going to succeed. And succeed they would, he did not doubt it.

Because they always did.

2

Leia sat in a bad cantina in the bad part of Mos Eisley. You really had to work at it to earn both of those low distinctions. Calling this place a dive would have elevated it four notches. The table was expanded metal, aluminum plate turned into a cheap and easy-to-clean mesh—probably they used a high-pressure solvent hose to wash everything into that drain in the middle of a sunken spot over there in the floor. If they opened the door to the arid outside, it would dry in a hurry. The cup of whatever vile brew it was she had in front of her was certainly losing more liquid to evaporation than to her drinking from it. The air refreshing system must have had a bad circuit—the place was hot, the desert air outside seeping in along with the gutter scum who came to hang out here. It smelled like a bantha stable in the hot summer, and the only good thing about the place was that the light was dim enough so she didn't have to look too closely at the patrons—from a dozen different species and none of them particularly savory-looking examples at that.

Lando must have done it on purpose, picking this pit in which to meet, just to get a rise out of her. Well. When he finally arrived, she wouldn't give him the satisfaction. For a time, she'd hated him, until she understood his apparent betrayal of Han had only been a ruse to help save them from Vader. Lando had given up a lot for that, and they all owed him for it.

Still, this wasn't a bar she would have gone into without a good reason—a *very* good reason—and not a place she would have gone alone, despite her protests that she didn't need a bodyguard. But need one or not, she had one—Chewbacca sat next to her, glowering at the assorted patrons. The only reason Chewie had left her with Luke after the last encounter with Vader was to go with Lando to Tatooine to set up Han's rescue. Once Leia had arrived, Chewie had stayed as close to her as part of her wardrobe. It was irritating.

Lando had explained it: "Chewie owes Han a life debt. That's a big deal among Wookiees. Han told him to take care of you. Until Han tells him otherwise, that's what he's going to do."

Leia had tried to be firm. She told Chewie, "I appreciate it, but you don't have to."

It was no use, Lando told her. As long as he was alive, Chewbacca was going to be with her, and that was that. She didn't even speak Wookiee, save for a couple of swear words she thought she recognized, but Lando had smiled and told her she might as well get used to it.

She almost had, after a fashion. Chewie could understand a number of languages, and while he couldn't speak them, he could usually make known what he wanted somebody to know.

Leia liked Chewie okay, but here was another reason to find and free Han—so he could call the Wookiee off.

Then again, even though she would never admit it, there were times when having a two-meter-tall Wookiee around was useful. Such as in this wonderful place.

During the last hour, she'd had to look a little closer at several of the patrons than she liked. Despite the fact that she wore old and threadbare freight handler's coveralls spotted and stained with lube, had her hair wound into a tight and unattractive bun, and did not meet anyone's gaze, there had been a steady parade of various humans and aliens to her table, trying to pick her up—also despite the fact that a fully grown and armed Wookiee sat at the same table.

Males. Didn't seem to matter what species they were when they wanted female company. And it didn't seem to matter what species the female was, either.

Chewie made it clear they weren't welcome, and between his size and bowcaster, nobody much wanted to argue the point. But new ones kept coming.

Chewie growled at a bulbous-headed Bith who banged into the table. The alien, whose species was normally well behaved and peaceful, had obviously had way too much to drink, if he would even think it possible that he and Leia could find anything in common. The Bith looked at Chewie's bared teeth, hiccuped, then tottered off.

Leia said, "Look, I appreciate your help, but I can handle these guys."

Chewie turned his head to one side and regarded her, a gesture she was coming to realize meant skepticism and amusement mixed about equally.

She took it as a challenge. "Hey, next time somebody comes over, just watch me. You can do it without threats, you know."

It didn't take long. The next pest in the rotation was a Devaronian, a horned humanoid who—surprise—wanted to buy Leia a drink.

"Thank you, but I'm waiting for somebody."

The Devaronian said, "Well, why don't I keep you company until they get here? Perhaps they were delayed? It might be a long wait."

"Thank you, but I have company." She nodded at Chewie.

The alien ignored the gesture and, since the Wookiee didn't speak or point his weapon, kept right on talking.

"I'm really quite pleasant to have around, you know. Many fems have thought so. Many." He leered at her, his pointed teeth looking particularly white against his red lips. Shot his tongue out and sucked it back in; it was as long as her forearm.

Spare me, Leia thought. So much for the easy way.

"No. Go away."

"You don't know what you are missing, little one." His leer grew wider, making him look more demonic.

She glanced at Chewie, who was about to start laughing, she could tell. She glared at the Devaronian.

"I'll try to get over it. Leave."

"Just one drink. And I can show you my Weranian holocards; they are very, ah . . . stimulating."

He started to sit across from her.

Leia pulled the small blaster she had tucked into her coverall pocket, brought it out over the table where the Devaronian could see it. She pointed it at the ceiling and thumbed the power setting button from "stun" to "kill."

He saw that, too.

Very quickly he said, "Ah, well, perhaps another time. I, ah, just recalled that, ah, I left the converter charging on my ship. You'll excuse me."

He hurried away. Amazing what waving a blaster under an obnoxious would-be suitor's nose would do to improve his manners.

Chewie did laugh now. Said something, and she had a pretty good idea of what it meant.

"Nobody likes an obnoxious Wookiee," she said.

But she smiled. That point went to Chewie, and she was woman enough to admit it.

She put the safety on and tucked the blaster away. Fiddled with the stir stick in her drink. Lando was going to pay for calling the meeting in this hole. Somehow.

Somebody opened the door and a flash of hot light spilled into the dank bar. Outlined in the doorway was a human who, for just a second, reminded her of Han. *Han.*

She felt the grief start to well in her again, and she shook her head, as if that could stop the emotions from flowing. The last time she had seen Han Solo, he had been frozen in a block of carbonite. The last thing he had said to her was an answer: "I know."

Leia sighed. She hadn't really known until that moment that she loved him. When she saw Vader order him lowered into the freezing chamber, when she knew there was a chance he might not come out alive, she'd had to say it. It had come out of her unbidden, it had seemed as if the words had been spoken by another woman. It had been so . . . unreal.

But she couldn't deny it. Not then, not now. She did love him, pirate and rogue that he was. There was no help for it.

That feeling scared her more than anything she could think of. More than when she'd been in Vader's hands on the Death Star, more than when it seemed half the Imperial Army and Navy had been after them—

"Buy you a drink, beautiful?" somebody said from behind her.

Leia turned. It was Lando. She was angry at him, but glad to see him, too. "How'd you get in here?"

"Back door," Lando said. He smiled. He was a handsome man—tall, dark-skinned, a thin mustache above those shiny white teeth—and he knew it, too.

Behind him were the droids R2-D2 and C-3PO.

Artoo's dome swiveled as the droid took in the bar, and Threepio, the most skittish droid Leia had ever been around, managed to look nervous even though he could not change his facial expression.

Artoo whistled.

"Yes, I see that," Threepio said. A short pause. "Master Lando, wouldn't it be better if we waited outside? I don't think they like droids in this place. We're the only ones here."

Lando smiled. "Relax. Nobody is going to bother you. I know the owner. Besides, I don't want you alone outside. You might find this hard to believe, but this town is full of *thieves.*" He opened his eyes wide in mock amazement and waved his hands to take in the bar and the port around it. "You wouldn't want to wind up shoveling sand on some moisture farm, now would you?"

"Oh, dear me, no."

Leia smiled, unable to help herself. What a band of characters she'd wound up with. Two funny droids, Lando Calrissian the gambler, Chewbacca the Wookiee, Luke the—

What was Luke? Halfway to becoming a Jedi, at least. And awfully important, given how badly Darth Vader seemed to want him. She'd heard other rumors, too, that Vader wasn't particular how he got Luke, alive or dead. She loved Han, but she felt something for Luke, too.

Another complication she did not need. Why wasn't life simpler?

And Han . . .

"I think we've got *Slave I* spotted," Lando said quietly.

That was Boba Fett's ship. The bounty hunter who had taken Han from Cloud City. "What? Where?"

"A moon called Gall, circling Zhar, a gas giant out in one of the far Rim Systems. The information is thirdhand, but the informant chain is supposed to be reliable."

"We've heard *that* before," she said.

Lando shrugged. "We can sit and wait or we can go see. The bounty hunter should have delivered Han to Jabba months ago. He's got to be someplace. I've got a contact in that system, an old gambling buddy who does a little, uh, freelance cargo delivery. Name is Dash Rendar. He's checking it out for us."

Leia smiled again. "Freelance cargo delivery" was a euphemism for "smuggling."

"You trust him?"

"Well, as long as my money holds out, yeah."

"Fine. How soon will we know?"

"A few days."

Leia looked around. "Anything would be better than waiting here."

Lando flashed his bright smile again. "Mos Eisley is known as the galaxy's armpit," he said. "I guess there are worse parts of the anatomy where we could be stuck."

Chewie said something.

Lando shook his head. "I don't know why he'd be there. There's a shipyard on the moon; maybe he needed repairs. Something serious had to hold him up because Jabba won't pay him until he gets here."

Chewie said something else.

"Yeah, I'm afraid so." Lando looked at Leia. "Gall is an Imperial Enclave. Got a couple of destroyers based there, plus all the attendant TIE fighters. If Fett's ship is there, it won't be easy to get to him."

"When has anything been easy since I met you?" she said. "Let me ask you something. Of all the crummy places in this port, why did you choose this one?"

"Well, I *do* know the owner. He owes me for a bet we once made. I get to eat and drink here for free whenever I'm in town."

"Oh, boy. What a thrill that must be. You ever try to eat anything in this place?"

"I haven't been that hungry yet, no."

She shook her head. Her life had certainly been interesting since she'd fallen in with these guys. But it was like Lando had just said about Boba Fett: Everybody had to be someplace.

Until they found Han, this was as good as any.

Leia said, "Maybe we better go tell Luke."

Xizor left his four bodyguards in the antechamber and went into Darth Vader's personal meeting room. The guards were trained in half a dozen forms of hand-to-hand combat, each armed with a blaster and each an expert shot; still, if Vader wanted to harm him, it wouldn't matter if he took four or forty men with him. The mysterious Force would let Vader block a fired blaster bolt with his lightsaber or his hands, and he could kill with a gesture, could freeze your lungs or stop your heart, just like that. It was a lesson many had learned the hard way: One did not stand toe-to-toe with Darth Vader and challenge him directly.

Fortunately, Xizor enjoyed the Emperor's patronage. As long as that was the case, Vader would not dare harm him.

The room was spare. A long table of polished, dark greel wood, several nonreactive chairs made from the same kind of wood, a holoplate and viewer. A faint tang of something spicy hung in the air. There were no pictures on the walls, no conspicuous signs of the wealth Vader commanded. He was nearly as rich as Xizor and, like the Dark Prince, cared little for wealth itself.

Xizor pulled one of the chairs away from the table and sat, allowing himself to appear completely relaxed, legs stretched out in front of him, leaning back. Somewhere in Vader's castle monitoring technicians would be watching every move he made, recording it all. Xizor knew that Vader's spies followed him everywhere he went, on- or offplanet; here in the dark heart of the serpent's nest itself, there could be no doubt that his slightest gesture would be watched and analyzed. If Vader wished it, he could likely know how much air Xizor breathed, the volume, weight, and composition of that air, the percent of carbon dioxide in the residue.

Xizor allowed himself a tight grin. Give the techs something to think about: *Uh-oh, he's smiling—what do you suppose that means?*

Of course, he had Vader under constant surveillance, too, every time he set foot outside his castle. On Coruscant—yes, it had been renamed the Imperial Center, but Xizor did not care for the new name—virtually everyone of any importance had his or her own spynet keeping track of all the other people of importance. It was necessary. And Black Sun's spynet was second to none, not even the Empire's own. Well. Perhaps the Bothans were slightly better . . .

The wall at the opposite end of the room slid aside silently, and Vader stood there, quite dramatic in his cape and black uniform, his breathing audible inside the armored helmet and mask.

Xizor stood, offered a military bow. "Lord Vader."

"Prince Xizor," Vader offered in return. No bow—he bent the knee only to the Emperor—but Xizor did not acknowledge the small breach of etiquette. This was all being recorded. The recording might find its way before the Emperor—in fact, Xizor would be greatly surprised if it did *not* come under the Emperor's scrutiny; the old man was not one to let much get past him. Instead, Xizor intended to be the soul of grace, the epitome of politeness, the acme of good manners.

"You asked to see me, Lord Vader. How may I be of service to you?"

Vader stepped into the room, and the door slid shut

behind him. He made no move to sit, no surprise.
Xizor also remained standing.

Vader said, "My master bids me to arrange for a
fleet of your cargo ships to deliver supplies to our bases
on the Rim."

"But of course," Xizor said. "My entire operation is
at your disposal; I am always happy to aid the Empire
in any way that I can."

Xizor's legitimate shipping operations were quite extensive, among the largest in the galaxy. Much of the
money from Black Sun's illicit activities had been fun-
neled into Xizor Transport Systems, and XTS alone
was enough to make him a wealthy and powerful man.

Vader was also aware that the holocams were upon
him. He made a comment for the record. "In the past,
it seems as if your company has been slow to respond
to Imperial requests."

"It embarrasses me to say that you are correct, Lord
Vader. Certain individuals who worked for me were
lax. However, those individuals are no longer employed by my company."

Point, counterpoint. Vader jabbed, carefully, using a
fine point, and Xizor parried. Each conversation he had
with the Dark Lord of the Sith was thus, an obvious
surface dialogue with much hidden in the depths below
it. It was a kind of fugue, in which each player tried to
score, like two brothers trying to outdo each other in
the eyes of a critical father.

Xizor did not consider Vader anything like a nest-
brother, however. The man was an impediment to be
removed and—though he did not know it—a mortal
enemy.

Ten years ago, Vader had a pet project, research on a
biological weapon. He established a hazard lab on
Xizor's home planet of Falleen. There had been an accident at the supposedly secure facility. A mutant tissue-
destroying bacterium somehow escaped quarantine. In
order to save the planet's population from a horrible,

rotting, always fatal infection for which there was no cure, the city around the lab had been "sterilized."

Sterilized, as in: baked, torched, seared, burned to cinders; houses, buildings, streets, parks—

And people.

Two hundred thousand Falleen had been killed by the sterilization lasers crisscrossing the doomed metropolis from orbit. The Empire counted itself lucky to have lost only that number when the necrotizing bacteria could have killed billions, maybe even escaped offworld to infect other planets. It had been a close call, but the cost had been relatively minor—in the opinion of the Empire.

In Darth Vader's opinion.

Among the dead had been Xizor's mother, father, brother, two sisters, and three uncles. He'd been offworld at the time, cementing his control of Black Sun into place; otherwise he would have been one of the victims himself.

He had never spoken of the tragedy. He had, through the offices of Black Sun, caused his family's deaths to be erased from Imperial records. The operatives who had done that deed had been themselves eliminated. Nobody knew that Xizor the Dark Prince had personal reasons to detest Darth Vader. It would be natural to see the two as rivals for the Emperor's favor, and there was no way to hide that, but of the other, no one save Xizor had any inkling.

He had been patient, Xizor had. It was never a question of "if," only a matter of "when" he would repay Vader in kind.

Now at last, revenge was in the making. Soon he would have it. He would spear two fleek-eels with the same trident: Vader the impediment to his power and Vader the killer of his family would both be . . . removed.

Xizor felt a smile but held it from observation by Vader and his hidden holocams' gazes. Killing the Dark

Lord might be possible but much too good for him—
and dangerous in the extreme. Dishonor and disgrace
were ever so much more painful at this level of existence. He would break Vader, would cause him to be
tossed upon the trash heap by his beloved master.

Yes. That would be justice—

"We shall need three hundred ships," Vader said,
cutting into Xizor's thoughts. "Half of them tankers,
half dry cargo transports. Standard Imperial delivery
contracts. There is a large . . . *construction* project of
which you are aware. Can you supply the vessels?"

"Yes, my lord. You need but tell me where and when
you desire them and I will make it so. And Imperial
terms are acceptable."

Vader stood silently for a moment, the only sound
the mechanical wheeze of his breathing.

He didn't expect that, Xizor thought. *He thought I
might argue or try to haggle over the price. Good.*

"Very well. I'll have the fleet supply admiral contact
you with details."

"It is my honor to serve," Xizor said. Again he gave
Vader a military bow, a bit lower and slower than before.

Anybody watching would see only how courteous
and eager to please Xizor was.

Without another word Vader turned. The wall slid
back again, and he swept from the room.

And anybody watching would see how close to the
edge of rudeness Lord Vader walked.

Again Xizor allowed himself a tiny smile.

Everything was going according to plan.

3

Luke stared at the little furnace, as if so doing could hurry the process. Inside, the ingredients for a lightsaber gem cooked at an incredible heat and pressure, hot enough to melt denscris, intense enough to collapse durasteel into a liquid ball. And yet from a meter away, except for the red operating diode, you couldn't tell the thing was even on. Well, except maybe for a little bit of a smell something like a blaster bolt, a kind of ozone odor.

The furnace had been working for hours and the little yellow diode had not yet begun to blink, the signal that the process was in the final stage.

He looked around at the inside of what had been Ben Kenobi's home. It was a small place on the edge of the Western Dune Sea, made, as so many of the local structures were, of synstone—crushed local rock mixed into a slurry with dissolvants and cast or sprayed onto frames to harden. The resulting buildings were sturdy and proof against the sandstorms. Ben's house looked almost as if it could have been a natural rock formation, smoothed and rounded by centuries of too-hot-by-day and too-cold-by-night desert weather.

Ben. Struck down by Vader on the Death Star. The memory was equal parts grief and rage.

His teacher hadn't left much behind, not for a man who had once been Obi-Wan Kenobi, a Jedi Knight and a general in the Clone Wars. Perhaps the most valuable thing was the old and intricately carved boa-wood trunk and its contents, including an ancient leather-bound book. A book that contained all manner of wondrous things for a would-be Jedi, such as plans for building a lightsaber. The thumbprint clasp on the volume had accepted Luke's right thumb to unlock it, and once it was open, he saw the flashpacket rigged inside the cover. Had anybody tried to force the clasp, the book would have burst into flame.

Somehow, Ben had known Luke would find this book. Somehow, he had prepared it so that only he could open it safely.

Amazing.

According to that book, the best lightsabers used natural jewels, but there weren't a lot of the kind he needed lying around where he could find them on Tatooine. He'd managed to collect most of the electronic and mechanical parts in Mos Eisley—power cells, controls, a high-energy reflector cup—but he had to make his own focusing jewel. Ideally, the best lightsabers also had three of those, different densities and facets, for a fully adjustable blade, but for his first attempt at building the Jedi weapon, Luke wanted to keep it as simple as possible. Even so, it was trickier than the book made it out. He was pretty sure he had the superconductor tuned right, the amplitude for the length set where it was supposed to be, and the control circuitry boards correctly installed. He couldn't be positive until the jewel was finished, and the book didn't mention exactly how long that took. Supposedly the furnace would shut down automatically when it was done.

If everything went right, he'd be able to cut the jewel, polish and install it, tune the photoharmonics, and then he'd only have to hit the switch to have a working lightsaber. He had followed the instructions to the letter; he was pretty good with tools and it *ought* to be okay, but there was a small worry that when he switched it on it might not work. That would be embarrassing. Or worse, it might work in a way it wasn't supposed to. That would be worse than embarrassing: Luke Skywalker, up-and-coming Jedi Knight, a man who had gone one-on-one with Darth Vader and lived to tell of it, vaporized when his faulty lightsaber blew up. So far he'd been very careful constructing the thing, triple-checking each step, and to get this far had taken almost a month. The book said a Jedi Master in a hurry could construct a new lightsaber in a couple of *days*.

Luke sighed. Maybe after he'd built six or eight of them he might be able to speed it up, but he obviously had a long, long way to go to get there—

Suddenly he felt something.

It was like hearing and smelling and tasting and seeing somehow combined, and yet it was none of those things. Something . . . impending, somehow.

Could it be something coming from the Force? Ben had been able to sense events happening light-years away, and Yoda had spoken of such things, but Luke wasn't sure. His own experiences in his X-wing and in his practice had been so limited.

He wished Ben were here to tell him.

Whatever it was grew stronger. For a moment, he had a flash of recognition: Leia?

He had been able to call to her when he was about to fall from beneath Cloud City after his encounter with Vader. She had somehow received his cry for help.

Was it Leia?

He buckled on his blaster, adjusted the belt on his hip so he could draw the weapon quickly if needed, and went outside. Normally the Tusken Raiders—the Sand People—stayed clear of Ben's house. They were superstitious, Ben had told him, and with his control of the Force, he had shown them a few tricks, enough so they marked his place as haunted. But Ben was gone, and whatever he had done might not work forever. Luke didn't have Ben's control; the Raiders might not be so impressed with him picking up a few rocks with the Force. Then again, there was nothing wrong with his aim, and however inelegant it was, a blaster bolt splashing off a rock next to them would make just about anybody stop and think.

Once he got the lightsaber built and working, he hoped he could put the blaster away. A true Jedi did not need any other weapon to protect himself, Ben had told him.

He sighed. He had a way to go to get to that level, too.

A hot wind blew grit off the desert, abrading and drying his skin. In the distance, he saw a thin dust cloud. Somebody approached across the barrens from Mos Eisley, probably in a landspeeder. Since nobody else was supposed to know he was here, it was probably Leia or Chewie or Lando—if the Empire had located him, they would have dropped on him from the air, raining ships and stormtroopers. In that case, he'd be lucky to get to his camouflaged X-wing before they blasted the place to a smoking ruin—as they had blasted Uncle Owen and Aunt Beru at the farm . . .

Luke felt his jaw muscles go tight at the memory.

The Empire had a lot to answer for.

The protected corridors in the core of the Imperial Center were available only to those with proper identification, and admissions were, supposedly, strictly limited and enforced. Such corridors were large, well lighted, lined with fanciful botanicals, such as singing fig trees and jade roses, and often patrolled by hawk-bats, which preyed on the rock slugs that sometimes infested the granite walls. These corridors were designed to be pathways in which the rich and famous could stroll without being bothered by the rabble.

But as Xizor walked along one such enclosed path, his four bodyguards ahead of or behind him, an interloper appeared in front of them and started shooting at the Dark Prince with a blaster.

One of the pair of bodyguards in front took a bolt in the chest that pierced his concealed hardweave armor and dropped him. Xizor noticed the chest wound smoked as the guard groaned and rolled onto his back.

The second guard, whether through skill or luck, returned fire and scored a direct hit on the assassin's blaster, knocking it from his hand. The threat was over.

The attacker screamed and charged at the remaining guards and Xizor barehanded.

Intrigued, Xizor watched the man come. The assassin was big, bigger than any of the guards and much larger than Xizor himself, built like a heavy-gravity weight lifter, and he was obviously crazed if he would charge three armed men without a weapon.

How interesting.

"Don't shoot him," Xizor said.

The running man was only twenty or so meters away and closing fast.

The Dark Prince allowed himself one of his tight smiles.

"Leave him alone," he said. "He's mine."

The trio of bodyguards tucked their own blasters away and moved aside. They knew better than to question Xizor's orders. Those who did could wind up like the still-smoking guard lying on the polished marble floor.

The assassin continued his run, screaming incoherently.

Xizor waited. When the man was nearly upon him, the Dark Prince pivoted on the balls of his feet and slapped a hard palm against the back of the man's head as he charged past. The extra momentum of the strike was enough to off-balance the yelling man so that he overstepped and fell. He managed to turn the fall into an awkward shoulder roll. He came up, spun, faced Xizor. He was a bit more wary now. He moved in, more slowly, hands held in tight fists.

"What seems to be the problem, citizen?" Xizor asked.

"You murdering scum! You bog slime!"

The man lunged in closer, swung a roundhouse punch at Xizor's head. Had it connected it would have shattered bone. Xizor ducked and sidestepped, kicked the attacker in the belly with the toe of his right boot and knocked the man's wind out.

The attacker tottered back a few steps to catch his breath.

"Have we met? I have an excellent memory for faces, and I don't recall yours." Xizor noticed a bit of lint on the shoulder of his tunic. He reached up and brushed it off.

"You killed my father. Have you forgotten Colby Hoff?"

The man charged again, fists swinging wildly.

Xizor stepped aside and almost nonchalantly slammed a hammerfist into the man's head, knocking him down.

"You are mistaken, Hoff. Your father committed suicide, as I recall. Stuck a blaster in his mouth and blew the back of his head off, didn't he? Very messy."

Hoff came up from the floor, and his rage drove him at Xizor again.

Xizor V-stepped to his right and drove his left boot

heel at Hoff's left knee, hard. He heard the joint go with a wet snap as he connected.

Hoff fell, his left leg no longer able to support him. "You ruined him!" He struggled up to his good knee.

"We were *business* competitors," Xizor said matter-of-factly. "He gambled that he was smarter than I. A foolish mistake. If you cannot afford to lose, you should not play the game."

"I'm going to kill you!"

"I think not," Xizor said. He stepped in behind the wounded man, moving fast for one his size, and grabbed Hoff's head with both hands. "You see, to contend with Xizor is to lose. As far as any reasonable person is concerned, attacking me will also be judged a suicide."

With that, Xizor gave a sharp, hard twist.

The crack of vertebrae was quite loud in the corridor.

"Clean up this mess," he said to his guards. "And inform the proper authorities of this poor young man's fate."

He looked down at the body. He felt no remorse. It was like stepping on a roach. It meant nothing to him at all.

In his most private chamber, the Emperor sat staring at a life-size holographic recording: Prince Xizor breaking the neck of someone who'd attacked him in a protected corridor.

The Emperor smiled and turned in his floating repulsor chair to look at Darth Vader.

"Well," the Emperor said, "it seems that Prince Xizor has kept up his martial arts practice, does it not?"

Unseen under his armored mask, Vader frowned.

"He is a dangerous man, my master. Not to be trusted."

The Emperor favored him with one of his unattractive, toothy smiles. "Do not trouble yourself with Xizor, Lord Vader. He is my concern."

"As you wish." Vader bowed.

"One wonders how that hotheaded young man managed to get into a protected corridor," the Emperor said. But there was no wonder in the Emperor's voice, none at all.

Vader's face froze. He *knew*. It was not possible, for the guard who had admitted the would-be assassin into the corridor was no longer among the living, and none but that single man had known who ordered him to allow the young man access—but somehow, the Emperor knew.

The Emperor's mastery of the dark side was great indeed.

"I will look into it, my master," Vader said.

The Emperor waved an age-spotted hand in dismissal. "Don't bother. There was no harm done. Prince Xizor was hardly at risk, after all, was he? He seems quite capable of taking care of himself—though I would hate to see anything happen to him as long as he is useful to us."

Vader bowed again. As usual, the Emperor made his point in a subtle manner, but in such a way that it could not be ignored. There would be no further attempts to test Xizor's ability to defend himself against deadly attack.

Not yet, anyway.

Meanwhile, Vader would keep a close watch on the Dark Prince. The Falleen was all too devious, and whatever his twisted mind was up to would serve the Empire only if it served Xizor himself.

Xizor was, after all, a criminal. His morals were perverse, his ethics situational, his loyalties nonexistent. He would stop at nothing to get his way, and Vader was fairly certain in his own mind that what Xizor wanted did not include a galaxy in which there was room for Vader or the Emperor.

To contend with Xizor is to lose?

We shall see.

4

As the landspeeder carrying them neared their destination, Leia saw Luke standing next to the house, watching. Odd, that he would somehow know of their approach.

Of course, out here in the middle of nowhere, nothing but sand and rocks and scrub, he could have seen them coming for a long way. It might not be the Force at work here but simple observation.

Chewie brought the speeder to a stop. Dust kicked up by the repulsors floated around them for a moment before the nearly constant wind swirled it away. This climate would leach you dry if you stayed out in it unprotected for too long. The dunes shifted and revealed more than a few crisp white bones of those who had thought they could move around the desert with impunity.

Luke smiled at her, and once again Leia felt that sense of confusion. She loved Han, but here was Luke, and she certainly felt a connection to him, too. Was it possible for a woman to love two men at the same time? She returned his smile. It was not the same with Luke as with Han, but there was something there.

"Hey, Luke," Lando said.

Chewie added what had to be a greeting.

"Master Luke, it's so good to see you again," Threepio said. His normally bright golden color was somewhat dimmed by a coat of dust. It seemed as if the protocol droid somehow attracted more dirt to himself than the rest of them did, though Leia felt a little gritty herself after the long ride from town.

Even Artoo whistled a happy greeting.

They all liked Luke. There was something about him that seemed so natural and so attractive. Maybe it was the Force flowing through him. Maybe it was because he seemed like such a nice person.

"We would have called," Lando said, "but we didn't want to risk having our com overheard. Chewie saw a couple of those new Imperial codecracker slicer droids in town; he thinks they might be monitoring local calls. No point in taking any unnecessary risks."

Luke nodded. "Good thought. Come on inside."

There was a faint smell of something cooking in what had been Obi-Wan's simple home. The aroma reminded Leia of a time she'd gone camping as a girl and had sat around an open fire. She saw a small blast furnace set up on a table. Was Luke making some kind of jewelry?

They told Luke why they'd come.

He was immediately excited. He was ready to hop into his X-wing and leave right now.

"Hold on a second," Lando said. "First we have to make sure Fett's there. Then there's the little matter of the Imperial Navy."

Luke shrugged. "Hey, we can fly circles around those guys."

Lando and Leia exchanged glances. Whatever else

Luke was, he was not lacking in self-confidence when it came to his piloting.

Chewie spoke up.

Threepio translated: "Ah, Chewbacca wonders if perhaps the Rebel Alliance might not be willing to help, given Master Han's services to them."

Luke grinned like a child seeing a new toy. "Sure they would. Wedge is in command of Rogue Squadron now, and he told me if I ever needed them they'd come running."

"They can drop whatever they are doing, just like that?" Lando asked.

Leia nodded. "I don't see why not. The Alliance's chain of command is a lot looser than the Empire's. We have to be more flexible, given the numbers. The Rogues don't have any permanent assignment, and I'm sure I can convince the Alliance that Captain Solo is worth rescuing. He was instrumental in the destruction of the Death Star; plus we need all the good pilots we can get."

Leia glanced at the others quickly, to see if her somewhat shaky reasoning covered her true feelings.

Luke didn't seem to see past what she said, eager to fly as he was; Lando's small grin could mean anything; the droids and Chewie were unreadable.

"Great," Luke said. "Let's do it!"

"Not so fast," Lando said. "First what say we wait for the confirmation that Fett is actually *on* Gall before we take off? That's a long trip to make for nothing."

Leia could see that Luke didn't want to wait—patience didn't seem to be his strongest virtue—but he could see the wisdom of what Lando said. "Okay. But in the meantime, let's contact Wedge and have the Rogues standing by."

"I'll speak to the leadership," Leia said.

She hoped that Lando's informant—what was his name? Dash somebody?—would get the information to them quickly. And she hoped that the rumor was true. Nobody wanted Han back more than she did.

Xizor sat at the head of the long table in his private meeting room, watching the nervous faces of his lieutenants. Guri stood behind him at a modified parade rest, her hands out of sight at the small of her back.

They had reason to be nervous, his lieutenants. By ascending to this level in Black Sun, they had each earned the honorific "Vigo," from the old Tionese for "nephew." It fostered the illusion that the top managers of the organization were family and thus made them appear stronger to outsiders.

Unfortunately, the appearance was not always the truth.

One of them at the table was a spy.

Xizor did not know for whom the spy worked— could be the Empire, the Rebel Alliance, even a rival criminal organization—and he did not particularly care. Everybody spied on everybody in this business, it was a given, but the fact that it was normal did not mean that you let it pass when you found it.

Now, at the beginning of this meeting, he had nine lieutenants at this table, each of whom was responsible for several stellar systems.

At the end of this meeting, he would have eight lieutenants.

But first, the normal business of Black Sun must be attended to and properly settled.

"I will have your reports," Xizor said. "Vigo Lonay?"

Lonay was a Twi'lek, sly, clever, and cowardly. He wore his prehensile head-tails wrapped and draped over one shoulder, his usual garish jewelry and decorative coloration toned down for this meeting. "My prince, the spice trade is up twenty-one percent in our sector, the gambling casino ships have increased their

business by eight percent, and the arms dealers are doing a brisk business; current estimates indicate a thirty-
one percent increase. Unfortunately, slave revenues are
down fifty-three percent. Several planets have fallen under the sway of the Rebel Alliance and passed local
laws forbidding slavery. Until the Empire chooses to
intercede, I am afraid revenues in this area will remain
depressed."

Xizor nodded. Lonay would always be too much a
coward to risk death by betraying his "uncle." His
whole species was that way.

The Dark Prince said, "Vigo Sprax?"

Sprax, a Nalroni whose dark fur had begun to gray,
though he dyed it to try to appear younger, began to
rattle off his statistics. Xizor watched him, listened
with half his attention—he already knew all of what
was being officially delivered.

Sprax was too smart to try to cross Xizor.

The Nalroni finished his report.

"Vigo Vekker?"

Vekker, a Quarren, flashed a nervous smile and
started his recitation.

The Squid Head had no ambition to rise any higher,
was content with his job and the status quo.

One by one Xizor called for the Vigos to speak, and
one by one the rest of them did: Durga the Hutt,
Kreet'ah the Kian'thar, Clezo the Rodian, Wumdi the
Etti, Perit the Mon Calamari, Green the Human.

It was hard to believe any of his Vigos would be so
foolish; after all, one could not get to this elevated
status without years of loyal effort. Some of them had
come up through the ranks—smugglers, thieves, busi-
nessmen—and some of them had been trained from
birth and had inherited their places from their fathers,
or, in the case of Kreet'ah, his biological mother. Several of these nine had been Vigos before Xizor himself
had attained that rank before moving to head Black
Sun.

And yet, there it was. Life was full of treachery.

He let them all sit and worry for a few moments. Then he nodded at Guri. His most trusted bodyguard and employee began to walk behind the seated Vigos.

They all had their own intelligence operations, and they all knew at least what Xizor had allowed them to find out about the traitor—not much save that there was one. And that he did not know who it was.

A calculated bit of prevarication, this last. He *did* know who it was. And now the matter would be . . . corrected.

"A final item on our agenda, my Vigos. One of your number has seen fit to use his office to betray us. Not content with the millions of credits he has made by my largesse, the awards, bonuses, dividends, and unreported skim that all of you indulge yourselves in, this . . . person has dishonored the title of Vigo."

Guri strolled behind the seated lieutenants slowly. Xizor watched them. Those who could, sweated or flushed or otherwise showed signs of fear they could not hide.

She passed Durga, Kreet'ah, Clezo, reached the other end of the table and circled around it.

Xizor continued speaking, slowly, evenly, betraying nothing in his tone. "There are sublieutenants among your ranks who would cheerfully wipe out entire planets to be given such an opportunity as you all have been given. To be a Vigo in Black Sun is to enjoy more power than all but a handful of beings in the entire galaxy."

Guri passed Lonay, passed Sprax, then Vekker. Paused a moment behind Durga the Hutt.

Tension thickened in the room, became almost tangible.

Xizor thought that was a nice touch. Durga was nobody's fool and would never risk himself as a spy; no, the Hutt had ambition enough for ten; *he* would go for a coup. Having Guri pause behind him let him know

Xizor was keeping an eye on him. A warning that he should think long and hard before trying to climb from his lofty plateau to the top of the mountain.

Guri moved on, and the sense of relief that came from Durga was, like the tension, something you could very nearly collect from the air and use for a doorstop.

The droid who could pass as a woman sauntered past Wumdi the Etti and Perit the Mon Calamari.

She stopped behind Green the Human.

Xizor smiled.

Green tried to stand, but Guri was incredibly fast. She whipped her arm around the man's throat and locked it with her other arm into a choke hold.

Green struggled briefly, but he might as well have been wrestling with a durasteel clamp. The blood that fed his brain shut off, and he lost consciousness.

Guri tightened the hold and held it, held it, held it . . .

A long time passed. None of the other Vigos moved.

When Green was no longer among the living, Guri released him, and he fell forward; his head thumped loudly upon the table.

"I will accept nominations for a new Vigo now," Xizor said.

Nobody spoke for a moment, and Xizor kept his face bland. A pity about Green; he was one of the smartest of all the Vigos. But humans were quick to treachery and could hardly ever be trusted.

He looked at his lieutenants again, waited for them to speak. Here was an object lesson they would certainly remember.

To contend with Xizor is to lose.

Never forget that.

After the Vigos had gone and the body had been removed, Guri returned.

"I thought that went well," Xizor said.

Guri nodded once, not speaking.

"You have assembled all the information on Skywalker?"

"Yes, my prince."

He stared into space. His organization was huge, the people working for him numbering in the tens of thousands, but some things he had to deal with personally. Especially something this . . . sensitive.

"All of the material has been checked and rechecked?"

"As you ordered."

"Very well. Let the bounty hunters know the price for Skywalker's head. Black Sun's hand must be invisible. There must be no mistakes."

"There will be none, my prince."

"Oh, I would like to speak to Jabba the Hutt."

"He will be online when you return from midday meal, my prince."

"No. Have him come here by the fastest ship; I would speak to him personally."

"As you wish."

Guri stood silently as Xizor considered his plan.

Vader wanted Skywalker, wanted him alive to give to the Emperor. Xizor's memory of that conversation he'd been privileged to overhear some months back was that the Emperor very much wanted the young man alive and in his control.

Black Sun's reach was long and wide, and what information there was on Vader's quarry was now in Xizor's personal computer system. The Dark Lord of the Sith had all but promised to deliver Skywalker not only alive but made pliable to the Emperor's wishes.

If Vader should fail in his promise, if it could be made to appear that he had never really intended to produce this young would-be Jedi for the Emperor, if it could be made to seem that he had killed the boy rather than risk facing him . . .

Well. The Emperor put great stock in Vader's abili-

ties, probably trusted him as much as he trusted anyone. But the Emperor demanded total loyalty and total
obedience. If he could be made to believe that Vader
was disloyal or disobedient or had simply failed in his
assigned task, things would not go well for Vader.

The Emperor was capricious. He had been known to
have whole cities destroyed because a local official defied him. He'd once had a wealthy and influential family banished from the core systems because one of the
sons had plowed a ship into one of the Emperor's favorite buildings, damaging it—and not incidentally killing the pilot responsible.

If the Emperor thought that his trusted right hand,
Darth Vader, his own creation, was any kind of threat,
even the Dark Lord of the Sith would not be immune
to Imperial anger.

Yes, it was a good plan. A bit complicated, but all
the possible sequels had been examined and considered
and covered.

In the end, he knew he had found the perfect
weapon with which to finally defeat Darth Vader:

The death of Luke Skywalker.

5

Darth Vader sat naked inside his hyperbaric medical chamber. The interior lighting was turned off, and he was free of the armor that he had to wear to sustain himself in public. The Force was powerful; Vader thought the dark side even more so, but he had never been able to use it to heal his badly burned body to the extent that he wished. That he was alive at all was something of a miracle, but he had somehow failed to master the energies needed for complete regeneration. He believed that it was possible; that with sufficient meditation and training, he would someday be able to rebuild himself into the man he once had been.

Physically, at least.

He would never go back to what he had been mentally. Weak, foolish, idealistic. Anakin had been much like Luke Skywalker was now. Mere . . . potential.

Yes, the Force was strong in Luke, perhaps even stronger than it had been in Anakin. But the boy needed to embrace the dark side, to learn where the real power was, to achieve his true promise. If he did not, the Emperor would destroy Luke.

Vader did not want that.

When they fought, he had also tried to strike the boy down, but that had been merely a test. Had he been able to kill Luke easily, Luke would not have been worth the effort to recruit. But although he had certainly attempted to defeat Luke, the boy had held his own. Despite Vader's superior skill, despite his experience, Luke had survived with no more damage than an easily repaired amputated hand.

The meeting had made Vader *feel,* not a normal occurrence lately. There had been the thrill at meeting a worthy opponent and pride that the one so strongly opposing him was his own son.

Vader smiled into the darkness surrounding him. Obi-Wan had not told Luke that Anakin Skywalker had become Darth Vader. Luke's anger at the man who had slain his teacher had been potent, had allowed the dark side to claim him. If Vader hadn't broken that anger with fear and confusion by telling the boy that he was his father, Luke *could* have defeated him. A Jedi does not fight in anger; he holds his emotions in check and allows the Force to move through him. But the dark side needed to be fed with strong emotion, and when it was, it repaid that sustenance tenfold.

Luke had felt the power of the dark side. It was up to Vader to find him and allow him to feel it again. The dark side was addictive, more potent than any drug. When Luke accepted it, he would be more powerful than Vader, more powerful than the Emperor. Together they could rule the galaxy.

Enough. It was time for another test.

Vader waved his hand over the motion-sensitive controls in his chamber. The spherical chamber opened and the lid lifted with a hydraulic hiss and escape of pressurized air. He sat exposed to the surrounding room, unprotected by the supermedicated and oxygen-ated field inside the chamber.

He concentrated on the injustice of his condition, on his hatred of Obi-Wan, who had made him so. With the anger and hatred, the dark side of the Force perme-ated Vader.

For a moment, his ruined tissues altered, his scarred lungs and dead alveoli and constricted passages smoothed out and became whole.

For a moment, he could breathe as normal beings breathed.

His sense of relief, his triumph, his *joy* at being able to do so drove the dark side from him as surely as a light chases away shadow. The dark side eagerly con-sumed anger, but it was poisoned by happiness. It left him, and when it did he could breathe no longer.

Vader waved his hand, and the half-dome lowered and sealed him into the chamber once again.

He had achieved it briefly, as he had done several times before. The trick was to maintain it. He must not allow himself to feel relief, but must somehow cling to his rage even as he healed.

It was difficult. He had not purged all of Anakin Skywalker, that blemished and frail man from whom he had been born. Until he did, he could never give himself over totally to the dark side. It was his greatest weakness, his most terrible flaw. A single spot of light amid the dark that he had been unable to eradicate over all the years, no matter how hard he tried.

Vader sighed. He would have to try harder. He could not afford any weaknesses, given his enemies—and more especially, given his friends.

Luke reset the jewel in the clamp and took a deep breath. He had the first few facets done, and now the cuts were getting trickier. If he tapped the shearing tool too hard, he could shatter the jewel, and if he did, he'd have to cook another one and start over.

Chewie sat watching him, apparently very interested, while Leia napped in the bedroom. Lando had left them all at Ben's and taken the landspeeder to town. He was due back soon . . .

Chewie looked away, hearing something. He spoke.

Threepio, who was playing some kind of word translation game with Artoo, turned. "Chewbacca says Master Lando has returned."

Luke nodded but concentrated on his task. He tapped the cutter with the little wooden hammer . . .

A flat sliver of the stone flaked off. All right! Perfect—

Lando came in, grinning.

"What are you so happy about?" Luke said.

"I just got a coded call from Dash Rendar. That is Boba Fett's ship on Gall."

In theory, only the Empire could use the expensive and restricted HoloNet; in practice, anybody with a little primary electronic education could tap into the net, use a few relays, and make calls easily. And to add insult to injury, make the Empire pay for it, too.

Luke jumped up. "When can we leave?"

"I've got the *Millennium Falcon* ready to go. How long will it take you to get your X-wing operational?"

"Soon as Artoo and I get on board!"

"Get on board what?" Leia said from the doorway. She rubbed sleep from her eyes.

"It looks as if we've found him," Lando said.

"I'll meet you in orbit," Luke said. He grinned. The waiting was over.

Leia said, "I'll get off a coded call to the Rogues."

Luke nodded.

They were going to get Han.

·   ·   ·

Jabba waited in the visitors' chamber. The Dark Prince entered and looked at the Hutt. Such gross and ugly creatures they were, but no less useful for that.

"<Greetings, Prince Xizor,>" Jabba said, in Huttese.

"Speak Basic," Xizor said.

"As you wish."

"How goes your business, Jabba? Are things well in your sector?"

"They could be better. Revenues are up, generally. Of course, the cost of Imperial bribes has also risen. As have shipping and salaries. But one does what one must."

"I understand you have had some dealings with high officials in the Empire of late."

Jabba looked quizzical. As quizzical as Hutts could look.

"I speak of Lord Vader."

"Ah. Not directly, Highness. I recently engaged several bounty hunters to, ah, collect a bad debt. As it happened, one of them—Boba Fett, I believe you have utilized him yourself a time or two?—managed to locate the, ah, *source* of the debt in Imperial hands. Lord Vader was in command of the situation. A coincidence, I am told."

"You are speaking of Captain Solo, I believe."

It was not a question, and it was meant to remind Jabba that Xizor had more than a few sources of intelligence himself. This was a tricky game, and it had to be balanced precisely. Xizor needed information, but he could not reveal what it was and thus must circle around it. He also had to let the Hutt know who was in charge, and showing him he knew trivial things was part of that.

He saw Jabba get it.

"A minor smuggler," Jabba offered. "He has had his uses in the past, but he joined the Alliance and does owe me money."

"Some refreshment, Jabba?"

"Thank you. Something crunchy?"

Xizor waved a hand and a serving droid appeared almost instantly, bearing a tray of insectoids and some vile liquid Hutts were known to favor.

"Ah, thank you, Highness." He picked up one of the wiggling things and ate it.

Xizor leaned forward, as if to convey a sense of closeness. "I have had some dealings with Vader myself of late," he said. "Your presence here is most important, Jabba; information, even the smallest details about the Dark Lord of the Sith, will be most helpful to me in my present situation. This deal with Boba Fett, has it been finalized yet?"

"Not yet, my prince. I am awaiting delivery of Captain Solo."

As if remembering a small and insignificant fact, Xizor said, "Hmm. Wasn't this Solo part of a Rebel force that attacked the Death Star?"

"Yes, Highness. He and his friends were instrumental in its destruction. The Wookiee Chewbacca, Princess Leia Organa, and a young unknown player by the name of Skywalker, all were involved in the debacle."

"Skywalker?"

Jabba laughed, a deep rumble that echoed from his huge bulk. "Yes, he thinks he is a Jedi Knight, so I understand," he said when he'd finished laughing. "He was until recently on Tatooine."

"Where is he now?"

"Who knows? He took his X-wing offplanet only a short time ago."

Xizor leaned back. "Hmm. It probably means nothing, but perhaps these things will be of use to me. If any of these people return to Tatooine, I would greatly appreciate knowing it."

"Certainly, Prince Xizor."

Xizor nodded. He was essentially done, but he continued to carry on a conversation with the Hutt, pretended that Jabba's opinion was worthwhile and that he needed to hear it. He let it run for another ten minutes, asked a few questions about Imperial troop movements and naval deployment so that Jabba would think that was the reason he'd been summoned. When he had done what he thought was enough of it, Xizor smiled. "Old friend, this information is most confidential," he said. "It must remain between us. Your cooperation will be suitably . . . appreciated."

The Hutt mirrored Xizor's smile. Sometimes the touch of a soft word was more powerful than the impact of a hard staff. Jabba was not stupid, and he knew what happened to anyone who crossed the Dark Prince. But—let Jabba think instead he was privy to some vital bit of business, some twisted plot, that he was a trusted confidant. It would do the Hutt's reputation no harm if his underlings and enemies thought he had the ear of the leader of Black Sun. Fear was good; fear and greed were better.

Xizor nodded and took his leave.

His spies had learned that Darth Vader had turned Solo, a small-time smuggler and sometime Alliance pilot, over to the notorious bounty hunter Boba Fett on Bespin. Sooner or later, Fett would show up on Tatooine to deliver Solo and collect his credits. But Xizor's spies indicated that Fett's ship, *Slave I,* was not on Tatooine. And so far those spies had not been able to locate the bounty hunter.

Well. It was a large galaxy, and such searches took time.

But he was willing to bet that Skywalker knew about the bounty on his friend and had returned to Tatooine to wait for Fett to show up. That he had left could indicate a lot of things. Perhaps he had gotten tired of waiting, though Xizor did not think that likely. Or perhaps he had pressing business unconnected to Solo. Or perhaps he had, through the Alliance, discovered where his friend was. That was possible, given that the Alliance's contacts were fairly extensive and included much of the famed Bothan spynet.

Well. There was nothing to be done about it, if that was the case. But he could increase his agents' chances of finding Skywalker.

He reached his sanctum and called Guri. She glided in silently.

"Put out the information that those seeking to claim the reward for Skywalker would be advised to locate the bounty hunter Boba Fett. Sooner or later, Skywalker will likely do so, and appropriate plans can be made for that instance."

Guri nodded, not speaking.

Xizor smiled.

Leia sat in the *Millennium Falcon*'s lounge, watching Chewie and Threepio play on the hologame board. Lando was in the galley making something that smelled awful for their dinner. Luke sat next to Leia, cleaning the lenses on Artoo's electrophoto receptors. Luke's X-wing was locked onto the *Falcon*'s hull—the trip was possible in the fighter, but it was also a long jump to make without sleeping or eating or using the 'fresher.

The *Falcon* hummed along through hyperspace on autopilot, running much better than it had any right to, looking as it did. The first time Leia had seen the Corellian freighter she'd almost laughed. The ship appeared to have been rescued from a scrap pile. But while it had a few glitches, it was obvious the craft had been heavily modified to fly faster and shoot harder than the Corellian designers had ever intended. Lando had owned the ship once, until he lost it to Han in a sabacc game.

Han—

No, don't think about him now.

Chewie said something that sounded angry and impolite.

Threepio said, "Well, I'm sorry, but it was a fair move. It's not my fault you didn't see it."

Chewie said something else.

"No. I'm not going to take it back. And don't threaten me. If you pull my arm off, I won't play with you anymore."

Chewie muttered something, then leaned back on his seat and looked at the game board.

Leia smiled. Like a couple of small children, the Wookiee and the protocol droid.

She turned and watched Luke as he cleared the micrometeor dust from Artoo. Luke wanted to rescue Han as much as she did. Which was interesting, given that she'd felt the competition from them for her attention. A lesser man than Luke might take advantage of a rival's absence, but so far he had not. That was the thing about Luke. He wanted to win, but he wanted to win fairly.

Lando came into the lounge bearing a tray with several steaming plates and bowls upon it.

"Dinner is served," Lando said. He smiled. "Giju stew."

They all glanced at him, then went back to what they were doing.

"Don't everybody rush in at once," Lando said. His smile faded.

To Leia, the stuff on the tray looked like a cross between melted boot plastic and fertilizer, with a sprinkling of pond scum over it. Stank like she imagined that combination would smell, too.

"Come on, I spent an hour in the galley fixing this. Everybody dig in!"

Chewie said something that didn't sound particularly complimentary.

"Hey, pal, you don't like it, you cook next time."

Luke looked up from his work on Artoo, made an oh-yuck face. "Giju stew?" he said. "It looks like old boot plastic and fertilizer drenched in pond scum. Smells like it, too—"

Leia chuckled.

"Fine, fine!" Lando said. He put the tray down in the middle of the hologame board. The tiny game figures suddenly seemed to be buried to their hips or chests in the steaming goo. "Don't eat it, that'll just mean more for me."

Lando snatched up one of the bowls and dipped a spoon into it, shoved the spoon into his mouth. "See?" he said around the mouthful of stew. "It tastes great, it—" He stopped talking. The expression on his face went from irritated to amazed, slid to horror, then right into disgust.

He forced himself to swallow. Then he blew a quick breath and shook his head. "Oh, man. Maybe I did use a little too much Boontaspice," he offered. "Maybe I'll just open a couple of packets of beans for dinner."

Luke and Leia laughed at the same instant. Looked at each other.

There were worse places she could be than with her friends, Leia decided.

A lot worse places.

6

When the *Millennium Falcon* broke from hyperspace in the vicinity of the gas giant Zhar, Luke used one of the vacuum suits to transfer to his X-wing for the rest of the trip. Lando and Leia would have preferred that they all stay together, but if any trouble showed up, better there were two armed ships to meet it than one, Luke argued. They saw his point.

After he and Artoo were in the fighter, Luke felt a lot better. Yeah, Lando was a good pilot, but Luke trusted his own skills more. Not that he was necessarily a better flier—though he was pretty sure he was—but at least he didn't have to sit and watch. The vac-suit made things a little tight, though.

He kept the little ship close to the *Falcon* as they entered the system. What was Boba Fett doing this far out on the Rim? It didn't seem to be on the way to anywhere.

He saw the blips on his scope about the time he got the call over his comm.

"Hey, Luke! Welcome to the end of the galaxy."

"Hey, Wedge! How's it going, buddy?"

"So-so. Another day, another credit—before taxes, of course."

Luke smiled. Wedge Antilles had been one of the Alliance pilots who survived the attack on the Death Star. He could fly, and he was braver than he had any right to be. Good old Wedge.

Here they came. A dozen ships like his own.

"Good to see you again, Luke. I hope you've got something interesting cooked up for us; things have been a little slow lately."

"Well, if you want to talk about bad cooking, you'll need to speak to Lando—"

"I heard that," Lando said over the comm.

Luke grinned at the *Falcon* where it flew on his port side.

"Just a joke, Lando."

"Hey, Calrissian, long time. I figured you'd be in jail by now."

"Not yet, Antilles, not yet."

"Follow us, Luke," Wedge said, "we've got camp set up on a little moon called Kile in the planet shadow opposite Gall. We've fixed it up real nice, got air, gravity, water, all the comforts of home."

"Lead on," Luke said. "We're right behind you."

"You call this 'real nice'?" Leia said as she looked around at the interior of the cast-plast prefab building Rogue Squadron had set up as a base. It was basically four walls and a roof and looked like a cross between a warehouse and a hangar, with exposed plastic beams and not much else. It was cold, and it smelled like burned rock. "I'd hate to see a place you thought was not real nice."

Wedge smiled. "Well, you know the Rogues. All we need is a ship and rock to land it on."

"You got that second part right."

Wedge led them to a corner of the chilly building where a table and a holoproj unit had been set up. A man sat sprawled in one of the one-piece cast-plast chairs, looking as if he were asleep.

He didn't really look anything like Han—he had red hair and pale skin—but something about the way he sat . . .

He might have been asleep, but his eyes flicked open fast and he looked awake by the time they got there.

He was tall, lean, had green eyes. He wore freighter togs, a gray coverall, and a holstered blaster slung low on his hip. He looked to be about Han's age, Leia figured, and he had that same lazy, insolent look about him. He came to his feet and made a low, sweeping, theatrical bow.

"Princess Leia," he said. "How delightful of you to visit us here in our humble castle, Your Highness." He waved at the big empty room and grinned.

Leia shook her head. Could Han have a long-lost brother? Did these guys take lessons in how to speak smartmouth?

Lando said, "This is Dash Rendar, thief, card cheat, smuggler, and an okay pilot."

Dash's grin increased. "What do you mean, 'okay pilot,' Calrissian? I can fly rings around you in a one-winged hopper with a plugged jet."

"And modest, too," Leia said.

Dash bowed low. "I see that the princess has a keen eye to go with her stunning beauty."

Oh, brother, Leia thought. *This* guy was going to lead them to Boba Fett?

"Bottle the serpent oil, Dash," Lando said. "Let's take care of business."

"First good idea you've had in years, Lando," Dash said.

Lando made introductions. "So you know who Princess Leia is, and you know Chewie. This is Luke Skywalker."

Luke stepped forward, and the two men nodded at each other.

"Have we met? You look familiar."

"You might have seen me on Hoth," Dash said. "I was delivering a shipment of food stores when the shield went up. I flew a snowspeeder during the battle while waiting my turn to leave."

Luke nodded. "That's right. You took down one of the Imperial walkers, I remember now. You were pretty good."

Dash flashed the bright smile again. "Pretty good? I *slept* through most of that battle, kid. I could have stayed and knocked those walkers over all day without raising my heartbeat, if I hadn't had an appointment to pick up paying cargo elsewhere."

Leia shook her head. What was it with men? It was a wonder they didn't knock themselves down, patting themselves on the back so hard. Did she really need to get involved with another hotshot braggart?

Well, yes. If he could take them to where Han was being held prisoner, she could stand it.

Wedge said, "We've done a little recon work, couple of flybys. Let me show you the layout." He moved to the holoprojector controls.

Luke watched as Wedge began showing them the holographic maps and recorded images of the moon where Boba Fett's ship was supposed to be docked. *If* they could believe this Dash Rendar. He was pretty good at shining his own light, that was for sure, and yeah, he had done okay during the fight on Hoth, but Luke wasn't so sure about this guy.

Still, Lando seemed to think they could trust Dash's judgment, as long as he was well paid.

Luke had to smile at that. Han had seemed like

nothing more than a mercenary smuggler when they'd first met, and pretty quick to let people know what a terrific pilot he was, too. It wasn't until later that Luke realized that was just a public mask, a facade behind which Han hid so nobody would know how much he really cared. Maybe there was more to Dash Rendar than met the eye, too.

Wedge said, ". . . moon has some bad atmospheric conditions, big cyclonic storms that get real mean, mostly in the southern hemisphere. You wouldn't want to try to fly through one of those."

Dash laughed. "Maybe *you* wouldn't want to, Antilles, but I eat thunderstorms for breakfast."

Or maybe there isn't more to him, Luke thought. *Maybe he's just crazy.*

Wedge continued the briefing. The Imperial Enclave was home base to two Star Destroyers—turned out the carrier was just a rumor—but that was plenty. Luke knew that a standard Destroyer carried a wing of TIE fighters, each wing made up of six squads, which meant seventy-two TIEs per Destroyer. A hundred and forty-four of them against the twelve in Rogue Squadron.

Well. Thirteen, counting Luke's ship. That made the odds a hair less than twelve to one. Not so bad compared to some battles they'd been in.

He grinned. It was a measure of how lopsided the war between the Empire and the Alliance was when twelve-to-one odds didn't seem so bad.

As Luke listened, he started thinking about a plan. Simpler the better, he figured.

Wedge finished his briefing. "That's about it. What do you think, Luke?"

"Piece of cake," Luke said. "I know just how to do it."

Leia and Lando both looked at him as if he'd turned into a big spider. He grinned again.

.   .   .

In his sanctum Xizor grinned at the information floating holographically before him. Well, well. The misguided young man who had seen fit to try to kill him—what was his name? Hoff?—had gained access to the protected corridor through an Imperial checkpoint a mere few hundred meters away. And here was an odd coincidence—the guard who had been on duty at that checkpoint had mysteriously vanished. So whatever subterfuge the dead man had used would never be known, him being dead and the guard having disappeared.

Xizor would bet half his fortune against a bent decicred that the absent guard would never be heard from again, either. Somebody had caused the guard to allow the would-be assassin to pass, and whoever that was, they did not wish their involvement known, Xizor was also sure of that.

He considered it. His enemies were legion, were myriad, at the very least, and many of them would happily see him dead. A single guard would be easy enough to bribe and get rid of; a hundred of his foes here on Coruscant might be in a position to do that.

Who hated him the most? A difficult question, there being so many.

Who was likely to have the nerve to make such an attempt? Here was another matter. Black Sun was nearly invulnerable, and while many would cheerfully lop off its leader's head if they thought they could get away with it, not many would be so certain they could do the deed undetected. So narrow that down to somebody powerful, somebody who might, should it become known, survive not only Black Sun's wrath, but the possible ire of the Emperor himself.

Well, that narrowed it down a whole lot more.

Xizor leaned back in his chair and steepled his fingers. This was a little game he sometimes played with himself, pretending that he was using reason and logic to arrive at a conclusion he had already made intuitively. He *knew* who had caused the attack, just as he knew it had not really been meant to succeed. It was no more than a small thorn set in his path, a tiny sticker upon which he was to step and be irritated, no more.

A small grief offered to his person by a man who feared neither Black Sun nor the Emperor's displeasure. There was only *one* such man.

Xizor was tempted to hire a dozen assassins, not tell them who their target was, and loose them on Vader. The killers would fail, of course, be squashed like insects by Vader with less effort than Xizor had expended on the man in the walkway. Vader could kill with a wave of his hand, though he enjoyed a chance to use his lightsaber from time to time.

But—no. That might foul Xizor's plans to appear to be Vader's friend—or at least, not his enemy. If Xizor could figure out who had been party to the pathetic attempt on his life without any evidence save his feeling, Vader could also determine who might be brave enough to send shooters after him.

Certainly he would be quick to at least consider that it was a retaliation in kind for the attack on Xizor.

No. Satisfying as it might be to worry Vader with an attack, it would not be prudent, given the larger plan.

But it was good to know that Vader disliked him enough to want to see him dead.

Leia laughed. "*That's* your plan?"

Luke looked indignant. "What's wrong with it?" His breath made fog-vapor in the cold room.

"You and Rogue Squadron will attack the Imperial Enclave, keep a hundred and some-odd TIE fighters and two Star Destroyers busy while Dash leads the *Millennium Falcon* to where Boba Fett's ship is docked? We'll just land, rescue Han, and fly away? Why, nothing is wrong with that plan. What could I possibly be thinking was wrong? It's perfect." She shook her head.

"Okay, so it's simple—" Luke began.

"Simple*minded*," Leia said.

He set his jaw. Uh-oh. She'd insulted his manhood. She knew that look.

"If you have a better idea . . . ?" Luke said, his voice tight.

Leia sighed. That was the problem. She didn't have a better idea. Luke's plan was straightforward, and while it might be foolhardy enough to get them all cooked by Imperial turbolasers, it might also be just crazy enough to work. If she were the local commander, she'd never expect anybody to do anything so stupid. "Well . . ." she began.

"That's what I thought," Luke said. There was a small note of triumph in his voice when he said it, too.

"Not to put a governor on your drive or anything," Dash said, "but if we're going to sneak in the back way, it'll take some pretty fancy flying. Treetop-level stuff to avoid local sensors. Might have to drop into the Grand Trench canyons." He looked at Lando. "Even if that piece of Corellian junk you're in doesn't fall apart, you think you can manage it?"

Lando said, "You flew it? *I* can fly it."

"Yeah, well, I was in the *Outrider* when I did it."

"The *Millennium Falcon* has had a few modifications since I owned her," Lando said.

Chewie said something.

"That right?" Dash said. "Where'd you get sublight engines that fast?"

Chewie said something else, waved his left arm.

Dash grinned. "Yeah, I guess Solo would be dumb enough to do something like that." He nodded at Luke and Wedge. "Okay. If you can keep the TIE fighters and the Destroyers busy, I can get Lando to where Boba Fett's ship is."

Chewie said something. Leia figured she knew what it meant. He was offering to go along.

"You don't have to, pal," Lando said.

Chewie spoke again.

"Thanks, I appreciate it."

"Count me in, too," Leia said.

"I don't know if that's a good idea—"

Leia interrupted him. "You don't think the Imperial commander is going to send all his TIEs out to deal with a dozen X-wings, do you? He's bound to have somebody on the planet. If they start shooting at the *Falcon,* you'll need somebody to shoot back. If Chewie is in the dorsal turret, who is going to cover your belly?"

Lando and Luke looked at each other. Luke shrugged. "She's right. And she's a good shot."

"Thank you," Leia said.

"Okay, I guess that's it," Wedge said. "The boys'll be glad to fly under your command for this mission, Luke."

"Thanks, Wedge."

Dash said, "Want to see something, kid?"

Luke looked at him.

"Through that door there."

Luke walked toward the door. Curious, Leia followed them.

Dash opened the door, into another large, hangar-like room.

"Wow," Luke said.

Leia looked through the doorway.

A ship sat perched on the cheap plastic flooring. It had smooth lines, heavy cannon mounted above and below, and it shined with a dark gleam, like chrome. It was almost the size of the *Millennium Falcon* and had an offset cockpit module, but that was as close as it got. This ship was a top-of-the-line, state-of-the-art craft; Leia had seen enough ships to recognize that it was something special.

A droid stood next to it, a stripped-down skeletal model with a tool bag slung over one shoulder.

"The *Outrider,*" Dash said. "And my droid, an LE-

BO2D9—he answers to 'Leebo,' when he bothers to answer at all. He thinks he's funny."

"How'd you afford a ship like that?" Luke said.

"Well, it wasn't clean living. You like it?"

Luke nodded. Leia could see he itched to inspect the vessel, to climb into it, to see what it would do with him at the controls.

Like boys with an expensive toy, she thought. She hoped the mercenary who owned it could fly half as well as he claimed. This didn't sound as if it was going to be an easy trip.

Leia stared at the *Outrider*. She was about to risk her life again, and that wasn't something you got used to doing, even when it was necessary. That she was going to risk it to rescue Han somehow made it worse. That she would be that . . . vulnerable, to want something—no, some*one*—so badly was scarier still. She could justify putting herself at risk for the Alliance; that was of galactic importance. But to do it for the love of a man . . . ?

She'd never thought it would happen. Her dedication to the Alliance, to defeating the Empire, had never allowed for much of a personal life. Oh, sure, there had been friends, even some with whom she'd been close, but she had always thought that her life would be spent fighting against the Emperor and his evil. She'd never seen herself falling in love, settling down, having a home or children. Probably that wouldn't happen anyway, given all that could get in the way, but at least it was a possibility now. Assuming they could find and free Han. Assuming they could escape and not get killed in the process.

Assuming Han had any real interest in her. He hadn't said the words. She'd believed he felt the same thing, but he hadn't said it.

Big assumptions, those.

Well. They'd just have to see. One thing at a time. One thing at a time.

7

Darth Vader held his lightsaber firmly, wrists locked, and watched the killer droid circle to its left. The droid was a new model, one of a dozen identical units constructed to his personal specifications. Like Vader, it also held a lightsaber. It was tall, spindly, looked something like the general-purpose Asps to be found all over the Empire, but with a number of special modifications. The unit was faster than an ordinary man, stronger, programmed with the knowledge of a hundred sword masters and a dozen different fighting styles. Against a normal person, the droid would be unbeatable and deadly—

The droid stepped in fast and cut at Vader's head. Vader blocked, and the droid chopped again, circling the humming blade in a second cut at Vader's side. Fast, but again a block—

The droid's third attack came from the opposite side as its blade flashed in a large half circle—

Vader parried and riposted, angling a slash at the droid's head—

The droid blocked and slid back a meter, out of range, blade held over its head, point angled down.

The slight ache in Vader's shoulder where Luke had cut through his armor during their fight was definitely better. He hardly felt any soreness at all with that series.

He moved in, swung a feint at the droid's neck, twisted his wrists, and pivoted the lightsaber for a second feint at the same side, then a third feint, a jab at the midsection.

The droid stepped back and crossblocked the final feint—

Vader V-stepped to his left, cocked his blade over his left shoulder, and hacked forty-five degrees at the base of the metal neck—

The droid's block was a quarter second slow. Strong as it was, it was not strong enough to offset the power and momentum of Vader's strike. The blades met, hissed and sparked, but Vader's sword shoved the droid's blade to the side. It tried to backpedal—

Too late. The lightsaber hit midway between the droid's neck and shoulder joint, sheared through the exoframe and halfway through the chest. Circuitry sparked, shorted out. Sparks and acrid smoke erupted from the droid's body. It dropped the lightsaber as its hand controls died. Fell to its knees.

Vader cocked the weapon over his right shoulder and swung in a flat horizontal arc—

The lightsaber sliced through the droid's neck and took its head off. The head fell, bounced, and the droid's decapitated body fell backward.

Vader stood over the downed droid. Soon he would have to order another dozen of them produced—this was the eighth one of the originals; he had but four left. And the next batch would need to be improved. It was getting too easy.

His shoulder definitely felt better.

He shut off his lightsaber and turned away from the droid.

An aide stood in the doorway, looking impressed and nervous.

"Clean up the mess," Vader said.

He strode away. He did not look back.

Inside his X-wing, Luke took a deep breath. "You ready, Artoo?"

Artoo whistled assent.

"This is Rogue Leader," Luke said. "Lock your foils into attack position, accelerate to sub-six and acknowledge."

"Rogue One, copy," Wedge said over the comm.

"Rogue Two, that's affirmative, lock and load."

"Rogue Three, I copy."

The rest of the squadron acknowledged Luke's orders. They were ready, as ready as they were going to get. The dayside Destroyer lay dead ahead, and by now its long-range sensors would have spotted the incoming X-wings, and the commander would have started scrambling his fighter force. The latest TIE fighters were a couple of sublight units faster than an unmodified X-wing, TIE interceptors faster still, but they couldn't get to top speed immediately, so Rogue Squadron would get one relatively free pass at the Destroyer before the TIEs got clear and moving. Not that they'd be able to do much to the Destroyer with fighter-wattage laser cannons or proton torpedoes; Destroyer shields and armor were too thick. But a lucky shot might do a little damage, and it would make the Imperials keep their heads down—they couldn't know if the Alliance might have outfitted its snub fighters with some new weapon. It would make them sweat a little.

TIEs were faster but no more maneuverable, and the X-wings had the advantage in shielding—TIEs didn't have any, save for a few of the specially equipped interceptors, like the one Vader had.

"Here they come," Rogue Six said. That was Wes Janson, an old hand.

A score of TIE fighters spewed from the Destroyer's flight bay ports.

"I see them, Wes," Luke said. "Everybody stay alert!"

Took them long enough, Luke thought. *Must have thought it was a drill; they probably don't get much action out here.* Maybe they'd gotten fat and lazy. Well. He could hope they had.

"Double up on the forward shields," Luke ordered. "Attack speed, targets of opportunity."

"Yeeehhaaawww!" one of the squad yelled into the comm.

Luke had to smile. He really should tell whoever it was—sounded like Rogue Five, that was Dix—to bottle the unofficial commspeak, but he knew just how the pilot felt.

There was nothing else in the universe that felt like flying into combat.

"Watch yourselves," Luke said.

Then he was cutting across the Destroyer's axis, laser cannons spitting high-energy beams, no time to talk now.

The battle was joined.

On the *Millennium Falcon,* Leia crouched down behind Chewie and Lando in the control cockpit. Threepio stood behind them, braced more or less in the doorway.

"Do be careful, Master Lando. We're awfully close to the tops of those trees!"

"Oh, really?" Lando said. "I hadn't noticed."

"Well. There's no need for sarcasm."

Ahead of them a couple hundred meters, Dash flew

the *Outrider*, and the wind of his passage was enough to fan the tall evergreens below; you could see the air wake ripple through the foliage. The chrome-silver ship cleared the tops of the highest trees by no more than five meters.

"Any closer and we'll get green stains on our belly," Leia said.

"Tell me about it," Lando said. "He said we'd have to fly low but I didn't realize he meant this low. Chewie, what's our altitude?"

Chewie looked at a control panel and said something in that half gargle, half moan of his.

"Oh, my!" Threepio said.

"Do I want to know?" Leia said.

"I don't think so," Lando said.

Over the comm on a shielded opchan, Dash spoke. "You nervous back there, Calrissian?"

Lando glanced at Chewie. "Who, us? Nah. I thought you said we were going to be flying *low*, Dash. We're practically in the stratosphere way up here." He cut the comm off.

Lando grinned at Chewie. "Guess I told him, didn't I?"

Dash didn't respond in words; instead, the *Outrider* dropped four meters lower. If a passenger on the smuggler's ship could have reached through the floor, he would have been able to touch the tops of the trees with his fingertips.

He's crazy, Leia thought.

"He's crazy," she said.

"Yeah, but he can fly, you got to hand him that," Lando said. "Give me a little more thrust, Chewie."

"Master Lando! What are you *doing*?"

"I can't let him think he's scared us, can I?"

"Certainly you can!" Threepio said. "He has!"

"You're crazier than he is," Leia put in.

The *Millennium Falcon* lost four meters of altitude. Chewie said something.

Threepio said, "Oh, dear!"

"What?" Leia asked.

Threepio waved his arms. "He says that another centimeter and we'll snag the laser cannon!"

Leia shook her head. "What's with this guy? What's he trying to prove?"

Lando concentrated on his flying—that was good— so he didn't look at her as he spoke. "You never heard the story of the Rendars?"

"Should I have?"

Chewie yelled something.

"I see it, I see it!" Lando said. The ship lifted a meter to avoid a particularly tall tree directly in its path.

After they'd cleared it, Lando continued. "Dash was at the Imperial Academy, a year or so behind Han. His family was wealthy and highly placed. Dash's older brother was a freighter pilot working his way up through the family shipping company. There was an accident. A control system blew out, not the pilot's fault, and the freighter crashed on liftoff from the Coruscant spaceport. Killed the crew, destroyed the ship."

Leia nodded. "Terrible. So?"

Chewie started to speak, but Lando beat him to it. "I *see* it. Do you want to fly it?"

Chewie grunted. Leia didn't need to speak Wookiee to understand that one.

"Then be quiet and let me do it."

The *Falcon* did another little hop behind the *Outrider,* settled back into its dangerous dance with the treetops.

"So, the building the freighter hit was the Emperor's private museum. Had a lot of his mementos in it. Most of them were lost in the ensuing fire.

"The Emperor was not happy. He had the Rendar family's property seized, then had them banished from Coruscant. That included Dash. They kicked him out of the Academy on Carida and off that planet, too."

Leia ground her teeth. That kind of thing was one of

the reasons the Alliance was fighting the Empire. No one should have that much power, that he could arbitrarily do such things unchecked. And Leia knew of worse, knew of much worse. The Death Star had destroyed her homeworld, killed millions, as a test of its power. Just to see if it worked. It had meant nothing to the Empire, less grief than swatting a fly.

"I can see that he wouldn't have any love for the Empire," Leia said. "Why isn't he working for the Alliance?"

Lando shrugged. "He doesn't want to owe anybody, doesn't want anybody to owe him. He works for whoever pays the most. He's downright magic with anything that flies, and he can pick wing nuts off a tabletop with a blaster without scorching the finish. He's a good man to have at your back when the going gets hot—as long as your money lasts."

Leia nodded. The Empire had ruined a lot of good people. Looked as if Dash Rendar was one more casualty.

Four TIE fighters roared in, spewing death.

Luke yelled at Wedge. "Rogue One, look out! On your port, bearing three-oh-five!"

Wedge's X-wing immediately peeled left and down. "Thanks, Luke!"

Luke punched it, swung a shallow turn, and headed straight for the attacking quad.

Use the Force, Luke.

Luke grinned. The first time he'd heard that, during the attack on the Death Star, he hadn't understood. He knew what it meant now.

"Targeting sensors off, rear shields off, reroute more power to the guns."

Artoo was not pleased and said so.

"Sorry, buddy, but this way is better."

Luke reached out. The Force was here, as it was everywhere, and it was no harder to touch deep in space than it was in the swamps on Dagobah. He let it fill him.

The TIE fighters suddenly seemed to be moving slower. Luke's hands flew over the controls; he moved the stick with sharp and precise movements. Swung to his starboard and lit the lasers, double-tapped the fire button.

Lines of fire lanced out and shattered one, two of the four TIE fighters. The explosion spat a hard spray of wreckage at him as Luke looped away. Shards of the destroyed TIEs sleeted against the X-wing's transparisteel canopy, a metal and plastic hail.

"Fine shootin', Rogue Leader," Rogue Five said.

"Thanks, Dix."

"More coming in, six blips at one-seven-five," Rogue Four said.

"Watch your back, Luke!" somebody said. "You got a tail!"

But Luke had already felt the approach of the TIE and had put his fighter into a hard downturn. He flew an outside loop and came up behind the TIE.

Luke stroked his fire button once, and the TIE shattered into expensive scrap.

"Rogue Two, you got a pair of 'em coming in at two-two-four, move it!"

"Ah, copy that, Wes. I owe you one."

"Pay me back later."

The X-wings and TIE fighters streaked back and forth through the blackness of space, tossing incandescent spears of hard light at each other.

"I'm hit," Rogue Two said. "Got my Artoo unit and punched a hole in my canopy. I've got a patch here . . . Okay, the leak is plugged."

"Break off and return to base, Rogue Two," Luke said.

"Hey, I can still shoot and I got manual."

"Negative, Will, there's too many for that. Take a walk."

Artoo whistled rapidly.

"Doesn't apply to me," Luke said. "I've got an edge."

"Copy, Rogue Leader. Rogue Two returning to base. Good luck, guys! I'll put the kettle on for tea."

Two more TIEs came at Luke, and he moved instinctively, pulled the stick and soared away from the attackers at almost ninety degrees, then looped at the top and dropped back toward the attackers in a power dive, lasers blinking.

One of the TIEs exploded; the other's engine flamed and went out, and the wounded TIE coasted out of the fight without main power.

"Here comes another wave," Wedge said. "Twelve blips at three-zero-three and closing fast."

The odds were getting worse, the dangers increasing by the second, and Rogue Squadron was down one member. Things didn't look good.

Despite that, Luke was having a great time. He might not be much of a Jedi, but he could fly.

He hoped Lando and Leia and Chewie were doing okay.

Acceleration pulled at his body as he swung the X-wing into a hard power turn.

The battle continued.

8

Late afternoon shaded into evening as Xizor left the house of his mistress, an almost palatial dwelling he had bestowed upon her as a going-away gift, though she did not yet know the affair was over. Xizor never spent more than a few months with any female. Because of his hormonal makeup, his ability to produce overwhelmingly powerful pheromones, he never had any trouble attracting new companions. But because it was so easy, he quickly tired of them, no matter how beautiful, no matter how clever. He had never found a companion he could consider his equal, and if he ever did, well, how would he be able to trust someone that adept? An interesting conundrum.

Moreover, once a meal was eaten, no matter how delicious, he preferred to dine on a different delicacy the next time . . .

A warm rain drizzled down from a condensation cloud hanging low over this section of the city. Such microweather cells were quite common at this season; a short distance away the skies might be crystal clear. As the darkness thickened and where clouds did not interfere, one could view the colorful discharge auroras and the red and blue running lights of the constant stream of ship traffic going to and coming from orbit, even here in the center of the cityglow.

The two bodyguards waiting at the exit accompanied Xizor to his armored luxury coach, where two more guards and the droid chauffeur waited. Xizor entered the vehicle and leaned back on the cloned-leather seat. His mistress would receive a call from Guri shortly, a generous severance payment and good wishes for her future. She would also be told never to attempt to contact Xizor again. Should she do so, the consequences would be . . . dire.

Thus far, only one of his ex-companions had tried to see him after their arrangement had been terminated. That unfortunate woman, he was told, had become part of a tall commercial plex on the Southern Enclave, courtesy of a giant factorylike construction droid that had somehow, alas, accidentally mixed her in with a vat of duracrete.

Life was full of dangers, even here.

"We'll have dinner at the Menarai," Xizor told the droid.

The coach lifted and swung smoothly up into the traffic pattern, bracketed front and back by bodyguards in their own airspeeders. The trio of vehicles reached cruising altitude and headed for Monument Park, where the planet's single uncovered mountain peak jutted above the surface's otherwise all-encompassing building complex. There was a restaurant that catered to the wealthy and powerful on a spire near the park, and from the shelter of the building one could view the mountain, even see through the restaurant's transparisteel walls the religious fanatics who maintained vigil over the peak to prevent tourists from stealing the bare rock for souvenirs. One booked reservations for the Menarai months in advance and then only if one's name was on the approved list. It was the most exclusive restaurant on the planet.

Exclusive, but even so, no matter how crowded the Menarai, no matter how it might upset a rich man to see an empty space when he'd waited months for a chance to dine there, a place was always kept open for Prince Xizor. If he took it upon himself to drop in, he was ushered to his private booth without delay. To most of the diners, Xizor would be simply another wealthy shipping magnate, no more important than a thousand other rich beings in the Imperial Center. They would wonder why he deserved such treatment when they did not—given that many of the patrons had more credits in their accounts than Xizor, at least in his guise of shipper.

None of them had more money than Black Sun.

Besides, Xizor was one of the place's owners, though that was not common knowledge, and word had filtered down from the top: If Prince Xizor has to wait to be seated, the manager who allows such stupidity to occur will be looking for another job before he can stammer an apology. If he is lucky.

Xizor smiled as the coach looped away from the central nexus toward the mountain. He did not often flaunt his power, but good food was one of his small pleasures, and there was no cuisine better than that of the Menarai.

The rain had stopped, and now the shadows of night condensed and intensified. Soon Coruscant would be ablaze with its own light, quite a view from a ship as it approached from space. Nowhere else in the galaxy had nearly the entire surface of a world been covered with the building blocks of civilization. To live here was truly an experience, to be at the center of everything. Coruscant was the Empire's acme; the head of Black Sun could hardly live anywhere else.

Now. What should he have for dinner? The fleek-eel

was good. Kept alive until the moment of being dipped in boiling pepper oil, the eels would have been light-years away and swimming in the Hocekureem Sea that same morning. Also, the stuffed yam and plicto steak was excellent, as was the Giant Ithorian snail in flounut butter. Or perhaps the Kashyyyk land shrimp?

So many choices, none of them bad. Well. Rather than order in advance, perhaps he would just wait until he arrived at the restaurant and decide then. True, he would have to wait for it to be prepared, but then, patience was one of his virtues, after all.

Yes. That was what he would do. He would be . . . spontaneous.

It would be refreshing.

"Heads up, boys, another wave coming in," Luke said into his comm.

"Copy that, Rogue Leader," came a chorus in return.

"Uh-oh, I see a couple of TIE interceptors in this squad," Wedge said.

"I got 'em, Wedge," Luke said. He leaned on the stick and put the X-wing into a sharp turn to port. Interceptors were faster, and the newer ones wore heavier guns. He hoped the Force would stay with him. This was getting trickier by the moment. He couldn't afford to fail; Han's rescue depended on his keeping things going—not to mention the Rogues and his own life.

He hoped Leia and Lando were doing okay wherever they were.

Lando flew past jagged outcroppings of reddish rock that looked like giant fangs. The *Falcon* zipped through a three-sided tunnel with what seemed like very little clearance below and to both sides. The sky above was like the surface of a river, blue and serene.

Threepio said, "I think perhaps one of my circuits is overheating. I really ought to sit down and power off." But the droid didn't move. Like the rest of them, he seemed hypnotized by the flight through the canyon.

There was a long-range Imperial sensor post at the edge of the great plateau into which these deep canyons had been carved by time and water, Dash had said. The only way to avoid being spotted was to sneak in below the sensor scan.

It reminded Leia of Han's desperate flight into the asteroid field after they'd fled Hoth, and the hiding place into which they'd scurried to avoid being captured by Vader—a place that had turned out to be something other than what it had first seemed.

Ahead of them, the *Outrider* flew. As Leia watched, the ship rolled, twisted on its long axis like a screw.

"Oh, man," Lando said. "A couple meters either way and we're bugs on a canopy and Dash is doing barrel rolls. He *is* crazy."

Chewie said something.

"I hear that," Lando said.

Threepio translated for Leia: "Chewbacca says that Master Dash must be part bird."

Leia found herself nodding. Lando had been right. Whatever else he was, Dash Rendar could fly.

Luke kept the Rogues spiraling in and out, drifting the skirmish several degrees one way, then the other, to keep the Destroyer's big guns from locking on them. They were doing okay so far.

"Look out, Dixie!" Wedge yelled.

Luke saw the danger. A TIE fighter had gotten below Dix and now bored in, firing at the X-wing's exposed belly. Dix cut hard to his right and began a sharp starboard turn—

Too late. The deadly lasers raked the X-wing like fiery claws and ripped into it.

Dix's ship blew apart in a fireball that ate the craft's oxygen, then winked out, leaving nothing but blasted and ionized wreckage.

Luke felt his stomach roil. *Oh, no.* They'd lost Dix.

Suddenly it wasn't a game. People were dying. Good people. He could never lose sight of that, not for a moment. It was only fun as long as nobody got hurt and that part never lasted. War was ugly. It got bad.

Now it got worse. The nightside Destroyer came around the terminator and began unloading its fighters.

No more time to think, no time to worry. Luke abandoned himself to the Force.

"Terminator coming up," Dash said. "And we're past the plateau's sensor station. Ready to go up top?"

"I was just beginning to enjoy this," Lando said. "But I suppose if we have to . . ."

They were approaching the nightside of the moon, and while the darkness wouldn't hide them from Imperial sensors, it would offer them some cover from curious eyes.

"We're about four minutes away from the shipyard," Dash said over the comm. "Any luck at all and the tooloos operating the scopes there won't notice us until we're a minute or so out. Time they get their fighters scrambled, we'll be right on top of 'em."

"Copy," Lando said.

Leia felt her stomach twist, go fluttery. The flight so far had been dangerous, but this was going to be a whole lot more so.

Lando shook his head, said, "This was not my idea, right? I want it on record that this was not my idea."

Dark shadows began to paint the rock, lengthening so fast they could see them move as the *Falcon* flew deeper into night.

"Going up," Dash said.

The *Outrider* lifted from the canyon.

"Blast!" Lando said.

Directly ahead of them, no more than a few hundred meters and getting closer fast, the canyon ended in a wall of dark rock.

Chewie roared.

Lando didn't bother to answer as he pulled the *Falcon* up in a climb that made Leia's stomach feel a lot worse.

They missed the collision by centimeters.

"Oh, better be careful," Dash said as the *Falcon* rose into the night. "Did I mention the canyon dead-ends pretty soon?"

"Just wait, Rendar," Lando said. "Next time I see you I'm going to punch you in the nose!"

"Yeah? You and what army?"

Chewie snarled.

Leia could figure that out easily enough.

Over the comm, Dash Rendar laughed.

Wedge's voice over the comm seemed calm, but there was a lot of emotion under it. "Luke, we aren't going to be able to keep this dance going much longer. Once that second Destroyer sets up a south pole, we'll be in range of the big guns on one or the other."

"I hear you," Luke said. "Artoo, would they have had time to make it to the yard yet?"

Artoo whistled. Luke glanced at his sensor screen, saw the translation of the droid's whistles. They could have made it, but barely.

"One more minute," Luke said. "Then let's make a pass at the daysider and get out of here."

"Copy, Luke. You heard the man. Let's throw a few more rocks and keep 'em jumping."

Around Luke, TIE fighters and interceptors swarmed like saurian hornets from a disturbed nest. The Rogues had taken out a score of them, maybe more, and lost one of their own, plus another one damaged. Good flying, but given the odds, they couldn't keep it up forever. He had to hope they had bought enough time.

A TIE fighter appeared in front of Luke, coming right at him.

Luke thumbed his own fire button, and the two craft sped directly at each other. Neither pilot blinked.

The TIE exploded, and Luke flew through the fireball.

Artoo's exclamation sounded like "Yeeooww!"

"You okay, Artoo?"

The droid whistled. Yes, he was okay. He had been better, however.

Luke smiled. The party was getting raucous. It was time to pack it up and leave.

"There it is, dead ahead," Dash said.

The lights of the shipyard blazed in the darkness, a beacon visible for a long way.

"We'll pass right over your target in . . . thirty seconds."

Leia leaned forward. Strained to see . . .

"There it is! There's Fett's ship!"

"Been fun, people," Dash said. "See you around."

Ahead of them, the *Outrider* pulled up in a hard climb and rocketed toward space.

"Where are you *going*?" Lando said.

"Hey, you didn't pay me to shoot, only to guide. I'm outta here."

"Dash, blast you!"

"Never mind," Leia put in quickly. "We don't need him."

Chewie pointed at the sensor screen and said something.

"Oh, dear!" Threepio said.

"I wish you'd stop saying that," Leia said. "What?"

Lando spoke before the droid could. "Company. We've got half a dozen TIE fighters on our tail!"

"Is that all? For a hotshot pilot like you, that shouldn't be a problem, right?"

Lando shook his head. "Yeah, right. But just for fun, why don't you and Chewie go see if the guns still work?"

The Wookiee came up. Leia was already on the way. "I'll take the dorsal turret," she said.

Chewie growled, and she took that for agreement.

Now things were really going to get interesting.

9

"Luke . . . ?" Wedge said over the comm.

"Right, Wedge. Rogue Squadron, this is Rogue Leader. Break off your attack, go to lightspeed—repeat, break off and jump to hyper!"

The leap into hyperspace was a trick—they weren't going far enough to need it, and they'd reenter normal space in a few seconds. But better that the Imperial fighters thought they were going far away; maybe nobody would bother to look for them at a moon just around the bulk of the huge gas planet right in front of them. That was the hope.

Rogue Squadron peeled away from the engagement in a shallow arc.

The TIE fighters, who'd obviously been ordered to defend but not to pursue, allowed them to go. Most of them.

As the Rogues sped from the battle, Luke felt a sudden wave of something he couldn't quite identify wash over him. Like a sense of danger that couldn't be ignored, some kind of warning—

Luke!

Obi-Wan!

He jerked the control stick between his knees to the side without questioning further.

The beam from a laser cannon flashed past.

If he hadn't moved it would have cooked him.

But there weren't any TIEs behind him! Only Rogue Six. As he watched, Wes's X-wing altered course to follow him. What—?

"Wes! What are you *doing*?"

Wes yelled, a short burst of expletives, then, "Luke! Something's gone wrong with my Artoo unit! It's taken control of my ship! My stick is dead!"

Yeah, Luke thought, *I'll be dead, too, if I don't do something!*

To complicate things, one of the TIE fighters who decided to give chase did get within range. The TIE let loose with a blast of its weapons, barely missing Luke.

Luke pulled the stick back into his belly and hit full thrust. The X-wing responded; acceleration mashed him into the seat; his face stretched and flattened as if a giant hand pressed hard fingers against the skin and muscles.

"Everybody get clear!" Luke managed to say through peeled-back lips. What was going on? He'd almost been fried, by one of his own! At the moment, he couldn't think about it—but he couldn't *not* think about it, either.

He could have died. If not for the Force, he would have died. Whatever he might have been would never have come to pass—

Behind him, Wes's X-wing replicated Luke's maneuver, trying to stay with him.

The TIE fighter kept shooting, too.

Blast!

This was bad, this was very bad. What was he going

to do? He couldn't fight, not one of his own people! And if all he did was run, sooner or later the out-of-control X-wing would blast him.

First things first. The TIE fighter.

Luke looped around, trying to shake Wes and lock on to the TIE at the same time.

He didn't manage either very well. The TIE fighter zipped away, and Wes kept shooting at Luke.

Luke felt the sweat seeping from him, soaking his suit. He wasn't prepared for this; it had never crossed his mind.

If Wes could bail out, that would solve it. Thing was, he couldn't eject; like the others, he wore only a lightweight flight suit, not suitable for protection against the vacuum of deep space—

Another blast of laser fire stabbed out from the pursuing X-wing.

Missed, barely!

The TIE fighter swung around. Probably didn't have any idea what was going on, but he was going to take advantage of it for sure.

Luke felt himself gripped by the fear, an icy sensation that turned the perspiration cold. What was he going to do? He had to figure it out, and he had to figure it out *fast*!

He had an idea. It was risky, but his choices were getting real limited.

Here goes—

At the apex of his climb, Luke killed his thrust and shoved the control stick forward. Inertia kept the craft going, but its relative speed compared to Wes's out-of-control craft made it seem to stop as Rogue Six rocketed past before his malfunctioning R2 unit could compensate.

The TIE fighter had looped and was opposite Wes, trying to track Luke.

Luke punched in full thrust again and swung the

stick hard to port, spiraling away in a left turn. He gave the little ship all it—or he—could take.

The TIE fighter ran into Wes's fire and shattered.

That was something, at least.

Luke felt better, but it wasn't over yet.

He jockeyed the X-wing around. Wes copied his move and fired.

Luke had never asked the X-wing for more.

Artoo shrilled, and Luke tuned it out. He had to trust the Force now; normal skill wouldn't get him out of this.

He dodged.

Another blast cooked the vacuum.

Luke stalled and dived.

Wes's ship hammered at him, splashing a glancing shot off the rear shields.

He had to shake him!

Come on, come on—

He knew the Force was powerful, but he wasn't sure his control of it was enough. A mistake and a good man would die.

A mistake and they might *both* die.

He focused himself. Cut hard to port, then starboard, gave his engines full power, pulled up and into an inside loop, circled down and *behind* Wes, almost blacking out from the G-force . . .

Help me, Obi-Wan.

Luke fired . . .

The beam splashed against the runaway X-wing's main engine precisely, cut through and killed it.

Rogue Six's thrusters flamed out.

Luke was close enough to see the R2 unit on Wes's ship try to effect repairs as he flew by, but it surely wasn't going to fix that.

Rogue Six couldn't fly very well, but it could still shoot.

It did shoot, tracking him and lancing out with pow-

erful beams. Like a wounded firecat, it was still dangerous to approach.

Luke dodged, abandoned himself to the Force again,
let the X-wing become an extension of his body. The
little ship danced, hopped, slowed, sped up, and managed to avoid being speared.

Luke felt the sigh slip from him.

Steady . . .

Luke made another pass.

Wes's R2 blasted at him. Luke imagined he felt the
heat of the beam.

Maybe it wasn't his imagination.

Come *on* . . .

"More of those TIEs coming back, Luke," somebody said.

"Not now!" Once again he let the Force direct his
aim, gave himself to it. Pinpointed the targeting sensors
in the nose cone. Felt the *rightness* of it—

Fired again . . .

A hit!

Now Wes's guns were dead and he—or his crazed
droid—couldn't fire the lasers or the torpedoes.

Luke sighed again. *Thank goodness.*

What in the galaxy could have caused it to malfunc-
tion that way?

"Wedge, see if you can get a magnetic line on Wes
and let's get out of here, fast!"

"That's affirmative, Luke."

Bad enough when it was the enemy shooting at you;
much worse when it was your own men.

"Hey, I'm sorry, Luke, I don't know what happened!" Wes said.

"Don't worry about it. We'll sort it out later. Right
now, we'd better go before the Empire decides we
might be worth chasing after all."

"Copy that, Luke."

But now that the heat—and sweaty cold—of the incident had passed, the fear oozed back, the taste of it sour in him.

He could have been blown apart.

If not for the Force warning him, he would have been fried, would have winked out like an overloaded glowbulb, never knowing what had hit him. Dead, gone, no more.

"Those TIE fighters are coming back, Luke."

"Let's move it!"

Until now, that had never seemed a real possibility to him. Luke had always thought that somehow all the lasers would miss, all the missiles would sail past harmlessly, that he would live forever. It hadn't seemed real that he could actually cease being.

Now it seemed real.

Leia fired, and the quad-barrels of the *Falcon*'s dorsal guns pistoned, spat its hard energies at the incoming TIE fighter.

The Imperial craft flew right into the beams. Exploded.

That was three she'd gotten, and Chewie had hit some of them, too, but there were more of them swarming in.

Too many more.

"We can't land," Lando said over the comm. "If we put it down on the deck, we'll get blasted!"

"What are we going to do?" Leia said.

"I don't know; we can't keep flying around—uh-oh."

" 'Uh-oh' what?"

"Boba Fett's ship—it's taking off."

"Follow it!"

"How? There's a wall of Imperial fighters between it and us!"

"Go around them!"

She was too close to lose Han now.

"I'll try."

The *Falcon* lurched, fell in a belly-twisting dive. Because they were in a gravity well and they needed the power for the shields, the artificial gravity was turned off. Leia felt herself go weightless; only the safety straps kept her from floating out of the seat. Abruptly she grew heavier as the power dive bottomed out and Lando hit the throttles hard in a climbing turn.

Another TIE fighter came into view. Leia started the guns working, but the fighter zipped past, too fast. Missed it.

She felt the *Falcon* rock as the shields were hit by enemy fire.

"I sure hope that bootleg shield generator Han installed holds up," Lando said.

Leia didn't answer; she was too busy trying to shoot down the next pair of TIE fighters coming at her.

Her gun beams lanced out and pierced one of the fighters, sent it spinning away, control surfaces riddled with holes.

She missed the other one.

She heard Chewie yelling something, and she wished she could understand him other than from context.

"I hate to be the one to say it," Lando said, "but I have a bad feeling about this."

Back at Rogue Squadron's secret moonbase, Luke and Wedge hurried from their fighters to where Wes's X-wing had been towed. Wes stood there staring at his ruined ship.

Wedge said, "You all right?"

"Yeah, I'm fine. I'd sure like to know what my Artoo unit ate for breakfast, though. What could have gotten into it?"

Luke hoped he looked better than he felt. He was still rattled, his knees a little rubbery. He took a deep breath, fought to keep his voice calm. "Why don't we see if we can find out?" he said. He waved at the crew chief. "Get a coupler on this Artoo unit, would you?"

As the chief hustled her crew over to do just that, Luke heard a whistle behind him.

Luke turned. "I don't know, Artoo. You ever heard anything like it before?"

Artoo chirped and whistled.

Luke took that for a negative.

The malfunctioning R2 unit settled to the ground. The crew chief stepped in and stuck a restraining bolt on it before it could move.

Artoo moved closer, extruded an interface, and plugged it into the other unit. Somebody plugged a translation screen into the damaged R2 unit.

Artoo whistled frantically.

"Uh-oh," Luke said, looking at the translation screen.

"What?" Wedge said.

"Look. According to this, the droid wasn't malfunctioning. It was *programmed* to shoot at me."

Wedge whistled, a counterpoint to Artoo's astromechspeak. "Who would do that? Why? *How?*"

The chief pulled her comlink from her belt and spoke into it, listened. Luke couldn't hear who was on the other end of the comlink.

"That's Rendar coming in," the chief said.

"What about Leia and Lando?"

The chief shrugged. "He didn't say."

To the chief, Luke said, "Keep an eye on this droid. Don't let anybody touch it." To Wedge, he said, "Let's go."

Luke hurried to the second hangar, where Rendar's ship would arrive shortly.

"We can't get through!" Lando said. "They'll pound us to pieces unless we get out of here! We'd better—"

His voice shut off.

"Lando? Lando!"

No answer.

"Chewie?"

No answer from there, either.

The *Falcon* seemed to be flying okay, but the comm was out.

Leia yelled, "Threepio! Where are you?"

"R-R-Right here," came Threepio's nervous voice from above her gun turret.

"Go find out what happened to the comm. Check and see if Lando is all right."

"Yes, Princess Leia."

Another TIE shot past. Leia fired at it, missed. The blasted things were fast.

The *Falcon* swung a hard turn to the left, then the right. Well, *some*body was flying it.

Threepio leaned over her turret. "Princess Leia, Master Lando says the comm unit has been damaged; we no longer have internal or external communications. Master Lando says we must leave immediately or we'll be destroyed!" There was a tinge of hysteria in Threepio's voice.

"We can't!" Leia said.

But they were already doing so. The *Falcon* arced away from the shipyard and dived between two half-constructed towers, twisted so it flew sideways. The metal support struts of one tower passed so close to Leia's guns, she could read the part numbers stamped into them.

"No!" she yelled.

One of the TIE fighters chasing them wasn't so well flown. Leia saw it smash into the tower and shatter into a fireball.

The *Falcon* twirled and flew parallel to the ground again, but only for a few seconds before Lando took it almost straight up.

Leia looked, saw they were outrunning their pursuers. She unbuckled herself from the turret. Hurried to reach the control cockpit. Threepio followed her, prattling on about something she couldn't catch.

Lando was sweating when Leia arrived.

"What are you doing?"

"Saving our lives," he said. "I used every trick in the manual, plus a few I made up, and I couldn't get past those fighters. There were too many of them. It was just a matter of time before they knocked us down."

"What about Boba Fett?"

"I lost sight of him."

"He's probably trying to run to hyperspace. Luke and Rogue Squadron . . ." she trailed off as she realized the problem.

"Yeah," Lando said. "Our comm is dead. We can't call Luke to tell him to chase Boba Fett."

"Maybe we can circle around," she said.

He shook his head. "He'll be long gone."

Chewie arrived, asked a question.

"No," Lando said. "Sorry, buddy."

Chewie expressed anger.

"Yeah, me too," Lando said. "But we can't do Han any good if we get scattered all over the landscape."

Leia felt a great weight settle upon her. Like a blanket made of soft lead, it pressed on her; she could hardly sit there without bowing.

Han. I'm so sorry . . .

"Listen," Lando said, "I don't want to add rocket fuel to a burning building, but we don't even know for sure that Han is *on* that ship. Boba Fett might have stashed him somewhere."

Leia couldn't speak. It was too much effort.

Chewie said something.

"Chewbacca is right," Threepio said. "Sooner or later Master Han will be delivered to Jabba. We can always go back to Tatooine and wait. I think that is a very good idea."

Nobody spoke for a moment.

Threepio continued, "Well, at least we're *alive*."

• • •

Luke almost took a swing at Dash; it was all he could do to restrain himself.

Wedge saw, said, "Easy, Luke."

Dash, if he was worried, didn't show it. He stood there, relaxed, and shrugged.

"You just *left* them there?"

"Hey, kid, I was paid to show them where *Slave I* was. I showed them. My job was done. If they'd wanted me to do anything else, they should have contracted for it up front."

"If anything happens to them—"

"What, kid? You gonna shoot me? I didn't make them go there. I was hired as a guide, so I guided, end of story." He turned and ambled off.

Wedge kept one hand on Luke's shoulder. "Don't do it, Luke. It won't help them."

"Maybe not, but it'll make me feel a lot better!"

Even as he felt the anger flush through him, Luke also felt a coldness, a kind of . . . slyness within it. He knew what it was.

Obi-Wan had warned him. He couldn't give in to his anger. If he did, the dark side would be there to claim him. He could feel it, waiting, ready to fill him with its bleak and unclean energies. He could feel that to allow it in would give him abilities he did not have, would give him powers ordinary mortals could not withstand. He would be able to bring Dash Rendar to his knees with a gesture—

No. Don't even think it. To give in to the dark side would be to become like Vader, like the Emperor, to become that which he fought against.

He took a deep breath, and when he blew it out, much of his anger flowed with it. Dash even had a point: He hadn't forced anybody to do anything.

One of the sensor crew ran over to where they stood. "We've got a ship coming in," he said. "No communications, but the scopes say it's a Corellian freighter."

The *Millennium Falcon*! They were alive!

"They're about fifteen minutes out," the man said.

Luke felt a vast relief. Leia. She was all right. Even though he felt that he would have known if anything had happened to her, it was still a relief to hear that the ship was in one piece.

"That gives us a few minutes," Wedge said. "What say we go and see what we can dig out of that rascaled R2 unit?"

"Good idea," Luke said.

But when they reached the place where the bollixed astromech droid had been, what they found was a smoldering pile of debris.

Somebody had blasted the droid into rubble.

Luke spun around, looking for the crew chief who was supposed to be watching the unit. He spotted the woman quickly enough.

She was pointing a blaster right at him.

10

Luke saw Wedge reach for his blaster. He yelled, "No!"

Too late.

The chief saw Wedge go for his weapon, turned slightly, and shot at him. The blast sizzled between Luke and Wedge, missed Luke by centimeters. He smelled ionized and burned air as he jumped to the side—

Wedge didn't have any choice. His blaster beam caught her square in the center of mass and knocked her sprawling.

The burned smell grew stronger and more unpleasant.

By the time Luke got to her, the chief wasn't going to be answering any questions ever again.

"Well. I guess we know who rascaled the droid," Luke said, his voice quiet. "I would have liked to know why."

Wedge shook his head. "Maybe we can find out. I'll see what the operations computer has on her."

"Do that."

It was only a few minutes later that the *Millennium Falcon* put down on the moon. Once it was stowed out of sight inside the hangar, the hatch opened and the ramp came down. Lando and Chewie walked down the ramp, followed by Threepio. Where was—?

There she was. She looked terrible. She walked as if she were a thousand years old.

"Leia?"

Her face was a study in misery. Luke moved to her, hugged her, but she was limp in his arms. "What happened?"

"Boba Fett got away," she said.

Behind them, Lando said, "Yeah, and we were lucky to get away ourselves. The place was thick with TIE fighters. I'm sorry, Luke. I tried."

Chewie nodded and said something.

Luke nodded. He turned, one arm still around Leia. Holding her thus brought up all kinds of conflicting emotions. As if he didn't have enough to sort out about Vader and the Force and the dark side, how he felt toward Leia was another whole unprobed universe.

"Come on," Luke said to her. "We'll figure something else out."

Leia was depressed, but the news of the malfunctioning droid broke through the blanket of despair shrouding her. It frightened her.

When Wedge and Lando came back from checking on the former crew chief through the opcomm, they looked grim.

"What?" she asked.

"Well," Wedge said, "it seems there was a transfer for ten thousand credits into the chief's account a few days ago, just after Rogue Squadron arrived here.

Lando managed to access the account, using, uh, a borrowed command override code."

"And . . . ?"

"The money came from a dummy corporation," Lando said. "I managed to backwalk it through two more dummy corporations. Wound up with something called Saber Enterprises. Last I heard, Saber was a front organization for the Empire's secret undercover antiespionage operations."

"You think somebody paid the chief to rig the droid to shoot Luke?" Leia said.

"Seems awfully coincidental to me otherwise," Lando said.

Leia nodded. "It's got Vader's gloveprints all over it."

Luke shook his head. "That doesn't make any sense."

"Why not?"

"He wants me alive," Luke said. "He wants me to join the Empire."

"Maybe he changed his mind," Lando said.

Leia stared off into the distance. This was bad. She'd lost Han, maybe forever—*no, don't think that*—and she didn't want to lose Luke, too. He was too important, not just to the Alliance, but to her.

She loved Han, but she loved Luke, too. Maybe not in the same way, but she didn't want to see him hurt. She had a feeling about this, an . . . intuition. This attempt on Luke's life was just the tip of something much larger, something hidden under a great depth of murky water. She had to find out what it was and stop it.

"There was another thing," Lando said. "The chief's account had a pending file of credit in it from the same dummy corporation."

"Meaning what?" Luke asked.

"Meaning there was probably going to be another transfer of funds. My guess is that the ten thousand was just a down payment. If you had gotten blown up on that run, I'd also guess that a much larger amount would have wound up in the chief's account. Sure brings up a lot of questions, doesn't it?"

Lando looked at Wedge.

"She was going to shoot Luke," Wedge said. "Second rule of self-defense is to shoot first and ask questions later."

Leia turned around and looked at Lando. "What is the first rule?"

"Be somewhere else when the shooting starts."

They looked at each other. What did all this mean?

Xizor knew that exercise was necessary, was essential for optimum health—and it helped keep underlings in line if they knew you were physically powerful. He practiced martial arts now and then, but he knew that wasn't enough. And exercise bored him. He hated to do it. Thus it was that he sat in the myostim unit when Guri came to see him. The unit was simple enough, a sensor field coupled with an adjustable, computerized electromyoclonic broadcaster. Turn it on, set the level, and the myostim unit worked the muscles, forcing them to contract and relax in sequence. You could get stronger just lying there, develop powerful mass without having to do any heavy lifting. A great toy.

Guri seemed to materialize from nowhere.

Xizor lifted an eyebrow as his thighs clenched into hard knots, relaxed, then contracted again.

"The first attempt on Skywalker's life has failed. The bribed crew chief is dead."

Xizor nodded as his calves hardened and softened under the electrical stimulus.

"No surprise. We knew the boy was extremely lucky."

"Or skillful," Guri said.

Xizor shrugged as his feet tightened and slackened.

"Either way. I've had some thoughts about the matter. Allow our agents to proceed, grease bearings as necessary. Be certain it looks as if they are in the employ of the Empire, linked directly to Vader. If they get Skywalker, good. If not, I have another idea that might be even more beneficial to us."

"As you wish."

He gestured with one arm as the stim wave began to move back up his legs toward his belly.

"This is not our only concern. We have a business to run." He paused for a moment, and when he spoke again there was a sharp edge to his voice. "Ororo Transportation."

Guri nodded.

"I do not believe the Tenloss Syndicate knows that Ororo is trying to take over our spice operations in the Baji Sector. I suppose we could make them aware of it and allow them to handle it, but that doesn't suit me. I want you to go there and meet with Ororo. Indicate our . . . *displeasure* at their ambition."

Guri nodded again.

"Before you leave, put in a comm to Darth Vader. I would like to see him at his convenience."

"Yes, my prince."

"That will be all."

She left, and Xizor watched his bare stomach ridge under the hard stim contraction, forming symmetrical and rounded rectangles. No fat coated those muscles.

Sending Guri to deal with Ororo was necessary; greed never slept, and it was incumbent on Xizor to make certain that everyone knew that to cross Black Sun was to court ruin. Guri by herself would probably be enough to knock the transportation company's leaders back into line, but Xizor never used a wrist slap when a hammer fist was called for. If you damage an enemy, you should damage him enough so that he cannot retaliate; that was a simple truth.

He had plans for Ororo, plans that would not only

chastise them for their stupidity but would also further Xizor's aims on other fronts. Everything in the galaxy was interlinked; a spark here could become a conflagration there, if you knew how to fan it properly. He was always looking for links, always checking to see how an event on that side of the galaxy could be made to serve his ends on this side. As in a tridimensional hologame, there were small moves that would add up to larger ones; a push at precisely the right place and exactly the right time could, in theory, topple a mountain. And it was his business to know when and where to push.

Yes. Ororo would pay for its temerity, and in ways it could not begin to imagine.

He leaned back and allowed the myostim machineries to make him stronger.

Darth Vader stared at the hologram of Xizor's human droid Guri.

"Very well," he said. "Tell your master I will see him. I have business on the Emperor's skyhook. Have him meet me there in three standard hours."

Vader broke the connection. What did Xizor want? Whatever it was, he did not believe for a moment that it was to serve the Empire—unless it served Xizor first.

The Dark Lord of the Sith stalked through the bowels of his castle to where his personal shuttle was kept. He could have taken the turbolift to the skyhook; most passengers and cargo were moved to the giant orbiting satellites through their tethers to the surface of the Imperial Center; but he had not stayed alive this long by taking foolish chances. Skyhook lifts seldom malfunctioned, but they were vulnerable to attack, from within and without. No, better to be in control of his own armored craft, where the dark side could be unleashed —along with laser cannon—if need be.

As he walked through one of his spare hallways, Vader considered another problem. For now, the Emperor did not want him to hunt for Luke Skywalker, at least not personally. While the Emperor had not yet spoken of it directly, the construction of the new and more powerful Death Star was behind schedule. Those in charge offered many excuses—material, workers, constantly changing plans—and the Emperor was growing impatient. Vader was fairly certain that it would be only a matter of time before the Emperor sent him to oversee the lagging project. It was amazing how a general who would drag his feet while out of the Emperor's sight would suddenly learn how to run when paid a visit from one who could call upon the dark side. Those Imperial officers who scoffed at the Force did so out of ignorance.

Those who did not fear the power of Darth Vader were those who had never stood face-to-face with him.

Vader did not agree that the Death Star was the invincible and omnipotent weapon its designers had promised the Emperor. He had heard that tale before, and the ill-equipped Rebel forces had shown just how wrong *that* was with the first Death Star.

No, that was not strictly true. It had been Luke Skywalker who had struck the deadly blow, proving to Vader's satisfaction that the Force was more powerful than the most sophisticated and deadliest technology. But—the Emperor did not agree, and there was nothing to be done about it. Nor was there anything to be done about being made to wait here. What the Emperor willed was so.

Vader reached the shuttle's bay. A guard stood at the door.

"Is my shuttle ready to launch?"

"It is, Lord Vader."

"Good." The example he'd made of the technicians in charge the one time it had *not* been ready when he wished to use it had thus far been sufficient to keep that from happening again.

Vader swept past and marched toward his vessel.

Very well. He could not seek Luke out in person, but he could arrange for others to do so. Those wheels had already been put in motion. A very large reward and the gratitude of Darth Vader had been offered for whoever brought Skywalker to him alive. That would have to do for now.

"Why me?" Luke said.

They were next to the *Falcon*. Support techs from Rogue Squadron moved in and out of the ship, repairing damage done during the failed attempt on Boba Fett's ship. The big makeshift building hadn't gotten any warmer since they'd arrived.

Leia said, "Because it's your homeworld and you're the most familiar with it. Somebody needs to be there to keep an eye out for Boba Fett. You need to practice your Jedi skills, and you need a quiet place to do it. You're the logical choice."

Luke shook his head. He didn't like it. And he didn't think Leia was being completely frank with him.

"Can't your Alliance business wait?" he asked.

"No. Take Artoo and go back to Ben's house. Lando and Chewie and Threepio and I will meet you there as soon as I am done."

Luke sighed. She was probably right, but that didn't make it any easier. "All right. But you be careful."

After Luke had taken off in his X-wing with Artoo—it was a long trip and they'd packed food and water for him, though he'd be ready for a shower when he got there—Leia spoke to Dash Rendar.

"Are you available for a job?" she asked him.

"Sweetie, I'm always available—if the money is right."

"I want you to go to Tatooine and keep an eye on Luke."

Dash raised an eyebrow. "Bodyguard? Sure, I can do that. Kid won't like it if he finds out."

"So stay out of sight," Leia said. "Somebody tried to kill him, and I think they'll try again. How much?"

Dash named a figure.

Lando whistled. "Man, you are a bandit, aren't you?"

"The best don't come cheap, Lando. In advance, Princess."

Leia smiled. "You think so little of me, Dash? Do I look that stupid? One-third in advance, two-thirds when we arrive—*if* he's still alive."

"I can't guarantee that."

"I thought you were the best."

Dash grinned. "I am. Half up front, half when you get there."

"All right."

After she'd paid Dash and he was gone, Leia turned to Lando.

"All right. Let me pose a hypothetical question."

"If you don't mind a hypothetical answer, go ahead."

"What would be the best way to contact somebody high up in Black Sun?"

Lando stared at her as if she'd just told him she could fly by waving her arms. He shook his head. "The *best* way? Don't."

"Come on, Lando. This is important."

"Princess, Black Sun is bad news. You don't want to get into bed with them."

"I'm not planning on getting into bed with them. I just want to rummage through their wardrobe chest."

"What?"

Leia said, "Somebody just tried to kill Luke. Maybe it was Vader. Maybe not. Black Sun has a vast spynet of its own, older, maybe even wider than the Alliance's. They can find out who is responsible."

Chewie half grunted, half moaned something.

"I'm with you, pal," Lando said. He exchanged glances with Chewie. "This is a big mistake."

Leia continued. "But you have the connections and can put me in touch with them, right?"

"It's still a bad idea."

"Lando . . ."

"Yeah, yeah. I know a few people."

She smiled. "Good. Where do we find them?"

11

The Emperor's skyhook was half again as large as Xizor's and far more opulent. The Dark Prince preferred to keep his best treasures on the ground; he felt they would be safer there. Not that there was any real danger of a skyhook dropping out of the sky—it had happened on Coruscant but once in a hundred years, and that had been a freakish combination of a power failure, a solar storm, and a freighter collision.

Then again, the Emperor had a lot more treasures than anybody else in the galaxy, and the loss even of a city-size skyhook would be but a small pail subtracted from his vast sea.

Xizor stood on a high, wide terrace overlooking the central park of the huge space habitat. His bodyguards, now at travel strength of an even dozen, formed a semicircle from the balcony's edge with Xizor alone inside it. Here he stared out at full-size evergreen and deciduous trees, some of which topped thirty meters. A section of the park immediately below him was planted and climate-controlled into a fecund jungle, a riot of colorful flowers, electric reds, bright blues, phosphorescent oranges among the verdant hues, those ranging from the palest of greens to a broad-leafed vine whose waxy leaves were almost black.

Xizor did not care much for botany, but he knew good work when he saw it. Perhaps he could entice the Emperor's gardener away for his own skyhook?

He felt Vader approach before he heard or saw him. The man did have a presence, no doubt about that. Xizor turned and offered a small bow. "Lord Vader."

"Prince Xizor. You had something to discuss?"

No polite small talk, no social niceties from Vader. Almost refreshing, given some of the toadies Xizor encountered. Almost.

"Yes. The location of a secret Rebel base has come to my attention. I assumed you would want to know of this."

Vader was silent save for his measured, mechanical breathing, which suddenly seemed quite loud. Xizor could almost see Vader's brain working, measuring, calculating. Wondering: What was the head of Black Sun up to?

Xizor kept his face carefully neutral for the recording holocams he knew were watching. His, the Emperor's, Vader's—and whoever else might be good enough to get past the Emperor's security to be spying on them.

"Of course," Vader finally said. "Where is this base?"

"In the Baji Sector, out on the Rim. The Lybeya System, hidden on one of the larger Vergesso Asteroids. It is my understanding that there is a shipyard full of vessels undergoing repair. Scores, perhaps hundreds, of Rebel ships, ranging from fighters to troop carriers."

Vader said nothing.

"Destruction of such a base would no doubt greatly cripple the Alliance," Xizor continued. A bland understatement, offered as if ice would not melt upon his tongue.

Again, a protracted silence. Then: "I'll have my agents check it out," Vader said. "If it is as you say, then the Empire will be . . . indebted to you."

Oh, that must have hurt, to have to say that. Xizor gave Vader a courteous nod. "Merely my duty, Lord Vader. No thanks are necessary."

He could almost feel Vader squirming. To have to owe Xizor must have rankled. But what could he do? If this report was true—and certainly it was—it was a succulent and ripe offering. The Rebels didn't have so many ships that they could afford to lose any, much less an entire yard full of them. This truly was a service to the Empire.

That the shipyard was, unknown to either the Rebels *or* the Empire, owned by Ororo Transportation, the same company that had dared tread on Black Sun's spice operations in that sector—well, so much the better. Here was another way to skewer two eels with one spear: Ororo would be much damaged, and the Emperor's trust in Xizor would be greatly enhanced at the same time.

It truly was an ill wave that washed no good ashore.

Vader turned and left, black cape flagging behind him. Xizor's bodyguards prudently stepped well aside to allow him to pass.

Vader would have to verify the report. The Emperor would send forces to attend to the base. With any luck at all, Vader would be the one dispatched, given the Emperor's well-known disposition regarding such things: You found it, you take care of it. That would get Vader out of the way and allow Xizor a bit more freedom to continue the unfolding of his plan.

He turned and looked down at the miniature jungle below. Schemes were like plants in many ways. You put them where you wanted them, fed and watered them, pruned them as needed, and they grew as you expected. By and large.

He waved one of his bodyguards over.

"My lord?"

"Find out who is in charge of this." He waved at the park. "Offer him twice the credits he is being paid to come to work on my skyhook."

"My lord." The bodyguard bowed and hurried away.

Xizor took a deep breath and inhaled the oxy-rich and jungle-scented air. It smelled very alive. Like wet mushrooms and leaf mold and fresh grasses all mixed into a fine odor. Very alive, and he never felt more so himself than when he was manipulating things to his satisfaction.

Luke covered the X-wing with the camo-netting and stood back next to Artoo. "There. That ought to do it." From the air, the ship should be invisible, and with all its power systems shut down and offline, a flyby wouldn't pick it up on a quick sensor scan. Not that he was particularly scared after the incident with the crew chief; it just made good sense not to let passersby know there was an Alliance ship parked here.

Heat rose from the ground in shimmery waves, and the suns seethed and offered yet more light and warmth than the desert could absorb. The reflections from the sand were actinic and bright, and Luke had to squint against the hard light. He didn't worry too much about somebody just happening to pass by—nobody came out here without a really good reason.

He walked back to the house—he still thought of it as Ben's—with Artoo rolling along the bumpy ground behind him. The short droid chirped and whistled at him. He sounded concerned, and Luke guessed he was talking about Leia and the others.

"Yeah, I know, I worry about them, too. But they'll be all right."

He hoped.

Inside, Luke touched a control, and a panel of syn-stone on the curved roof slid back and exposed the so-lar panels hidden underneath. The house had been running in reduced mode on battery power while he'd been gone, and it was not much cooler inside than out. With the panels suddenly feeding the system more power than it could use, the air conditioner kicked on and a welcome cool breeze blew through the small house.

Luke felt grubby from his flight. He stripped and took a long shower. Fortunately, the water condensers had filled the underground tanks while he was away, and he had enough water to lather and rinse twice. When he was done, he felt a lot better. It was a long hop from Gall, and he was looking forward to stretch-ing out and sleeping in a bed for a change.

But maybe he would just finish the facets on the lightsaber jewel first. He had a lot to think about, and he didn't think he would be able to take a nap just yet; too many things buzzing around in his head. Might as well do something useful.

He put on a robe and moved to the worktable.

"Rodia?" Leia said.

"Rodia," Lando said.

They were in the *Falcon*, moving through hyper-space. Chewie was asleep in the bunk behind the lounge—the only one long enough to hold him stretched out—and Threepio had powered down. So it was just the two of them in the cockpit.

"Why Rodia? That's a long way from here, halfway to Coruscant."

"I know, but that's where my contact is. Name is Avaro; he owns a small casino in the gambling complex in Equator City. The complex is run by Black Sun. Avaro will know who to contact."

"Okay."

"Might be a little tricky, though."

"Why is that?"

Lando shook his head. "Well, before Vader showed up on Cloud City and gave him to Boba Fett, there were other bounty hunters looking for Han. I found out when we were poking around in Mos Eisley that a Rodian thug named Greedo caught up with Han in one of the cantinas there. Greedo was going to blast him for the reward. There was a shootout. Han walked away. Greedo didn't."

"So?"

"Greedo was Avaro's nephew."

"You think he'll hold that against us?" Leia asked.

"Maybe. Maybe not. All I know about Rodian customs is that they are big on hunting. If somebody had shot my nephew, I might be unhappy with them."

"We didn't shoot him, Han did."

Lando grinned. "Well, yes, that's true. But we *are* his friends."

Leia leaned back in her seat. Always more obstacles. Then again, maybe this wasn't really a problem. No way to tell until they got there.

Around them, hyperspace flowed as the *Falcon* carried them to whatever awaited.

Vader knelt on one knee as the Emperor stared through his viewer plate at the spires of the city. Abruptly he turned. "Do get up, Lord Vader."

Vader obeyed.

"So our agents have verified this report?"

"They have, my master."

"A hundred Rebel ships? Plus, no doubt, their pilots and officers."

"Likely, yes."

"That's Grand Moff Kintaro's sector, is it not? He has been lax in allowing such a base to become established. We will speak to him."

Vader said nothing. Grand Moff Kintaro would likely be out of a job soon and also likely out of breath —permanently.

"Well. You must take part of the fleet and go there immediately. Destroy the base. The loss of ships and troops will be most damaging to the Rebels."

"I thought perhaps Admiral Okins might command the expedition."

The Emperor smiled. "Did you?"

Vader felt his hope evaporate. "But if it is your wish, I shall lead the attack."

"It is my wish. You may take Okins if you like, but you are to personally ensure the assault."

Vader bowed. "Yes, my master."

As he left the Emperor's most private chamber, Vader fumed. The base was there, just as Xizor had said. It would be a powerful victory for the Empire and relatively easy—ships under repair would not be able to lift to defend themselves, and it would be like shooting game birds at roost, but he did not trust the Dark Prince, and he knew the man did nothing for free.

What was in this for Xizor? What did he hope to gain?

Vader brooded as he walked. At least he had not conveyed to the Emperor who had given the Rebel base's location. He'd had the recordings from the skyhook's holocams erased and his own recordings locked away. A small victory, but any such triumph over Xizor was better than none.

Vader was met at the exit of the Imperial Palace by Admiral Okins. "Prepare your ships, Admiral. I shall be carrying the flag on my Destroyer."

Okins bowed. "At once, Lord Vader."

Vader looked up into the night skies over Imperial Center. The darkness was held at bay by the millions of lights on the surface, and up where the glow dimmed, the tiny dots of spacecraft arriving and leaving looked like a swarm of Belvarian firegnats, reds and greens and blinking white ventral landing beacons. He would take his ships and crush the Rebel shipyard, smash it flat, and then he would hurry back here. Xizor was up to something, and it would be best if he found out what quickly.

12

Luke took a deep breath. He stood outside Ben's house, the first stars of evening aglimmer, the moon still on the rise. The air was warm but not as scorchingly hot as it had been. He held the completed lightsaber in his right hand. He had assembled it according to the old book's direction; everything should work.

Should work. But he'd come outside to test it. That way, if it blew up, at least it wouldn't take Ben's house with it.

Artoo stood nearby, watching. Luke could have had the droid try it without any risk to himself, but what kind of Jedi would do that?

"Go back inside," he told Artoo.

Artoo was not happy with that and said so, ending in an air-forced-through-rubbery-lips noise.

"Go on. If something happens, I need you to tell Leia."

Yeah. Tell her Luke, the galaxy's biggest idiot, flash-

*flamed himself into a black crisp because he couldn't
follow an elementary circuit diagram.*

Artoo left, whistling his protest as he went.

Luke let his breath out. He waited until Artoo was
out of sight, then took another deep breath, held it, and
pushed the control button—

The lightsaber glowed; the blade extruded to full
length, just under a meter, and began to hum with
power. It gave off a green gleam that was quite bright
in the early night.

Luke grinned and let his indrawn breath escape.
Whew.

Well, it wasn't like he *really* thought it was going to
explode.

He waved the lightsaber experimentally. It had a
good balance, maybe even better than his first one. He
drew himself up into a ready stance, slid forward, and
swung through a series of downward cuts, alternating
from left to right and back.

Yes!

There was a thin spire of rock jutting up from the
dry ground a few meters away. He moved to it, cocked
the lightsaber, and whipped it down at a forty-five-de-
gree angle. The humming blade crackled, sheared
through a wrist-thick chunk of rock, left a smooth cut.

He nodded and relaxed his fighting stance. He held
his left hand near the blade. No sensation of heat; that
was good; it meant the superconductors were working.

Behind him, Artoo chirped and rolled to a stop.

Luke shut the lightsaber's power off. Saw the droid
and shook his head. He had a mind of his own, Artoo
did.

"Hey, it works great," Luke said. "I knew it would,
you know."

Did Artoo's whistled agreement have a sarcastic
tone?

Luke chuckled. Well. No matter. He had built the
elegant weapon, and it worked. That was something.

Maybe he would learn how to be a Jedi Master after all.

He looked up at the stars. He hoped Leia and the others were doing okay.

Leia, Chewie, and Lando sat in Avaro's private office, facing him across a large desk made of some kind of carved yellowish bone.

Avaro's skin had faded to a dull green; he was much fatter than most of the Rodians Leia had seen, and he spoke Basic with a lispy accent.

"I thee no prowblemth," he said. "Gweedo thouldn't have twied to take Tholo alone. He wath not vewwy bwight, my nephew. Tholo ith fwothen, Kenobi ith dead, yowah money ith ath good ath anybodyth."

Well. So much for family ties. Made things easier, though she wished Avaro would speak some language in which he was more proficient. She didn't know what, given that her Rodian was elementary. Oh, well. She could understand him with a little work, and that was all that was necessary.

"So you will put us in touch with the proper people?"

Avaro nodded. "Yeth. It will take a few dayth. Local contakth won't do you any good, you need an off-planet wepwethentative."

"Fine."

"Meanwhile, feel fwee to enjoy owah cathino. Woomth will be made available fowah you."

Leia nodded. "Thanks."

If Mos Eisley was bad, this place was worse, Leia thought, as they left Avaro's office and moved toward the hotel section. There were electronic gambling devices, card games, wheels of fortune and the like, with players and dealers and operators busy at them, but the floor was worn and dirty, the air filled with smoke and an odor of spice that indicated some of the patrons

might be chemically enhanced—or chemically debili-
tated, depending on how you viewed such things. Large
armed guards stood at regular intervals, looking, she
thought, for somebody to shoot. It all looked seedy and
unkempt.

Lando glanced around with a critical eye.

"See anything you like?" Leia said.

"Couple of the card games look as if they might be
honest. Place like this in a complex with so many other
casinos pretty much has to be on the up-and-up. House
percentage ensures a good profit, and if there aren't a
few big winners now and then, the customers go elsewhere. Better stay away from the credit disk machines
and the wheels, though. Those'll be rigged."

"Don't worry, I don't gamble."

Lando grinned.

"Something funny?"

"Princess, you're the biggest gambler I've ever met.
But you don't risk money, you risk your neck."

Leia also had to grin a little at that. He had a point.

Threepio waited at the entrance, and he did not
seem happy to be there. He did seem relieved to see
them return. "I hope your meeting went well," he said.

"Yeah, it did," Lando answered. "Though I think
we might take you to translate for us next time. Avaro
has a slight problem with Basic."

"Happy to be of service," Threepio said. "I'd much
rather stay with you than out here alone. Some of the
patrons seem quite unsavory."

Leia smiled again. There was an understatement.

"We'd better get checked in," Lando said. "Then we
can come down and see just how honest this operation
is."

It was nearly a standard week after his meeting with
the Emperor, and Darth Vader now stood on the bridge

of his *Super*-class Star Destroyer, about to leave hyperspace. They had entered the Baji Sector and would soon be in the Lybeya System. In formation with him were two *Victory*-class and one *Imperial*-class Star Destroyers, more than sufficient firepower to destroy a single shipyard.

Better too much than too little, the Emperor had said.

Vader took no particular joy in this kind of mission, it was so impersonal; but it was a necessary part of the war. The enemy could not fight without equipment, and depriving him of it was much better in the long run than waiting to meet in battle, no matter what Vader's personal preferences might be.

"We are dropping to sublight, Lord Vader."

He turned and saw a junior officer standing there. He had heard that the officers drew lots when it came time to deliver messages to him, and the loser had to go. It was good that they feared him. Fear was a better weapon than a blaster or a lightsaber.

Vader was silent, allowing the man to worry for a moment. "Very well," he finally said. "Set a course for the Vergesso Asteroids, using the coordinates for the shipyard. I will be in my chambers. Call me when we get there."

"Yes, Lord Vader."

After the frightened officer hurried away, Vader stood there staring after the man. He would much rather be hunting Luke Skywalker than playing figurehead on a mission any line officer with half a working brain could manage. True, he had his agents in the field —some volunteers, some conscripted—many of whom were quite adept, but it was not the same as doing it himself.

He blew out a particularly labored breath. Unfortunately, he had not been given a choice. The Emperor did not ask for opinions when he issued a command.

The best Vader could do was to hurry and finish as quickly as possible.

He headed toward his chambers.

Lando sat at a table with five other cardplayers, engaged in a game Leia didn't recognize. Each player was given seven thin electronic rectangles by the dealer droid, allowed to discard up to four of them, then to draw replacements. The game seemed to involve sorting these card plates into colors and numbers, then betting that the resulting combinations would either total more points than the other players' or come closer to some ideal. Leia wasn't quite sure about that part yet. Apparently each player was given the same number of points on a counter to begin with, and the winner was the one with the highest total when the session ended.

Lando seemed to be doing well at the game. The electronic counter in front of him showed a positive balance higher than all but one of the others.

"The bet is fifteen," the droid said. "The sum is minimum and the color is open."

"Match," the bald man next to the dealer said. "In green."

"Match, in blue," a young Rodian female next to him said.

"Double," Lando said. "In red."

The other players groaned.

Lando smiled.

Threepio stood nearby, watching, as did Chewie. Threepio kept his voice quiet and said, "I don't understand how he keeps winning. He isn't playing correctly. The odds on the match he just offered are eight hundred and six to one. It would be very difficult to achieve that combination."

"He's bluffing," Leia whispered.

Threepio turned to look at her. "That doesn't seem very wise."

Three of the players tossed their cards into the retrieval tray.

"Sure it is," Leia said. "He's winning and they are intimidated. Rather than risk losing more, they prefer to drop out."

"But what if one of the other players has a superior hand and doesn't drop out?"

"Watch," she whispered.

Now just Lando, the bald man, and the Rodian female were left in the round.

"Match," the bald man said.

"Plus a tenth," the Rodian said.

"Redouble," Lando said. "In red, maximum count."

"He can't possibly achieve that," Threepio whispered.

Chewie growled at him.

"How rude. I was merely stating the truth—"

"Be quiet," Leia said. She was interested in seeing how the others reacted to Lando's gambit.

The bald man shook his head and tendered his cards. "Too steep for me."

The Rodian looked at her cards, held in such a way that Leia could not see them, then glanced at Lando.

Lando smiled at her. The expression was at once warm and mocking. He looked self-satisfied, confident, even smug.

Oh, he was good.

The Rodian muttered something Leia didn't catch, though she guessed it was probably a curse of some kind. She shoved her cards into the collector.

"Round to player number three," the droid said.

Lando tossed his cards into the collector and turned to grin at Leia.

Threepio said, "I can't believe it."

Leia said, "Sometimes the appearance of strength can be as effective as strength itself. Think about the Bulano serpent, which has no teeth or claws or poison but which can blow itself up to five times its normal size, making itself look fiercer and more dangerous. It might not really matter whether you can beat an opponent if *he* believes you can."

"I suppose you have a point," Threepio said. But he did not sound convinced.

Leia hoped Lando was having fun; she wasn't. They'd been here for three days, and since she didn't care to wager on the games of chance in this pit, it wasn't interesting for her. She'd practiced with a Rodian electrodictionary and learned a few words and phrases. She'd gone outside a couple of times, Chewie staying with her like a shadow, but that wasn't much fun, either. Like Mos Eisley this time of year, it was hot. Unlike that wretched place, there was an ocean not too far away from the gambling complex, so the humidity was much higher. It was thus hot *and* sticky, hardly an improvement.

She could, she supposed, go to that body of water and sit on a beach or something. Avaro had made it known that many tourists did that, swam or motosurfed while their friends or relatives spent time in the casinos. Of course, sitting on a beach and enjoying the breeze and a cold drink might be fun, but probably not as much fun with a grumbling Wookiee complaining about the sand in his fur.

Besides, if something came up, she wanted to be right here.

There was a row of holoboard games set up in one corner of the casino, with players betting on their skills there, and Chewie seemed interested, the way he kept looking in that direction.

She shook her head. "Come on," she said to Chewie. "You want to play, play. I'll watch and Threepio can stand behind you and offer bad advice."

The Wookiee raised his eyebrows.

The three of them left Lando and headed toward the board games. Amazing how fast a path cleared for them. Leia didn't know if that was because of their connection to Avaro, who deigned to pass through the smelly room from time to time, or because Chewie led the way. There was a "no shooting inside" policy, they'd been told, but almost everybody seemed to be sporting a weapon of some kind, and Chewbacca's bowcaster looked particularly lethal.

She was surprised there didn't seem to be any Imperial presence. No stormtroopers, no off-duty officers, nothing. Maybe it was because Black Sun had some interest in the complex.

She sighed. Somehow when she'd signed on to help the Alliance, she'd never pictured herself in a ninth-rate, bug-chewed casino waiting to be contacted by a representative of the galaxy's largest criminal organization. If somebody had told her that even a few months ago, she would have laughed and told them to see a medic.

Trying to guess your own future turned out wrong almost all the time.

Life was strange that way.

13

Artoo fired a crackling beam of electricity at Luke. Tatooine's desert morning air sizzled with a spark that arced a full two meters long.

Luke, in the grip of the Force, had already snapped the lightsaber over to block the artificial lightning bolt. The charge cascaded harmlessly from the blade.

"Too easy," he said.

Artoo whistled.

"I know, I know, it's not your fault you're no Darth Vader."

Luke relaxed a hair. It took a few seconds for the capacitor that ran Artoo's electroprod to build up enough of an electrical overload for another discharge. With the Force, the blue flash was easy to deflect; without the Force, it would zap him pretty good, since there was no way he could dodge the bolt.

Not that there was any danger. The electrostatic charge would make his hair stand on end and tickle some, but even with almost two hundred thousand volts, the amperage was so low that it couldn't do much more than that, unless he was standing in a puddle of water.

Freestanding water was unlikely out here in the Wastes.

Luke heard a distant drone. It was a faint noise but quickly grew louder. He turned and looked into the morning desert—

Bzzzhhtttt!

Luke jumped a meter, came down rubbing at his backside. "Hey, ow!"

Artoo made a noise Luke had come to believe was his version of a laugh.

"That's not funny!"

Artoo chirped and whistled, punctuated his reply with a bladder squeeze.

"I know I didn't tell you to quit, but you saw me turn and look away!"

Artoo said something that was probably derogatory.

"Yeah, well, you just remember that next time you need a lube."

Artoo whistled, sliding up and down the scale.

Master Yoda would be shaking his head. So much for Luke's control of the Force. One little slip in concentration and *poof!* it was gone.

Luke quickly forgot his irritation at himself and the little droid. Those sounds were getting louder, and he could see the dust trail now, pointing like a comet right at him. Engines.

Somebody was coming to call, and there appeared to be a lot of them.

"Maybe we'd better get out of sight," Luke said. "Hide inside, Artoo."

With Artoo safely in Ben's house, Luke circled around to a sandy hillock and crouched down. He couldn't be bolting every time some passing dune rat coughed. He had to stay and see what was going on.

The noise of the engines was an echoing racket now, and Luke finally recognized the source: swoops.

Swoops were long, raked repulsor craft with a plowlike scoop on the front. The vehicles were capable of seating two, were fast and maneuverable but hard to control well. They weren't much more than huge engines with seats and controls, and the combination of big repulsors and hot turbothrusters made for a mean, fast, noisy flier. A speeder bike was a child's toy compared to a fully dressed-out swoop. Most people associated the small, unprotected craft with gangs, outlaws who did almost anything as long as it wasn't legal. Some of them were famous, like the Nova Demons and the Dark Star Hellions. They could make their swoops do everything but dance. They ran spice, smuggled weapons, did odd jobs for various factions of the underworld, and generally raised a lot of grief wherever they went.

Of course, not everybody who flew a swoop was a thug.

He'd spent quite a bit of time riding a borrowed swoop himself when he'd been a teen, darting in and out of the canyons and roaring through the streets of Mos Eisley late at night when the traffic patrol was thin.

Question was, what was a swooptroop gang doing out here? He was the only person around for a hundred kilometers. Had they gotten lost?

Not likely, given their time in the seats.

No, if this was what he thought it was, they were coming to see him.

And he didn't think they were coming out to wish him a nice day. Well, he'd wanted a real test for his lightsaber. Looked as if he might be about to get one.

Luke looked for insignia as the swoops roared in and began to circle Ben's house. There were eight, nine . . . a dozen of them, and they all wore protective goggles and shock helmets, but their flight suits weren't matched. A couple of them wore blue neocels; a couple wore orange and tan; one was in green puff sleeves; another sported dyed red bantha hide; and about half of them wore freight handler grays.

All had the same insignia on their jackets—Luke couldn't quite place it, though it looked vaguely familiar somehow.

All carried blasters.

He wasn't as well hidden as he'd thought. One of them spotted him, jerked his blaster up, and fired. The beam sizzled past him, turned sand into muddy glass. Not even close, but it didn't look as if they were here to take any prisoners.

Uh-oh.

He heard one of the bikers yell above the engine racket: "Blow the little runt to Bespin, boys!"

Luke hurried to find better cover. There were a couple of large boulders that would keep most of their fire off him. He ran. His own blaster was in the house; all he had was his lightsaber and—ten-to-one, twelve-to-one odds? That could be a lot better. He'd never outrun them on foot. Not a whole lot of places to hide out here.

Why were they trying to kill him? Who sent them?

He needed to know that. He also needed to stay alive.

The engines rumbled; the vibrations of the repulsors shook the ground; the sound washed over him in hard bass, and the subsonics made his head ache. He could see their mouths working, but he couldn't hear what they were yelling.

Okay, Luke. Think *of something.*

The swoopers roared in, snapped off shots at him. Most of the bolts didn't come close, and he was able to block those that did with his own unaugmented skills. He tried to let the Force fill him, but it didn't happen. Hard to concentrate with all that racket and a dozen armed thugs taking potshots at him that way.

Two of the riders headed for him; both fired again. Neither was even close; their beams missed by a meter.

Fortunately the swoops kicked up a lot of grit. A cloud of dust surrounded them and offered a translucent tan screen.

Again a blaster beam went wide as Luke jumped and swung his glowing green blade.

Behind him there came a crash. Luke spun, saw that two of the swoops had collided. One of them angled off and smashed into a clump of rocks, the rider leaping free at the last second. The other bike settled to the ground, damaged but probably not unusable. They couldn't shoot and they couldn't fly. Lucky for him.

A roar to his left. Luke twisted.

A biker roared in; he had what looked like a giant ax in his hand!

Another engine screamed closer than the axman. Luke set himself, and as the second swooper came in, he swung his saber in a feint and slammed his boot into the rider.

Luke's kick toppled the attacker from the swoop. The deadman switch in the grips immediately killed the turbine, but not the repulsor engine. Luke hopped onto the swoop, grabbed the handlebars, and twisted the start ring. The swoop's turbine grumbled back online.

Now the odds were better. He couldn't keep riding his luck; better to take his chances riding one of these.

He opened the throttle a little, hit the retros, turned, put the swoop into a one-eighty and kicked up a sandwall, just like he'd done as a teen. He pointed the swoop at the axman and opened the throttle wide.

The acceleration nearly unseated him, but he managed to stay in the saddle.

Oh, boy! He'd nearly forgotten how much fun one of these was!

The axman's weapon shattered when it hit Luke's saber. Luke twisted the throttle, turned, roared away.

The next rider nearest Luke was the one dressed in

puffy green. With the swoop's turbos open wide, it didn't take long to reach him.

Green saw him coming, and by the time he figured out Luke wasn't one of his gang, it was too late. He tried to turn away at the last second, but Luke's cut sheared through Green's right thruster-control line. The right jet shut down, but the left jet did not, and the swoop immediately spun out of control. Luke was past him and safe, but the wildly twirling and gyrating little craft flew into the path of another of the gray riders. There came a crunch of metal and plastic as the two swoops smashed into each other and crashed to the ground.

Well, well. Three down, nine to go. So far, so good.

It was too good to last.

The leader saw Luke and used hand signals to move his troops. They scattered and re-formed in a unit.

Luke swung the swoop into a wide turn and hit the throttles. If he took this baby a few hundred meters up and out of the sand and ground clutter, he could open it up to racing speed. He could be at Beggar's Canyon in minutes. He'd explored just about every centimeter of that place in his T-16; no way they'd run him down there. He could pick them off one at a time, disable their machines—shoot, he could capture the whole gang!

There was an extra set of goggles clipped to the handlebars. Luke belted his lightsaber, pulled the goggles free, and strapped them on. He'd need them—when the afterburners kicked in on a hot swoop, it could hit a good 600 kph. A bug would put an eye out at that speed. He hoped the machine's owner kept this rake tuned.

Beggar's Canyon, here I come.

Beggar's Canyon was actually a series of interlinked canyons. Long ago, there had been a lot of water on

Tatooine, and much of it had flowed as rivers. Beggar's Canyon had been the confluence of at least three rivers, and, along with millions of years of wind and rain and sunlight, the flowing water had carved deep and twisted valleys into the rock.

It had been a while since Luke had flown the canyons. Then again, they hadn't changed since his last visit. He and a few of the other local would-be star pilots had engaged in mock firefights here, using harmless light beams for lasers. Plus he'd hunted womp rats, some of them three meters long, but hard targets to hit with a low-powered sporting blaster while traveling at speed.

The pack of swooptroops was still behind him as he dropped below ground level. They hadn't gained on him, save for one of the riders, who was only a hundred meters or so back. But the pack hadn't lost much distance, either; it was only a few hundred meters behind the rider dressed in blue, and holding steady.

Luke grinned. *Let's see how they like playing in my territory.*

The route called the Main Avenue went more or less straight for nearly two kilometers before it made a sharp-angled turn to the right. Dead Man's Turn, they called it, and for good reason. Luke dropped his airspeed as he approached the intersection. Try to take it too fast and you'd turn yourself into a gooey paste on the far wall of the turn.

He hit the retros as he adjusted the turbojets for a hard arc to the right. The swoop slewed a little, drifted to the left; then the thrusters straightened it out with a heavy shove.

Easy as sneezing.

The rider behind him, apparently unfamiliar with the canyons, didn't slow down enough.

Luke heard the crash as the swooper hit the far wall of the turn. The fuel cell let go, and a brilliant yellow-orange flash and fireball rose into the air.

No time to worry about that; another turn was up-coming, a long zigzag to the left, right, then left again, and he needed to keep to the center of the corridor, which narrowed in the middle of the stretched-out Z.

He didn't see the rest of the swooptroops behind him, but if they wanted to catch him, they'd have to be back there somewhere. They could stay high, but to see him they'd have to be so high they couldn't possibly catch up. And if they got that far away, he could find an overhang and hover under it and they'd never find him.

Four down, eight to go.

Seconds later one of the graysuits appeared in Luke's rear viewer.

He was pretty good, to have gained so fast. Or pretty stupid.

Gray gained. He was within sixty or seventy meters now.

Time to thread the needle. There it was, just ahead.

The Eye of the Needle was a narrow slot with jagged rock teeth lining it.

Luke gunned the turbojets. Went through the slot. Close enough so he felt a shard of rock catch his jacket and tear it. *Man—!*

Gray, hot on Luke's tail, tried to follow him.

Didn't make it.

Boom . . .

The rest of them were still after him. And the bad odds were still bad. It might be a long afternoon. Or a short one . . .

As he throttled back for a sharp turn, Luke heard a hoarse yell: "He's got help! We ain't gonna win this one, Spiker! Let's burn!"

Huh? Help?

Luke looked over his shoulder.

A swoop, engines off, dropped silently in free fall. The man on the machine wore black, his head shrouded in a flight helmet and polarized shield, a blinking blaster held in his outstretched right hand. He was shooting at the swoopers.

If that guy on the swoop didn't light his engines real soon, he was going to turn that expensive machine and himself into a big smoking crater—

As if he'd heard Luke, the falling swoop's engines ignited. The little craft continued to fall, but more slowly.

It didn't look as if he'd kicked the repulsors on in time—

He kept firing as he fell, missing but making the swoopers scatter. Who—?

The swoop got to within a handspan of the ground and stopped. It hovered, dead still.

Man, that was flying.

The swoopers took off. After a moment, the stranger eased his craft toward where Luke had put his swoop into a hovering idle.

The man pulled off his helmet and face shield.

Dash Rendar!

"What are you doing here?" Luke said.

Dash shrugged. "Saving your butt from swoop scum, it looks like."

"You know what I mean. *Why* are you here?" Luke looked at the fallen attackers. "Well?"

"Well, here's the thing. Leia—she's a hot package, that one—Leia kinda wanted me to keep an eye on you until she gets back."

"She *what*?"

"Ease up, you'll blow a fuse. No big deal."

"Listen, pal, I don't need a baby-sitter!"

"Oh, yeah, you coulda taken these melloons all by yourself, right?"

"I wasn't doing so bad."

"No, you're right, you weren't. But you *were* gonna lose."

Luke held his temper as best he could. He didn't like this braggart, but Dash was right. It would have taken a miracle, one he wasn't capable of just yet, to beat the last of the swooptroop alone. Like it or not—and he didn't like it at *all*—Dash had saved his neck.

"Thanks." It was a mumble.

"Excuse me, I didn't hear what you said."

"Don't push it, Dash."

The older man grinned.

Boy, was he going to have words with Leia when she came back. As much as he was attracted to her, as much as he thought she was the toughest, most beautiful woman he'd ever known, where did she get off sending this guy to watch him? And he knew she had to be paying Dash to do it—Dash wasn't the kind of guy who did stuff for free.

Dash said something, and Luke blinked at him. "Huh?"

"I said, did you see their tattoos? This gang works for Jabba."

Luke looked. That was where he recognized the insignia from. Jabba's men.

Dash continued, "I was in Mos Eisley, kinda . . . hanging around, when I heard them talking. They had orders to kill you."

Kill him, yeah, he'd figured that out. Dash kept talking, and Luke tuned back in to what he was saying. ". . . Vader is no longer your number one admirer."

"He never was. If it's him behind it."

Was it? Luke shook his head. That still didn't make sense.

14

"Lord Vader, we are closing on the Rebel asteroid."

Vader turned away from the viewport to behold the junior officer who had drawn the duty this time.

"Good. Have Admiral Okins meet me on the bridge."

"At once, Lord Vader."

Vader adjusted the controls on his armor for an increased supply of oxygen and started for the bridge. It was not his choice of chores, this surprise attack on helpless vessels, but he would do it well.

"Ah, Prince Xizor," the Emperor said. "How good to see you again."

Xizor nodded and bowed low. "The pleasure is mine, my Emperor."

"Do come in. What brings you to my chambers?"

"I was just curious, my master, as to the progress of

Lord Vader's attack upon the Rebel shipyard in the Baji Sector."

The Emperor's ravaged face revealed nothing, but Xizor was certain his comment had come as a surprise.

"I really must see about hiring your spies away from you," the Emperor said. "Especially after you stole my best horticulturist. A pity the man had that fatal lift accident before he could start working for you."

"Yes, a pity," Xizor replied. If ever there was a poor loser, it was the Emperor. "However, it was not my spies who gave me this information."

"Tell me, then, how did you come to know of it?"

"I'm surprised Lord Vader didn't mention it to you, but what my spies *did* discover was the location of the Rebel shipyard. I, of course, immediately offered this information to Lord Vader."

"Of course," the Emperor said, his voice as smooth as lube on transparisteel plate. "I am expecting a report from the fleet shortly. Perhaps you would join in some refreshments and wait with me?"

"I would be honored."

Xizor kept his smile in check. Vader had not told the Emperor who had given him the Rebel shipyard. No surprise. More, he had somehow gleaned the recordings from the Emperor's own skyhook to keep him from finding out. Xizor himself would have done the same in Vader's position. Which was, of course, why he was here. To make certain the Emperor knew whom to credit for this bit of business.

And whom to blame for his not knowing that, too.

Ah, but he was going to enjoy watching Vader become aware that his little game had gone awry.

He was going to enjoy it greatly.

"Admiral?"

"We will be in range shortly, Lord Vader," Okins said.

"Good. Commence firing as soon as we reach optimum distance. I want no mistakes."

Vader stood in front of his vessel's main viewport, looking out at the large asteroid looming ahead of them. Big as a small moon, the rock was pocked with craters from collisions with its smaller brothers, and looked to be nickel-iron, very common in this region.

Suddenly a pair of ships came around from the opposite side of the asteroid.

"Two Nebulon-B Escort Frigates," an officer said to his left.

Vader looked at the pair of ships. The frigates were long and lean, with control and weapons pods in the front connected to the massive drives and TIE decks at the rear by a long and relatively slender tube. "Our own ships," he said, angry.

Nobody spoke to that.

Early in the Rebellion, a number of the frigates had been captured or had defected to the Alliance.

"At least they won't have any operable TIE fighters," the admiral said.

As if his words had been a signal, a dozen X-wing fighters boiled out of the frigate and began accelerating toward the Imperial fleet.

"I see they have been modified to carry X-wings," Vader said. His tone was very dry. "It seems the shipyard will not be such an easy target after all."

Okins turned to his TIE operations officer. "Scramble our fighters. I don't want to waste firepower swatting these annoying . . . flies with our big guns."

"At once, Admiral."

Vader saw a third ship round the asteroid, much faster than the frigates. He identified it as the officer spoke: "Here comes a Corellian corvette."

Inside his mask, Vader smiled. *Good.* Better a fight than a slaughter of crippled, roosting birds. He turned to the operations officer. "Have my Interceptor readied."

The admiral glanced at the TIE OpOff, then at Vader. "My lord, do you think that is—?"

"—wise?" Vader finished. "It has been too long since I flew in combat, Admiral. I need to flex those muscles. You can handle the shipyard. I will clear the vacuum of the fighters."

The admiral inclined his head in a military bow.

As if the admiral could do anything else.

Vader had forgotten how much he enjoyed piloting his Interceptor, it had been so long. It came back quickly.

The enjoyment did not last. Almost effortlessly, he blew three, four, five of the Rebel ships into smoking pieces.

It was . . . disappointing. The Force was not strong in any of them; it was no real challenge. Some were skilled, true, but mere skill could not defeat the dark side. He had hoped for better competition.

Any competition.

An X-wing in a hard power climb tried to attack him from below, but he looped away and came around fast, punched it with his lasers, turned it into scrap.

He was aware of the destroyers firing at the frigates, disabling one and holding the other at bay. A frigate was no match for the pride of the Imperial Navy.

As he chased another X-wing into oblivion, he felt the disturbance in the Force as the fleet pounded the Rebel shipyard apart, pouring destruction upon the helpless grounded ships, pilots, and troops. Multicolored streams of light burned all they touched.

Another X-wing darted and twisted and turned, tried to avoid his fire. The Rebel pilot was good, but he had no chance of escaping.

Vader let the dark side guide his aim. Felt his weapons lock on . . .

Held his fire.

Disgusted, he broke off his attack and allowed the X-wing to escape. This was beneath him. Since he had fought Luke on the balcony of the city in the clouds, no other opponent had been any real competition. Well. Perhaps the criminal Xizor offered something, but that was different, that was not a warrior's challenge. Xizor was merely duplicitous and devious; he would never dare stand eye-to-eye with the Dark Lord of the Sith.

Vader watched the X-wing scurry away. The battle was over, such as it was. The Rebel shipyard burned, its own air and fuel feeding the conflagration. Hundreds of ships gone, thousands of troops wiped away, a great victory for the Empire.

Vader shook his head. A great victory. Once that would have been something to make him proud. Now? Now it was as hollow as smashing these weak X-wing pilots.

A warrior needed to contend with equals. Obi-Wan was gone, and the other Jedi were all extinct, save one, who was the strongest of them all. His own son.

He had told the Emperor that Luke Skywalker would join them or die. The real truth was only slightly different: Luke would join Darth Vader or die.

It would be something to look forward to.

That would be the duel of a lifetime. This wasn't even exercise.

He headed his fighter back to the ship.

Vader stepped onto the holocam field and initiated the transmission. The holonet made its shortcut through hyperspace and achieved its considerably faster-than-light connections. The air shivered and shimmered as the Emperor appeared from nothingness.

Vader lowered himself to one knee. "My master," he said.

"Ah, Lord Vader. Your report?"

"The Rebel shipyard is no more. They put up a

fight, but it was of brief duration. We destroyed hundreds of vessels and thousands of the enemy within them."

"Good, good." The Emperor waved his hand, and his image became smaller as the holocam on his end adjusted to a wider angle.

The new angle revealed Xizor standing a couple of meters away.

Vader's involuntary reaction overrode his mechanical breather. He realized the Emperor would be able to hear his breathing. He forced himself to allow the breather to resume its normal function.

"Prince Xizor was just telling me how happy he was to provide the Empire with the location of the Rebel base. It seems we owe him much gratitude, don't you think?"

Vader gritted his teeth. He would rather bite off his own tongue and swallow it than offer such gratitude, especially in front of the Emperor, but he had no choice. The Emperor did like to crack the whip now and again, to show that he still held it and was not averse to using it.

Vader looked at Xizor. It was good that they could not see his face when he spoke. "The Empire owes you thanks, Prince Xizor."

The Emperor smiled.

Xizor smiled even more widely. Said, "Oh, think nothing of it, Lord Vader. I am always happy to serve."

Had the man been any more self-effacing and servile in his tone he would have had to look up from licking the Emperor's boots. It was good that he was light-years away; Vader's anger was such that he wasn't sure he could have stopped himself from destroying Xizor had he been within reach, despite the Emperor's admonitions.

"I expect to see you soon, Lord Vader."

"Yes, my master. We are returning even as we speak."

"Good."

The image swirled and faded.

Vader stood. Turned to leave the holo chamber.

A junior officer approached him as he exited. "Lord Vader, I—"

That was as far as he got. Vader clenched his fist and called upon the dark side.

The officer fell, clutching his throat.

"I do not wish to be disturbed," he said to the man lying on the deck. "Is that clear?"

Vader opened his fist.

The officer inhaled noisily. When he could manage it, he said, "C-C-Clear, L-Lord Vader!"

With that, the Dark Lord of the Sith stormed away to his own chamber to brood.

Xizor felt the glory of his triumph over Vader almost as a tangible thing, a shower of pleasure that rinsed him and filled him with a warm glow.

"You must come and visit me more often," the Emperor said. "I do enjoy our conversations. I'm sure Lord Vader would also enjoy seeing you when he returns."

Xizor bowed. Most unlikely that Vader would enjoy that. "My master."

He left, and the feeling of power was unabated. The Emperor was, of course, aware of what Xizor had just done to Vader; indeed, he had enjoyed being a part of the process, of pitting his two servants against each other and watching to see how the play would go. He was like a man who owned a pack of semitame wolf cats. He enjoyed throwing a single bone into the pack to see which would outfight the others to claim it. He was as devious as any man, the Emperor was, and Xizor resolved to take extreme care during the remainder of this endeavor.

Extreme care.

15

Xizor leaned back in his form-chair and looked at the small holoproj floating on his desk. "Magnify image," he said. "Full scale."

The computer obeyed, and the simulacrum increased sixfold.

Standing on his desk now was a strikingly beautiful woman, unaware that her picture had been captured by a hidden holocam.

"Move image to floor holoplate."

Again the computer did as it was ordered.

Xizor nodded. "So this is Princess Leia Organa. My. How interesting."

He knew who she was, of course, though he had never bothered to scan her image closely before. He'd always assumed that she was some hardened battle-ax of a woman, all for the Cause, one of those androgynous and ugly zealots who couldn't be bothered with worrying about her appearance. A mistaken assumption, that.

Behind him, Guri said, "She approached the owner of one of our protected casinos on Rodia, in the gaming complex. Looking to set up a meeting with somebody of stature in Black Sun."

The Dark Prince steepled his fingers and regarded the image. "Now, why would one of the leaders of the Alliance be interested in our organization? They have repeatedly rebuffed our overtures, not wishing to sully their clean revolutionary hands with common criminal dirt. A change of heart? I wouldn't think so."

Having been asked nothing, Guri did not reply.

Xizor continued. "It must be important. Let's see what she wants, shall we? Go and find out."

Again Guri refrained from speaking, but Xizor detected something unsettled in her manner. "A problem?"

"The task does not seem particularly challenging."

Xizor laughed. One of her few foibles, that, wishing to be pushed to find her limits. "Perhaps not. Still, it is important for another reason. If our intelligence and that of the Empire are both correct, Princess Organa is close to only a few people. One of them is Luke Skywalker. It is a strong possibility that she knows where he is. Find out what she wants and report back to me. She may well be the easiest way to find Skywalker. In any event, I may find a . . . use for her. After you take care of that other business we discussed. That should be more . . . challenging, I believe."

"As you wish."

Xizor touched his finger to his forehead and sketched a mock salute.

Guri left.

He returned his gaze to the counterfeit of Leia Organa. "Computer, rotate image, normal speed."

The hologram turned on an invisible axis.

She looked just as good from behind.

Xizor took a deep breath and let it out. Here was an interesting woman. Attractive, adept, well educated, and dangerous. She was, according to the files, as good with a blaster as she was beautiful.

The Dark Prince felt a stirring inside him. He was aware of his skin color shifting, going from the cool green to a warmer pale orange. He smiled. He had dismissed his most recent mistress. The idea of female company was not repellent. Especially a female who had more to offer than mere good looks. He wondered what she might be doing just now. Probably eating a fine meal or spending money on expensive entertainment. Females did love such things.

Leia watched as Chewie played another hologame, this one against a Twi'lek with a gaudy dye job and cheap jewelry on his tentacled head.

Chewie made a move and leaned back.

"Very good, Chewbacca," Threepio said. "Excellent move."

The Twi'lek glanced at Threepio and gave him a rather sick, toothy grin.

Leia leaned over to the protocol droid and whispered to him, "What's going on here? I saw this Twi'lek win four in a row against other players who were a lot better than Chewie is."

Threepio looked at her. "Ah, well," he said, *sotto voce*, "I took the liberty of mentioning to the Twi'lek before the game what happens when Wookiees lose such entertainments."

Leia looked blankly at him.

"You recall what Master Solo said about pulling arms off?"

Leia shook her head. Han had been teasing Threepio with that comment. Chewie was fierce enough in battle but actually very even-tempered. She hadn't ever believed that arm business. Though it appeared the Twi'lek did.

If Black Sun didn't show up pretty soon, she was

going to develop a bad case of ship fever cooped up in this place.

Guri sat across the table from three others. Two of them were men; one was a Quarren. Behind her, a pair of Gamorrean bodyguards stood watching. Guri was unarmed.

"Your sources are mistaken," one of the men said. That was Tuyay, the chief operating officer of Ororo Transportation. A fitness buff, he bulged with muscle even under his expensive tailored zeyd-cloth suit. Supposedly, he could squat holding four times his own weight on his shoulders without breaking a major sweat. He did not look happy. In fact, he looked as if he was about to burst a blood vessel.

"Are they?" Guri said. She slouched in the chair, looked totally relaxed.

"M. Tuyay is correct. Ororo would not presume to contend with Black Sun." That from Dellis Yuls, the Squid Head and chief of security for the organization.

The other player, a thin, short, and nervous man, nodded his assent. "No, of course not, we would never tread in Prince Xizor's territory." This was Z. Limmer, the chief financial officer.

"So," Guri said, "I should tell Prince Xizor that this was all a mistake—that our agents are idiots who couldn't find their backsides with both hands?"

"I would not put it precisely so," the Quarren said.

Tuyay looked at the other two sitting next to him and snorted. "Sack this scat! I'm done playing doormat to your boss. Yes, tell him that your agents are idiots! Tell him that *he* is an idiot! Ororo isn't quaking in fear of the terrible and mighty Dark Prince! We're out on the Rim here, a long way from a soft bed and the decadent pleasures of the Imperial Center, where Xizor feathers his nest with our tribute. We earn our way here; we deserve every decicred we collect! Tell him if he doesn't like it, he can come out here and *do* something about it."

Limmer swallowed and went pale. "I—I—I think perhaps what M. Tuyay m-m-means to say is—"

"Shut up, Limmer, you little revo-worm! Don't try to sweeten it." Tuyay glared at Guri. "Go home, little girl. Leave now while I still permit it. And don't come back. You do, and I might find a use for you you wouldn't like." He grinned, and it was a wicked expression.

Guri smiled and stood, still looking as if she'd just awakened from a long nap.

When she moved, it was incredibly fast. She hopped up onto the table, threw a front somersault and landed behind Tuyay, spun, and picked him up, chair and all. Then she threw him at the two Gamorrean guards before either could clear his blaster. The impact knocked both of the piglike aliens flat.

Dellis Yuls pulled a small blaster from inside his tunic, but before he could line up, Guri grabbed his wrist, broke it, and removed the weapon from his hand. She tossed it aside, grinning.

Limmer tried to stand, and she speared his throat with her fingertips, paused long enough to twist Yuls's neck until it cracked like a wet branch breaking, then leaped over the table.

Tuyay came to his feet and turned. Guri grabbed him around the throat as he did the same to her. For a moment they stood there locked in stasis.

Tuyay crumbled, his face full of horror at her strength. He lost consciousness as the blood was kept from his brain.

Guri dropped him, reached down, pulled the blaster from the belt of one of the stunned Gamorreans, then used it to shoot both the bodyguards. One bolt each, in the head.

She hopped up onto the table and down next to

Limmer and Yuls and shot each of them at the base of the skull.

Then she returned to where Tuyay lay trying to breathe through his bruised throat. She squatted next to him and waited until he came to and looked up at her.

"I'll tell Prince Xizor what you said." She smiled and almost carelessly shoved the blaster against Tuyay's left eyeball and pulled the trigger.

Then she stood, walked to where a hidden security wallcam recorded the entire scene, and ripped the unit out of the wall.

The picture went black.

"Stop the recording," Xizor said.

He sighed and shook his head. The recording showed him what he already knew. Guri was the deadliest weapon in his arsenal. He wondered how she would do in a one-on-one against Vader. Probably better than he would, though he was fairly certain that Vader, who had hunted down and killed Jedi adepts, could take her.

Even so, it would be interesting to watch.

And at nine million credits, a very expensive entertainment, should she lose.

"Run it again," he said.

He did love to see a professional at work.

16

"So, where *is* Leia?" Luke asked.

He and Dash had returned to Ben's, each on a swoop. The two swoops were under the camo-tarp with the X-wing now. Dash's ship was in Mos Eisley at the port.

"Gone to Rodia to connect up with Black Sun."

Luke nearly dropped the container of cold water he held. "Black Sun! Is she out of her mind?"

Dash smirked. "Oh, you're an expert on them, are you?"

"No, but I talked to Han a lot while we were cooped up on Hoth during the cold, stormy nights. He had dealings with them. He said they were more dangerous than the Empire." He paused a second. "Why would Leia want to contact Black Sun?"

Dash shrugged. "Got me. Maybe they might know who wants you dead. The princess is fond of you, though I can't see why. You gonna hold on to that water until it evaporates?"

Luke glanced at the forgotten container. "Oh, sorry." He handed the water to Dash, who poured himself a large cup, then drank noisily from it.

The idea of Leia fooling around with a vicious underground criminal organization didn't sit well. Still, what was he going to do about it? She was a big girl; she'd been taking care of herself okay before they'd met. Well, if you didn't count getting captured by Vader. Sure, he and Han and Chewie had rescued her from that, but they hadn't exactly covered themselves with glory doing it. They *had* covered themselves with a stinking effluvium in that garbage pit . . .

"So, what's the drill, kid?"

"Huh?"

"We gonna sit around here and wait for them to come back? Or you maybe want to go ask the Hutt why he sent that comedy troupe out to zap you?"

"Jabba's got no reason to be after me."

"Unless somebody put him up to it. That's why I'm here, remember? Since it's nice and quiet, I could teach you how to fly those swoops right."

"Listen, they'd have *never* caught me in Beggar's Canyon—"

Artoo began whistling and beeping frantically.

"I don't like the sound of that," Luke said.

"What is it?" Dash said.

"Something outside, sounds like. We'd better go see."

Artoo beeped again.

Dash pulled his blaster and checked the charge reading.

Luke reached down to touch his lightsaber to assure himself it was still hanging from his belt.

Artoo chirped and rolled toward the door.

Outside, they saw the fire of a braking rocket high overhead.

"Looks like a message droid," Luke said.

Artoo seemed to affirm that.

Dash blew out a breath and reholstered his blaster.

Message droids weren't something you had drop in on you every day. They were used when fast delivery was needed and you didn't want to risk the holonet and its relays, but they were expensive and good for only one shot; unless you had a new booster lying around, you couldn't reuse them.

Artoo whistled again.

"That's awfully fast. I hope they shockproofed it," Luke said.

Dash had already started for the door.

Outside, the incoming vessel, tiny as it was, was visible as it fell toward the desert floor half a klick away.

"Who knows you're here, kid?"

Luke shook his head. "Leia, Lando, Chewie, Threepio."

"And Jabba," Dash said. "Though I don't think he'd spend the money for a droid when he could make a local com, he wanted to talk to you. Not to mention kill you."

"Maybe it's for you," Luke offered.

"I doubt it. I don't leave forwarding addresses. Nobody knows I'm here except your friends, and they have no reason to call me."

Luke watched as the little message ship plummeted. It began firing retros and slowing, but it was still coming down pretty fast. The droid must've underestimated the gravity or something.

Maybe it was for Ben. Somebody who had been out of touch for a long time and didn't know he was . . . gone.

The message carrier hit hard enough to splash sand and make a noise they could hear five hundred meters away.

"Let's go see," Dash said.

Luke ground his teeth. He started to say something

about giving orders, but held himself in check. Jedi Knights were supposed to be even-tempered. He'd have to work on that.

They started toward the ship.

In his inner sanctum, Xizor awoke from a light doze to the sound of his personal and private comlink speaking his name softly.

"Incoming call for you, Prince Shheezzorr."

Was that his imagination, or did the voxchip slur his name as the chair he'd replaced had done?

Nothing lasted these days. Everything started to break down before it was properly broken in. The Empire was going to entropy in a turbolift.

"Put it through. And do a self-diagnostic on your voxchip."

The small-scale holoproj flowered on his desk. It was one of his local spies.

"Yes?"

"You asked me to inform you when Lord Vader returned to his castle, my prince. He has just arrived."

The Dark Prince nodded. "Good. Maintain normal surveillance procedures."

The spy nodded and broke the connection. His image blinked out.

So, Vader had returned from the wars, having unwittingly done Xizor's bidding by hitting Ororo where it hurt the most, in the credit balance. Along with Guri's little demonstration to the ranking officers, Ororo would be well-behaved, at least in the near future.

Best he not call on Vader just yet. Doubtless the Dark Lord of the Sith needed some time to cool down a bit from the slap on the hand the Emperor had delivered. Vader's main problem was that he allowed his temper to rule him. A legacy of his mammalian heritage —it was that way with many species and detrimental nearly always. Cold allowed precision; heat threw caution aside and plunged in rampantly. Cold was the process of deliberation and planning, heat the result of unbridled passion. Passion was fine, but only when controlled and channeled properly.

Take Princess Leia, for instance. She attracted him, but he would bring her to him slowly and with care, not in some wild chase in which he cast off his intellectual moorings and sailed out on the sea of lust. Ah, no, that was not the Falleen way. The Falleen way was cold.

Cold was better than heat.

Always.

Darth Vader watched the spy via the holocam hidden at the top of a street-cleaning droid. The droid moved down the avenue like a giant mechanical snail, leaving a trail of cleanliness behind it instead of slime, washing the hard road with powerful jets and ablutants that caused the surface to sparkle.

Xizor's spy sat at an outdoor food bar, pretending to read a hard-copy newsfax as he dawdled over a hot drink long gone cold.

Vader sighed and waved the picture off. This was such a convoluted business, all this spying and intrigue. True, he had learned the game; he played it well, as one must to live on this world, but he did not enjoy it. Men like Xizor and the Emperor took pleasure from their manipulations, but Vader always felt . . . soiled when he mucked around in all this double-dealing and triple-crossing. He was a warrior, and as such, he would prefer to plant himself in the path of an advancing army alone to all this smiling-to-his-face while plotting an enemy's ruin, which was the political core of Imperial Center. Striking a man down with your blade was clean and honorable. Shooting him in the back from the darkness of an alley and hurrying to blame it on another was something else altogether.

He turned away from the monitors. Yes, he could *do* it, and yes, it was necessary; still, he did not have to like it.

Sooner or later, he would have the evidence he needed against Xizor. The more tangled the web, the more likely it was that the weaver would eventually trap himself in it. Sooner or later the man would make a fatal mistake, and when he did, Vader would strike Xizor down—and explain why to the Emperor afterward.

There was a thought he enjoyed.

The message droid, a compact, rounded box with an antigrav unit that allowed it to hover and move a couple of meters off the ground, was apparently undamaged by the delivery vessel's hard impact on the desert. The box, half the size of Artoo, floated in front of Luke and Dash now in Ben's house.

It didn't *look* damaged, but something must have rattled loose inside it. "I have a message for Princess Leia Organa," it said for the fifth time.

"How many times do I have to tell you she isn't here?" Luke said. "Artoo, can you talk to this thing?"

Artoo moved closer to the droid, whistled and beeped rapidly, and ended by flashing lights from its holoprojector at the thing.

There was a pause as some system adjusted itself inside the droid.

"I am empowered to deliver the message to an authorized representative of Princess Leia Organa, in her absence," it said.

"Now we're getting somewhere," Luke said. "Tell me. I'm her, uh, authorized representative."

He grinned at Dash, who shook his head.

"Password?" the droid asked.

Password? What would Leia use as a password?

"Uh, Luke Skywalker."

"That password is incorrect."

Dash laughed.

"Uh, Han Solo?"

"That password is incorrect."

"We could be here a real long time while you rattle off all the names you know, Luke."

"Shut up, will you? I'm thinking."

"Ah, well, wouldn't want to interfere with *that,* would we?"

Luke did think about it. It had to be something simple, he figured, something Leia wouldn't forget. What was the first thing that came to mind when he thought about her?

Forget *that.*

"Uh, Alderaan?"

"Password correct."

A sliding plate on the droid moved and exposed a holoprojector. After a second a holoproj blinked on.

A short, long-haired, and bearded Bothan stood there, dressed in a forest-green overtunic, pants, and boots, a long military-style blaster strapped to his waist and right leg.

"Greetings, Princess Leia. Koth Melan here, speaking to you from my homeworld of Bothawui. Our spy network has uncovered information vital to the Alliance, and the nature of these data are of such significance as to justify sending this messenger droid. You must come to Bothawui *immediately.* I cannot overemphasize the importance of this information, or the urgency. Time is of the essence. I will be at the Intergalactic Trade Mission for five days. The Alliance *must* act in that time or the information may be lost."

The projection shut down.

"Well, well," Dash said. "Somebody is in a big hurry. We could just make it to Bothawui before his deadline if I pushed my ship hard. Even that X-wing crate of yours might do it, though I wouldn't bet on it."

"We need to get this information to Leia," Luke said.

"Not a chance, kid. We can't use the holonet 'cause we don't know where she is exactly. We can't just call and ask, now can we? 'Excuse me, can you tell me where one of the Empire's most wanted enemies is, please?' "

"All right, I get it."

"Yeah, well, time we got to Rodia, found her, and *she* got back to Bothawui, it'd be a standard week at the least."

Luke stared at the message droid. What were they going to do? This sounded big, really big.

"Well," he said. "I guess we'll have to go in her place, then."

"Why? The message was for her."

"I'm her designated representative. I got the password right. Whatever this Koth Melan has got, he can tell it to me."

"Doesn't sound too bright to me. A Bothan spymaster is just going to roll over and give it up, just like that? And his name doesn't sound right, either. 'Melan'? That's not Bothan."

"Nobody asked you. You're supposed to be a bodyguard, right? You don't care about the Alliance."

"Not unless they want to hire me, you got that right."

"Fine. I'm going. You do whatever you want."

Dash grinned. "Well. You're worth more to me alive than dead; I'd better protect my fee. I'll take one of the swoops into town and get my ship. Meet you in orbit."

Luke nodded. He didn't much like Dash, but the guy was good with a gun, and he could fly. That counted for a lot. "Let's go get the X-wing, Artoo. We're going for a ride."

Artoo didn't seem to think it was a particularly good idea, either.

Too bad, Luke thought. A Jedi Knight wouldn't just sit around when there was vital Alliance business in the works, would he? No. He wouldn't.

17

"I'm thowwy," Avaro said. "Black Thun dothn't hop when I thay tho."

Leia shook her head in disgust. She and Chewie were in Avaro's office, and once again he put them off. Lando was happy as a stilepig in warm mud; he was winning most of the card games he played. Even Chewie was enjoying the casino, but if something didn't break pretty soon, Leia was going to start pulling her hair out. Sitting around and doing nothing was not her style.

"Okay," she said. "Tell you what. If somebody doesn't show up here in the next week, we'll try elsewhere."

Avaro shrugged. "Thuit yowahthelf."

Little chance of that, Leia thought. It would suit her to be moving, to be doing something, to find out who was after Luke and why. It seemed awfully clumsy of Vader to have engineered that attempt by the crew chief so that it could be traced back to the Dark Lord of the Sith so easily. She didn't have any other ideas as to who might be gunning for Luke, but sometimes when a thing looked too easy, it was.

Other times, it wasn't.

She stood and left Avaro's office. She didn't have a lot of choice here. She'd wait, but she wouldn't like it.

Guri was about to leave for Rodia when Xizor stopped her. "Before you go there, I have another errand for you. There is a secret document in my personal files under the heading 'Route.' You know what it is."

"Yes."

"Download it and see that it gets into the hands of our Bothan double agent on Bothawui. Make certain he knows that we are responsible for its delivery."

Guri said nothing, but he could feel her reluctance. He said, "You disapprove."

"It does not seem to be in your best interests to do this," she said.

"Ah, but it is. Having Black Sun put this tidbit into the Rebels' hands gratis will make them much more apt to trust us. In the unlikely event the Empire should lose this war, the Alliance will remember us as friends and not enemies."

Guri nodded. She understood, whether she agreed or not. "Highness."

She left.

Xizor considered Guri's worry as he went over the plan again. The new information was in addition to intelligence he had already caused to be discovered by the Bothans. There was some slight risk, but not much, given that which was to be gained. The Empire was strong, and he did not really think that the Alliance would triumph, but it was a stupid man who never considered remote possibilities. Stranger things had happened. People were struck by lightning; meteorites

hit them out of a clear sky; the beating of a moth's
wings on the north coast could be the breeze that
helped spin a tornado on the south coast. A prudent
player took no unnecessary risks, but there were times
when a calculated leap had to be made over a deep
abyss. This was one of those times, and as usual, it was
a double-edged blade. Swung with care, it would cut
both ways.

Just as it was supposed to cut.

Reaching Bothawui wasn't so hard, though it got a
little tricky when they dropped back into realspace. An
Imperial patrol buzzed the planet. Luke and Dash had
to do some fancy flying to avoid them.

There didn't seem to be any quarantine, and they
made it to the surface of the world. Caught a pubtrans
flitter from the port into the city.

Luke had never been on Bothawui, and he was interested in how clean and well maintained it was compared to his homeworld. It was a sunny spring day
locally. There was a token force of Imperial stormtroopers hanging around in small groups, but it seemed
as if the Bothans had control of the port itself. The
streets were wide, many of the tall buildings were glit-
tery with some kind of natural stone. Most of the people he saw were, of course, Bothans, but there were a
fair number of other aliens out and about. Very cosmo-
politan, given the war and all. He said as much to
Dash.

"Yeah, well, a lot of spying goes on," Dash said.
"And Bothawui is one of the more active hubs for operatives from around the galaxy. The Empire has its
own spies here; so does the Alliance, and they've all
pretty much decided to let the place be neutral territory."

They made it to the Intergalactic Trade Mission,
paid the fare, and got out.

Getting inside to see Koth Melan was a little harder. The Bothan guard wanted to see a pass, and they didn't have one. Luke wasn't particularly interested in telling the guard who he was, given that he was a wanted man.

Maybe he should try to use the Force on the Bothan? He'd done Ben's trick a couple of times, and it had worked for him. Plus he could impress Dash a little.

But before Luke could gather the Force to sway the guard, Dash pulled the Bothan aside, spoke a few words, and pressed something into his hand.

The guard smiled and waved them into the building.

"What'd you say to him?" Luke asked.

"Not much. But that hundred-credit coin I gave him said, 'Hey, these are good guys—what say you just let them in?' "

"You *bribed* him?"

"You don't get out much, do you? That's how things work out here in the real galaxy. Money is the lube that makes all things move. We're inside, so we're happy. The guard can buy his spouse or his femfriend a nice gift, so he's happy. Nobody got hurt. If we get caught, the guard never saw us before. It's the cost of doing business."

Luke shook his head. But maybe Dash had a point. Was giving the credits any worse than clouding his mind with the Force? Yeah, it was for a good cause and it would have been justified, but wasn't a few credits also justified?

He'd have to think about that a little more.

Dash, meanwhile, walked up to an information droid parked in the lobby of the building. "Where might we find Koth Melan?" he asked it.

The droid had a deep, sonorous voice. "Level sixteen, number seven," it said.

"Thanks."

They moved toward the turbolifts.

.   .   .

Another droid, this one a protocol model much like Threepio, staffed the desk in the anteroom of the office to which Luke and Dash had been directed. The droid's metal skin was polished to a gleaming gold.

"Good morning. How may I assist you?" he asked them.

"Princess Leia is supposed to see Koth Melan," Luke said.

"*You* are Princess Leia?"

Luke frowned, "No, no, *I'm* not Princess Leia. I'm her . . . representative. Luke Skywalker. We don't exactly have an appointment. But he wants to see her, so he'll want to see us."

The droid said, "I don't believe that is a logical assumption."

"Look, just tell him we're here, okay?"

"I'm afraid I cannot admit you without an appointment. Master Melan is a very busy Bothan. Nor can I bother him with every little thing. Perhaps I can arrange for you to see him in, oh, perhaps a standard week? Your names?"

Luke frowned. How could they convince this droid to let them in? Couldn't bribe him, the Force wouldn't work—

Dash grinned and pulled his blaster. Pointed it at the droid. "Okay, Goldie. My name is Man with a Blaster About to Cook You. Either you open the door or your busy Bothan is going to have to get himself a new receptionist."

"Oh, dear," the droid said.

"And no security alarms, either," Dash said. "I'm watching you real carefully. Up, and do the door manually."

The protocol droid said, "Very well, Man with a Blaster About to Cook You."

Luke and Dash exchanged wry looks. Droids could be too literal at times.

The droid tapped a code into the keypad next to the inner door. It slid open.

"Inside," Dash ordered.

The droid preceded them into a large office. Sitting behind a desk in front of a clear wall of transparisteel was the Bothan who'd sent the message to Leia.

Well, at least Luke thought it was the same one. They all looked pretty much alike to him.

"Master Melan, I'm sorry to interrupt, but—"

"It's all right, R-Zero-Four. Go back to your desk. I'll see these gentlemen."

"Hardly gentle, sir," the droid called R0-4 said. "They said to me they were Princess Leia. They threatened me with bodily harm!"

"Never mind, R-Zero-Four." To Dash, the Bothan said, "Put away the hardware, Rendar. You don't need it."

Dash blinked, surprised, but holstered his weapon.

The droid left, closing the door behind him.

Luke stepped forward. "Excuse the way we came in, but we had to see you."

Melan smiled. "I know. You're Luke Skywalker, and you are Dash Rendar. I've been expecting you. Please, take a seat."

Luke and Dash exchanged quick glances.

"Perhaps I should explain," Melan said. "I discovered that Princess Organa was no longer on Tatooine a short time ago, too late to recall the messenger droid I sent. Because you are here, I assume you knew the password she and I agreed upon."

He looked at Luke. "I know your reputation and your work for the Alliance."

He glanced over at Dash. "I also know your reputation, M. Rendar, though I'm surprised to see you working for the Alliance."

Dash shrugged. "I'm not. I'm working for the princess."

"Ah, well. No matter. You're here and now we can get to the business at hand."

"You took kind of a risk letting us barge in here with a blaster that way," Dash said. "We could have been Imperial assassins in disguise."

Melan treated them to another smile. "Not really. I've known you were here since you landed at the port. You were scanned first at the doorway to the building by the guard you 'bribed,' then on the turbolift, and positively identified. If you had been assassins in disguise, you would have arrived on a level with a dozen armed guards pointing their weapons at you when the lift doors opened."

Luke and Dash glanced at each other.

"I have many enemies," Melan continued. "I have learned to be cautious."

Luke moved to one of the chairs and sat. Dash did the same.

"What is so important that you sent a message droid to Leia?" Luke asked.

"The Empire has embarked on a new military project," Melan began. "We do not yet know what or where the project is, but we do know it is vast—the Emperor has diverted huge amounts of money, material, and men for this secret enterprise."

"How did you come by this information?" Luke asked.

"The Bothan spynet is second to none," Melan said. There seemed to be a touch of pride in his voice. "As you thought you did with the guard on the street, we bribed a high-ranking Imperial officer. With what he gave us, we tried to infiltrate a slicer droid into the main computer complex on Coruscant to locate and copy the plans for this secret venture. Unfortunately, this portion of the plan failed.

"What we have learned as a result of this failure is

that the plans are kept closely guarded in special computers with no outside lines. There is thus no way to
obtain this information from a distance by comlink, no
access to these systems save by direct hands-on contact.

"From what little else we've learned of it, this project does not bode well for the Alliance."

Luke nodded. "So, what are we supposed to do
about it?"

"Our operatives have collected intelligence that indi-
cates one of the secured computers is being sent from
Coruscant to Bothawui. We believe the Alliance would
be served by obtaining this computer and cracking it
open, to see what the Empire is up to."

Luke nodded again. "That sounds reasonable."

Dash said, "Excuse me, but why are you so hot to
help out the Alliance? I thought the Bothan spynet's job
was to gather and sell information, not get involved
with strategy and tactics."

Melan looked grim. "Twenty years ago the Empire
had my father executed for espionage."

"That's one of the risks of this business, isn't it?"

"Yes, and one I take. But all Bothans are not spies,
M. Rendar. My father was a teacher. He was guilty of
nothing save trying to educate his students about the
Empire. You will have noticed my name doesn't end in
the normal 'y'lya' honorific. Until the Empire is defeated, I can have no true honor."

Dash nodded. "That explains that."

Luke thought about his aunt and uncle, turned into
smoldering corpses at the farm on Tatooine. He understood how Melan felt.

"I would think that you might have a grudge against
the Empire yourself," Melan continued, staring at
Dash. "After what the Emperor did to you and your
family."

Dash gritted his teeth; Luke saw his jaw muscles
flex. "That's none of your business," he said.

Luke didn't say anything, though the question

leaped to the top tier of his mind: *What did they do to you, Dash?*

Instead, Luke said, "If the Empire is going to all this trouble, we'd best find out why. How do we get our hands on this computer?"

Melan nodded. "Our operatives have learned that the Empire intends to send the plans incognito, on an unescorted ship posing as a simple freighter carrying fertilizer. They reason that such a ship will not draw the attention of the Alliance the way a heavily armed convoy would."

"A freighter full of fertilizer?" Dash said. "That is devious. Who'd hijack that?"

"Our operatives inform us that they will be able to obtain the route of the disguised ship shortly. When they do, it will be but a matter of a day or two before the vessel arrives. There are Bothans who have Alliance sympathies willing to help secure the freighter, but they are relatively unskilled at such sorties. It would help if they had a commander with some experience in space battles to lead them."

Luke smiled. "That's me." He turned to Dash. "What about you? You in?"

"Risk my ship and neck? For what?"

"I thought you wanted to keep me alive."

"You ain't worth that much."

"One freighter? Against a squad of Bothans and me in my X-wing? How dangerous can it be? A piece of cake."

Dash appeared to consider it.

"Besides, if the information in the computer is as valuable as it seems to be, the Alliance might be willing to give you a bonus for helping collect it. Could be worth a few thousand credits, maybe more."

Dash looked at him. "All right. I got nothing else to do. Why not?"

Luke grinned. This guy did remind him a lot of Han.

18

The Emperor was normally a clever man. He seldom did anything that Darth Vader thought particularly unwise, much less stupid.

Yet as Vader stood before his master in the Emperor's castle, this latest bit of twisted business fit squarely into the latter category. Stupid—and dangerous.

Not that he would dare say so—to the Emperor's face or behind his back. But the Emperor was not so powerful as to be able to read thoughts. Just as well, too, because if he could, surely he would destroy Vader here where he stood for his opinion of this foolishness.

Then again, Vader thought as he stared at his master, could he read thoughts, it was doubtful this . . . *plan* would ever have come to pass.

"You disapprove, Lord Vader?"

"It is not my place to disapprove, my master."

"Quite so."

Later, as he walked toward his castle, Vader consid-

ered his response to this new gambit. There seemed little he could do save to monitor the situation. To stand
still and *watch*.

This did not improve his mood.

Luke and Dash traveled with Koth Melan in his private landspeeder to a base hidden in the mountains two
standard hours away from the city. Here they met with
the squad of Bothan pilots and weapons officers and
inspected their ships.

The dozen fighters were BTL-S3s—two-seat
Y-wings, the Alliance's most common attack craft.
They weren't as fast as X-wings or TIEs, didn't have
the firepower, but were rugged and could take a lot of
punishment. Not the latest or the best ships in vacuum,
but they ought to be more than enough to stop a single
freighter. They wore Alliance colors and ID codes.

"Buncha antiques," Dash said. "Probably have to
get out and push if you want to go any faster than a
broke-leg droid."

Luke ignored him. To the leader of the squad he
said, "You have astromechs for all of these?"

The leader, a Bothan who looked as young for his
species as Luke was, nodded. "Yes, we have droids.
And all the ships have Taim & Bak IX-Four laser cannons run off standard Novaldex generators. Unfortunately, we don't have proton torpedoes for the Arakyrd
launchers."

Luke shrugged. "Doesn't matter. We don't want to
blast the freighter anyhow, we want it in one piece.
How much flying time does your squad have?"

"Not much, I'm afraid. Most of us are relatively
new. A hundred hours or less in these birds. But the
boys are quick, and the gunners are pretty fair shots,
though we haven't gotten much practice."

That wasn't so good. "We have a few days before

we get our target location," Luke said. "Maybe we can find a place to do a few maneuvers."

"We'd love that, Commander Skywalker. The squad is at your disposal."

Luke grinned. He did still like the sound of that. *Commander Skywalker.* He could see it becoming Colonel Skywalker, *General* Skywalker. Wouldn't interfere with his Jedi studies to be a general—Ben had been a general, hadn't he?

That path would have to begin later. First this; then Han had to be rescued. That might be tough, but for a slow run against a dung freighter, surely he could get these guys into shape in a couple of days?

Leia was contemplating putting a credit coin into one of the rigged gambling machines. She was so bored, she was about ready to give it a try.

Avaro approached her. "I just got a com fwom off-planet. Black Thun'th wepwethentative ith en woute. Thee will be hewah in thwee dayth."

Leia felt a rush of relief. *Thank goodness.* Then, as Avaro waddled off, she thought about what he'd just said. *"Thee"* will be here in three days?

She?

Well, why not? No rule said a woman couldn't be a criminal.

In a perverse way, it pleased her that the representative from Black Sun would be a woman.

And about time she got here, too.

The operative they were awaiting arrived at the hidden base on Bothawui three days after Luke and Dash. Koth Melan ushered the operative into a private room, where the four of them met.

"Here are the coordinates of the flight plan," the

agent said. He produced a tiny computer and laid it on the table.

Melan said, "Any more information on what the project might be?"

"Not even rumors. This is closed up tighter than a Corellian clam."

"Too bad."

The agent looked just like a hundred other Bothans Luke had seen. Put him in a crowd and he'd disappear.

"You believe these directions to be valid?" Melan asked. He nodded at the small computer.

"I do. I received them from our underworld contact. She has never delivered false information before."

"Underworld contact?" Luke said.

"Black Sun," the agent said.

Luke and Dash glanced at each other. Luke said, "Black Sun?"

Melan answered. "It appears that the organization is courting the Alliance," he said. "They have several times provided us with valuable intelligence. I believe they think the Alliance will win the war against the Empire."

"They must be the only ones," Dash said.

Melan looked at Dash but ignored what he'd said. "War, like politics, sometimes makes for strange bedfellows. One uses the tools one has."

Luke shook his head. "I don't like it. They must expect something in return." And it seemed awfully coincidental that Leia had gone to seek out Black Sun and here they were delivering invaluable information. Something wasn't quite right about that.

"They have not asked for anything."

"Yet," Dash said.

"Okay," Luke said. "Put that aside for now. If this information is right, how long before we need to launch and get ready?"

"Your squad of volunteers has already been put on

alert," Melan said. "We'll need to be in position in less than three standard hours to make the rendezvous."

" 'We'?"

"I'll be going along," Melan said. "If Dash Rendar has room on his ship?"

Dash gave the Bothan a lazy grin. "No problem. Can you cook? Might want to grab a bite while we collect this freighter."

"I doubt we'll have time to eat," Luke said.

"Maybe you won't, kid, but I can fly and eat at the same time."

Luke had to grin. This guy was so full of himself it was a wonder he didn't explode and spew ego all over the place.

"Better get to our ships," Luke said.

Dash gave him a mock salute. "Aye, aye, Commander."

Time to go.

Luke led the dozen Y-wings away from the planet in the sensor shadow of the local moon, to help them avoid Imperial patrols. Although the formation was a little ragged, they flew pretty well for a group who'd had only minimal time in the craft. He wouldn't want to take them into battle against the best TIE wing in the Imperial Navy, but they ought to be able to help surround a freighter and stop it.

The coordinates and time were coming around, and he turned his attention to the ambush.

Behind him, Dash flew his chrome ship, nearly invisible against the backdrop of airless space, with Koth Melan as a passenger.

"Keep in tight, boys," Luke said into his comm. "We're almost on station. Let's hear you sound off, Blue Squad."

The pilots of the Y-wings logged in. He'd kept it

simple; each of the attack ships got a number, and he'd christened the unit with a color.

"Copy," Luke said. "We're there. Stall 'em in position."

Blue Squadron obeyed, bringing their fighters to a halt. They floated in the middle of nowhere, waiting. If the information was correct, the freighter ought to be popping out of hyperspace less than a hundred kilometers dead ahead—

The freighter pilot must have overslept. The ship dropped into realspace, all right, but only fifty klicks away.

It was a stock light freighter, Corellian, though different in configuration from the *Millennium Falcon*. Instead of the saucerlike body with the twin nose and offset control cockpit, this was a long oval with the ends squared off, with a rectangular, detachable cargo container slung under its belly. It looked kind of like a graphic of a giant blaster.

"Heads up, Blue Squad, there's our target. Attack formation!"

The ship came out of hyperspace relatively slowly, but since it was closer than anticipated, they didn't have much time. Luke switched to a standard operations channel and hailed the freighter.

"Attention on board the freighter *Suprosa*. This is Commander Skywalker of the Alliance. Shut down your engines and prepare to be boarded."

If everything went as planned, Koth Melan, in a vacsuit, would be escorted on board the freighter by a couple of guards and technicians also riding with Dash. They'd be in and out in a few minutes.

"This is the captain of the freighter *Suprosa*. Are you crazy?" came the reply. "We're hauling fertilizer here! What kind of pirates are you?"

"We're not pirates. Like I said, we are with the Alliance. And maybe we have a big garden. Pull it up, Captain, and nobody gets hurt."

There came a long pause. It was possible the pilot didn't know what he was hauling, but Luke didn't believe that. If he didn't know, he'd have no objection to being boarded. If he did—

"Listen, pal, I'm working under contract to XTS and my orders are to deliver my cargo to the agent on Bothawui. Why don't you go bother somebody smuggling guns or spice or something?"

"Captain, either you shut down your engines or we'll shut them down for you. Some of my gunners can pick flies off a wall with their laser cannons." Well, it was possible, though he hadn't seen any of them shooting quite that well during maneuvers. The freighter pilot didn't know that.

The freighter suddenly dropped its cargo module, speeded up, and turned to starboard.

It was going to make a run for it.

Luke switched back to the tactical opchan. "Gotta do it the hard way, boys. Target the engines only! If you aren't sure, don't take the shot—we don't want to blow this baby up. Move in!"

The distance between Blue Squadron and the freighter decreased in a hurry. This was stupid; the ship was unarmed and much slower than the Y-wings. If they wanted to cook the captain, he was dinner—and he had to know it.

The freighter tried to move at a right angle to the incoming fighters, but they were almost in range. Luke was in the lead; his ship was faster than the Y-wings, and it would take only a couple of blasts to knock out the engines, assuming they had standard shields.

Another two seconds . . .

Artoo whistled.

Uh-oh. Luke didn't like what he heard. "Put it on screen, Artoo."

The image of the freighter appeared on Luke's screen.

Where there had been four smooth sections of hull

before, red lights now blinked. Another two spots flashed blue.

Plates had slid back on the freighter to reveal hidden weapons.

"Heads up, everybody, this thing has got teeth! He's got laser cannons fore and aft and what looks like missile launchers ventral and dorsal. Watch yourselves!"

Luke put his X-wing into a sweeping turn as the freighter's port laser fired. The blast was close enough to scramble his comm.

One of the Y-wings, Blue Four, dived at the freighter, targeting its engine compartment. Luke saw the fighter's beam stroke the target, but the bright blue splash as the beam hit revealed that the freighter had augmented shields.

Not such an easy target after all—

The freighter's cannon found Blue Four, and the ship blew apart.

Man, that must be some wattage behind those guns!

"Break off, circle, and regroup!" Luke called into his comm.

Blue Two was on the way in, and it aborted its attack run.

Too late. Blue Two became shattered history.

Four of the Bothan ships looped away in pretty good formation, Dash in the *Outrider* in tandem with them.

Luke was close enough to see the missile port on top of the freighter blow a cloud of gas into space that crystallized and glittered under the local sun's light.

"He's got a missile off!" Luke yelled.

"I got it," Dash said. "I'll hammer that spike into scrap."

Luke watched Dash's ship roll and dive, and his robotic guns began spewing coherent bolts of energy. He couldn't see the missile, but he saw Dash continuing his attack, saw the guns spraying their hardlight spears.

"Blast!" Dash said. "I've got to be hitting it! Why doesn't it stop?"

"Dash! Come on!" Luke yelled.

"Shut up, I've got it, stop, you blasted piece of junk, stop!"

"Move, Dash!"

"No, I'll get it!"

"Incoming!" Blue Six yelled. "Scatter!"

The four fighters tried to split up, separated like an opening fist.

Too late.

The missile exploded among them, and when the blast cleared, all four ships, eight Bothans, were gone.

"I can't have missed," Dash said, his voice incredulous. "I can't."

Luke's anger swept over him as he put the X-wing into a sharp and twisting turn. He headed right at the freighter. Six of his squadron had been destroyed, just like that. And Dash, hotshot Dash, he'd screwed up royally. If it hadn't cost lives, Luke would have felt that the braggart got what he deserved. If he'd had any doubts that the crew of the freighter knew what they carried, they were gone now.

He was too incensed to use the Force. He ignored the energy beams stabbing at him, ignored Artoo's cacophony of whistles and bleats, ignored everything but the engine compartment of the freighter under his guns. Fired. Fired again and again. Saw the radiation absorbed by the shields, saw the blue glow brighten. Saw the force field give way under his attack. Saw the engine compartment rupture, smoke, flash red and purple as his laser beams baked and killed it.

"I couldn't have missed," Dash said. He sounded dazed.

"Stow that, Dash," Luke ordered. "It's too late to worry about it now. Get ready to bring your ship in."

Luke switched channels. To the freighter, he said, "Your engines are dead, Captain, and that's what you and your crew will be if you fire another laser or missile, do you copy?"

A brief pause. "We copy."

"You are hereby considered prisoners of war. Stand by to be boarded. If you value your lives, best you don't mess with your real cargo. If anything happens to it, you will suffer the same fate."

Luke shut off his comm. Oh, man. He'd lost half his squad. He should have *known* it was too easy to be true. A dozen Bothans had died to secure this vessel and its computer. He should have been ready for a trick. He should have known better than to trust the Empire. He should have realized that Dash was more talk than substance.

He was a lousy commander. Every time he went out, he lost people. And there was nobody else to blame for this. Yeah, Dash had failed him, but it was his responsibility, *he* was the commander of the mission. He'd thought it would be so easy. A piece of cake, he'd told Dash.

Yeah. He was too cocky, too self-confident, too certain the Force would show him the right path. Wrong.

On some level, it made him angry. The Force didn't always come when he needed it.

But the dark side would be there if you needed it. Always.

Oh no you don't. Don't even think about going down that road.

But it was tempting. All that power. He had felt it . . .

He shook his head. He hoped whatever was in the computer the freighter was carrying was worth what it had cost to collect it. It had better be.

19

Avaro sent a menial to tell them that the representative from Black Sun had arrived. He offered to provide a room, and Leia politely declined. She'd had Lando rent a place two casinos away from here, and he and the droid had recently checked it carefully for spy devices. She trusted Avaro about as far as she could throw him.

"Tell her to meet us at the Next Chance," she told the flunky, who bowed and left.

Leia approached Chewie where he was playing a board game with Threepio, the other gamblers in the place having been convinced it was wiser to let the Wookiee win than not.

"Let's go, boys. We have company."

Chewie and Threepio stood and followed her from the casino.

Lando was on the way to their rented suite, to do another fast pass on the place and to set up security. He'd be hiding with his blaster drawn when the Black

Sun rep showed up. Chewie would watch the door from the hall, and Threepio would stay with her.

Outside, the day had shaded into early night, damp and hot still, and the facades of the gambling casinos might not have seemed quite so run-down if not for the garish lighting installed on the exteriors. Clear plastic pipes full of electroreactive gases that glowed in a dozen different colors, most of them bright, cast multi-colored glare and shadows in all directions. The lights went with the rest of it: Everything in the complex seemed to be artificial; even the bioengineered lawns and shrubbery looked fake.

Somewhere in the darkness somebody yelled. Leia heard the sound of boots running, followed by more hoarse screams. She touched the butt of her blaster, tucked into a holster inside the waistband of her pants. Even with Chewie looming over her, she felt better knowing she had a weapon. The night here was as dangerous as a skirmish with the Empire. People who had lost big money gambling sometimes did desperate things. The local news stat listed the number of murders on its back page every morning—a slaying had to be particularly gruesome or spectacular to make the front of the stat.

They arrived at the Next Chance without incident, however, and went straight to the suite.

Lando, blaster in hand, met them at the door when they buzzed.

"Everything set?"

"Yes," he said. He waved at the suite's meeting room. There was a desk with a computer inset at one end of the room, two couches, three chairs, and a small table. A bar and a cooler were tucked into the corner opposite the door. Two sliding doors led to the refresher and an adjoining bedroom. "I'll be behind the bedroom door," Lando said. "In case the Black Sun rep needs to use the refresher."

"Good. Chewie, you've got the hall."

Chewbacca nodded and moved out into the hall, his bowcaster slung over his back.

"Okay, Threepio, you stand over there, next to the bar."

Leia moved to the desk and sat behind it. Might as well try to keep this on a businesslike basis. She sat, took a deep breath, blew it out.

She'd met with Alliance officials, generals, heads of planets, as well as Imperial governors and Senators, so rank didn't scare her. But she'd never had a face-to-face meeting with a major underworld player before. At least not that she knew about. She was a little nervous. She didn't know quite what to expect.

Chewie called from the hallway.

Sounded as if their caller had arrived.

"Send her in," Leia said.

The door opened.

The computer was the size of a small carrying case. It was black and nearly featureless, save for a control panel along one edge. Koth Melan held the thing easily on his palms.

They were on board the *Outrider* in the ship's lounge. Dash sprawled on a built-in chair, staring at the wall, not saying anything. He was stunned at his failure to stop the missile that had taken out four of the Y-wings. As much as Luke had wanted to see Dash taken down a notch, that was not how he would have seen it done. Dash was disappointed that he wasn't as good as he'd thought he was, but at least he was alive —more than he could say about half his attack unit.

Luke also stared, but at the small computer. Once again, he hoped whatever was in it was worth the lives of a dozen Bothans.

"Can you access the program?"

Melan shook his head. "No. It will be encrypted and protected by an automatic destruct device. Only an expert can circumvent the wards. Our best team is on Kothlis, a Bothan colony world a few light-years from here. We'll transport it there and find out what we've got."

"I'd like to go along," Luke said.

"Of course. I'll give you coordinates; you can reach it easily in your X-wing."

"Dash?"

The man didn't answer but continued to stare at nothing. This had really hit him hard. Luke even felt sorry for him.

"Dash," he said again.

Dash blinked, as if coming out of a trance. "Huh?"

Luke had seen it before. Battle shock.

To Melan, Luke said, "Are we apt to run into any Imperial problems on the way to Kothlis?"

Melan shrugged. "Who can say? It is possible."

"Would it be possible for your organization to locate Princess Leia?"

"As of yesterday, she was at Avaro Sookcool's casino in the gambling complex on Rodia."

Luke shook his head. These guys were good. He looked at Dash. He couldn't bring him along, not the way he was now. He was too rattled.

"Dash . . ."

"I had it in my sights," Dash said. "No way I could have missed."

"Dash!"

"Huh? What?"

"Go to Rodia. Find Princess Leia and tell her about the computer and the secret plans. You got it?"

"I should go with you."

"No, it's more important that you find the princess." Luke felt as if he were talking to a child.

Dash blinked. Stared at Luke. "All right. Rodia. Plans. Got it."

"We'll meet later," Luke said. "Okay?"

"Meet you later, uh-huh."

"You going to be all right?"

"Yeah."

Luke turned back to Melan, who looked sympathetic. "It is war," Melan said. "Bad things happen."

Luke nodded. One more thing the Empire had to answer for.

Whatever she had been expecting, Leia thought, Guri was not it.

The woman from Black Sun was gorgeous, strikingly beautiful, with long, blond hair and a trim figure. She wore a short black cloak over black thinskins and calf boots, with a belt of pebbly red leather slung low over her hips. If she had a weapon Leia couldn't spot it. She moved with the grace of a professional dancer.

She sat across from Leia and smiled. When she spoke, Guri's voice was cool and even: "How may we serve you, Princess?"

Leia repressed a smile. Direct and to the point, this woman. But Leia had been too long a diplomat to blurt out what she wanted to a stranger. There needed to be some ritual circling, a few feints, a bit of misdirection. One did not leap from a high cliff into unknown waters; there could be dangerous things lurking just under the surface. It was a good idea to probe carefully first. She didn't know anything about this icy blonde, what her status was in her organization, what their goals were, what they wanted from those they dealt with. While the Alliance would not enter into a partnership with criminals, Leia was not above using whatever eyes and ears she needed to keep Luke alive, and she did not represent the Alliance in this meeting—though she would keep that to herself.

"I understand that Black Sun has a first-rate intelligence-gathering capability," she said.

Guri flashed a smile. "We hear things from time to time."

"Care for some refreshment?" Leia nodded toward the bar and Threepio.

Guri looked that way. "Tea, if it is not too much trouble. Hot."

Leia looked at Threepio. "And the same for me, please."

"At once," Threepio said. He began making the tea.

"Your flight was pleasant?" Leia said.

Guri smiled. "Very. I trust that Avaro has made your wait here equally pleasant?"

Well, at least she knew how to play this game. It had been a while since Leia had occasion to sit and chat with another woman, being around all these men and males lately. They would have tea, they would dance their diplomatic dance, and eventually work their way to matters of substance. Like Lando's card game, it was wiser to keep your hand hidden until you had some knowledge of the other players.

The tea came and went; the conversation stayed bland, and while there was nothing upon which Leia could put a finger, something was wrong. Guri didn't feel right, somehow. She was polite, well-mannered, willing to follow Leia's lead in the game they played, and despite all that, Leia wanted to be rid of her visitor.

What was it?

So far, they hadn't come anywhere near the subject of Luke, and eventually she'd have to work her way to that, but not yet. Not until she could get some handle on what was bothering her about the woman from Black Sun.

"We are more than willing to accommodate the Alliance," Guri said, leaning back in her chair. She looked so relaxed. Much more so than Leia felt herself. "We would not be unhappy if the Empire were to lose this war and the Alliance were to ascend to power."

"The Alliance might be worse than the Empire, as

far as criminal organizations are concerned," Leia said. *Let's see how she handles that.*

Guri shrugged. "The truth is, Black Sun is less and less interested in illegal activities. Most of our revenue these days comes from investments in legitimate industries and strictly legal operations. There are many in our organization who would have it become completely aboveboard, nothing under the table. Such a thing is difficult under the weight of the Empire. Perhaps under the Alliance the transition might be better effected."

Good response, Leia thought.

"And, as I mentioned, we are in sympathy with the Alliance. We have . . . aided you a number of times. In fact, we have recently aided the Alliance in obtaining the plans for a supersecret Imperial construction project, by way of the Bothan spynet."

"Really? I hadn't heard that."

"It was very recent. The news would not have had time to reach here."

Hmm. Leia leaned back, tried to mimic Guri's relaxed pose. That would bear investigating. She was fairly certain that if Black Sun had given something of great value to the Alliance, there would be something asked in return. If not now, then later.

Guri leaned forward. "I regret that I must ask if it might be possible to continue this meeting later. I have pressing business on one of the local moons, and I'm afraid my launch window is coming up soon."

"Of course," Leia said. Whether Guri had such business or not was hardly important. If she did, then she could attend to it. If not, then cutting short the meeting was a gambit, and Leia would accept the move, to see where it led.

"Perhaps we can talk again in, say, three or four days?"

"I will look forward to it," Leia said, smiling.

Guri stood, smooth as an acrobat in peak condition.

Smiled, gave Leia a nod that was something a little softer than a military bow, and left.

After she was gone, Lando and Chewie came into the room.

"What do you think?" Leia said.

"Man, she's a smooth piece of work," Lando said. "You could stack ice cubes on her head and they wouldn't melt. Unarmed, unless she was hiding a weapon somewhere *I* couldn't spot it. Very attractive, too, but there's something spooky about her."

Leia nodded. She was glad that Lando had noticed. "Threepio?"

"I was unable to place her accent," he said. "Which is decidedly odd, given my extensive experience in languages. Her Basic was flawless, her inflection precise, but I am afraid I cannot tell you her planet of origin."

Chewie said something.

Nobody spoke for a moment. Leia said, "Well, is somebody going to tell me what he said?"

Threepio got it out first: "Chewbacca says the woman made him very nervous."

"He didn't say 'very,' " Lando said. "Just plain 'nervous.' "

"Excuse me," Threepio said. "I inferred the modifier from his tone. Wookieespeak allows for such shadings."

"You saying my Wookieespeak is bad?" Lando said.

"Don't start again, you two." "Very" or not, few things made a Wookiee nervous. Certainly not normal women. Something to consider.

Maybe the next time the woman from Black Sun visited they ought to prepare their reception a little better.

20

Princess Leia leaned back in her chair and smiled. She looked relaxed, comfortable, in charge.

Guri leaned forward. Told Leia that she had to break the meeting off now.

Leia was not the least nonplussed. "Of course," she said. Again the small and polite smile.

"Freeze it right there," Xizor said.

The holoproj of Leia shuttered and held, sharper as a single image than it was as a moving one. Perhaps he would have this particular frame installed as a permanent holographic duplicate on one of his private chamber walls. It would be better, perhaps, had she been nude, but it was fine just as it was. It seemed to catch the essence of the woman. He could get the nude one later.

Without taking his gaze from the full-size three-dimensional picture on the floor in front of him, he said, "What did you think of her?"

Behind him stood Guri. "She's adept at meaningless

small talk, as befits a skilled diplomat. She revealed nothing of what she really wanted except that it might have to do with intelligence gathering. She is physically attractive for one of her species and related species. She is intelligent."

"And . . . ?"

"And it would seem more than coincidental that this woman who is known to be close to Luke Skywalker is probing Black Sun."

Xizor glanced away from the holoproj at his most trusted lieutenant. *There* was a dry understatement. A man who believed in such heavy coincidences was a fool. Somehow, Leia—he was already beginning to think of her on a first-name basis—somehow she had figured out more than she should have been able to figure out. Although he had taken great pains to separate himself from the planned assassination of Skywalker, she had happened upon the plot and managed to connect it to Black Sun. It was not good, but it was somewhat amazing. Another point in her favor.

"Your suggestion?"

"Kill her. Kill her Wookiee and gambler companion. Wipe the protocol droid's memory and melt it down. Eliminate Avaro as well, just to be sure. And anybody in the casino who might have recognized her."

Xizor smiled. Guri was ruthless and efficient; that was part of her charm. If she had to flame a building to rid it of termites, so be it. Given leave, she would do exactly what she suggested.

"I think not," he said. "Go back and meet with her again. We should find out exactly how much she knows and to whom she has told it, if anybody."

"I can get that information before I terminate her."

"No, I would rather conduct this particular interrogation myself. I want you to bring her to me."

Guri was silent.

"Go ahead, speak your mind."

"You are attracted to this woman in a romantic way."

"So?"

"Such attractions have been known to cloud the minds of otherwise rational beings."

He laughed, something he did all too seldom these days. Nobody but Guri would have the nerve to speak thus. Another of her endearing traits. "Do not fear, my dear Guri. She could never replace you in my affections."

Guri did not speak. He didn't think that thought had crossed her mind. She was immune to jealousy as far as he'd been able to determine. Guri would stand by and hold the clothes of his mistress while Xizor had his way with her, apparently unaffected by what she saw. "Princess Leia will surely be useful in locating Skywalker, one way or another. After that, then you can dispose of her."

Guri nodded once.

"Go."

When she was gone, Xizor considered what she had said, then dismissed it. He walked the cold road, and his passion was always safely leashed until he let it free. Guri worried; that was her job and how she had been programmed, to protect him at all costs, even if it extended into his love life. He did not need to be protected there. In such matters a Falleen was quite capable of taking care of himself.

And in this case, it would be a pleasure to do it, too.

Luke's X-wing dropped from hyperspace in the vicinity of the planet Kothlis. The world had three small moons, was the fourth of seven planets circling the local primary, and did not appear to be swarming with Imperial Navy, at least not where Luke was. He scanned the local comm bands and picked up normal traffic, nothing alarming.

"Artoo, lay in a course for the rendezvous Melan gave us."

Artoo whistled his acknowledgment.

Darth Vader's spies told him that Xizor had gone once again to see the Emperor. The man was involved in something dangerous to the Empire, he was certain of it. But he had to have proof before he went to the Emperor. Xizor was currently enjoying favor, and if Vader wished to stop that, he must find out exactly what the Dark Prince was up to. He must have evidence that was irrefutable.

"Bring one of my dueling droids," Vader said to the air. "No. Bring *two* of them."

The Rebel fighter squadron bore in, a dozen Y-wings led by a single X-wing, and a larger unidentified and heavily armed vessel.

The target of the attack took evasive action and opened fire.

The fight was furious but over quickly. The pilot of the X-wing came in fast and crippled the freighter by killing its main engines after the larger ship had destroyed half of the attackers.

"I think we've seen enough," the Emperor said.

The recording of the attack, taken from within the freighter and without sound, vanished.

"It went exactly as we planned, I see," Xizor said. "They had to work a little for it. We didn't want it to seem too easy."

A long silence passed before the Emperor spoke. "I do hope you know what you are doing, Prince Xizor. I agreed to allow the plans for the new Death Star to fall into Rebel hands on your advice. You had best be right."

Xizor said, "I am, my master. Once the Rebels find

out exactly what it is they have been given, their trust in me will be complete. It will be an easy matter to lure the leaders of the Alliance into your grasp. I will deliver the Rebellion and you can crush it at your pleasure."

The Emperor said nothing, but Xizor heard the unspoken threat: *If you are wrong, you will be most sorry.*

To someone watching from outside who knew even most of what Xizor knew, his position might seem precarious. As with a juggler who had half a dozen balls in the air, disaster seemed imminent. But Xizor had the skills and, more important, the will to keep the balls flying smoothly. All part of the game. And what made it so interesting. Anyone could juggle with fewer items; it took a master to do what he was doing.

"You sure this thing is going to work?" Leia asked.

Chewbacca, busy working on the doorjamb with a small power wrench, said something. It sounded snide.

Threepio quickly translated: "He says that if it doesn't, it won't be because it was improperly installed."

Leia turned and looked at Lando, who shrugged.

"The guy who sold it to me said it was top-of-the-line," he said. "Got the latest doppraymagno scanner, full-range sensor, a self-contained power supply good for a year. It better work, it cost me enough."

"Hardly a dent in your winnings, I would think," Leia said.

"Oh, it was a dent. I hope it's worth it."

So do I, Leia thought.

Chewie gargled something.

"He says it is ready for testing," Threepio said.

Leia walked to the desk and sat behind it. The computer inset into the desk was off, and she switched it on.

"The unit is under the file 'Bioscan,'" Lando said.

Leia opened the program. A hologram appeared over the desk. "Nonholographic mode," she said. "Flatscreen only."

The image vanished. She looked down at the desk. The words "Scanner offline" appeared on the screen. It would be invisible from the chair opposite the desk. "Bioscan on," she said.

The screen lit up with an image of an eye, an ear, and a nose. Oh, how cute.

"Okay, everybody out. Let's test it."

Threepio, Lando, and Chewie trooped out into the hall.

"Close the door."

They did.

"Okay," Leia yelled. "Lando, you come in first."

The door opened and Lando sauntered in. He turned around as if modeling the latest fashions. "Here I am. Enjoy."

Leia grinned. He was endearing for a rogue. She looked down at the screen.

The scanner newly inset into the frame of the door picked up Lando's image, and it appeared on the screen. An infocrawl moved up the side of the image as the sensors examined Lando and fed the result to the computer: Human, male, armed with a blaster and a small vibro-shiv in his pants pocket on the left side, heartbeat, respiration, muscle tone index, height, weight, body temperature. Even a refractive index indicating how old his skin was, plus or minus a standard year.

Lando, according to this device, was a little older than he looked.

No bombs or poison gas or commactive material hidden upon his person. No hidden holocams or recording devices.

"Seems to be working on you. Chewie, come on in."

Again the device scanned and reported. She didn't know what the normal readings for a Wookiee were, but the program that came with the scanner apparently did, and it told her that Chewie was within normal limits for one of that species.

She was sure Chewie would be happy to know that. Finally she called Threepio in. The program had no trouble at all recognizing him as a droid.

"Well. It seems to be working just fine," she said.

"Why don't we test it on you?" Lando offered.

"I don't think that will be necessary," she said. "You were plenty."

Lando's comlink bleeped. He pulled it from his belt. Leia looked at him.

"I've got an eye at the port," he said. He lifted the comlink. "Go ahead."

"A ship has just arrived," the tinny voice said. "The *Outrider,* piloted by—"

"—Dash Rendar?" Leia finished. "What is he doing here? He's supposed to be watching Luke!"

"Thanks," Lando said into the comlink. He shut it off. To Leia he said, "Maybe we better go find out."

They met Dash halfway. He was in a pubtrans cab heading away from the port. Chewie swung their rental vehicle around, and they quickly caught up with the cab and waved it over.

When Dash got out, he looked terrible.

"Is Luke okay?" Leia said in a rush.

"Yeah, he's fine."

"Why are you here? You're supposed to be guarding him."

Dash stared at her. "He's fine. He doesn't need *my* help."

"You don't look so good," Lando offered. "Trouble?"

"Long story," Dash said.

"Get into the speeder," Leia said. "You can tell it to us on the way back to the casino."

He got into the speeder, and they started off.

When he was finished, Leia shook her head. Luke was okay, that was the important thing. And it appeared that Guri had told the truth, at least about the secret plans.

"Any idea what these plans are?" Lando asked.

"No. The Bothans have some kind of hot specialists on Kothlis who are going to pull them out of the computer." His voice was almost a dead monotone.

Lando said, "Hey, lighten up, Dash. Things get heavy in the middle of a battle. Anybody can miss—"

"Not me! I don't miss. I should have clipped that missile! Bothans *died* because I missed, you understand?"

Leia was silent. She didn't like Dash Rendar; he was a braggart and stuck on himself; but at least he had some feeling for others. Maybe it was more because his self-confidence had been shattered, but she could tell it had really rattled him. It must be terrible to think you are the sharpest thing in the skies and then to find out you have a dull spot on your edge.

Nobody said anything for a while.

Well. As soon as this business with Black Sun was finished, they would go and find Luke. Somehow it would all get sorted out.

Luke left Artoo to watch the X-wing and made his way to the lounge where he was supposed to meet Koth Melan.

The Bothan was waiting.

"Any problems?" Melan asked.

"No. Now what?"

"We have a safe house here, a few kilometers away, on the outskirts of the city. The computer is already there and the team working on it. We'll go there and wait until they are done."

"How long will it take?"

Melan shrugged. "Who can say? Hours, perhaps, if we are fortunate; days if not. The team is very good and won't take any chances. After what we paid for it, it would be terrible to slip up and lose the information."

"Yeah, it would."

"I have a speeder waiting outside."

"Lead on," Luke said.

Outside, the daytime air had a funny smell. It took Luke a moment to place it. The odor was of warm and moldy cheese. He smiled to himself. He knew he would get used to it pretty quick and tune it out. That was something they almost never mentioned in the travel ads, that every planet had its own smells and feel. The light was a little redder here than on Tatooine; it was a little cooler than Bothawui, and there was that smell. The thing about alien worlds—well, alien to somebody not born there—was that each one was unique.

Moldy cheese wasn't so bad. He'd smelled worse.

They walked to Melan's speeder and got in. Time to go find out what the Empire thought was so valuable.

21

The safe house was a clever setup, Luke saw. What looked like a row of old storage units and run-down office space in an industrial park turned out to be something else behind the facade. Past a security checkpoint with a trio of large armed guards was a modern complex of interconnected units, bright and gleaming with the latest computer and electronic gear, plus a bunch of technicians to operate it. Most of them were Bothans, but there were several other aliens at work.

It was a smart camouflage. From outside, you'd never expect to find all this.

"This way," Melan said.

Luke followed the Bothan spymaster down a gleaming corridor to a room with yet another armed guard posted at the door. Melan showed an ID, and they were admitted.

Inside the room were half a dozen Bothan techs. One of them tended leads plugged into jacks in the computer Melan had collected; others sat at consoles tapping keyboards or using voxax controls. Information danced in the air as holographic images formed and re-formed.

"There's not much to see, I'm afraid," Melan said. "Unless you're an expert in this, the information looks to be pretty much a jumble of numbers and letters."

Luke nodded. "What do they mean?" He waved at one of the screens.

"Got me," Melan said. "I'm a spymaster. What I know about programming you could inscribe on a microdiode lead with a dull sword."

Luke smiled.

"Hey, hey, hey!" one of the Bothan techs said. "Look at this, boys! Scan sector Tarp-Hard-Xenon."

Luke heard the tap of keys, the commands of voxaxes.

"Wow!" said one of the other techs.

"Oh, sister," said another. "I can't believe it!"

"What?" Luke said. "What is it?"

Before anybody could say, the door exploded inward and somebody came in shooting.

Leia smiled at Guri, who was once again seated across from where she herself sat at the desk in their suite. But the smile was to cover her puzzlement.

According to the computer screen inset into the desk and the scanner that fed it, Guri was not human.

What she was, the scanner program could not say.

"Care for some refreshment?" Leia asked.

"Tea would be fine."

"Threepio, fix two cups of the special tea blend, would you, please?"

Leia turned back from the droid and flashed her smile at Guri again. She caught the computer screen peripherally as she glanced at Black Sun's representative. According to the scanner, Guri's skin was around ten standard years old.

Wasn't *that* interesting?

"I trust your business went well?"

"It did."

It would be no trouble to keep her talking for a few minutes, until the "special blend" tea Threepio was preparing did its job. The sleeping potion he was instilling into Guri's cup would put her out harmlessly for a couple of hours, during which time Leia and the others could make a closer examination of Guri's person and effects. This was the plan they'd agreed upon if the scan didn't check out the way it should. After a couple of hours, Guri would awaken and—if the potion worked as it was supposed to work—not remember having fallen asleep. Maybe they could figure out who and what she was during that time. At least Leia's instincts had been right: There was something odd about Guri. Very odd.

Threepio brought the tea. Leia hoped the droid had gotten the stuff into the right cup. It would be embarrassing if Lando or Chewie had to come in and take over while she took a nap.

Threepio had his back to Guri. Leia glanced at him. His left eye illuminator winked off, then back on.

Leia picked up her tea and smiled again.

When a man comes at you with a blaster spewing, you don't stand there asking stupid questions. Luke snatched his lightsaber from his belt, lit it, and whipped it up in a right inward block as he slid to the side.

A blaster bolt splashed from the blade in a shower of red and orange sparks. The air stank suddenly of ozone.

The techs were unarmed, and Luke saw two of them take hits and go down. The others scrambled for cover.

Koth Melan produced a small weapon and returned fire, hitting the lead attacker right between the eyes. The attacker fell backward.

There were more behind him, boiling through the shattered doorway.

Luke leaped forward, circled his lightsaber into a horizontal slash, and took down the next man through the door.

Melan fired. The bolt sizzled past Luke's left ear and hit the third man incoming.

Beyond that, Luke saw, there were at least a dozen more shooters crowding toward the doorway. Maybe more. It wasn't as if he had time to do a precise count here—

More energy beams cooked the air, scorching past Luke and spearing computer consoles and technicians alike.

"Too many of them!" Melan yelled. "This way!"

Luke wove a curtain of hard light with his blade, deflecting blaster bolts and driving the attackers back temporarily. He leaped to the side, and Melan fired repeatedly into the opening, momentarily clearing it.

"Come on!"

Luke turned and ran. Discretion here was definitely the better part of valor. Who were these guys? They wore black, but didn't have any insignia he could see. Some kind of new Imperial strike team? Mercenaries?

Never mind that now. Worry about who they are later. This party is over, Luke, it is time to leave!

Luke hurried after Melan.

After twenty minutes of small talk, Leia realized the sleeping potion wasn't going to work. It was supposed to take five minutes, eight minutes at the outside, if you had the constitution of a rock.

Guri continued their diplomatic back-and-forth without any apparent effects from the powerful potion.

Maybe Threepio had fouled up somehow? Not put the stuff into Guri's cup?

The computer was still processing information and

displaying it for Leia. The . . . person sitting across from her breathed air and her heart pumped blood, but the lungs weren't normal, and neither was the heart. The muscles under the supposedly ten-year-old skin weren't made of any tissue the scanner could recognize. Her body temperature was ten percent cooler than normal. A human that cold would be dead.

On visual inspection, Guri looked like a perfectly normal and attractive young woman in her early twenties. According to the scanner and computer, she was not human; nor was she any one of the eighty-six thousand alien species it was designed to recognize; nor was she any kind of standard droid. And she was, it seemed, immune to a sleeping potion that should work on anybody human.

What was going *on* here?

No doubt about it, this was a problem, and not one that Leia had anticipated.

Now what were they going to do?

Guri helped her resolve the problem. She said, "All right, Leia Organa, I think this has gone on long enough."

"Excuse me?"

Guri held her empty container up. As Leia watched, she squeezed the heavy ceramic mug in one hand. Her hand shook a little, but the cup shattered into tiny bits. Guri smiled. "I can do that to your head if I wish. You probably have a weapon hidden somewhere, but I warn you, I am much faster than you, and if you attempt to reach your weapon, I can get to you before you get to it."

Leia played it out. "Suppose I believe you. What do you want?"

"You are going to accompany me from this place. You will tell the Wookiee in the hall to stay here as we leave; convince him, otherwise he dies."

"Where are we going?"

"Do not concern yourself with that. Just do as you are told and you will survive to get there."

"I don't think so," Leia said. "Whoever—or whatever—you are, I bet you aren't faster than a blaster bolt. Lando? Dash?"

The door to the bedroom slid open. Lando and Dash stood there, blasters aimed at Guri. They stepped into the room.

"You might be wrong," Guri said.

The door to the hall also slid open, and Chewie stood there with his bowcaster leveled at Guri's back.

"Could be," Leia said. "But you'd have to be real fast to avoid being hit by three bolts."

Guri turned her head slightly to glance at Chewie. Turned back to look at Leia. "You have the advantage, it would seem. What do you propose?"

There was a good question. What *were* they going to do now?

One of the Bothan techs leaped up, grabbed the computer, and jerked it loose from the leads. The undamaged screens went blank.

"Go!" Melan yelled at the tech. "We'll cover you!"

The tech ran for the rear of the room. A section of the wall slid back to reveal an unmarked emergency exit. The tech with the computer barreled through the opening.

Melan, meanwhile, emptied the charge in his blaster at the attackers coming in again. The weapon clicked dry, and he tossed it aside.

"Run!" he yelled.

Luke didn't need to hear that twice. But before he could take a step, a blaster bolt hit Melan.

The Bothan went down.

Luke dropped to one knee.

"G-G-Go!" Melan said. "Leave me, get out!"

Luke saw the black-clad attackers stream in. You

didn't leave your wounded comrades in battle. He stood between Melan and the incoming tide.

"Idiot! L-L-Leave!"

Luke chopped the blaster from the hand of the first man to reach them. Wondered briefly why the man didn't cook them, but had no time to reflect on it as five or six more shooters came in.

"Luke," Melan said. "Thanks. I—"

Luke glanced down. Melan went limp and his eyes rolled back, showing only the pale sclera. A final, shuddery breath escaped, and he was still.

Dead.

The number of men crowding into the room increased. There were ten, fifteen of them now, all pointing blasters at him but not firing. What—?

"Turn off your saber," one of them commanded in a rough voice. "You can't win."

Luke looked at the speaker. The figure stood in a shadow, was hard to see until it stepped out into the light.

The reptilian alien was about his height, covered with black scales, with a mouth full of pointed teeth. Definitely a meat-eater. He thought he recognized the species as that of a Barabel, but he wasn't sure; he hadn't seen a lot of them. Barabels didn't leave their homeworld very often.

Luke saw that he didn't have a chance, even using the Force. He clicked his lightsaber off.

"Wise move," the Barabel said. "My people have great respect for Jedi Knights and I am sorry I must do this, but it is business. Take his weapon."

One of them moved in and removed the lightsaber from Luke's grasp.

Luke looked back at the Barabel. "What do you want?"

"Sorry, but we want you, Skywalker."

·   ·   ·

Chewie said something. He didn't sound happy.

"Chewie doesn't think this is a very good idea," Lando said. "I agree with him."

Leia said, "Look, I know you owe Han and you want to take care of me, but we need to do this."

Dash leaned against a wall, a blaster trained on Guri, who sat in a chair and was bound with cuffbands and a steel cable. They weren't taking any chances with her. Dash said, "You're going to waltz into the heart of the Empire, just like that?"

"I have some connections on Coruscant," Leia said. "That's where our friend here came from." She nodded at Guri, who offered nothing. "Somebody is playing games I don't much like. Luke is in danger; this . . . person who says she represents Black Sun is our only link to them."

Lando said, "You know, there were rumors a few years back about human replica droids. Seems like I heard somebody had perfected the method, got them good enough so you couldn't tell the difference between one of the replicas and a real human by looking. That was about ten, twelve years back. It would fit with the age the scanner gives us about her." He glanced at Guri.

Guri smiled but said nothing.

"So what if she is a droid?" Dash said. "What good does it do for you to know that?"

Leia shook her head. "Not much good at all," she said. "But if we can get to whoever sent her, maybe that does. She's got to be worth a lot to them."

Chewie moaned something.

"Chewbacca says that if you go to Coruscant, he is going as well."

Leia glared at Threepio.

"Don't blame me, I'm only translating what he said."

"Fine, you can go with me. Lando, you and Dash

wait here for Luke. We'll take Guri with us. Whoever or whatever she is, she's our pass."

"How are you going to get there?" Dash asked. "Book a compartment on a liner? They check those things going into Coruscant, you know."

"I'll contact the Alliance and have them supply us with a small ship."

"I don't like it," Lando said.

"Why not just take her ship?" Dash asked. "It's bound to be cleared."

"And maybe blow ourselves to tiny pieces? We've already determined she's not the most trustworthy being we've ever met. Could somebody steal your ship?"

Dash laughed. "They wouldn't get very far if they tried."

"I still don't like it," Lando said.

"I'm not asking you to like it, I'm telling you to do it."

Which pretty much ended that conversation.

Leia tried to sound as if she were in charge and as if she knew exactly what she was doing, but that was a stretch. If Guri was a replica droid, surely she must be valuable to whomever had sent her. Maybe that person would be willing to talk to get her back. Conventional wisdom had it that the best plans were usually the simplest ones, and if that was true, this was a *great* idea.

Conventional wisdom aside, it wasn't much; still, it was what she had, and she would follow it up as best she could.

"Excuse me," Guri said.

Leia turned to look at her. "What?"

"There is an easier way."

Leia stared at her, then at the others. "What are you talking about?"

"You want to go to Imperial Center and meet with the leadership of Black Sun, correct?"

"That was the general idea."

"That is why I was sent—to provide you escort for such a trip."

"Then why the threats?"

"It was the fastest way."

"I wouldn't trust her, Leia," Lando said.

"I don't, but I'm reasonable. Go on."

"It will be very risky for you to try to sneak past the Imperial pickets around Imperial Center. I can greatly lessen that risk."

"No offense, but Lando is right. Why should we trust you?"

"Because I work for Prince Xizor."

Lando and Dash both inhaled sharply.

Leia looked at them.

"Xizor is the *head* of Black Sun," Dash said.

"I can arrange for you to speak with him, if you like."

Leia frowned. "He's here?"

"I have his private comlink codes."

"I don't like this," Lando said. He waved the blaster.

Lando didn't much like anything lately.

Chewie growled and harned.

Neither did Chewie like it.

"You are wanted by the Empire, as are your companions. I can arrange disguises, get you past customs and straight to the prince," Guri said. "It would eliminate much of the risk."

Leia sighed. It sounded reasonable, despite Guri's attempt to capture her.

"All right, we can at least listen to what your master has to say." Before the others could protest much, she waved them silent.

"May I stand?" Guri asked.

"Yes."

Guri came to her feet in a smooth motion.

"Dash, unbind her," Leia ordered.

"There is no need," Guri said, smiling. She flexed

her arms. The bands around her wrists popped as if they were made of cheap plasto. She took a deep breath and strained; the cable around her shoulders gave a metallic groan, stretched, then snapped.

"Oh, man," Lando said.

Guri moved to the room's com, waved her hands at it. A few moments passed. Then a deep, masculine voice said, "Yes?"

"Guri, Highness. I have Princess Leia Organa here. She would like to speak with you."

"Where's the image?" Lando asked.

"My master prefers not to send it out, even on a shielded channel," Guri said. She looked at Leia.

Leia said, "Greetings, Prince Xizor."

"Ah, Princess Leia. How delightful to make your acquaintance at last."

His voice was compelling, at least.

"Your . . . droid here says you wish to see me."

"Indeed. I have information that might be of use to you."

"Concerning . . . ?"

"The attempted assassination of Luke Skywalker. A friend of yours, is he not?"

It took much of Leia's control to avoid gasping. Xizor knew about the plot!

"We are comrades, yes," Leia said. "Tell me, how do you know of the attempts on Luke Skywalker's life?"

"Not over the comlink," he said. "We must discuss such matters face-to-face. If you will allow Guri to escort you, I will explain all when you arrive."

Leia looked around the room. This certainly was unexpected. What was she going to do?

22

The building to which Luke had been taken was only a hundred kilometers or so, he guessed, from the Bothan safe house—that hadn't stayed safe very long, had it?—and he was now locked in a strongly reinforced cell. The technology here was a whole lot lower than the Bothans' had been. The walls were plain, of some hard substance, a neutral gray. The heavy door was sheathed in durasteel plate, and a window at eye level was crisscrossed with metal mesh, the strands of which were as thick as his little finger. A guard pushing two meters tall and probably half that wide stood across the hall with a blast rifle, staring at the door. There was a heavy plastic cot bolted to the floor, with a thin pad and a blanket on it. A dim light overhead cast faint and fuzzy shadows. In one corner was a shallow depression in the floor with a fist-size round hole in the middle of it. He had a pretty good idea what that was used for.

Other than those things and himself, there was nothing in the cell.

Well. It could be worse. There could be vermin.

Luke sat on the cot. They'd taken his comlink and lightsaber, but they hadn't roughed him up or tortured him. Yet, anyway.

Who were they? What did they want?

As if in answer, the lock on the cell door clicked and the door swung inward. The Barabel stepped into view. Luke couldn't see her very well—he was pretty sure now it was a her—she seemed to find the darkest of the shadows as if she belonged there. Well. That didn't matter, either. He could hear her well enough.

"I don't suppose you want to tell me what's going on?"

The Barabel made a gesture Luke interpreted as a shrug. "No reason why not. No point in being unpleasant. There's nothing you can do about it."

There was a happy thought.

"I am Skahtul. I make my living as a bounty hunter, as do the others with me. It seems there is a large reward—a *very* large reward—offered to whoever delivers Luke Skywalker to them, alive and well, no questions asked. Realizing what a difficult chore this might be, a group of us decided to band together. Better to have a portion of a lot of credits than none. Lucky for us, you and those blasted Bothans have increased the amounts of the shares the survivors of the attack will collect. It's the same pie, but there are now fewer of us to divide it among."

Before he could speak, she continued: "Oddly enough, there is a *second* reward being offered for Luke Skywalker; this one is for him—you—dead.

"Fortunately for you, the second amount is not quite as large as the first, so we plan to keep you healthy until we can collect it."

"Here's a third option," Luke said. "How about I give you more than either bounty to let me go?"

Skahtul laughed, a hard-edged sound that lapped against the solid walls and bounced back at them. "Oh, certainly, we—my colleagues and I—would be open to such an offer."

Here was a chance. He could borrow the credits from Leia and pay her back later. "How much are we talking about?"

Skahtul named a figure.

"Whoa! You could buy half a city with that many credits!"

"With enough left over for you and six or eight of your friends to retire upon and live happily ever after," the bounty hunter said. "Did we miss something in our search? You have a credit tab with that much in your pocket, perhaps?"

"I wish." If Leia *had* that much, he'd never live long enough to pay it back, even if he made it to general. Unless he was out walking and tripped over a mountain of platinum that didn't belong to anybody. Not much chance of that.

Skahtul laughed. "It is good that you maintain your sense of humor." Her voice turned serious. "But be warned. Any attempt to escape will be met with maximum resistance. We know how resourceful Jedi Knights are. You are worth a few thousand more alive than dead; however, better to collect the smaller bounty than to risk losing it all. Is this understandable?"

"Yeah, I get it."

"Good. It's not personal, you know. Some of us even admire what you've done against the Empire, having some sympathies in that direction, but business is business. Behave yourself and you will be treated well. You'll be kept in here, but you'll be fed and unmolested until we arrange for our benefactor to pay us and collect you."

"You want to tell me who this 'benefactor' is?"

"Not to worry, you'll find out soon enough."

With that, Skahtul oozed back through the door and shut it behind herself.

Luke stared after her. Well, this was great. Captured by a bunch of bounty hunters and sold to the highest bidder. Good thing the one who wanted him dead—and who might that be?—was not as generous as whoever wanted him alive. Given the money involved, he had no idea about who the latter could be.

Darth Vader could throw that many credits out a window and never miss them, were the stories true. According to what he'd heard, if Vader's personal fortune was changed into credit coins and dumped in a pile, you could spend the rest of your life digging in it with a shovel and not get to the bottom.

Leia sure didn't have that much. Probably the whole Alliance didn't have that much.

He'd better think of something fast. He had an idea that if he stood face-to-face with Vader unarmed, he wasn't going to have much of a chance of surviving that meeting.

Good idea, Luke. Think of something.

What?

The droid who looked like a woman had hidden her ship in a small clearing centered in a vast rain forest two hundred kilometers away from Avaro's casino. The ride didn't take long by landspeeder, and it was just the three of them: Guri, Chewie, and Leia.

Storm clouds gathered in layers of purple and gray as they arrived. The rumble of thunder followed close after the bright flashes of approaching lightning. The air had that damp, wild smell that ran before a hard rain.

Leia and Chewie stared at the ship.

It was a sleek, somehow almost feminine craft, shaped vaguely like a figure eight lying on its belly, bristling with guns fore and amidships, a quad of powerful-looking engines mounted aft.

"My vessel, the *Stinger*," Guri said.

"Very nice."

"Named by my master," she said. "An appropriate designation."

"We'd better get on board before the storm gets here," Leia said.

The trio started for the ship. Dash and Lando weren't particularly happy being left behind, but Leia wouldn't risk any more people than she had to. Chewie was enough. If this turned out to be what Guri and the mysterious Xizor claimed, it would be fine—assuming they got past the pickets around Coruscant and on-planet customs. If not, no point in all of them getting into trouble.

Well. Any more trouble than they were already in.

The rain let go in earnest, and they ran for the ship. They got drenched anyhow.

A couple of days had passed, at least. Luke had lost track of the time, since there wasn't any light except for the dim one in the cell and no transparisteel on the outside.

He was practicing his levitation, hovering a few centimeters over the cot, when he heard approaching footsteps. He allowed himself to drop to the cot. He didn't want to reveal he knew how to do this. There weren't any holocams in the cell that he'd been able to detect, and the guard usually stayed across the hall.

The door clicked, and Skahtul slipped silently into the room.

"So, has my buyer paid up?"

"Not exactly."

Luke slipped off the cot and stood, facing the shorter Barabel. "What does that mean?"

"It means that after a discussion with my . . . colleagues, we realized that you might be even more valuable than we thought."

"More valuable? Come on."

"There are two factions who want you. It was suggested that we might be able to pump up the price by playing them off against each other."

Luke blinked. "You're going to have them *bid* for me? Like a slave?"

"Something like that."

"Who are these people?"

Skahtul did something like a shrug. "To be honest, we don't know. Our contacts have been very, ah, circuitous. Agents of agents of agents kind of thing."

Luke couldn't think of anything to say.

"Of course, we must be very, ah, circumspect in our dealings. Players with the kind of money we are talking about must be very powerful. A misstep might be most dangerous. Fatal."

"So you solicit higher offers from them. What if the ones who want me dead come up with more credits?"

"Like I said before, it's not personal, just business."

Luke stared at the Barabel. "You'll excuse me if I take it personally." His voice was as dry as his throat had suddenly become.

In his lair, Xizor smiled. Guri had the princess, and they were on their way here. Perfect.

He leaned back in his chair and steepled his fingers. Sometimes it was almost disappointing how easily he accomplished his ends. It would be good to have a challenge now and then, as he had in the old days before he was master of so much. When he'd had to work a little.

Ah, well. Better to win easily than to lose.

The Emperor sat in his favorite throne, the one set a meter higher than the rest of the room. Vader entered, dropped to one knee.

"My master."

"Rise, Lord Vader."

Vader did so. He hoped whatever the Emperor wanted was something easy and brief. He had just received word from his agents that Luke had been found. His captors, it seemed, were a ragtag band of bounty hunters who were demanding more money. Vader's agents knew who they were but not precisely where they were hiding. And it seemed there was another bidder who also wanted Luke. Vader would have his people offer whatever it took; money meant nothing when compared to the dark side, and he fully intended to turn the boy in that direction. He considered going to collect Luke himself, to Kothlis, where he was reportedly being held, but to leave Imperial Center just now would be dangerous. He needed to be here to watch Xizor. The criminal's twisted plans had ensnared the Emperor, and to walk away might well be a fatal mistake—

"You will go to Kothlis," the Emperor said. "And collect young Skywalker."

Once again Vader was glad his face was masked. He had not expected to hear this. How did the Emperor know? Who in Vader's organization had betrayed him? There was no way the Emperor should be privy to that information, not yet. Only a handful of Vader's most trusted agents knew it.

Unless . . . unless the Emperor was the other bidder for Luke?

No. That made no sense. The Emperor had given the task to Vader; he would not enter into a bidding war against himself.

"I have already sent my agents for him," Vader tried.

"Agents are not to be trusted. Skywalker grows stronger in the Force each day. I remind you that he has within him the power to destroy us. Only you are potent enough to capture him."

"Yes, my master." There was no arguing with him once he'd made his mind up.

Surely Prince Xizor's foul hand was involved in this. It would not be wise to bring that up; the Emperor had made it quite clear that the Dark Prince was his concern, and it would not be a good idea to reveal that Vader had plans of his own concerning Xizor.

"There is another reason. You are aware that Prince Xizor's scheme to allow the plans for the Death Star to fall into Rebel hands has been implemented."

"Yes, my master. The plan proceeds over my objections."

"Those objections have been noted, Lord Vader. As it happens, the plans have been transported from the freighter hijacked off Bothawui to Kothlis. Quite a coincidence, don't you think?"

That Luke and the fruits of Xizor's twisted plot were on the same planet at the same time, a coincidence? Doubtful.

"We must appear to make an attempt to recover the plans," the Emperor continued, "to convince the Rebels that the plans are genuine and that we are distressed by their loss. Therefore your trip will serve two purposes. You can fetch Skywalker, and you can destroy some of the local scenery so that the Rebels will be gulled into believing we are concerned over the theft."

He had to at least try: "Any of our admirals could go and wave the flag and fire the guns. I have many pressing matters here."

"More pressing than my commands, Lord Vader?"

So much for that idea. "No, my master."

"I thought not. I will have Skywalker with us or destroyed, the sooner the better. And the end of the Rebellion is near. If *you* personally lead the attack, the Rebels will be convinced that we think these plans of great value."

"Yes, my master."

Vader left the chambers, and once again his simmering anger threatened to bubble up and overcome him. Xizor's touch was like a thick night fog: dark, clammy, seeping into the smallest cracks to chill and dampen. Once again, he had maneuvered the Emperor into getting his rival out of the picture. With Vader on Kothlis, who knew what cloying webs that reptilian spider would spin for the Emperor?

Vader resolved to make it a fast trip.

The call came from the picket line of Imperial Star Destroyers and frigates posted around the planet:

"Entry code?" the bored voice said.

Inside the *Stinger,* Guri responded with a number.

A moment went by. "Pass. Lock into the landing grid and put it on auto."

Guri operated the ship with an offhand expertise that was most impressive. She tapped controls, her hands dancing rapidly.

Leia and Chewie looked at each other.

"They will check for contraband at customs," Guri said, as if reading Leia's mind. "Black Sun has contacts there, but we cannot make it too obvious that you are under our protection. Time to go change."

Chewie said something. It didn't sound happy.

"You wanted to come along," Leia said.

He didn't like it, but he left and went to the 'fresher.

Once the ship was on auto, Guri stood and walked to a locker. She removed some clothes and a full-head muzzle-mask helmet from the locker, tossed them at Leia. "Here. Put these on."

The clothes stank. Leia wrinkled her nose at them.

Guri said, "They belonged to Boushh, an Ubese bounty hunter. Boushh was quite good at the trade. He did a lot of contract work for Black Sun. He . . . retired recently."

"As it happens, I speak a bit of Ubese," Leia said.

"We know. The costume is not a coincidence."

Leia looked at the clothes. "What happened to this Boushh? He retired?"

"Quite suddenly. He tried to rascal Black Sun for more credits on a delivery for which there was an agreed-upon contract. That was . . . unwise."

The sound of the last statement gave Leia a chill. She moved to don the clothing. She had a feeling Boushh would not be needing these smelly clothes again.

When Chewie returned in a few minutes, it was all Leia could do to keep a straight face. Where his fur had been brown and gray, it now was mottled with large patches of black. A raccoonlike mask encircled his eyes, and the fur on his head had been trimmed into a short spacer's cut. She turned to Guri, who said, "Meet Snoova, a well-known Wookiee bounty hunter."

Chewie was unhappy, and that came through in whatever it was he said.

"Stop complaining," Leia said. "The dye will wash out and your fur will grow back. In a couple of weeks you'll be back to normal."

Leia put her helmet on and tested the built-in vox-scrambler. When she spoke her voice was electronically altered. She knew enough Ubese to get by, and as long as she didn't run into a native of that place, she should be okay. Her speech buzzed and clicked and sounded to her own ears as if it were indeed coming from an alien throat.

Chewie gargled and moaned, and Guri nodded. "Yes. It will do. We'll be landing soon."

Leia nodded and removed the helmet. She hoped Guri knew what she was doing.

23

A thin man brought Luke food and drink twice a day. He had eaten worse, eaten better, too. The routine was usually the same when breakfast or supper arrived: The thin man carried a tray to the door. The guard unlocked the door, leveled his blast rifle at Luke, and backed him to the cot; the thin man put the tray on the floor just inside the door, then left, with the guard.

This time, Luke asked the thin man for the time.

"Whyddya care?" the thin man said.

"Why do you care if I care?" Luke returned.

The thin man sneered, but he told Luke what time it was and departed.

This was the evening meal, as Luke had suspected.

The reason for his question was simple. He was planning on leaving, and he wanted the cover of darkness. Once he got out of the building, better they were not able to spot him, that he could use the night for camouflage.

Luke ate. The liquid was sweet, brown, and fizzy;

the food was bland—soypro cutlets, some kind of orange vegetable, something green and crunchy—but there was no point escaping on an empty stomach. Once he got to his X-wing and lifted, there was no telling how long it would be before he had a chance to eat again.

Once he got to his X-wing.

He grinned around a mouthful of the green stuff. Like that was going to be the easy part.

It would not be wise for them to be seen together, Guri told Leia.

"After you clear customs, meet me at these coordinates."

Leia and Chewie agreed.

There were a few tense moments at customs.

A guard examined the holocard ID that said Leia was Boushh, tapped it against the table in front of him. "Purpose of your visit?"

"Business," Leia said in Ubese. Her voice clicked and buzzed through the mask.

"I see you are licensed to carry that weapon, but we do not take kindly to people who use them on Imperial Center."

Leia said nothing.

"I think we'll have to take that helmet off," he said. "Just to be certain you match the holograph." He tapped the card again, looked at it. "One can't be too careful."

Leia said, "It will damage my lungs to breathe this air without my filters."

"I can arrange an atmosphere room—" he began. He stopped.

Chewie moved close to Leia and the guard, rumbled something.

She realized how used to him she'd gotten every time

she took in his disguise. Good old Chewie, he was as dependable as sunlight, loyal to a fault.

"What is your problem?" the guard said.

Chewie babbled something that sounded angry.

"I don't care if you are late for an appointment," the guard said. But the line of people waiting to pass through customs was starting to lengthen, and the guard suddenly thrust Leia's ID card back at her. "Move along, bounty hunter. I have others to process."

Once Chewie was through, he and Leia moved quickly away from the area.

"Okay, now we go and see my contact. This section of the Underground is relatively safe," she said, "but still not a place where you want to relax your guard."

Chewie nodded and patted his bowcaster. Said something.

"If you just asked why we aren't going directly to see Guri, I want to see if I can't hedge our bets a little first."

Aboard the *Executor,* Vader considered his upcoming meeting with Luke. Since last they'd met, the boy had had time to come to terms with what he'd been told. On some level, he must know the truth, that Vader was his father. Of course, that had been in another lifetime, when Vader had still been Anakin Skywalker, but the fact of it remained.

He would turn him. He knew he could, because he had felt the dark side rise in Luke, had felt the power of his anger. The boy had loosed it once; he could be made to free it again. Each repetition became easier. The dark side was a path that grew wider and deeper each time you trod upon it. Soon it would be no effort at all for Luke to allow the dark side to rule.

And the Emperor was right. Luke had much power in him. It was raw, unchanneled and untrained, but it was vast. His potential was larger than the Emperor's, larger than Vader's.

But it was still only potential and not focused energy. When next they met, Vader would still be more adept, still the master. He would defeat the boy and bring him to the dark side. They would be in accord, father and son.

And when that happened, nothing in the galaxy could stop them. None would dare oppose them. All would bow before them. Worlds would tremble at their approach.

Under his mask, Vader smiled.

Luke took several cleansing breaths, as he had been taught, and tried to release his thoughts at the same time. Ben—Obi-Wan—could plant suggestions in a stormtrooper's mind without apparent effort. It was not so easy for Luke. A couple of times he had managed it, but it required a lot of concentration to summon enough of the Force. You couldn't be worried about whether or not it was going to work, or what would happen if it failed halfway through. You pretty much couldn't have anything else on your mind—well, at least *Luke* couldn't—and that made it tricky, given that if it didn't work or if it quit before he was done, he might wind up dead.

No. *Put those thoughts away. Remember that the Force is with you. You can do this.*

He took another breath, let half of it out, and allowed the Force to connect him to the mind of the guard in the hall.

The sensation was strange, as it always was. It was not as if he were really in two places at once, but more as if there were a part of his own mind that was somehow not quite connected, not quite accessible. A kind of muzzy feeling.

Luke became aware that the guard's feet hurt, that he needed to visit a refresher, that he was tired of standing here holding a blast rifle, watching a meadle-blasted door when there was no way anybody could get through it, no way—

"Open the door."

"Huh? Who's there—?"

"You must open the door."

"I . . . must open the door."

"You must put down your rifle and open the door now."

"I must . . . put down my rifle. Open the door now."

Luke watched the guard through the barred window. Watched him put his rifle down.

Got him. Luke grinned. A mistake.

"What—?"

Lost him. Concentrate, Luke!

"Open the door."

Luke put the thoughts of victory and loss out of his mind. The only thing that mattered was the guard.

"Open the door."

"Yes. Open . . . the . . . door . . ."

The guard's keycard slipped into the slot. The lock clicked.

One of the sweetest sounds Luke had ever heard. He didn't dwell on it.

"You're very tired. You need to come in and lie on the cot and take a nice nap."

"Cot. Take a nap . . ."

The guard moved into the cell, walked past Luke. Luke took the keycard from the guard's hand. He glanced out into the corridor. Nobody else around. He stepped out of the cell, shut the door carefully, dropped the keycard on the floor, and picked up the blast rifle. He looked back. The guard snored on the cot.

Now. This was more like it.

He started down the corridor. He felt pretty confident. This guard had been easier than the one at the carnival where he had practiced walking on the tightrope. He ought to be able to take care of any others he ran into, either with the Force or the rifle. He also ought to head straight for the nearest exit and leave. With any luck it would be hours before anybody even knew he was gone.

But he wanted to see if he could find his lightsaber first. He'd spent a lot of time building it, and since the escape had been so easy, he was pretty sure he could retrieve his Jedi weapon and leave just as easily. The Force was with him. He could do it.

He was sure of it.

As Leia and Chewie made their way down a dark and twisted passage into the heart of the Southern Underground, she shook her head. The casino complex on Rodia made Mos Eisley look good. But it seemed that no matter how awful a place was, there was always another spot that was worse.

The Southern Underground made the casino complex look like a vacation paradise.

Beggars were everywhere, dressed in rags, gaunt and demanding. Whatever had driven them underground must be terrible if this was their only option.

All manner of illicit offerings were made as she and Chewie moved farther into the maze of underground tunnels. Corridor dwellers would sell them whatever they wanted, and the particulars made Leia's stomach roil.

Yes, there had always been such people, but the Empire had caused their numbers to rise tremendously. That which had been a small stain on the joy of the Republic was a blight on the bloated body of the Empire.

Chewie growled at a partially clad woman who smiled as she approached them. The woman hastily backed off.

The corridor in which they walked was ill lit, splotched with graffiti in half a dozen common languages and pictographics, the walls themselves beaded with liquid as if they had sweated.

A planet whose surface was completely built over must have a big foundation. In places, the vast complex of tunnels and artificial caverns was a kilometer deep and continuing to go deeper. Here were locales where the sun's rays never came, where blue-gray mold sometimes grew ten centimeters thick on walls and ceiling, where the dank and fecund air stank permanently of fungal rot—and worse.

A black-hooded and robed figure moved out from the darkness under a shattered glowstick, a green four-fingered hand extended for alms.

Chewie said something, and the figure moved away. A wave of the unwashed creature's body odor joined the other smells.

Chewie wrinkled his nose.

The stench was worse than the garbage compactor in which she and Han and Chewie and Luke had found themselves at first meeting.

Fortunately for her, her bounty hunter's disguise filtered out the worst of the odors. Poor Chewie. She hoped where they were going had a good filtration system for its air, ozone generators or air fresheners, at least.

Ahead, a glowstick sputtered, painting the dim corridor with flashes of faltering light before it blinked out.

Somewhere in the corridor behind them, somebody —or some*thing*—screamed. The cry dwindled into a liquidy gargle at the end.

Leia kept her hand on her blaster.

·   ·   ·

"How long until we leave hyperspace?" Vader asked.

"A few hours, my lord," his captain said.

"I will be in my chambers. Send someone to tell me when we arrive at the system."

"Yes, my lord."

I will be there soon, my son.

This was almost too easy, Luke thought as he picked his lightsaber up from the table. The little storage room was empty; no one seemed to be awake or about, and there was his comlink right there on the table. He would call Artoo, have him warm up the X-wing and send Luke a homing signal. Once he got into his ship, these cloobs would never catch him again.

Luke put the blaster rifle on the table and reached for his comlink.

"Who's there? Move and I'll shoot!"

Uh-oh—

Deep in the Southern Underground the corridor opened up into a huge hemispherical chamber, as big as a city square, with a high roof, good lighting, and a circle of shops around the perimeter. Here the thick smells thinned. People and aliens moved about, protected by armed guards in some kind of uniform who were obviously here to maintain some semblance of order. It could have been a small-town shopping area almost anywhere on any civilized planet.

Around part of the circle where they stood were a bakery, a weapon shop, a shoe store, a clothing kiosk, an electronics market. Here a restaurant, there a cantina, and there, a plant store. Leia sighed, relieved. The place had changed since she'd been here, but their destination was still here.

"There," she said to Chewie.

The inside of the plant store smelled great, would have been delightful anywhere but more so given these surroundings. There were platters of gray stikmoss, potted stretchy plants, flowers of all kinds, colored from red to violet, and thick, billowy sheets of yellow fungus draped on the walls and ceiling. This latter produced oxygen without a need for sunlight and was thus particularly suited for underground habitat. The amount of oxy in the air here was so great it made Leia lightheaded to breathe it.

The ceiling was four meters high, necessary because the original owner of the plant shop had been an old Ho'Din named Spero. Ho'Din were usually at least three meters tall themselves, counting their vermis-like hair, which looked like nothing so much as a nest of snakes covered with bright red and violet scales.

Leia looked around and spotted the tall and spindly alien as he moved from behind a display of feather trees that brushed against the ceiling. Old Spero was still alive. Another stroke of good luck.

"Good meeting," Spero said. "How may I assist you?"

Leia spoke. "We're here to collect a debt, Master Gardener."

Since many Ho'Din were famous for their ecological work, especially that with plants, "Master Gardener" was considered a high honorific among them. Spero had earned his title by creating the strain of yellow fungus that hung on his walls and was used all over the galaxy.

"I cannot recall that I owe anyone a debt," the old Ho'Din said. "Certainly not strangers." He looked amused.

"Not even Leia Organa?"

Now he did smile. "Ah, yes. The princess. I owe her my life and those of my entire family."

"She would have you aid us."

"And how do I know you are from Princess Organa?"

"How else would we know of your debt?"

He nodded. "Reasonable. What would you have of me?"

"We need to know about Black Sun. Who runs it, how we might contact them."

Spero sighed. "I was about to make tea. Would you care for some?"

"Another time, perhaps."

"Well, then. Black Sun is led by the Falleen, Xizor. He is known variously as the 'Dark Prince,' or sometimes 'Underlord.' He is also the owner and president of XTS—Xizor Transportation Systems—a more or less legitimate concern worth billions in itself. He seldom leaves Coruscant, has a palace that ranks with those of the Emperor and Darth Vader." Spero pointed up at the ceiling. "On the surface, though portions of it extend deep into the ground."

Leia and Chewie looked at each other. This confirmed what Guri had told her. It was what she needed to know. Leia nodded and started to turn away. "Thank you, Master Gardener," she said.

"You are welcome, princess."

Leia turned back to stare up at the old alien. "Excuse me?"

"Ho'Din are not limited to their eyes and ears, princess." The thick fleshy "hair" on his head stirred and waved, flashing bright under the shop's lights. "We never forget our friends."

Leia bowed. "Then consider our debt balanced."

The Ho'Din bowed in return. "Nonsense. My grandchildren's grandchildren could never live long enough to repay you. But I am happy to have been of some small service. Move with care, princess. Black Sun is a formidable foe."

"I will. Thank you again, Master Spero."

Outside in the open area, Leia nodded at Chewie. "Well, it seems as if that much of Guri's story is true. Best we go and meet her."

Chewie growled, and she wasn't sure if he was agreeing or disagreeing with her.

24

Luke still held his lightsaber loosely in his right hand. He gripped the weapon tighter, thumb on the control as he slowly turned to face the owner of the voice behind him.

"Sorry, I thought this was the 'fresher," Luke said. Well. It was worth a try.

The alien facing him was a Nikto, and the comment must have puzzled him, at least for a second. Then his horn-rimmed eyes went wide as he recognized Luke. He thrust the blaster out one-handed.

Luke thumbed the lightsaber control. The glowing blade added its light to the dim room.

The Nikto fired, and a red bolt speared at Luke. He let the Force flow, and the bolt ricocheted from his blade, bounced back . . . and hit the shooter in the foot. The Nikto dropped his weapon, grabbed at his wounded extremity, and began hopping on his other foot, yelling.

"Ow, ow, ow, ow, *ow*!"

If it wasn't so dangerous it would have been funny. So much for sneaking out undetected.

Luke ran at the injured shooter, hit him with his shoulder in passing, and knocked him sprawling.

As the swoopers had been, the Nikto also was more adept at cursing than he was at shooting.

Doors began to open into the hallway, and armed bounty hunters, most of them dressed for sleep, emerged.

He was in for it now.

He swung the lightsaber and tried to cut a path to freedom.

Leia and Chewie worked their way to where they were to meet Guri. The place was a public park on the surface, a small dab of planted greenery surrounded by plasticrete and durasteel.

"It took you longer than expected," Guri said when she saw them.

"We stopped to see the sights," Leia said.

Guri glared at her, and Leia felt strongly that the woman—no, the droid—didn't like her.

"Follow me," Guri said.

A horizontal hail of energy bolts stabbed at Luke—

The Force let him move faster than he thought possible, and he wove a defensive tapestry with his lightsaber that turned the hard rain away. Ricocheting beams hit and pierced walls, bounty hunters, the floor, the ceiling. It was dangerous to be here, no matter where you stood.

Amazed as he was at his speed and skill, Luke knew it couldn't continue. He had to miss only one block and he would be a goner. Sooner or later, they'd get him.

He ran forward down the hall, and the shooters ahead of him gave way against their own reflected fire-power.

There was a lot of yelling going on with the blasting:

"—look out, you fool—!"

"—there he is, get him—!"

"—watch it, watch it—!"

"—I'm hit—!"

He didn't know how far he had to go to get to the exit. He had a good idea that if it wasn't pretty close, he wasn't going to make it.

But Luke went with the flow of the Force, continued to cut and block, to parry bolts and flesh and bones as the bounty hunters tried to stop him. There wasn't a lot of choice; he couldn't exactly stop to think about things.

Ahead and to his left, the wall suddenly shattered and imploded.

Smoking debris spattered in all directions. Some of the bounty hunters were blown down by the implosion; others fled. Smoke roiled and filled the corridor; acrid vapor burned Luke's nostrils.

The general chaos increased.

What—?

"Luke?"

He knew that voice.

"Lando? Over here!"

Yet another blaster joined the fray, only this one wasn't aimed at Luke. Bounty hunters fell.

"Regroup!" somebody yelled. "We're under attack!"

The confusion increased.

Luke saw Lando stride through the smoke and smelly vapor, saw him fire with offhand precision, nailing several of the confused bounty hunters.

"Like shooting snakes in a shoe box," Lando said. He grinned. "You called for a cab?"

"Me? What makes you think I want to leave? I'm

having fun here." Luke pivoted and chopped the barrel off an outthrust blaster. The weapon began to hiss and spew sparks, and the startled owner dropped it and fled.

"Yeah, right you are. This way."

Lando led the way, blaster working. Luke followed, blocking shots from behind.

They went through the ruptured wall and into the night.

It wouldn't take long for the bounty hunters to pull themselves together. They had better get far away before that happened.

"I've got a, uh, *borrowed* landspeeder parked over there," Lando said. He paused, fired at the building behind him. "What say we go for a ride?"

Somebody in the ruptured wall yelled in surprise and pain as Lando's blaster bolt found him.

"The *Falcon* is in the middle of a public park five minutes away. I left Threepio watching it."

"Threepio? Where are Leia and Chewie?"

"That's a long story. Better we get back to the ship before I tell it."

"How'd you know where to find me?"

"Dash gave me the planet. I got here and found out about the raid on the Bothan safe house. I know a few locals who owed me favors; they told me where these yabbos had set up shop."

Lando ducked. A blaster beam sizzled overhead, missed by a good two meters. "Can we go now and play Question the Quarren later?"

"Good idea."

They ran.

Behind them, the bounty hunters kept shooting.

Xizor observed with a critical eye the lower branches of his six-hundred-year-old miniature firethorn tree.

The small plant had been a gift from a former rival seeking to make peace with Black Sun after a . . . business disagreement. Less than half a meter high, the tiny tree was a nearly perfect replica of the hundred-meter-tall firethorn trees that grew only in a single small grove of the Irugian Rain Forest on Abbaji. The dwarf tree had been in the former rival's family for ten generations and was, to one who knew the value of such things, most precious. Were his fortunes to evaporate and leave him completely broke, Xizor would still not sell this plant, not if somebody offered him a decamillion credits.

There were those who would offer that much and more. Little trees such as this had connected to them a great deal of history.

He moved the tiny mechanical scissors in with great precision. Centered the almost hair-fine branch between the blades . . . cut . . .

Ah. Perfect. That single cut was all the trimming needed this year. Perhaps next season he would take off that obtuse-angled branchlet on the next ascending branch. He had a year to think about it. He pulled the scissors away carefully. Regarded the firethorn. Beautiful, it was. Beautiful enough to excuse the mistakes of its former owner. The man had made errors in judgment, but this gift showed he was also a man of some taste and intelligence. Errors could be forgiven if there were other mitigating reasons. Xizor was, after all, a civilized being, not a reflexive thug.

He would allow Princess Leia to find that out about him. Just as he would allow her to find out other, more intimate things about him . . .

"It's so good to see that you are all right, Master Luke."

"Good to see you, too, Threepio," Luke said.

Lando hurried past them for the *Falcon*'s cockpit.

"Move it, Luke," Lando called back. "Not only do we have the bounty hunters to worry about, there's an Imperial convoy heading this way. They've just dropped out of hyperspace and into the system."

Luke hurried. He reached the control seat and sat, strapped himself down.

"Yeah? Anybody we know?" He was already reaching for preflight switches.

"I didn't get close enough to read nameplates, but the lead ship is a Star Destroyer."

"*Victory*-class?"

"Bigger than that."

"*Imperial*-class?"

"Try again."

Luke looked away from the controls at Lando, eyes going wide. "No."

"Yep. *Super*-class."

"Is it . . . *Executor*?"

"Like I said, I didn't get that close. But how many of those are there? They don't crank those babies up just for fun."

Luke stared into infinity. Was it Darth Vader? What would he be doing here?

"Let's finish the flight check fast," Lando said. "I don't think we want to stick around here."

"I hear that. Wait. Artoo is in my X-wing."

"I know, I spotted it. I've got a tractor beam with his name on it. I'll overfly the X-wing and pull it up; we'll stow it in the hull clips." Lando pointed at the control screen. "We're going to slingshot out of here and hit lightspeed fast. Even if it isn't Vader on that monster, we don't want to tangle with it."

Luke nodded and reached for the comm. "Where are we going?"

"Back to Tatooine. That's where Leia wants us to go."

"Where is she?"

"Let's talk about that later, okay?" Lando touched controls, listened as the ship's engines came online.

"Better sit down back there, Goldie," Lando yelled. "We are about to be gone!"

25

A hundred stormtroopers surrounded the building, blasters ready to cook anybody who twitched.

Darth Vader stood in the darkness staring at the breach that had been blown in the building's wall. Night insects hummed, and the air smelled of burned insulation. He didn't need to go inside to know that Luke was not there; if the boy was anywhere within fifty kilometers he would certainly have felt him.

These bounty hunters had captured him—then they had *lost* him.

Vader was not pleased.

The commander of the stormtroopers stood nervously nearby, waiting for a command. Vader gave him such: "Bring me the highest-ranking survivor."

"At once, my lord." The commander waved, and a squad moved into the building. Shots were exchanged. Time passed.

Two troopers emerged, dragging a man between

them. They brought him to where Vader stood and released him. The prisoner tottered but stayed on his feet.

"Do you know who I am?"

"Y-Y-Yes, Lord Vader."

"Good. Where is Skywalker?"

"H-H-He escaped."

Vader clenched his fist, and the man clawed at his throat. "I *know* he escaped, fool."

The man choked; his eyes grew wider. Vader waited for a few seconds, then opened his hand.

The man gasped, sucked in air. "I was a-a-asleep, my lord. I awoke to blaster fire. I left my quarters and saw Skywalker in the hall. It—it didn't seem real. A dozen of us shot at him and he waved that lightsaber back and forth and *blocked* the bolts!"

Despite his anger, Vader was pleased. The boy's skill and power were increasing. "Continue."

"More of our men arrived. We were sure to overcome him, but then the wall blew in. We were attacked. I couldn't tell how many there were, fifteen, maybe twenty. We were outnumbered. When the fighting was over, Skywalker was gone."

Vader glanced up into space. And offplanet, too, he would wager. He would take his shuttle back to the *Executor;* perhaps it was not too late to catch him.

He glanced back at the bounty hunter. "I understand that someone else wanted Skywalker. Who?"

"I—I don't know, Lord Vader—"

Vader raised his hand again, started to curl his fingers into a fist.

"Wait! Please! I don't *know,* we—we dealt with agents."

He looked at the bounty hunter. Felt something more there.

"You have a suspicion," Vader said. Not a question.

"I—some of us heard rumors. I don't know if they are true."

"Tell me."

"We—we heard that it was . . . Black Sun."

Vader stared at the man. Of course.

"And this other . . . bidder wanted Skywalker alive and well?"

"N-N-No, my lord. They wanted him dead."

Abruptly he turned away, the prisoner forgotten. Of course. He had unconsciously suspected it all along. Now that it was out, it made perfect sense. Xizor wanted to thwart Vader in any manner he could. What better way than to kill his son, and by the same act embarrass him in front of the Emperor?

"Back to the shuttle," he said to the commander.

"What about this scum?" He waved at the building and the prisoner.

"Leave them. They are worthless." Vader was already walking away.

The *Falcon* hung in high orbit, about to slingshot away. Artoo was safely on board, and Luke's X-wing was clamped in place. Luke didn't trust the haphazard rig that slung the fighter on the larger vessel, but it kept it out of the way of the guns, and it should hold. He hoped.

"Artoo! I didn't think I would ever see you again!" Threepio said.

Artoo whistled at Threepio.

"Yes, we have had our share of adventures, as well. I must say I don't like all this business the least bit. Couldn't we find a nice quiet planet and take a vacation? Someplace warm, with a deep pool of lube?"

Luke grinned. Artoo and Threepio were always amusing.

Lando broke from orbit and headed out into interplanetary space.

"How long before we can make the jump to hyperspace, Master Lando?"

"Couple of minutes," he replied. "And how's this

for a change of luck—there aren't even any Imperial vessels on our tail. About time something went our way."

Luke nodded. While waiting for Lando to bring the hyperdrive online, he said, "How's Dash doing? He was pretty upset after we hit that freighter."

"Not so good. Pretty depressed. He can't believe he actually failed at something. Had to happen sooner or later, but he isn't used to it."

"Stuff like that goes on in war," Luke said. "You get disappointed." Like he had been with Dash. Too bad.

"Yeah. What was in the computer that was so important, anyway?"

Luke shrugged. "I don't know. The Bothans had just broken it open when the bounty hunters hit the safe house."

"Did the bounty hunters get the computer?"

"I don't think so. I don't think they even knew it was there. They were after me. Last I saw, one of the Bothan techs had the computer. I believe he escaped with it."

"If he did, the Bothans will get it to the Alliance," Lando said. "They're pretty dependable. I guess we'll find out what it was eventually."

"Yeah."

"Stand by for the jump to hyperspace."

Lando hit the control.

Nothing happened.

Luke turned to stare at him.

"Oh, dear," Threepio said. "There seems to be a problem."

"It must be one of Han's modifications!" Lando said. "My people supposedly fixed this thing on Bespin! It's not my fault!"

"Fine. What do we do now?"

"Find a place to hide and fix it before we bump into the Imperial Navy."

"That sounds like an excellent idea," Threepio said. Artoo whistled his agreement.

Guri led Leia and Chewie back into the Underground. They walked for hours, turning and twisting into narrower and narrower corridors. Eventually they came to a heavy, locked gate that Guri opened. She locked the gate behind them, and they moved into what looked like a small repulsor train station.

A man waited there. He was short, squat, and bald, built like a freight handler from some heavy gee world. He wore gray coveralls and had a blaster strapped on his left hip. He smiled, revealing teeth he'd had done in what looked to be black chrome.

Guri said, "Go with him."

"Where are you going?"

"Not your business. Just do as you are told and you will see Prince Xizor soon enough."

She turned and walked away without another word.

The bald man came over to stand in front of Leia. "This way," he said.

Baldy led the way to a small motorized cart parked outside. There was barely enough room in it for the three of them. Fortunately, there was a convertible roof on the thing, so with the top down, Chewie could sit up without bumping his head. They drove into a tunnel halfway around the circle of shops. Baldy touched a control on the cart, and a heavy metal grate covering the mouth of the corridor slid into the ceiling. Inside, the tunnel was clean, well lighted, no mold or graffiti on the walls, the floor free of dirt.

They drove for a long time; they probably covered ten or twelve kilometers. Finally the tunnel opened out into a large chamber, in the middle of which sat a bullet car floating on magnetic repulsors over a single rail track.

Wherever they were going, it must be a way off;

maglev cars could cover long distances in a hurry, three, four hundred kilometers an hour, especially in a complete tunnel such as this one was. It didn't pay to get them up to speed for anything less than a fairly long run.

Chewie and Leia followed Baldy into the car.

When they were seated and strapped in, Baldy said, "Go."

The bullet car moved smoothly away from the chamber and into a dark tunnel. It picked up velocity fast. A row of small yellow service lamps ringed the tunnel every few hundred meters, and it wasn't long before the yellow circle seemed to be flashing over them continuously.

Wherever they were going, they were going to get there pretty soon, even if it was halfway around the planet.

Leia looked at Chewie and wished she could read his expressions better. He looked calm. Calmer than she felt.

She hoped she was doing the right thing, though it was a little late to worry about that now, wasn't it?

"What's the problem?" Luke said.

From the service well below him, Lando's reply was more than a bit irritated: "The *problem* is that Han and Chewie have completely reset, rewired, and screwed up this whole ship! I'm looking at a serpent's nest of *wires* where there is supposed to be a pop-out circuit board! The schematics don't apply to *any*thing here!"

"Well, can you fix it?"

"I'm *trying* to fix it! Pass me that jumper bypass."

Luke picked up the JB, which looked like a bar with two sharp fingers making the V sign on one end. He had to lie on his belly to reach Lando.

Lando submitted, in a colorful fashion, that Han's

ancestry was in question and that his personal habits left much to be desired.

Despite the danger of their situation, Luke grinned.

"Get Artoo to peek over the edge; maybe he knows what this blue wire is supposed to do."

Artoo heard. He rolled to the lip of the service well, "leaned" forward, and peered down into it. Whistled and chirred for a moment.

"Yeeowch!" Lando yelled.

"Probably you'd better not touch that one."

"Now you tell me. What about this yellow one?"

Artoo whistled.

It looked as if they were going to be there a while, Luke figured.

They had managed to find the remains of a small moon or maybe a large asteroid in a big parabolic orbit around the planet and had nestled the *Falcon* in among the larger rocks and matched their velocity. From a distance, with most of its power shut down, the ship should be just another one of the cluster of big boulders. Not enough gravity here to clump them back together; they'd be a known hazard for ships and probably avoided. Even a *Super*-class Star Destroyer didn't want a bunch of building-size rocks smacking into its shields at speed; that would be a lot of kinetic energy to have to bleed off all at once.

At least that was what Luke and Lando hoped.

"Pass me those needle-head pliers," Lando said.

Luke complied. "You need me down there to help? I'm pretty good with tools."

"I used to own this ship," Lando said. "I'll figure out a way around what Han has done to her. The man ought to be ashamed of himself."

"I'll mention that to him when we get him out of the carbonite," Luke said.

"So will I. High, loud, and repeatedly."

•   •   •

The bullet car slowed. The bands of yellow blinked around them at longer intervals. When the car came to a stop, it was inside a vast chamber, as big as a state ballroom. The platform at which it stopped had six large guards on it, each dressed in gray armor and armed with a blast rifle. Baldy stepped out and grinned his shiny black smile. "This way," he said.

Two of the guards broke away from the others and moved behind Chewie and Leia. "Take the helmet off," Baldy said. "You won't be needing it anymore."

Baldy led them to a door as thick as that of a bank vault. He pressed his hand against a reader, and the door clicked and swung open. He led them inside a tall, arched corridor wide enough for a dozen men to walk through side by side. The massive door swung shut behind them. It was very cold here, cold enough for their breathing to show as vapor.

A short distance ahead was another door, another six guards in armor in front of it. Not as heavy as the door behind them, it was still thick enough and run by a print-reader, and when they'd gotten through it, there were yet more guards.

It seemed as if whoever ran this place didn't want unexpected company.

They came to a bank of four turbolifts. Baldy punched a code into a keypad, and the door to the lift on the left opened. The three of them stepped in, leaving the two guards behind.

As the lift rose, Leia said, "Learned to trust us already?" She nodded at the guards they'd dropped off.

Baldy smiled. The lift stopped, and another pair of guards stood there.

Well. Perhaps Baldy hadn't learned to trust them after all.

A series of corridors branched away from the turbolifts, and Baldy led them down one that linked to a maze of other hallways. Leia tried to keep track of all the twists and turns—she had a pretty good memory for such things—but halfway through an intricate chain of left and right tacks, the lights went out. "Just keep walking," Baldy said. "I'll tell you when to turn."

They walked in darkness for five minutes, Baldy calling out now and then. "Turn left." "Turn right." "Veer forty-five to the left for five steps, then veer right."

When the lights went back on—how could he have seen to lead them?—Leia was thoroughly lost.

Whatever fat spider crouched in the center of this web, he truly did not want anybody just dropping by unannounced.

Eventually Baldy led them into a hallway. At the end of the hall were two tall, carved wooden doors and, standing to the sides, two more guards. These didn't wear armor, had no rifles but wore blasters on low-slung belts. They were big men who looked as if they knew how to use their hands. One of them reached for the doorknobs and opened the doors as they approached.

Baldy said, "In there." With that, he turned and walked away.

Leia looked at Chewie. Realized her pulse was racing and her stomach was fluttery. She took a deep breath and let part of it out.

She stepped into the room, Chewie behind her.

A tall man—no, not a man but an exotic-looking alien—rose from behind a large desk and smiled at her. "Ah," he said, "Princess Leia Organa and Chewbacca. Welcome. I am Xizor."

It was the voice she'd heard over the hotel's comm.

Leia's pulse speeded up yet more. She felt a sudden giddiness, as if her brain had fogged over. So here she was at last, facing the person in charge of the galaxy's largest criminal organization. That was strange enough all by itself, but to make it even more so, he was absolutely . . . *gorgeous*!

26

"How is it going down there?" Luke said.

"Don't ask," Lando said.

"I'm going to see what I can whip up in the galley, you want something?"

"Yeah, how about a beaker full of battery acid and bug poison."

Luke shook his head, stood, and headed for the galley.

Stopped suddenly as if he'd been touched by a cold hand.

"Master Luke? Are you all right?"

Luke ignored Threepio. There was a disturbance in the Force, a dark blot on its perfection. It felt familiar somehow . . .

Uh-oh.

Luke turned and hurried back to the service well. "You'd better get it fixed fast, Lando."

"What's the hurry?"

"I think we're about to have company."

Lando poked his head up over the edge of the well. "What? No way anybody could find us in here."

"Yeah? Want to bet?"

"Oh, man. Don't even say what you're thinking," Lando said.

"Huh?"

"Don't say, 'I've got a bad feeling about this.'"

Luke stared at him.

Lando disappeared back into the service well. "I'm hurrying, I'm hurrying!"

Luke headed for the cockpit to check the sensors. If it was who he thought it was, hiding in a clump of rocks wasn't going to do much good. You could run, but from some things, you couldn't hide.

Xizor was pleased. The young woman sitting across from him, backed by her furry bodyguard, was every bit as delightful as he had hoped, even more so. Thus far, they had spoken of trivial things, in generalities. He pretended to be honored that she was a high Alliance official come to call; she pretended that she wasn't disgusted that he was a criminal. And, in fact, it didn't really matter *what* she felt, now that she was here in his grasp.

No, the thing now was how best to proceed with his courtship, if he could think in such terms.

Already he had allowed some of his potent pheromones to seep into the air. He'd fought hard to keep his skin color from altering too much, but there was a definite warm glow to it. The Wookiee didn't seem to notice, but Leia had responded to the chemical attractants he exuded. She felt drawn to him; he knew this from long experience with women. He was not unattractive to look at, and with the added lure of his enhanced hormones, it would take a very strong and very determined humanoid female to resist him.

As a young man, he had felt the pull that Leia was

now feeling. Falleen women had their version, and it was hard to ignore when one of them . . . blossomed for you. Like a hothouse flower sending its fragrance into the air, Falleen pheromones swirled and wrapped anyone close enough into their urgent embrace. As strong as a durasteel vise . . .

If Leia had any sensuality whatsoever, she could only pretend that she wasn't attracted to him—as she now tried to do. He had to give her credit; she was not volunteering how she felt. But the flush of her cheeks, her slightly faster breathing, her . . . yearning, all were obvious to one who had seen them a thousand times before. To one who knew how to spot the signs and use them to his best advantage, as did Xizor. And use them he would.

"You must be tired from your trip," Xizor said. "You should refresh yourself, change clothes, relax a bit before we delve into serious matters."

"I didn't exactly bring my wardrobe with me."

Xizor waved a hand and affected a man-of-the-galaxy smile. "Such things are easily remedied. I'll have Howzmin show you to your quarters. We have had other visitors from time to time, and a gracious host looks after his company's needs. Perhaps there are a few articles of clothing you might find acceptable in your room. I have pressing business to which I must attend. Refresh yourself and rejoin me in a couple of hours."

Leia glanced at her bodyguard, then back at him.

Xizor favored her with his sexiest smile.

She looked flustered. "Yes. All right. We are a little tired."

Xizor waved his foot unseen under his desk, and a sensor there transmitted the motion to a paging device implanted in Howzmin. The door opened, and the bald servant stepped into the room.

"Show Princess Leia and Chewbacca to their rooms."

"At once, Prince Xizor."

After they were gone, Xizor sat, breathing slowly and deeply, enjoying the feel of imminent victory. Before their next meeting, he would do the meditation and exercises that brought his hormonal essences into full array. An excited Falleen who loosed his full pheromonal arsenal was, for all practical purposes, irresistible to a member of the opposite sex. It did not matter what a woman's stance was on fidelity, that she had been a faithful partner to another for years or decades. Falleen pheromones were more potent than the strongest spice. Leia might want to resist him with her mind, but her body would ache for him. There was no antidote save one.

Xizor smiled. He would enjoy administering the single antidote to Leia. He would enjoy it very much indeed . . .

Leia was shaken. As Howzmin led her and Chewie down another convoluted hallway, she had to take several deep breaths to calm herself. What had *that* been all about? That—That emotional *attraction* that rolled over her like a tropical ocean breaker? Sure, Xizor was good-looking in an exotic kind of way, but she'd never before been one to stare dumbstruck at a handsome face. What she had felt, what she had wanted to do, well, that wasn't like her at all. Besides, she was in love with Han. That wasn't something you just put into a drawer when you saw an attractive man—Falleen. That wasn't right.

Then again, she couldn't deny she'd felt it. The alien called to her somehow. It had been like a punch to the solar plexus; it had knocked the wind out of her.

Well. No matter. She blew out a sigh. She was back to normal; she would stay on target. She'd come here to help Luke. When that was done, they were going to rescue Han. She would put whatever it was she had felt for the mysterious Xizor out of her mind and never think about it again.

The part of her that sat somewhere in her mind watching and listening and refusing to allow anything but the truth to pass it seemed to chuckle: *Oh, really? You might not* do *anything about what you felt for him, sister, but you won't be able to* forget *it that easily.*

Shut up, she mentally told the little voice. *I don't need this.*

Maybe not, sister, but you have it.

"This is your room," Howzmin said. "The Wookiee will be in the next suite."

Leia shook herself from the interior dialogue and nodded at Howzmin.

Chewie said something that sounded like a question.

Leia said, "I'll be okay in here. If Xizor wanted to harm us, he could have done it before now. Go on. Wash that dye out, we don't need it anymore. Meet me back here when you're done."

Chewie nodded and followed Howzmin to the next door.

The portal in front of Leia slid back as she approached, and she stepped into the room.

It was a study in understated elegance, she saw.

The carpet was so deep she sank nearly to her ankles in it. Black neocel, she guessed, and probably a murderous job to keep clean. There was a white leather couch, probably cloned, which sat in stark contrast to the carpet, a round bed with black sheets and a comforter under a translucent white canopy held up by six carved posts. A white desk with a computer on it and a black chair tucked neatly under the desk occupied a niche next to the bed.

Simple, elegant, and probably as expensive as any Grand Moff hotel suite in the galaxy.

Leia submitted to an urge to remove her boots and walk barefoot across the rug. The material was either naturally warm or was kept heated somehow, and it felt wonderful between her toes.

There was a refresher on the other side of a closed door, also done in black and white, tile, sinks, tub, all of them sculpted into smooth and rounded shapes.

She found a closet door back in the main room and opened it.

There were clothes in the closet, all right. Unlike the rooms, they were all the colors of the rainbow: dresses, shirts, pants, jackets, jumpsuits. Leia removed a hanger upon which was draped a diaphanous dress of nearly transparent green material so light it weighed almost nothing and looked at it. Touched it. She was not somebody who spent large amounts of money on clothing, but she knew quality when she saw it, even without the tag that confirmed it. This dress was a Melanani original, made of Loveti moth fiber, and for what it cost, you could buy a new landspeeder.

A quick scan of the other clothes revealed that they were also first-class originals. Looked after his company's needs, indeed. There were probably enough credits represented by this one closet to buy and furnish houses on many planets, with enough left over to hire cooks and gardeners to go with them.

Leia started to close the closet, then stopped. She reached back inside and examined the label on the first dress she'd seen.

My. Look at that. It was just her size.

A sudden thought occurred to her, and she began checking the other labels.

They were *all* her size.

She blinked and stared into the closet. Could it be coincidence? The leader of Black Sun just happened to have a closet full of clothes in her size?

She didn't think so. Maybe Howzmin out there had gotten her measurements via sensor somewhere along the way and had done the fastest shopping trip in history. Xizor had credits to burn. Maybe there were a dozen rooms all stocked this way, each for a different-size visitor? Not likely, but possible.

Xizor had known she was coming, after all; perhaps he was just being a considerate host.

She shook her head. She was tired. Maybe she would bathe and stretch out for a few minutes. As for the expensive clothes? Well, he had gone to some trouble no matter what the explanation. If he found such things attractive, perhaps she should slip into one of the outfits and use that to her advantage. Keep him off balance. If he was busy ogling her, maybe he would be more likely to give away something she needed.

And her little voice said, *Really, sister, who do you think you're fooling here? You want to look good for him, admit it.*

Yes, all right, so what? She wasn't married. There wasn't any law against flirting a little, was there? She wasn't going to do anything with the head of a criminal underground, now, was she? What could it hurt to dress up a little? She hadn't gotten to do much of that since she'd thrown her lot in with the Alliance—not that she missed it much—but given the situation, who would be hurt by it?

Careful, sister. These are dangerous waters. Better watch out for sea serpents.

Oh, spare me. I'm a big girl. I can take care of myself.

She went to run hot water into the bathtub.

"I think that's got it," Lando said as he clambered out of the service well.

"You *think*?"

"Won't know for sure until we engage the drive."

"Master Lando, Master Lando!"

Threepio came careening in, waving his arms and throwing gold highlights every which way.

"What?"

"The sensors indicate that a ship is approaching! A very large vessel! An enormous ship!"

Lando looked at Luke. "I wonder who that could be."

"I hope you fixed the drive," Luke said. "Otherwise I think we're going to find out."

The two of them hurried past the droid for the cockpit.

On the way, Luke felt that cold touch reach him through the Force. He knew who it was. The only question was, could Darth Vader feel him as well?

"Lord Vader?"

Vader stared through the viewer at the rock field ahead of them. He didn't bother to look at his captain. "What is it?"

"We are approaching the asteroid field."

Now Vader turned to stare at the captain. "Do you mean that asteroid field directly in front of us?" He pointed at the viewer.

Flustered, the captain plowed on. "Yes, Lord. Our sensors cannot detect any sign of a ship in the region."

"Nonetheless, there is something in the field," Vader said. "I cannot pinpoint it, but there is a locus for the Force in those rocks and I mean to find it."

"Certainly, Lord Vader. Ah, might I suggest that we send out fighters? Entering the asteroid field at right angles will place a great deal of strain on the ship's shields."

"Very well. Tell them to look for anything unusual, anything at all. If they find something, they are not to engage it but to report back immediately."

"Yes, my lord. I'll send them out at once."

Vader turned back to the viewer. Was it Luke? He couldn't yet be sure. The dark side might not have limits, but *he* had, and all he could tell at this distance was that some powerful locus for the Force lay in that col-

lection of shattered rocks ahead of them. He didn't believe it could be anything else *but* Luke, but he was not
certain. He had to proceed with caution. With Xizor's
manipulations poisoning the well at Imperial Center, it
was more important than ever to capture Luke alive. A
little closer and the vagueness would undoubtedly resolve itself. He was too close to lose his son again.
Sooner or later, he would find him and turn him to the
dark side. He was sure of it. He was Darth Vader; he
had exterminated the remaining Jedi with his own
hands. All but the strongest of them, his own son.

Sooner or later he would face the last would-be Jedi.
One way or another, he would deal with him, too.

Leia used the blowers to dry off after her bath,
combed her hair out, and had to admit she felt a whole
lot better than she had in a while. It wasn't often these
days she got to soak in a hot tub. Most of the places
she'd been, the ships she'd traveled there on, you were
lucky if they had enough recycled graywater for a tepid
shower. You got in, sprayed just enough water on
yourself to get wet, lathered all over, and rinsed off
with a few liters before the automatic timer shut it off.
It was better than nothing but not nearly as much fun
as stretching out in a vat carved out of black marble
full of steaming water so hot it turned your skin red.
That had to be one of civilization's best luxuries.

She went to the closet, opened it. Noticed a small
drawer built into the wall and saw that it contained
undergarments. Well. Xizor thought of everything.

All right. Which of these dresses should she wear?

Xizor stared at the blank spot where the holoproj
would be if he lit it. There were hidden holocams
throughout the castle, of course, in virtually every
room.

Including the room in which Leia had been installed.

He toyed with the thought of running the recording, to see if she'd taken advantage of what the room had to offer.

But—no. He didn't want to spoil it. He would get a closer look at her later.

Much closer.

27

The *Millennium Falcon* left the asteroid field opposite the approaching megaship and was ready to make the jump to hyperspace.

Luke looked at his sensors. "We have TIE fighters coming in. I make it about three dozen of them. Any time, Lando."

"Here goes," Lando said. "If you believe in luck, wish for the good version."

He reached for the control. Engaged the drive—

Nothing happened.

Lando swore at the ship, a string of colorful phrases, including several graphic—if highly unlikely—descriptions of things he wished it would do to itself.

"I'd better get back to the guns," Luke said. He started to rise.

"No, wait—"

"We don't have *time* to wait; in ten seconds we are going to be swarmed with TIEs—"

Lando touched another control, made an adjustment.

"Now!"

The *Millennium Falcon* leaped. Space blurred around it in the familiar shift as the freighter transited to hyperspace.

"Ha-hah!" Lando said.

Luke, halfway out of his seat, was thrown back into it hard. When he recovered himself, he glared at Lando. "You cut that awful close."

Lando shrugged. "Hey, you wanted a boring life, you should have stayed on Tatooine." He smiled, pleased with himself. "I knew I could fix it."

Luke shook his head but had to smile in return. They were, for the moment at least, safe. What did it matter what had *almost* happened? Almost didn't count.

"Now, if some other special Solo modification doesn't put us into the middle of a star, our next stop should be Tatooine. As soon as Leia and Chewie are finished with their business, we can get back to rescuing Han."

"Fine by me," Luke said. "Haven't they finished yet?"

Lando shrugged. "They had to take a slight detour."

Luke got the feeling Lando wasn't telling him everything, but he let it slide. He was tired. He needed to rest, get something to eat; then he could follow up on this conversation.

Vader stared out into space as the captain nervously approached.

"M-My lord Vader," he began.

Vader repressed a sigh. "There is no need to say it, Captain. Your pilots lost their prey."

"The ship left the asteroid field and made the shift

into hyperspace as they approached. There was nothing they could do."

"And did your pilots identify the ship?"

"It was a small Corellian freighter."

Vader said nothing. Solo's ship, the *Millennium Falcon,* no doubt, now under Luke's control. Perhaps he had the young princess with him and that traitorous gambler Calrissian.

"Set your course for Imperial Center, Captain."

"But weren't we supposed to—"

"Let *me* worry about that." He paused.

The captain was correct. The Emperor had sent him here for reasons other than to fetch Luke. "Very well. There is a suspected Rebel base on one of the Kothlisian moons."

"I know of no such base, my lord—"

Vader turned his gaze upon the captain, who quickly shut up.

"As I said, there is a suspected Rebel base on the moon. Before we leave, you will allow your men to display their prowess by pinpoint-bombing that base."

"Yes, my lord."

Luke was gone, he couldn't tell where, and Xizor still up to his twisted trickery within sight of the Emperor. He would locate his son later; meanwhile, best he get back to where he could deal with Xizor. There was an old Sithian proverb that said, "Even when fighting the great sabercat, it is best not to turn your back upon the lowly serpent." A bite from a tiny spit adder could kill you just as dead as the arm-long fangs of a giant predator. And the snake's kiss would be slower and more painful, too.

"Hurry, Captain. I do not wish to be kept waiting."

"No, my lord."

Leia put on a dark bodysuit before she slipped into the nearly transparent green dress. It was probably not the designer's intent that her choice of undergarments cancel out the see-through cloth, but she wasn't interested in letting Xizor look at *that* much of her.

It felt vaguely decadent to be wearing several thousand credits' worth of clothes. She hadn't done that since she'd been a girl on Alderaan.

She went into the 'fresher and looked into the mirror. She had made use of a well-stocked makeup drawer next to the looking glass, just a touch, and managed to plait her hair and pin it up so it didn't resemble the nest of a crazed ship rat. At least it was clean. She tried a smile.

Chewie should be here by now.

She went to the room's door. Frowned when it didn't open automatically. She found the manual control, but when she tried it, the door still refused to slide aside.

Ah. It seemed that Lord Xizor didn't want guests running around loose in his castle.

But as she turned around, the door slid open. Chewie stood there, sans his dye disguise. The haircut still looked odd, but with the coloring gone the Wookiee looked more familiar.

Howzmin stood behind him.

She wanted to tell Chewie that she needed to see Xizor alone. "Give us a moment, would you?" Leia said to Howzmin.

The servant nodded, a choppy military gesture.

Chewie stepped into the room. The door closed.

He stared at Leia. Turned his head to one side quizzically.

"What are you staring at? I put on some clean clothes, that's all."

Chewie said nothing.

Leia felt a sudden stab of guilt. Chewie and Han were like brothers. She hadn't done anything wrong, but she felt as if she had, so she tried to explain it:

"Look, we need Xizor's help. There's no reason I can't look nice; maybe it'll throw him off guard."

Still silent, Chewie raised one eyebrow.

Leia felt herself flush. "Who is the diplomat here, anyway? I don't tell you how to fly, you don't tell me how to conduct interviews."

Finally the Wookiee said something. He punctuated it with a wave of one hand at the door, then at Leia. She didn't understand the comment, but she had a pretty good idea of what he was trying to convey: Chewie didn't approve. Would Han?

In a Gamorrean's eye he would.

"It's none of your business how I dress!" she said. Maybe that came out a little more snappish than it should have. She started to apologize but then changed her mind. She and Han weren't married; they hadn't had time to even *pledge* anything. Yes, she loved him and she thought he loved her, but he'd never *said* it. When he had the chance, he'd said, "I know." What kind of commitment was that? "I know"? Two words instead of three? How much harder was it to say one more short little word?

There was nothing wrong with trying to look nice for a handsome man, especially one who could help save Luke's life. It wasn't as if they were going to *do* anything! What was Chewie doing being so righteous? She had nothing to feel ashamed about. Nothing at all!

Then why do *you feel so guilty, sister?*

In his most private of chambers, Xizor sat alone on a pad in the otherwise bare room, eyes closed, fingers interlaced in his lap. His breathing was deep and regular, his mind clear. He began to concentrate as he called upon his special hormonal abilities.

The attractants in him built, began to seep from his pores. His pheromones came forth, colorless, odorless, save to receptors carried by humanoid females. To the bearer of those small organelles hidden and nearly invisible inside the olfactory channels, the attractants would be overwhelming; they would carry a compulsion stronger than a hypnotic command.

There was no way to stop the color of his skin from shading into the red. No matter. She wouldn't care what color he was, once she felt him call to her.

He had given her but a taste of them before. Now he would set before her a banquet. One she could not refuse.

He took a deep breath, let it out. Almost ready. The coldness was there, but soon, soon—soon the passion would be set free.

He smiled.

Artoo and Threepio held a quiet conversation in the lounge. Luke, on his way to the galley to fix the meal he'd never gotten to, paused and looked at the droids.

"Something up?"

Threepio said, "Artoo is a bit worried about Princess Leia. I told him that she is quite resourceful," Threepio said. "I'm sure she's all right."

Luke shrugged. He went into the galley. In that moment, he had the feeling that Leia, wherever she was, was in great danger.

His hunger vanished. He didn't feel like eating anymore. Maybe he'd better go and have that talk with Lando. Now.

In the cockpit, Lando said, "Sorry, buddy, but I'm not supposed to tell you."

"What?"

"The princess wants you on Tatooine, and she said when you asked, to tell you she took care of herself before she met you and she can take care of herself now."

Luke glowered.

"Besides, she's got Chewie with her. He won't let anything happen to her, you know that."

"Yeah, maybe."

"Look, she'll probably get to Tatooine before we do. And she's in charge, remember?"

Luke nodded. But he didn't like it. Something felt wrong.

When the door to Xizor's sanctum opened, Leia almost gasped. The crime lord now wore a long, flowing robe done in shades of red that seemed to reflect that color onto his uncovered skin. The clothing could have been made by the same designer who had done her dress. And he wasn't wearing a bodysuit under it. He was big under the thin cloth, hard and muscular, and if there were any visible anatomical differences between him and basic stock humans, she couldn't see them.

He smiled. "Do come in, Princess."

Behind her, Chewie said something. Xizor must have understood it because his smile dropped for an instant before he recovered it. "Perhaps your friend would care to take this time to dine while we conduct our negotiations?"

From Chewie's tone, he would not care for that at all.

Leia had forgotten to tell him that in her room, so defensive had she been about her clothes. Now she said, "Chewie, wait outside."

He *really* didn't like that.

She turned to face the Wookiee. "Han would trust me here. You should, too."

Chewie wasn't sure, but he shut up. Took a step backward and nearly knocked Howzmin over.

"I'll be fine."

The door slid closed between them.

When she turned back around, Xizor had moved to

a small bar behind the leather couch. "Something to drink? Luranian brandy? Green champagne?"

"Tea would be fine, Your Highness." No way she was going to drink anything potent around him.

"Call me Xizor, please. We can dispense with titles, now that we are alone."

Leia watched as Xizor poured her tea. He seemed almost to . . . glow, and she felt dizzy watching him. She moved to the couch, sat on one end. Tried to relax but felt a strange tension grip her.

When he rounded the couch to bring her the tea, his hip brushed against the back of her head.

It sent a shock through her, a rush that was kin to dropping in free fall, a stomach-full-of-moths kind of sensation. Whoa!

Xizor handed her the teacup and moved to the other end of the couch and sat.

Leia felt a brief pang of disappointment that he hadn't sat closer to her.

And a sudden stab of worry at that thought. What was she doing?

She tried to bring an image of Han to mind. But all of a moment, she couldn't see his face. It was as if she had somehow forgotten what he looked like . . .

Stop this!

Xizor said, "So, the Alliance might be interested in doing business with Black Sun?" He sipped at whatever it was he was drinking.

Leia thought he looked absolutely fascinating as he drank.

She scrambled to collect her thoughts. "Uh, yes, we, that is to say, the Alliance, we have been considering such an alliance."

Alliance considering an alliance? What is the matter with you, Leia? Have you lost your wits?

Xizor seemed to take no notice of her poor choice of language.

"Well, certainly there are advantages to such a . . . liaison," he said.

Leia felt hot all of a sudden. She wished she hadn't worn the bodysuit. She had an urge to excuse herself, find a 'fresher, and take the undergarment off. The cloth of the dress would feel so good against her bare skin.

And what would Xizor's hand feel like against her bare skin—?

She shook her head, trying to clear it. This was crazy! She didn't even *know* him! But he was so, so— so *something*.

"I—we—the Alliance, we feel that while Black Sun's aims are not the same as ours, the Empire is our mutual enemy."

"Yes, war does make strange bedfellows, doesn't it?" He smiled.

Bedfellows . . .

"Here, let me warm your tea," he said.

"No, it's fine . . ."

But he was already up. He bent, lifted her hand with one of his, took the cup from her.

His touch was electric; it sent a charge through her as if she had grabbed a live capacitor node. She gasped.

Again, he seemed to take no notice of what she said.

Time seemed mired in thick mud. Xizor moved away so slowly; sounds seemed muted; Leia felt the heat in her growing. Something was wrong here. She felt, well, she felt too good. As if being here were the best thing in the universe. Well. Almost the best thing. Xizor needed to forget about that tea and come back; then the best thing would start . . .

Leia! What is the matter with you?

Trouble, sister. Big trouble. You'd better leave. Fast.

But leaving was the last thing she felt like doing.

·   ·   ·

In hyperspace, Vader considered his next move. He had arrived too late to collect Luke, but he had waved the Imperial flag and blown up a small spaceport. Whether or not the port had anything to do with the Rebels didn't matter, only that they thought *he* thought it did, and thus reasoned that the computer they had stolen was important to the Empire.

Half his mission had been accomplished, though to his mind it was the lesser half.

He had no evidence against Xizor, only speculation and rumor. Thirdhand knowledge from a soon-to-be-executed bounty hunter would hardly be enough to indict one of the most powerful beings in the galaxy. He was convinced, but the Emperor would not be so easily swayed. He needed more before he could move against the Dark Prince.

Well. If there was more to be had, he would have it. Now that he knew what he was looking for.

Xizor leaned over and kissed Leia. Lightly at first, a mere touch of his lips on hers.

Delicious. Amazing. She drank him in, enraptured by his touch.

He pressed harder.

Leia found herself responding to the kiss. Returning it . . .

She broke away. "No. This isn't right," she said. But she kept one hand on his shoulder. It was hard, powerful, that shoulder, warm under her fingers. No. This was wrong.

"I came . . . to talk about . . . Luke Skywalker!"

"In due course. We have more important things to do first."

He leaned in and kissed her again. She felt the fire in him.

Leia put both her arms around Xizor, returned his

fire with her own. Would this be so bad? To let him continue? To save Luke?

Xizor moved his mouth from hers and put his lips on her neck, slid down her shoulder. The dress's strap fell off on that side.

Not just to save Luke. To enjoy this to the fullest, did she want to do that?

She did not. No.

But she *did* want it, at the same time.

His hands moved on her. Oh, yes . . .

28

Xizor pressed his lips against Leia's bare shoulder and felt her shudder with pleasure. He had her now. She was his—if not in mind and spirit, then certainly her body belonged to him. He was a little disappointed in how easy it had been. Ah, well.

He reached for the closure of her dress . . .

There came a pounding at the door.

What—? Who *dared*?

Leia jumped, pulled away from him, straightened her rumpled dress. She was breathing fast, and her face was red.

Somebody started braying outside. The pounding increased.

That blasted Wookiee! Why was he here? How had Howzmin allowed him to *get* here?

Flustered, Leia said, "I—I'd better see what he wants."

"Stay. I'll get rid of him." Xizor started to rise.

"N-No, I'll do it."

Xizor smiled. Felt her want him. "As you wish."

He watched her get to her feet. She swayed a little as she walked to the door. This was only a temporary setback. She would shoo the Wookiee away and return to him. Once he put a woman under his spell she belonged to him forever.

Leia touched the door controls—Xizor had locked them—and the door slid wide.

The Wookiee gargled at her. Xizor's command of the tongue was imperfect, but he managed to catch the gist of what the tall, furry one said. He wanted Leia to come with him, now.

"I'm in the middle of—of a, a . . . delicate discussion here," she said. "Can't it wait?"

Xizor smiled.

The Wookiee ranted some more. Maybe he was smarter than he looked; he knew something was going on that threatened her, if not precisely what. A human standing in the doorway would know by looking at Leia, at least a human with any brains.

Leia turned and glanced at Xizor. "He seems upset," she said. "Maybe I better go and see what he wants?"

Now that he had her under his control, Xizor could do as he wished with her. He toyed with the idea of commanding her to shut the door and to remove her clothes before she returned to the couch. But—no. Such was his belief in his power that he merely shrugged. "As you like. I'll be here." He made a deliberate pause. "For a little while longer." Let her think that he might be gone if she did not hurry. A small cruelty but a demonstration of his authority. *I might be gone, do you want to risk that?*

"I—I will—" She stopped. Shook her head as if trying to shake off his influence.

You don't rid yourself of my biological magic that easily, little one.

He waved her away, unworried.

She'd be back.

.   .   .

In the hall outside Xizor's sanctum, Leia glared at Chewie, who glared right back at her. "This had better be good!"

Howzmin lay on the floor in a heap. Unconscious or dead, she couldn't tell which. Chewie grabbed her by the arm and hustled her down the hallway.

"Let go of me, you overgrown stuffed toy!"

Chewie paid her no mind.

When they came to a small alcove a short distance away, Chewie shoved Leia into it and stepped in behind her.

"You are going to be sorry, you—"

He pressed one hairy hand over her mouth, pointed up at the ceiling with his other hand.

Leia looked. Saw a small parabolic microphone inset into the ceiling.

"Somebody is listening?" she whispered.

He nodded.

"Are we being watched, too?"

Chewie shook his head. That was why he'd brought her here, she realized. It must be a blind spot. He knew what she and Xizor had been doing in there; he'd sensed it somehow. He was protecting her. And protecting Han.

The desire she'd felt evaporated. Shame flooded into her.

How could she have let that go on? She loved Han. She had only just met Xizor; nothing like that had ever happened to her before. Not only was it *wrong*, it wasn't *natural*. That was not like her; she would never behave that way, certainly not with a stranger!

Was he using some kind of drug—in her tea, maybe? That would explain a lot. Could it be that, for whatever reason, he wanted to seduce her?

That would be terrible. And at the same time, it made her feel better. At least there would be a real ex-

cuse for the sensations that had taken her—an excuse
for how she'd behaved. She had come very close to disaster. And Luke—?

Of a moment, the knowledge came clear to her: It
wasn't Vader who wanted him dead—

"I think maybe we'd better consider an alternate
plan," she said. "Chewie, here's what you should
do . . ."

By the time the *Executor* arrived in the system, Vader was almost itching to be back. Patience had never
been his strongest virtue, and he was looking forward
to assembling his case against Xizor.

As the giant ship lanced its way toward the planet,
Vader thought about what he was going to do. He de-
bated with himself about mentioning anything to the
Emperor yet. On the one hand, since Xizor was currently high in Imperial esteem, any disparaging com-
ments might be brushed off as jealousy, even though
the Emperor should know better. On the other hand, if
he didn't say anything, he might be irritated at Vader
later for his silence. The Emperor wanted to know everything about everybody—except when he didn't want
to hear it.

As Vader expected, the Emperor was not convinced.

"You disappoint me, Lord Vader. I sense that your
judgment is shaded by something of a . . . personal
grudge here."

"No, my master. I am merely concerned about the
criminal's treachery. If he is in fact trying to kill
Skywalker—"

The Emperor cut him off: "Really, Lord Vader, I
would certainly need more evidence than a *rumor* from
some *bounty hunter* to move against so valuable an

ally. Did he not give us that Rebel base? Has he not put his vast shipping fleet at our disposal?"

"I have not forgotten these things," Vader said. He tried to keep his voice steady and even. "But I have also not forgotten my promise to bring Skywalker to the dark side. Skywalker turned would be much more important to the Empire than Xizor."

"Indeed he would—*if* you can turn him."

"I can, my master. But not if he is slain before I can get to him."

"Young Skywalker has managed to stay alive this long. If he is as strong in the Force as we assume he is, he will continue to do so until you find him, don't you think? And if he is not as strong as we believe, then we have no use for him anyway."

Vader ground his teeth. He had thought much the same himself when last he met Luke. If he could be destroyed easily, then he had no real value to the dark side. Still, he did not like having this used in an argument against him.

None of this was unexpected, but it was nonetheless a great irritant. That the Emperor would put so much faith in the Dark Prince, as sly and immoral a being as existed anywhere, was disturbing in the utmost.

"Since it seems so important to you, I give you leave to search for Skywalker. For a short while, for there are other tasks I would have you perform. Is this satisfactory?"

Not really, but what was there to be done? "Yes, my master."

He did want to find his son, but he also had to build a case against Xizor. Either of these would command much of his attention alone. Both of them at the same time would be difficult.

But he was Dark Lord of the Sith and one with the dark side. He would manage.

.   .   .

Leia took a deep breath, blew half of it out, and opened the door to Xizor's chamber.

The head of Black Sun sat on the couch where she'd left him, the glass in his hand. He smiled. "I was beginning to worry about you."

She smiled, hoped it didn't look too false. She could still feel the charisma he exuded, but now she could resist it. She couldn't say how, exactly, but she had some kind of strength she hadn't noticed before. Maybe it was that her anger had become a shield upon which his attraction splashed and was repelled. Maybe the drug had worn off. It didn't matter why, as long as it worked.

Now she had to keep Xizor busy long enough to give Chewie a chance to escape, or at least to get a good start on it.

Chewie hadn't liked the idea, but she'd convinced him he could serve her better if he could get away from here and bring help.

"Come back and sit here next to me," Xizor said. It was not a request but an order. He didn't seem at all curious as to why Chewie had been so anxious to see her.

Leia moved instead toward the bar. "Let me make myself some tea first," she said. "I seem to have gotten rather warm and thirsty."

She saw the mixture of emotions flit quickly across his features, but only because she was looking carefully. He was angry that she didn't instantly obey him —his brow furrowed in the slightest of frowns—but he was also pleased that she was disturbed. Or perhaps excited? A quick flex of his lips into a smile that lasted but a second gave her this part.

She took her time making the tea. When she was done, she sipped at it but made no move to approach him.

"Come here," he said. Definitely a command.

Leia put the tea down and started for him.

There came the smile again. He thought he had her under his control.

"You said you were warm. Why don't you . . . remove your clothes and get more comfortable?"

She moved slowly. "I've gotten a little cooler," she said.

"Take them off anyway." Now there was a core of durasteel under his words. "It would please me. You want to please me, don't you?"

No, what I really want to do is give Chewie another few minutes.

She stopped. Lifted one foot and removed her slipper. Smiled at Xizor and tossed the slipper aside. Put her bare foot down and lifted the opposite foot. Tugged the second slipper off and dropped it.

Now he smiled again. Sipped at his drink. It was green, whatever it was.

She reached up and touched the fastener of the dress. Wiggled it, twisted it, frowned as she worked it.

"What are you doing?"

"It's stuck," she said.

He leaned forward. "Come here. I'll do it."

"Wait. There it is." She unsnapped the fastener. She was fully dressed in a bodysuit; removing the see-through dress wouldn't reveal any more of her, but it would buy a little more time.

He leaned back on the couch.

She delayed the moves as much as she could before she dropped the green dress to the floor around her ankles. Thus far, all he'd gotten a look at that he hadn't seen before were her feet.

"Now the rest of it," he said. He waved the glass.

She hoped Chewie had had enough time, because this was as far as she was going to go with this game.

"I don't think so," she said.

He put the glass down and came to his feet. "What?"

"It isn't proper to remove one's clothes in front of a stranger," she said.

He moved toward her. Grabbed her shoulders and shook her. This close to him, she felt the allure wash over her. It was something from within him, some kind of attractant he produced. It was much stronger, but now that she knew what it was, she could resist it. Her body wanted one thing, but she was a civilized woman and her mind was what controlled her, not her hormones.

He bent to kiss her.

She slammed her knee up between his legs, hard.

He groaned and shoved her away, stumbled back a step.

Leia stood there, watching him. Smiled sweetly. *Don't like that, do you?*

When he could straighten up, he did so. His face was cold, his expression neutral. If he felt any pain, it no longer showed, and if he was angry, that was not evident, either. The passion he'd had was gone or at least well hidden now.

He seemed to have changed color, too, now that she noticed. He looked paler, cooler, an ashen green.

"So. You resist me."

"You got that right," she said.

He nodded. "It was something the Wookiee said." Not a question.

She smiled. "Sometimes Wookiees are very smart. And always very loyal."

He shook his head. "Ah. Here is the drawback to bright and strong women: Sometimes they are bright and strong when you least want them to be." He bowed. "I am pleased that you are a worthy adversary." He finished the bow. "Guri."

A panel slid aside in the wall behind him, and the HRD stepped into the room.

Leia gave her a military nod.

"It seems you were right," Xizor said to Guri. "Take

her to her room and lock her in." To Leia he said, "You and I will continue this discussion later. Sooner or later, I believe you'll find that I am not such bad company."

"Don't bet on it," she said.

Guri moved to where she stood, took Leia's arm. Her hand was soft, but her grip was like a steel clamp.

Leia hoped Chewie had gotten enough of a head start.

29

After Guri had taken Leia away, Xizor sipped at another glass of green champagne. Perhaps it would help ease the pain in his groin.

After a time, he called his chief of security.

"Did the Wookiee escape?"

"Yes, Highness."

"You did not allow him to think it was too easy?"

"He put five of our troops down, my prince. We singed him with a blaster beam as he ran down a hall. He won't think it was easy."

"Good."

Xizor broke the link and smiled into the green, bubbly liquid. His surveillance on the Wookiee had reported the escape attempt immediately. Before Leia had returned to him, Xizor had already put his alternate plan into effect. He had intended to let the Wookiee go all along, albeit not quite this soon. Well. No matter. The Wookiee would surely contact Skywalker, and the boy would come running to try to rescue the princess.

Xizor's agents would probably collect Skywalker before he got within hours of the castle.

So easy. The hot ones were so predictable.

A priority offworld message announced itself on his private channel. He didn't feel like talking to anybody just at the moment, but only a few people had access to the direct link, and if one of them was calling, it was likely something he'd best not ignore.

The connection was vox only, no image of the speaker. Understandable, considering the position some of his agents sometimes found themselves in regarding their security. He himself did not like to transmit his image. A personal quirk. You could scramble the transmission, of course, but in the field, paranoia was high. Many operatives reasoned that if a shielded pipeline was broken into and the com somehow unscrambled, better it should not have pictures attached to the speaker.

His computer had verified the caller from his voice patterns, else it would not have been put through.

"Yes?"

"My prince, there is news of Skywalker."

"And it is . . . ?"

"He has allegedly been captured by a group of bounty hunters. They would not say where they are precisely, but we have determined that they are on Kothlis. We expect to have that information updated momentarily. There is a problem, however."

"I see. And this problem is . . . ?"

"They say there is another bidder for their prisoner. One whose offer tops ours and who has . . . Imperial connections."

Hmm. Vader had just gone to that area. Ostensibly it was to give credence to the computer theft, but consider: Who in the galaxy wanted Skywalker as much as Xizor himself did? Vader, of course. Then again, Vader was already back here onplanet, had gone to see the Emperor, and there were no indications he had brought

Skywalker back with him. Perhaps the information had reached him too late for him to make proper use of it. Or not reached him at all.

Well. This ploy with the princess might not be necessary at all.

"Tell them we'll double whatever the other side has to offer."

"Highness, if we're bidding against the Empire, we can't match them."

"I know that. It doesn't matter since we aren't ever going to have to *pay* it. As soon as we find out precisely where they are holding him, we'll scramble a jade ops team and collect him for free. We don't need him breathing, only his body."

"Very well, Highness—wait. Your pardon; I'm getting a call from one of our operatives regarding this; it may be the location we need . . ."

Xizor gave the agent leave to answer the call. He sat and waited. Meditated on the ruthlessness of entropy. On the amount of time he had spent waiting for somebody to get back to him. Months, probably, maybe more. Of course, that happened a lot less now than once it had . . .

When his agent came back online, his voice was shaky and he had difficulty speaking without swallowing frequently.

"M-My prince, there has been a . . . complication." Fear lurked in the man's words like a desert scavenger circling a dying animal.

"A complication," Xizor repeated.

"It—It seems that Skywalker has escaped custody. And *Darth Vader* is now personally involved; he was seen near the site of the escape within hours of the event."

As the bearer of what he thought very bad news, the agent feared for his life. People had been killed for less when offering unhappy tiding to their princes, and the man knew it, knew his employer had done it himself.

Had doubtless heard the tale of the traitor Green by now, too.

Xizor laughed.

"M-My prince?"

Finally. Some good news. Vader had just missed Skywalker. The boy was free, and as long as Leia was safely installed here, sooner or later Skywalker would show up on Xizor's doorstep. The Wookiee would see to that.

"Do not concern yourself with Skywalker's escape," the Dark Prince said. "That situation is under control."

Someday, perhaps, he would allow this story to become public—once he was in control of the galaxy.

Ah, people would say, *how devious the Dark Prince is. Beware!*

Beware, indeed.

Leia tried the door to her room, but of course it was locked. She looked around. It didn't appear as if the last occupant had forgotten and left a spare blaster in the bedside table; there were no tools with which to open the door, no secret escape hatches she could find. She also couldn't spot the holocam, but she was sure the room was wired for surveillance, given what she now knew. If she had to stay here long enough to undress, she would do it in the dark and hope they didn't have a light-gathering scope on the lens. Although it was probably a little late for modesty.

She sighed. She hoped Chewie had gotten away. Not that it would do *her* much good, but at least if he'd made it, he could fill Luke and Lando in, so they'd know to get Luke as far away from Black Sun as possible. Luke would want to come and rescue her, but Lando was a realist; he should be able to talk Luke out of it. They needed to be free, to rescue Han. That was the important thing.

Forgive me, Han, for what I almost did. It was a drug, I know, but I'm sorry I was so weak.

When she saw him again—well, *if* she saw him again —maybe she would tell him about it. Then again, maybe not. No point in upsetting him, right?

The idea of seeing Han again made her feel momentarily better, but she had to admit that her chances didn't seem particularly good just now.

She sat on the bed and considered her options. At the moment, she didn't seem to have an awful lot of them.

She leaned back, stretched out. One of the things she'd learned while working with the Alliance's military personnel was: When in doubt, take a nap. Never knew when you would get the chance again.

Not that she thought she'd be able to sleep, given all that was going on. She'd just lie here and try to relax for a few moments.

She surprised herself by dropping into a deep sleep almost immediately.

Lando didn't want to stop, but Luke insisted.

"Look, I trust the Force and it's telling me Leia is in danger. So let's just put in a call and check, okay?"

"Can't it wait until we get to Tatooine?"

"No."

Lando sighed. "All right. But you remember I did this. You owe me one."

He dropped the *Falcon* out of hyperspace.

"How do we call?" Luke asked.

Lando smiled. "I've got a little surprise for you. Han isn't the only one who can rig the *Falcon*."

"What do you mean?"

Lando put the ship on automatic control and led Luke to the aft cargo hold. He pointed at a device mounted on one wall.

"That looks like a comm unit."

"Bright boy. Go ahead, make your call."

Luke punched in the relay codes that Lando gave him while the gambler kept fiddling with the override to make sure the communication wasn't tapped.

Dash didn't answer, but there was a recorded computer response.

Luke turned to Lando. "Do we have the 'play message' code?"

"Yes." Lando gave it to him.

The image that ghosted into being surprised them. A Wookiee with a bad haircut. Luke didn't recognize him at first. Until he started talking. Yelling was more like it.

Chewie!

"What?" Lando said.

"What is it?"

"Oh, no!"

"Lando!"

Lando translated. "Leia is being held on Coruscant by Black Sun. They tried to kill Chewie but he escaped —the princess made him go, it wasn't his idea—"

Abruptly the transmission ended.

"What happened?"

"I dunno, my codes just went blank. Somebody must have reported the override's theft." He pulled the override from the comm unit's slot and tossed the electronic card on the floor.

"Let's go," Luke said.

"To Tatooine, right?"

"Wrong."

"Somehow I knew you were gonna say that. We can't go to Coruscant! It's too dangerous."

"You can stay here if you want."

"Luke . . ."

"Leia needs my help. I'm going."

Lando stared at the ceiling for a moment, then shook his head. "Why me? Why do these things always happen to me?"

. . .

Time and space shivered, and the *Millennium Falcon* dropped out of hyper- and into realspace.

Luke glanced at the control screens. "We're still a pretty long way off," he said. "It'll take days to get there."

"Yeah, well, there's a reason for that," Lando said. "We're not talking about some backrocket world with two cities and a small town on it. Coruscant is one big building complex that almost covers the entire planet. The space around it is filled with skyhooks, wheel-worlds, power sats, and a whole river of commercial and private traffic, not to mention a great big chunk of the Imperial Navy. It's like a huge canopy, and the holes in it are real tiny. We aren't going to sail merrily past all that in *this* ship. My guess is that the *Falcon* is plastered on computer wanted screens all over the galaxy and, sure as lizards like sunshine, on every security scanner here in the center of the Empire. I don't think a swiped security code is gonna get us past. We won't do Leia any good locked in an Imperial prison."

"I get your point."

"So we work our way in slow and try to figure out something. Got any bright ideas?"

Luke thought about it. "Well, actually, yes."

Lando blinked. "Yeah? Let's hear it."

Luke told him.

"I don't know about this," Lando said.

"Hey, Han did it—and on a Star Destroyer and not a droid-operated robotic freighter, too." Luke paused a second. Then said, "If you want, I'll take over."

Lando raised his eyebrows. "Listen, I *taught* Han that trick."

Luke smiled.

In theory, it ought to work. They were near the freighter lanes leading to and from Coruscant. Here was where the big vessels lumbered along, bulk freighters or container ships, in restricted channels. To be there, you had to be flying something that hauled a couple hundred metric tons or more. While the law said there had to be somebody other than droids on board one of the big ships, that law was usually ignored and seldom enforced, especially when it was somebody delivering goods for the Empire. A droid programmed to ferry ships in and out of gravity wells wasn't apt to be paying a lot of attention to what went on around it once it got into the lanes—the system's vack-traffic-control took care of all that, so sneaking up to the belly or backside of a big freighter ought to be as easy as snapping your fingers. After that, you just had to stay in its shadow all the way down until you were off the grid and into planetary Doppler. The *Falcon* had jammers that should take care of that without any problems—a bright ten-year-old could build a decent jammer from an old microwave cooker and a couple of detuned repulsor grids.

The trick was to match the speed and course of the bigger vessel so you'd stay in exactly the same place relative to it. A good pilot should be able to manage it, but if he zigged when he should zag, well, that might mean getting vaporized by an Imperial picket ship or a planetary defense battery. But it was doable if you had the nerve and the skill. It ought to work—in theory.

Yes, the Empire had rings of ships around the planet, but they were designed to stop an attacking force. Space was too big for them to be able to see everything, and what was a single ship going to be able to do to a whole planet, especially if—as the Alliance did—your enemy refused to attack and destroy civilian targets anyway?

"Ready?" Lando said.

"Ready," Luke said.

"*We're* ready, too," Threepio said. "If anyone *cares*."

Artoo whistled.

Lando grinned. "Hang on. Here we go."

The freighter moving in their general direction was a big one, actually a modified tug towing a series of closely linked cylindrical cargo containers, arranged in a long ring. Each of these containers was as big as the *Falcon*, and each was hung with orbital braking rockets. It was a bit small for a supertransport, but the ship's cargo was probably pushing eight or nine hundred m-tons, not exactly tiny. The freighter put out a bounce signal identifying it as the ISO—Independent Ship Owners'—vessel *Tuk Prevoz*, registered on Imperial Center and flying under contract to Xizor Transportation Systems.

Lando brought the *Falcon* around in a long, shallow arc, almost a hemispherical 180, first heading away from the freighter, then behind and under its belly.

"This ought to be right in their sensor shadow," he said.

Luke nodded. Big ships had plenty of blind spots, especially those towing large cargoes. If they could stay in the sensor shadow as they approached, the crew couldn't spot them. Once they were safely next to one of the cargo containers, nobody in the ship would be able to visually tag them, and, unless they passed within spitting distance of one of the picket line ships, no Imperial eyes would be able to make them out, either.

Luke looked at the scopes. Lando was dead on his flight plan. A degree or two either way and the crew on the freighter might get a blip on their scopes, but so far, so good.

The cargo containers loomed bigger. Problem with visual flying out here in the outvack was perspective; movement became pretty subjective. Relatively speaking, either they were getting closer or the freighter was dropping down upon them, and when you got right down to it, it didn't matter—as long as they stayed on the line inside the sensor shadow.

Lando moved his hands precisely, like a microsurgeon splicing nerves. The *Falcon* slowed, slowed . . . stopped.

The surface of the nearest cargo pod was three meters away.

"Good job," Luke said. Despite his giving Lando a hard time, he was a good pilot.

"Yeah, but that's the easy part. Now we got to stay with this boomer until we get into atmosphere and he drops his cargo into a spiral-in orbit. I'm shutting down the transponder and nonessential systems. We don't want anybody seeing our lights or picking up active sensors. From here on in, it's seat-of-the-pants."

"You thought about what we're going to do once we land?"

Lando snorted. "Let's worry about landing first, how about? I know some people, I have a few contacts. We'll be okay."

Luke nodded. He hoped Lando was right.

Of course, they might stray off course on the way to the planet and get roasted by a coherent light battery and he wouldn't have to worry about it. Not that that made him feel any better.

He reached out, tried to find Leia, using the Force. Pushed to the limit of his abilities . . .

Nothing. If she was there, he was too far away to touch her.

Well. They'd be closer soon. If they survived, he would try again.

If they survived.

Sitting naked in his chamber and working on his healing meditation, Darth Vader frowned. There was a disturbance in the Force. He reached for it with the power of the dark side . . .

He could not connect with it, whatever it was.

Abruptly the sensation of a ripple passed.

The dark side still had surprises for him. Like a fire, it could warm or burn, and great care must be taken not to trip and fall into it. He had seen what extensive use had done to the Emperor; it had eaten away at him physically. But that would not happen to Vader, for he intended to master the dark side. He was well on the way. It would be only a matter of how long, of *when*, not *if*. And when he finally snared Luke, the process would go faster. Two powerful magnets would attract more of the dark energy than one. Together they would manipulate the Force quicker than either could alone.

So strong, the boy. Who could have known? Luke Skywalker—his *son*—might well be the most powerful man in the galaxy.

He allowed himself a smile, even though the expression stretched scar tissue and was painful. He could withstand pain.

He was the Dark Lord of the Sith, and he could withstand anything.

30

"I really don't think this is a good idea, Master Luke. I believe it would be much better if Artoo and I went with you and Master Lando."

Artoo cheeped his agreement.

"Look, you'll be fine here on the ship," Luke said. "We need you here in case we need help. Besides, it'll be a lot more dangerous out there than in here."

"Ah. Well, in that case, perhaps we *should* stay here."

Artoo cheeped.

"No, you heard Master Luke, he needs us on the ship in case anything goes wrong."

"Wrong, what could possibly go *wrong*?" Lando said. "Just because we've got huge rewards posted everywhere in the galaxy for us, dead or alive, and we've plunked ourselves down smack in the black and evil *heart* of the Empire?"

Luke shook his head. "Come on. Where would be

the last place you'd look for us if you were an Imperial operative or a bounty hunter?"

"Yeah, I guess you're right. They'd figure nobody would be that stupid. Lucky for us they don't know we *are* that stupid."

Luke shook his head. All this banter was an attempt to make light of the situation. The truth was, this was dangerous, no two ways about it. To Threepio, he said in a more serious voice, "Look, I'll be honest. There's a good chance we won't make it back. If that happens, don't call the Alliance for help. There's no point in putting any part of the fleet in jeopardy."

Threepio said, "I understand."

Artoo whistled and cheeped rapidly. The tone was upset.

Luke looked at the little droid. He squatted down and laid one hand on his dome. "Just stand by the comm, okay? We'll call you if we need you. If we get in trouble, you can try to come and get us. Threepio has the hands and feet, you have the astronavigational skills. I'm sure the two of you working together can fly the *Falcon* in an emergency."

"There's a happy thought," Lando said. "Han knew that, it would thaw him out faster than a laser torch." Lando was still trying to keep things cheery, but Luke imagined the gambler had a cold feeling in the pit of his stomach, too. This was not going to be a piece of cake.

Artoo did not seem to think very much of the idea of flying the *Falcon,* either.

"Don't be rude," Threepio said. "I wasn't always a protocol droid, you know. I've programmed converters, and I once ran a shovel loader for an entire standard month. I've watched Master Han and Master Lando and Chewbacca often enough. I daresay I can pilot this ship better than *you* can!"

Artoo made more rude noises.

"Oh, really? Well, at least *I* don't look like an overgrown garbage can!"

"Come on, Luke," Lando said. "If we're going to go, we need to get moving. We can get ourselves some disguises, and if we hurry, we can be underground before daylight. These two will argue all night."

"Okay." Luke rose from his squat. "See you in a little while."

"Do be careful, Master Luke."

Artoo seconded that.

Luke hoped he didn't look as grave as he felt. "We will."

Lando already had his disguise in place. His head was wrapped in a beggar's scarf and cowl, his normal clothes hidden under a ragged robe. Luke donned similar garb and covered the lower part of his face as well.

Outside the huge building, Luke and Lando worked their way through a relatively sparsely populated area. There weren't many spots completely void of occupants, but this area was in the southern hemisphere not far from the pole—and it was *cold*. There were apparently more comfortable places to live and work. Lando had a "business associate" who owed him a favor, and he paid it by allowing them to hide the *Millennium Falcon* in a warehouse that was half full of what looked like dried plankton and smelled a lot like a Tatooine landfill in the heat of summer.

"Just how many people owe you favors?"

Lando flashed his bright smile. "A whole lot of them who should never gamble. Lucky for me they do."

"So now what?"

"We catch a ride into the Southern Underground. Keep that lightsaber out of sight but close to hand— this is not the kind of place you want to take your granny for tea, if you know what I mean."

"Bad as Mos Eisley?"

"Parts of it are worse."

"Great. Why are we *going* to such a delightful part of this chrome-plated planet, anyhow?"

Lando led them down a narrow, twisting alley. Luke

saw that he kept his hand on his blaster as they moved. The air was frigid; it clawed at the jacket Luke wore, nipped at his ears, and turned their breaths to crisp, white fog as they moved.

Lando paused at the end of the alley, peeped out, then continued to the next confined passageway. "Well, it's like this. You ever hear of the celebrated shipjacker Evet Scy'rrep?"

"Sure, I used to watch *Galactic Bandits* on the holoproj as a kid. They based a whole series on him. He knocked off something like fifteen starliners, got away with millions of credits and jewels. But they caught him eventually."

"That's right. At his trial, somebody asked him why he robbed luxury cruisers. And Scy'rrep said, 'Because that's where the credits are.'"

Luke smiled and shook his head.

Lando said, "We're going into a cesspool of a place because that's where my contacts are."

"Lead on. I hope it'll be warmer than here."

Xizor was in his bath, a sunken tub carved from dense black garden stone and large enough to seat ten comfortably. He spent a lot of time bathing, part of his species' heritage. The Falleen were born of the water, and it was always nice to return to it. Vapor rose from the hot water, bringing with it the scent of the eukamint oil that swirled in the tub. Blowers sent soothing waves and bubbles circulating through the liquid. Here was a place where he allowed himself to relax totally. There was no holoproj, no comlink, no admittance, save for himself and any guests he wished to entertain. And Guri, of course. He would sometimes have music piped in, when the mood struck him, but otherwise, he wanted nothing to intrude on his peace while he soaked away the day's tensions.

He leaned back against the warmed stone and

sipped a mild after-dinner drink, a smoky blend of wormwood and spice extract, just potent enough to add an inner glow to the water's warmth around him. Life always looked better from in here. Things were almost perfect.

He'd invited Leia to join him but she had declined to do so.

Things were . . . *almost* perfect.

Guri strode into the bathroom and stopped next to the tub.

"You know I hate to be disturbed here," he said. Which was, he realized even as he spoke, a pointless thing to say. Guri would not have bothered him if whatever she wanted had been something that could wait.

She produced a small com. "The Emperor," she said.

Xizor sat up and grabbed the comlink. "My master," he said.

"I shall be leaving the planet shortly," the Emperor said. "To inspect portions of a certain . . . construction project of which you are aware. When I return, we must get together. I have a few things I would like to discuss with you."

"Of course, my master."

"Tales have reached me concerning one of the Rebels, Luke Skywalker. It seems you have an interest in him?"

"Skywalker? I have heard the name. I cannot say I have an interest in him."

"We shall speak of this on my return."

The conversation ended, the Emperor disconnected. He seldom bothered with opening or closing salutations.

Xizor put the small comlink cylinder on the edge of the tub and allowed himself to sink deeper into the tranquilizing water. Well. It was to be expected that the Emperor would find out about his plans sooner or later. It affected nothing, as long as Xizor remained cautious. Rumors were not proof.

Guri bent, picked up the comlink, and left.

As he watched her walk away, he briefly considered telling her to disrobe and join him in the water. He had made her do that a few times when he wanted company he could trust absolutely, and she had demonstrated to his satisfaction that she could pass for a woman in virtually every way during those times . . .

But—no. He was saving his energies for Leia. She would learn to see him in a better light, he knew. He could wait. Patience was one of the ultimate virtues.

He took a deep breath and sank beneath the water. His lung capacity was great and he could stay under for a long time, a throwback to his reptile heritage. The water warmed his face, and he luxuriated in it.

Overall, life was very good.

It was warmer in the Underground, but it smelled at least as bad as the warehouse where they'd left the *Falcon*. At least it did to Luke. The various humans and aliens they'd passed didn't seem to notice the stink. It bothered Luke that in order for you to smell a thing, tiny and invisible particles of it had to be inhaled and sampled by your olfactory system. Whatever was causing that awful rotting, fetid odor, he didn't like the idea of microscopic bits of it going up his nose.

They were in a maglev train station not far below the surface. The waiting platform was crowded, and there were Imperial stormtroopers in armor and uniformed officers circulating in the huge room.

"I think maybe it's time we got some better disguises," Lando said. "We wouldn't want some surveillance cam taking note of us in these rags."

"What did you have in mind?"

A Squid Head brushed past them, in a hurry to get somewhere. It had no regard for beggars.

"I've been thinking about that. Ideally, we want to look like somebody nobody'll pay any attention to."

"Stormtroopers?"

Lando nodded. "Yeah. Or maybe the Elite Storm-troopers would be better. Their faces are covered, and since they are so well regarded, nobody is apt to bother them."

Luke looked around. "I see one about my size, over there by the ticket droid."

"Yep, and there's one about my height and weight, by the periodical dispenser. Maybe we should do our duty to the Empire and report something strange going on in one of the 'fresher booths, you think?"

"Just as any loyal citizen would," Luke said.

He and Lando grinned at each other.

Leia awoke, feeling groggy. There wasn't any way to keep track of time that she could see. She had dozed for a while; Xizor had called and asked her if she wanted to take a bath with him—a bath! come on!—and she'd fallen back asleep.

She got up and moved to the computer console. "What time is it?"

The device told her.

My. She'd been asleep for almost six standard hours. Quite a nap, that.

She was also hungry.

Even as she thought this, the door slid open and Guri entered, carrying a large domed tray. She put the tray on the computer table in front of Leia. "Food," she said. She turned and left.

Leia lifted the dome. A seven-course dinner had been artfully arranged on a series of dishes. A salad, a couple of different kinds of soypro patties, cooked vegetables, fruit, bread, containers of drinks. It looked great and smelled pretty good, too.

Leia picked up a piece of bread and tasted it. It was

warm, chewy, had a slightly sour flavor. Excellent.
Might as well eat. If Xizor wanted to kill her, he could
have done it by now; probably he didn't plan to poison
her. Like sleeping when you could, eating was one of
those things you had to do when it was available. And
if it tasted as great as this stuff did, well, that was a
bonus.

The Luke-size lieutenant frowned as he entered the
stall, Luke right behind him. "What are you talking
about, I don't see any—uh? What . . . ?"

This last was uttered as Luke used the Force to take
control of the man's thoughts. You'd think a crack
trooper in the service of the Empire would have a
stronger mind than this guy did. Then again, if he did,
he probably wouldn't be in the Imperial military, he'd
be working for the Alliance . . .

Luke ordered the man to strip, then to have a seat
and a nice long nap. He shucked his own clothes and
hurriedly dressed in the borrowed uniform. He kept the
blaster, tucked his lightsaber into his waistband under
the jacket, moved into the communal part of the refresher, and examined himself in the mirror. Not bad.

Behind him, Lando emerged from a stall, dressed in
a similar uniform. Lando adjusted the belt with his new
sidearm and brushed lint from the right sleeve.

"Women love a man in a uniform," he said. He
lifted his helmet and slipped it on.

"Let's hope they don't see the man behind the armor," Luke said.

The two of them squared their shoulders, stuck their
chests out, and affected an Imperial swagger as they
exited the 'fresher.

Vader stood at the ramp leading to the Emperor's
personal shuttle, looking down at the shorter man.

"I anticipate that I shall return in three weeks," the Emperor told him. "I trust you can keep the planet from falling apart while I am gone?"

"Yes, my master."

"I expect no less. Any news of Skywalker?"

"Not yet. We'll find him."

"Perhaps sooner than you expect."

Vader stared at the Emperor, who wore a half smile that revealed his damaged teeth. Had he foreseen something? The Emperor was still more attuned to the dark side than Vader was. Had he gleaned some new information about Luke?

If he had, he was not ready to reveal it, for he turned and allowed himself to be escorted up the ramp by a squad of the Imperial Royal Guard in their ceremonial red robes and matching armor.

The tap of the Emperor's twisted walking stick on the ramp was quite loud in the silence.

Of all the people in the galaxy, the Emperor trusted Darth Vader most; at least that's what Vader liked to believe. And as far as he was able to determine, the length of that trust was no farther than an outstretched arm could reach.

No matter. He was right about one thing: Sooner or later Luke would surface. A light that bright could not be hidden for long. By his nature the boy would have to burn hot enough to be visible to one who had the power and the knowledge of how to look for him. Once a Jedi began to grow in the Force, the process was not easily stopped. In Luke's case, Vader doubted that it *could* be stopped.

They would meet again. A week, a month, a year—it did not really matter. It would happen.

Meanwhile, he would keep a sharp eye on the actions of an enemy all too close to home. Even now, Vader's agents sought every scrap of information they had not already found on the Underlord of Black Sun.

That, too, would simply be a matter of time. Once you knew the direction, the trip was made easier, and sooner or later, Xizor would make an error. He would stumble.

When he did, Vader would be waiting to catch him.

31

"Well," Luke said, "this is a better neighborhood than where we were before, but where exactly are we going?"

Lando pointed. "There."

"A *plant* shop?"

"Don't let it fool you. It's run by an old Ho'Din name of Spero. He's got a lot of connections, some Imperial, some Alliance, some criminal."

"Let me guess: He owes you a favor."

"Not exactly. But we've done some business in the past and he doesn't mind making a few credits passing along information."

They headed for the shop.

"We're getting a lot of dirty looks," Luke said.

"It's the uniforms. The Empire doesn't have many friends down here. Most of the locals are probably on the run, one step ahead of being arrested. They won't bother us as long as we don't stick our noses in the wrong place. Don't want to bring Imperial heat and light into their hideout."

Inside the shop there was no sign of the Ho'Din owner. Except for Luke and Lando, the place was empty.

"Nobody home," Luke said. "That's odd, isn't it?"

"Yeah, odd. I—"

Somebody said something behind them. Luke didn't understand what it was, but he recognized the language: Wookiee.

"Easy, friend," Lando said. "Nobody is going to make any sudden moves." He lifted his hands away from his body, told Luke to do the same.

The Wookiee speaker said something else.

Something about the voice . . .

"Turn around, nice and slow," Lando told Luke.

They turned.

Sure enough, there was a Wookiee standing there. One with a bad haircut—

"Chewie!" Lando said.

Despite the helmets, Chewbacca recognized them at the same instant and lowered the blaster pistol he held.

Lando smiled as he and Luke moved forward to embrace Chewie.

"What happened? Why is your hair chopped off?"

Chewie tried to answer at the same time Lando fired more questions, and Luke didn't get much of it. But he was glad to see the Wookiee.

Finally Lando began to translate for Luke.

"The shop owner is tied up in back; in case anybody spotted Chewie coming in, they wouldn't think the Ho'Din was helping, right, right, and—slow down, pal!"

Chewie kept talking a keening, harning noise.

"Okay, okay, Leia thinks it's Black Sun that wants you dead, Luke, they're behind the assassination attempts, not the Empire. Huh? Well, I don't know how, there's just the three of us, how can we get inside the place, that won't help her if we get caught, will it—?"

The dialogue ended abruptly as a blaster bolt lanced through the shop's open door and shattered a flowerpot hanging from the ceiling. Shards of the ceramic pattered against Luke's back, and clumps of moist dirt and humus fell around him. The junglelike smell inside the shop increased.

"Hey!"

Outside the shop, four men with blasters loosed more shots. They weren't wearing uniforms, whoever they were.

The three inside the plant store dropped to the floor. Chewie raised his blaster and blindly fired several rounds back at the shooters.

"Who are those guys? Why are they shooting at us?"

Lando said, "Who knows?" He pulled his borrowed blaster and added to Chewie's return fire. It didn't look as if they hit anybody, from the torrent of light that came back at them.

"Is there another way out of here?" Luke asked.

Chewie growled a reply. Luke thought it meant "Yes."

"In the back!" Lando yelled.

He and Chewie cooked off several more shots, and the three of them crawled toward the back of the shop.

They passed an old Ho'Din bound and gagged in a corner.

"Sorry about this," Lando said to the Ho'Din. "Send the Alliance a bill, they'll pay for it!"

Chewie reached the back exit and shoved the sliding door open.

Another high-energy bolt zipped through the door at chest height and burned a hole in an inner wall. Fortunately, they were all still stretched out on the floor, and the hole was well above their heads.

Lando cursed. "They've got us boxed!"

Before they could think about what they were going to do, somebody outside the back exit screamed. There came the sound of several blaster discharges—but no fresh beams poked into the shop.

"What the—?" Lando began.

Luke looked up from where he lay prone on the floor, plant dirt ground into the chest and belly of his stolen uniform, and saw a figure walking across an alley. Well, not walking so much as . . . *swaggering*.

Luke recognized the man.

Dash Rendar! Oh, man. Here he was saving Luke *again*. Luke hated this.

"Howdy, boys. Having a little trouble?" He spun his blaster on his forefinger and blew across the end of the barrel. It made a slight hooting noise.

Luke came up, saw Lando and Chewie do the same. He started to speak, but Lando beat him to it. "Rendar! What are you doing here?"

"Saving your butts, looks like. Seems to be my specialty. Better come on, we can talk as we move. Follow me."

Luke shook his head. He really didn't like this, but there wasn't much he could say about it. Rendar was, unfortunately, right.

In a conference room in his castle, Darth Vader stared at the small man who stood in front of him. "You are certain of this?"

"Yes, my lord, I am certain."

Vader felt a flash of triumph. It was not enough, not by itself, but it went a long way toward the proof he needed. "And you have the tape and documentation."

"Already in your files, Lord Vader." The little man smiled.

"You have served me well. I will not forget this. Continue your search."

The little man bowed and left.

So. There existed a recording of a freelance agent speaking to an Alliance crew chief, telling her she would be made rich if she could but kill Luke Skywalker.

Of course, no direct connection to Xizor had been discovered, but Vader's agents would find it, did it exist. The briber had talked to the crew chief, someone had talked to him. Vader's agents would backwalk every moment of the briber's life until they found out who had sent him. And who had sent the being who had sent *him*. And so on.

It was one more addition to the growing collection of circumstantial evidence his agents had gathered and were continuing to gather.

By itself a grain of sand was nothing, but with enough grains, one could cover a city. It would not do to tip his hand too early. As of now, he had enough sand to begin. A bit more and he'd be able to bury Xizor . . .

He must be removed, once and for all, and the day was coming when it would happen.

Soon.

It would be soon.

Dash showed the way. Chewie took the point and led them into a warren of twisted corridors and tunnels that should lose any pursuers, given how fast Luke lost his own bearings.

"So how did you get here again?" Lando asked Dash.

"The usual way. Sneaked in under the belly of a freighter in the sensor shadow. A trick I learned as a boy at the Academy. A good pilot can do it in his sleep. How about you?"

Lando's smile seemed a little sickly to Luke. He shrugged. "Yeah, we did that, too. Piece of cake. Could have done it on autopilot, it was so easy."

"Yeah, but how did you manage to get *here?*" Luke asked. He pointed at the ground.

"The Ho'Din's? Oh, everybody knows about Spero, don't they, Lando?"

"I guess they do," Lando said. "Okay, that's how, but—why?"

Dash sighed. "Something to prove, I guess. I felt pretty bad after that disaster Luke and I went through. Not something I'm used to, making mistakes. But I figure, you crash your ship, you better climb into the next one you see and get it back in the air. Too much time goes by and you don't, you get afraid to fly. I screwed up, and I'm still not over that, but you can only sit and bubble in your own juices for so long. I work for money, but I figure I owe the Empire a little something. When Chewie called, I decided it was time to pay the Empire back."

Luke nodded. "I understand how you feel."

"I have a few contacts here," Dash said.

"You must breakfast with me," Xizor said.

Leia looked at him. He had come to her room early, but she had already dressed, and her costume was once again that of the bounty hunter she'd affected earlier, sans the helmet. She didn't want to wear the clothes this scum provided.

"I'm not hungry," she said.

"I insist."

Even now that she knew he had tried to kill Luke, she could feel the ghost of that attraction to him. Fortunately, she was able to resist it. Anger made a good antidote.

She decided to see if Xizor would reveal anything to her. Said, "Will Chewbacca be joining us?"

"Alas, no. Your Wookiee friend has . . . taken his leave of us."

"Got away and you can't find him, huh?"

Xizor gave her a thin smile totally without humor. "You think he escaped on his own? Really, Leia. I allowed him to break free."

"Come on."

"I want Skywalker. Skywalker wants you. I *have* you. Surely I don't need to draw you a diagram?"

She felt her belly twist and go cold. He was toying with them. The whole reason to have her come here was as *bait* for Luke. Oh, no.

She'd been hungry, but breakfast no longer held any appeal. This creature was evil. Twisted, brilliant, and evil.

"Where are we going?" Luke asked.

Dash said, "I know a place we can hide. We can figure out what to do from there."

Luke felt a sudden rush of something in him. A kind of powerful knowledge that filled him, made him grin. Of a second, he had become one with the Force—and he hadn't even tried to do it. It just happened.

"What?" Lando said, noticing.

"We'll go to this place and make plans to rescue Leia," Luke said.

He wasn't sure what he expected, maybe that Lando or Dash or even Chewie would stare and shake his head, ask who had abdicated and left Luke in charge, something. But the other three exchanged glances, looked back at Luke, and when they did, it was apparent that something had changed.

"Right," Lando said. "Of course."

Chewie moaned his assent.

"What else?" Dash said.

It was simply the right thing to do, and it felt as natural as breathing. That's what the Force was, he realized. A natural phenomenon. He had struggled so hard to attain it, and all that it required was that he relax and *allow* it, instead of trying to create it. Simple.

Too bad "simple" and "easy" didn't mean the same things.

Never mind. Because a thing was difficult did not mean it could not be done. With the Force, many things were possible. He still had much to learn, more than he'd ever thought before. He smiled. What was it Master Yoda had said? Recognizing your ignorance is the first step to wisdom?

Yes.

Guri stood in front of Xizor as he stripped from his breakfast outfit and began to dress for his appointments. She took no notice of his lack of clothing.

"Our agents say that a Corellian freighter answering the description of the *Millennium Falcon* is hidden somewhere in the Hasamadhi warehouse district near the South Pole."

Xizor selected a tunic and matching pants from the closet and examined them under the artificial sunlight. "So? There are hundreds of Corellian freighters that look like that, are there not?"

"Not hidden in the Hasamadhi warehouse district."

"Are you saying you think Skywalker and the gambler have come here? Have eluded the Imperial picket line and landed on the planet as bold as you please?"

"Any halfwit pilot who knows the freighter trick can manage it. Our own smugglers do it all the time."

Xizor rejected the outfit. Tossed it onto the floor and picked another suit of a darker hue and more conservative cut.

"All right. Check it out. If it is Skywalker's ship, have it watched. When he shows up, have our people kill him. Circumspectly, of course."

She nodded. Turned and left.

Xizor considered his image in the mirror after he dressed. Very impressive. He also considered what Guri had just told him. He didn't really expect Skywalker to arrive here so soon, but it was possible. If it was him, so much the better.

Vader would be made to look a fool by having Skywalker killed under his very nose.

And there was Leia, a problem he would eventually unknot to his satisfaction. He had plenty of time to play with her.

Things could hardly be moving along any smoother, could they?

Business had to go on, however, and Xizor could delegate only so much of it. Certain matters required his attention. He finished his inspection and headed for his receiving sanctum.

Once there, Xizor said, "All right. Who is my first appointment?"

"General Sendo, Prince Xizor."

Well. The device had been repaired enough to get his name right.

"Send him in."

General Sendo entered, bowed low.

"Do sit down, General," Xizor said.

"Your highness." The man obeyed.

There was the obligatory chitchat. Then Xizor gave him a plastex envelope containing ten thousand in worn, used credit notes, his monthly stipend for keeping Black Sun abreast of things Black Sun might wish to know about. Sendo was a do-nothing officer in the Imperial Intelligence's Destab Branch who had never seen battle but who could access all kinds of information from where he worked keeping a chair warm.

Xizor put the envelope into the man's hand and waved him away. There was no chance of any betrayal here—every supplicant who arrived was scanned and body-searched for recorders or holocams, and any who happened to have such things upon his or her person was summarily executed once he stepped inside. The rules were simple, and everybody who entered Xizor's castle had those rules made known to them each visit.

And if the courier decided to try to tell what he saw without proof, he would be wasting his time. Not to mention that the high-ranking officers of the local police, the local Army garrison, and Imperial Navy Intelligence were also on retainer to Black Sun, and any such reports concerning Xizor would find their way to his desk within moments of being given. Such reporters would simply . . . disappear, courtesy of Black Sun's secret employees in the appropriate agency.

Mayli Weng arrived with a petition from the Exotic Entertainers' Union asking for general pay increases and better working conditions for the twenty thousand workers who were members. Xizor was disposed to grant her request: Happy entertainers made for happier customers. Black Sun's percentage of the profits—donated by the owners of the businesses in which the entertainers were employed—would thus increase. Weng always asked and never demanded. He'd never even had to use his pheromones on her, she was so polite. Of course, he could not actually make the change himself; that would still be up to the Owners' League; but they had yet to refuse a recommendation from Black Sun, and he thought it unlikely they would do so now.

"I'll see what I can do," Xizor said.

Weng nodded, bowed, thanked him profusely for his generosity, and left.

Bentu Pall Tarlen, the head of the Imperial Center Construction Contracts Division, arrived to hand-deliver the latest bids on major building projects on-planet. With these numbers, Xizor could have his favored companies bid at lower prices and win the jobs. Once construction was started there would, of course, be cost overruns and delays to bring the monies involved up to profitable levels. Black Sun's percentage of such deals was not inconsiderable.

Through a dummy consortium that hired "consultants," Xizor arranged a transfer into Tarlen's account.

The man left, pleased.

Wendell Wright-Sims dropped by to deliver ten kilos of the highest-grade spice. Xizor didn't indulge in such things himself, but sometimes he had guests who might wish to do so, and he wished to be hospitable as a host. He thanked Wright-Sims and sent him on his way. There was no question of payment; the man did it to maintain favor. It was cheap insurance for him, even though that much spice was probably worth a couple of million credits on the streets.

The head of Black Sun could have had these transactions handled by others, but he preferred to see his most valuable tools face-to-face now and then. It was part of the job, necessary to remind those in the know just who ran the system—and who would come looking for them if they ran afoul of Black Sun.

The work might have been called tedious by some, but Xizor had not been bored in years. There were too many things to think about, too many angles to consider in even the most humdrum situation. Boredom was for those who lacked imagination. Xizor could sit alone in a room for days staring at a wall and be as busy mentally as most men working a complex and demanding job.

The representative from the Jewelers' Guild arrived . . .

The place Dash led them to was a pit, dirty, smelly, and more of a cave than anything, bounded by raw sewage and rat-eaten power cables. At least that was what it looked like on the outside.

Once they moved past a guard and a gate as thick as Chewie, the inside was a considerable improvement. It might have been a second-rate hotel in any one of a dozen ports Luke had visited. Except that the prices for staying here would have bought them new houses on Tatooine. Each.

Or so Dash told them.

"Now, if we can come up with an idea of how to proceed, I can reach out to my contacts," Dash said. "Do we have any ideas?"

"Yes," Luke said. "I have one."

32

Luke took a deep breath, let it out slowly, and sought to clear his mind. Now that they had the time and space, he wanted to try again to reach Leia.

He had removed the stolen uniform and discarded the blaster, and now he sat in the kneeling posture Master Yoda had taught him for meditation. The new clothes Dash had gotten for him felt appropriate: a coarsely woven, dark gray hooded cape and cowl, a plain shirt and a simple vest, pants and jacket, knee boots, all in black, without any insignia. Maybe it was not quite the uniform of a Jedi Knight, but it was close enough.

Relax. Let go . . .

He concentrated, focused, said the name aloud: "Leia . . ."

Waited a moment. Then, "Leia, I'm here. I'm coming for you."

.   .   .

She was using the computer, trying to find a floor plan for Xizor's castle. He wasn't so foolish as to leave one where she could access it; too bad—

Leia . . .

It was not telepathy so much as empathy, and since it had happened before, on Bespin, she recognized the sensation quickly.

Luke.

She took a deep breath and let part of it out, held her silence. She was being watched; she must give no sign of the connection with Luke. She pretended to look at whatever the computer image was, but she was seeing through it, into the distance beyond it, beyond the walls.

Leia, I'm here. I'm coming for you.

That's what Luke was saying, if she could have put it into words. But it wasn't expressed in words; it was a feeling, and she felt the truth of it.

Luke was here, on Coruscant, not far away. He was coming for her.

There was a calmness about Luke she hadn't felt before. He had grown stronger; his control of the Force was better. She was afraid for him and at the same time heartened at the connection. The sense of his confidence was very powerful. Before when she'd felt him touch her this way, it had been when he'd been injured, when Vader was on the brink of destroying him, but now, now he felt strong, in control, potent. Maybe he could rescue her. Maybe they would survive all this somehow.

Leia . . .

She smiled. *Luke, I'm here . . .*

Luke Skywalker, Jedi Knight, smiled.

•   •   •

In his chamber, Darth Vader felt the ripple in the Force. It was elusive, but he recognized it this time.

Luke.

He was *here*. On Imperial Center.

The knowledge sent a chill through his body.

Vader reached out, tried to touch his son: *Luke* . . .

He frowned. The way was . . . blocked. It was not only as if Luke's power had increased; it seemed also to be in two separate places.

Impossible. He was interpreting the energies wrong. There could be no other as strong as Luke in the Force; the Jedi were all dead. The Emperor was gone, light-years away.

What could be causing that echo effect? Surely that was all it was, an echo, some reverberation in the Force.

Of a moment the ripple passed and Vader was alone again.

He waved his hand, raised the lid of his chamber. Stood and moved for his armor. Luke was here, and he was going to find the boy. Find him—

—and bring him to the dark side.

33

Xizor sat alone in his private dining room deep in his castle and lunched on thin slices of moonglow, a delicate, rare—and expensive—pearlike fruit from more than a hundred light-years away. As he ate, he frowned. It wasn't the fruit, which was crisp and delicious; no, that was outstanding, was exquisite as always.

But something was wrong.

What it was he could not say, but he had not gotten to the top of an organization where you were either quick and clever or you were dead and gone by ignoring any input, be it logical or intuitive. In the complexity that was Black Sun there were *always* problems—but there were no indications of any more problems than usual. No reports of treachery, no upstart rivals trespassing on forbidden territory, no idealistic and overzealous police officers snooping where they'd been paid to leave off. The machine seemed to be running fine.

But there was an edgy, pit-of-the-stomach, nervous feeling he had learned to pay attention to over the years. It was a *feeling*, yes, but it was not as if he had no emotions, merely that he controlled them.

He chewed thoughtfully on the fruit. Nothing had changed about it, but it seemed to be . . . not quite as good as it had been a few moments before.

Moonglow was found only on a single satellite world, in a small section of one forest; it grew naturally nowhere else in the galaxy; in fact, it could not be grown anywhere else. Many had tried to transplant the funguslike tree, and all had failed. About the size of a man's fist, the fruit contained in its natural state one of the most potent biological poisons known. A single unaltered slice divided into a thousand tiny pieces would be enough, if consumed, to kill a thousand people and to do it in less than a minute. There was no known antidote, but there was a way to neutralize the poison before eating the fruit. Such preparation of moonglow legally required a chef who had studied the technique for a minimum of two years under a certified Master Moonglow Chef, and the process itself consisted of some ninety-seven steps. Should any of the steps be omitted or performed incorrectly, the resulting dish might cause anything from a mild stomach upset to a painful, thrashing, hallucinatory coma, followed by death. If a would-be diner went into a restaurant that had the proper licenses to offer the dish, the price of a single serving of moonglow would be somewhere around a thousand credits. Xizor generally ate it three or four times a month and had the most respected moonglow chef in the galaxy on his payroll. Even so, a small thrill always arose when he consumed the fruit. Always the possibility, however slight, of an error.

It added a wondrous flavor to the taste.

Eating moonglow was somewhat like Xizor's contest with Darth Vader, when he thought about it. There was no thrill in contending with those you knew you would defeat beyond any shadow of a doubt. But with an opponent such as Vader, lapdog to the Emperor that he was, you had to remember that those teeth *were* sharp and always ready to bite. He did not think Vader would win, but there certainly was a slight possibility.

It added a wondrous flavor to the contest.

Was it Vader who tripped those warning jitters?

Or was it someone else?

He pushed the moonglow aside, no longer interested in it. He would have Guri run a full security check on his operations, onplanet and off-. And while she was here, he would have her remove the remaining moonglow, too. If his chef saw anything left on the plate, he would probably quit in high dudgeon. Or worse, he might be upset enough to miss a step next time he prepared the dish. Xizor did not want that. Artists were so temperamental.

He stared at the half-empty plate, whose cost would furnish food for a small family for several months. There was nothing else to be done about the edgy feeling. It probably meant nothing anyway. Jitters, nothing more.

He wished he could believe that.

They sat at a small table in the Underground hotel's restaurant, waiting for their meal to be served.

Dash began, "This is the center of the Empire—"

"It is?" Lando cut in, heavy on the irony. "Uh-oh. We shouldn't be here. Why, it could be . . . *dangerous.*"

"What's your point, Dash?" Luke asked, ignoring Lando's sarcasm.

"The Empire is corrupt. It runs less on loyalty and honor than it does on bribes and graft. Credits lube the gears, and nowhere more than here."

"So? You think we're going to be able to bribe a

guard? I don't think Black Sun is likely to put that kind of person on the door," Lando offered.

"Not a guard, an engineer."

"What am I missing here?" Luke asked.

Dash continued: "In a bureaucracy, everything has to be filed and copied and logged in quadruplicate. You can't build anything without permits, licenses, inspections, plans. All we need to do is find the right engineer, one who maybe gambles too much or has more taste than he's got money."

They still looked blank.

"All right," Dash said. "Here's the idea. We know that the really big buildings on this planet extend as far under the surface as they do above it. One thing I know is, no matter how much graywater recycling and reclamation you do, some of it is always going to be lost. Waste products, sewage, they have to be pumped away where bigger and more efficient systems can work on them."

"Basic stuff, don't foul your own nest," Luke said. "So?"

"A building as big as this one"—here he tapped a holographic postcard showing several huge structures that included among them the Emperor's castle—"generates a lot of waste. There has to be a way to get rid of it. I haven't seen any garbage vans or drain wagons on the streets or in the skies of Coruscant, so they have to break the solid waste down and pump it away, probably as a slurry. Therefore we are talking about pipes."

Luke got it. He looked around the table. Said, "Big pipes."

He saw the others get it.

Chewie said something.

Lando nodded and said, "Chewie is right. Those conduits, if they are big enough to admit people, will certainly be guarded."

Chewie said something else.

"Yeah," Dash said. "Chewie also points out such

drains would be hard to locate, given that every building will have similar systems. It's probably a monster
maze under the ground."

"Right. But there will probably be fewer guards
posted on a big sewage drain than the doors aboveground. They wouldn't really expect any kind of assault that way; you couldn't move a lot of troops in
without making noise their sensors would pick up. But
a few men would be lost in the background gurgle, if
they were careful."

Lando looked at Luke and Chewie, then back at
Dash. "Assuming we could find a guide, you are saying
you want us to wade through kilometers of *sewage* to
get into this place?" He looked at Dash as if he had just
turned into a big spider.

Dash smiled. "Exactly what the guards would think.
Who would be that stupid?"

Lando shook his head. "Us. Who else?"

"And finding a guide is no problem. I know somebody."

"I've heard *that* before," Luke said.

Vader took a deep breath, blew it out, then took another. The energies of the dark side filled him, and he
could once again breathe as a normal man did. He focused his anger. It was not right that he be crippled,
that he couldn't do this all the time. It was . . . not
. . . right!

The healing energies held.

As long as he could maintain his indignation, his
lungs and breathing passages stayed open and clear. He
fed the fires of his rage with the unfairness of a galaxy
that would not let him be whole.

Still the healing energies held.

He fought the sense of relief he felt. Fought it and
kept his anger pure.

And *still* they held. Almost two minutes now. A new record.

He would grow stronger. He would add Luke's power to his own, and he would eventually be able to shed the armor, to walk around as normal men walked.

Luke . . .

He tried to stop the smile. Failed.

Sank back into the protection of his breathing chamber, unable to maintain the energies any longer. But even so, he'd managed two minutes. Eventually it would be ten minutes, then an hour, then as long as he wished.

Eventually.

Leia was not the most patient woman in the galaxy, she knew. Being cooped up in a room, no matter how well appointed that room might be, was not her idea of fun.

She tried meditating, but her mind buzzed too much.

She worked on escape plans, but given how little information she had, that was also fairly limited in scope.

Finally she took to exercising. She knew some basic gymnastics, easy enough to do as long as you had a little floor space. The carpet was almost as thick as a tumbling mat, and while the roof wasn't high enough to allow flips—even if she could still do one—there was nothing stopping her from doing handstands and assorted presses. She stretched, twisted, did splits, pitted her muscles against gravity in a variety of ways until she worked up a healthy sweat.

When she was done and fairly exhausted, she felt a lot better. She padded into the refresher and cranked up the shower. Turned off the lights and undressed, showered, and got dressed again in the dark. Tricky business, but since she was fairly sure Xizor had a hidden holocam or three in her room, she was *not* going to give him a show.

Feeling a little sore but better, Leia once again considered ways to escape. Or, more likely, ways to help Luke with whatever plan he had. She was worried about him, but on another level, pleased that he would come for her.

It was nice to know somebody cared that much.

34

Dash's contact, one Benedict Vidkun, was more than willing to scan the systems, make maps, lead them himself or whatever else they might want—as long as they had plenty of credits.

They didn't really have a whole lot of money among them. Lando had a little stashed here and there, plus what he'd managed to get from the Galactic Bank before his accounts on Bespin were shut down by the Empire. But under a pseudonym, Leia had a line of credit from the Alliance for use in emergencies, and Luke knew the account's access code. He figured this was as good a time as any to use it. Vidkun was willing to sell himself cheaply, too. The engineer's integrity was apparently worth about three months' salary—and that was not very much.

He was a short, thin man, fish-belly pale, with bulging brown eyes, a wispy beard and mustache, and more than his share of nose. He tended to clear his throat a lot. According to him, he worked nights, slept days, and seldom saw the sun, save when he went to and returned from his duties under the Imperial Complex. His wife, a somewhat younger woman, apparently had very expensive tastes.

"—see this conduit? This is the subsewer for the entire sector. You could drive a landspeeder through it; it's huge. The branch we want is here." He pointed to the holograph floating over the table. "That one drains Xizor's castle. There's a locked grate to keep out rats and snake eyes and other vermin, but maintenance has the key codes. After that, it's a clear shot to the building pipes, here. About a half kilometer is all."

He touched a control on the projector and the picture changed, enlarged as the viewpoint zoomed in closer on the mass of noodlelike tunnels.

"How big are those?" Lando said.

"You can see, they're to scale. Big enough for a couple of men to walk side by side, if they ain't too tall." He glanced at Chewie. "The Wook here'll have to hunch down some."

Chewie growled at the little man.

"Those go into the building itself?"

The engineer cleared his throat, a phlegmy rasp. "Yuh. There'll be another rat-grate where they enter the structure. We're not supposed to have the lock codes for those, but, well, it so happens my brother-in-law Daiv works for the firm that got the construction of Xizor's castle and I can give you those. For a consideration." He grinned, revealing yellow teeth that looked sharper than they should.

Luke and Lando exchanged glances.

"How much of a consideration?" Dash asked.

"Two hundred and fifty credits?"

"A hundred and twenty-five," Lando said before Dash could speak.

"Save us a lot of trouble, we got those codes."

"Blaster energy is cheaper," Lando said. "We can blow the locks. One-fifty."

"Make a lot of noise, you don't want that. One-seventy-five."

Lando nodded. "Okay, deal."

The engineer smiled nervously and continued. "Now, we got to watch out for the varmint zapper, here." He waved his finger through the diaphanous image. "Walk into that field and *bzzzt!* it'll cook you faster'n a high-amp microwave blast. As it happens, my other brother-in-law, Lair, he installs these things, and I have the bypass codes."

"For a consideration," Luke said. His voice was dry.

"Same price as the other?"

Lando cut his gaze to the ceiling.

Dash said, "All right."

"After that, all you got to worry about is getting out of the gather chamber and past whatever guards are down there. I can't help you there; Xizor uses his own people and I don't know any of 'em."

"We'll manage," Dash said.

Vidkun nodded. He stood.

"Where do you think you're going?" Lando said.

"Huh? Home."

"I don't think so," Dash said. "I think maybe you'll stay here with us."

"But you said you ain't ready to go until tomorrow."

"We changed our minds," Dash said. "We want to go now. And since we don't want to find a squad of stormtroopers or Black Sun guards waiting for us when we start wading through the sewers, we'd rather you didn't make any calls."

"Hey, I wouldn't turn you in!"

"Not unless you thought you could get more for us from Black Sun or the Empire," Lando said. "But since you're going to be leading us, anybody starts shooting, guess who gets it first?"

Vidkun looked nervous. He cleared his throat, swallowed, said, "How about if I call my wife and tell her? She'll be really mad at me if I don't."

"So buy her a nice present when you get back," Dash suggested. "You'll have a pocketful of credits, you can make it up to her."

The engineer rubbed at his face, flashed his orpimental smile again. "Yuh. Well. I guess so, since I don't have much of a choice."

"That's right," Dash said.

The planet-glow was so bright, the incoming and outgoing ships so plentiful that it never truly got dark here on Xizor's private balcony. There was apparently a brisk convection-downdraft blowing, generated as the buildings cooled and the night air slid down into the artificial canyons toward the streets far below. Apparently, because even here, many stories above the surface, Xizor's protections included hand-thick transparisteel plate wrapped around the balcony in an armored bubble. He could see but not feel the night. It was a small price to pay for the safe view.

There was always the option of donning a disguise if he wanted to walk along among the rabble, and thus far, the lack of personal freedom had not bothered him *that* much.

Guri approached from behind him, her footsteps barely audible.

"All of our security systems have reported," she said.

"And . . . ?"

"No unexpected activity. Nothing more threatening than usual."

He nodded. Waited a moment, then said, "I invited her up here." He waved at the view. "She refused."

There was a pause, longer than Guri would normally allow before speaking. She said, "Your pheromonal attractant was insufficient to bend her to your will; that has never happened before."

"I *had* noticed that, thank you."

"This failure has made her more appealing."

Xizor said, "Your point?"

"One wants more what one cannot have. As long as she resists your advances, her charisma grows stronger. The more she resists, the more you desire her. It has become a contest of wills."

He smiled. "So it has. Which I will win, eventually."

Guri said nothing.

"You doubt me?"

"You have never failed before."

Not really an answer, but true enough. "And you, my ever-vigilant bodyguard, you do not approve."

"The more intelligent and dedicated someone is, the more dangerous she can be when threatened."

He stared at a particularly congested lane of ground-to-space traffic. The running lamps of the vessels seemed to form an almost continuous line of bright-colored light.

He said, "You of all beings should understand. Much of life is about the search for equals. You are unique. There are others similar to you, but none exactly like you. You are superior to any other HRD ever created."

"Yes," she said.

"Don't you ever want to meet one who is capable of moving, of feeling, of thinking up to your level? An equal?"

"Not particularly. What would be the point? Greater than I, lesser than I, what does it matter to my functioning?"

He turned away from the light show in the skies and looked at her. "Yet you wish for tasks that will challenge you."

"Of course."

"It is the same thing. Yes, it is dangerous to contend

with one who might defeat you, and perhaps it is even more dangerous to consort with one who might some-day stab you as you lie sleeping next to her; still, the possibilities are so much . . . more.

"There are billions of women, many of whom are more beautiful, more adept physically, even more dedi-cated," he continued. "Maybe even all three. But this one is the one I want and I *will* have her."

Guri nodded once. "Ah. This is why you eat moon-glow."

He looked at her. She did understand, at least on some level. He nodded. "After I have accomplished the conquest, when I have grown tired of her, then you may eliminate her."

"After you have accomplished the conquest."

He smiled. Heard the unspoken "*If* you do" in her voice.

After Guri left, he returned to his skygazing. Most people would be thrilled to have found a partner with whom they could live in stimulation for the rest of their lives. He was not most people. He was, just as Guri was, unique. He would wait as long as necessary to taste Leia, and when he had done so, he would be satis-fied and finished with her. In his search for equals, she was close, but not quite as good as he.

So far, nobody in the galaxy had been, and he did not expect he would ever find such a person. He was, simply, superior to everyone.

He had learned to live with it.

"Threepio?"

"Yes, Master Luke?"

"Everything okay on the ship?"

There was a short pause. Luke twirled the small comlink absently in his fingers.

Threepio's voice was somewhat tinny from the com-link. "On the ship, yes. But Artoo has overheard some tactical communications on a shielded operations channel. Apparently there are search teams in the area. They seem to be looking for a Corellian freighter."

Luke stared at the comlink. "Hmm. Okay. Keep a sharp eye out. If anybody starts snooping around you, call me."

"Certainly I shall. Right away," Threepio said.

Luke chewed at his lip. They were about to go into the sewers. He didn't need any more problems.

Vader stood on the balcony of his castle, immune to the night breeze that washed over him. He had tried to reach out with the Force and find Luke, but had failed. Surely it *was* Luke? Who else could it be? And if it was —*where* he was exactly was probably not as important as *why* he was here in Imperial Center.

Had he come to challenge Vader? Had he been sent on some Rebel scheme to attack the Emperor? The protective line of Imperial warships would stop any attack by the Rebel forces, but it was designed to detect large vessels and not mites. A determined pilot in a small ship could find ways through the Imperial skynet.

What is it, my son? Why have you come here? Let yourself hear me, reveal your whereabouts and I will come to you.

If Luke heard his call, there was no response.

"My lord Vader," came the voice from behind him.

He turned. The little man who had supplied him with the damning information on Xizor stood there. Vader had left orders he was to be admitted no matter when he arrived.

"You have something for me?"

"Yes, my lord. We have uncovered a pirated copy of certain of the planetary files for Falleen, thought to be destroyed."

"Why should I find this interesting?"

"It contains some material about Prince Xizor's family. His father was king of a small nation there."

Vader frowned. "I knew his father was royalty, but I have been given to understand that Prince Xizor was orphaned at an early age."

"Not precisely, my lord. You may recall a biological experiment on Falleen that . . . went awry a decade or so past."

"Yes, I recall."

"During the, ah, *sterilization* procedure, some Imperial citizens' lives were lost."

"A regrettable incident."

The little man touched a control on his belt. A hologram appeared between him and Vader. It appeared to be a family portrait of eight Falleen. Vader looked at the group. There was a certain familial resemblance among them—wait. One of them was Xizor. He looked much the same, a little younger, perhaps. It was hard to say; Falleen aged very slowly; they were a long-lived species.

"Prince Xizor's family," the little man said. "All of whom were killed during the destruction of the mutant bacterium that escaped from the lab."

A light dawned then, bright and clear and sudden in Vader's mind. Ah! That explained much. It was not simply that Xizor considered Vader a competitor for the Emperor's affection, not merely a roadblock to his ambitions.

It was *personal*.

"How did the records of this come to be destroyed?"

The little man shook his head. "We do not know. For some reason, all references to Xizor's family simply vanished, shortly after the destruction of the city."

Darth Vader had been in charge of that project. Xizor must consider him responsible for the deaths of his family. And now he wanted to kill Luke—Vader's son. Not simply to make him lose face in the eyes of the Emperor, but for revenge!

It made sense. Through Black Sun, Xizor had the means to get to and eliminate the records. He was Falleen and thus patient. Was it not the Falleen who said that vengeance was like fine wine? It should be aged until it was perfect. They were cold, the lizard men; they could wait for a long time to get what they wanted.

Well. So could he.

"Once again you have served me well," Vader said. "When you finish this project, you will no longer have need to worry about money, such is my gratitude."

The little man bowed low. "My lord."

Vader waved him away. He had things to think about.

Things to do.

35

By the time they were ready to leave, the small band was outfitted with all the gear they thought they might need for a long hike through the sewers followed by an assault on a heavily fortified building.

Luke certainly didn't consider himself a Jedi Master, but he elected to use his lightsaber as a weapon. Chewie managed to locate a bowcaster, and Lando and Dash stuck to their own blasters. Nobody offered Vidkun a weapon—if the shooting started, they weren't at all sure which way he might be firing.

Dash had expressed it by saying that people like Vidkun were useful—but you didn't trust them any farther than you could see them. You paid them what you owed and then got as far away as you could, fast.

They elected to go during the daylight hours. Vidkun would normally be off work and thus would not be missed. That far under the ground, it wouldn't matter what the sun was doing, either.

Luke shifted some of the gear on his belt, adjusted

the small backpack so it rode more comfortably on his shoulders.

Dash said, "Ready?"

Everybody was.

"Let's do it."

Darth Vader received a call from the Emperor, via the holonet:

"My master."

"Lord Vader. How are things there?"

Why was he asking that? "Calm. There are no problems."

"Stay alert, Lord Vader. I have felt a disturbance in the Force."

"Yes, my master."

When the Emperor had discommed, Vader stood and stared into infinity. Was it Luke the Emperor sensed? Or something else? Black Sun and its amoral leader?

Well. It was time, he decided, to see if he could back that particular adversary into a corner. To his computer, he said, "Get me Prince Xizor."

In his sanctum, Xizor was mildly surprised at the incoming call.

"Lord Vader. What a pleasant surprise."

The image of Vader looked, as always, imperturbable. But when he spoke, the durasteel in his voice was barely covered by a thin layer of civility:

"Perhaps not so pleasant. I have been made aware of your attempts to kill Luke Skywalker. You will cease all attempts to harm the boy immediately."

Xizor kept his face neutral, even though he felt a violent surge of anger. "Your information is in error, Lord Vader. And even if it were correct, I am given to understand that the boy is a Rebel officer, all of whom are traitors and wanted dead or alive. Is this sudden change of policy an official Imperial decree?"

"If Skywalker is harmed, I will hold *you* personally accountable."

"I see. I assure you that if I should happen to come across Skywalker, I will extend to him the same courtesy I would to you, Lord Vader."

Vader broke the connection.

Xizor took a deep breath and exhaled slowly. Again he told himself it was to be expected that Vader would uncover some information about Skywalker sooner or later, as had the Emperor. Few things of any real value could be kept secret forever; still, it was another irritant. This should have no effect on his plans, either; he would merely have to be more circumspect in his actions. When Skywalker could not be found, Vader might *suspect* who was responsible, but as long as he did not have *proof,* Xizor would be safe.

Knowing that did not quite erase the lingering echo of fear.

Of course, the Emperor could always shift his stance. He had done so more than a few times and for reasons that often seemed capricious at best. Still, if Xizor could deliver the leaders of the Alliance, that would go a long way toward keeping Imperial favor. With the Rebellion beheaded, a lot of effort would be saved; billions of credits and tens of thousands of men and machines would be freed for the Emperor's other pleasures, whatever those might be. The Dark Lord of the Sith might rant, but as long as he was that useful, Xizor would be blasterproof and untouchable.

Darth Vader was too much the Emperor's puppet to go against Palpatine's wishes.

This conversation was thus mildly upsetting, nothing more, and in fact had given Xizor knowledge he had not had before. Vader was not sleeping, and that was good to know. Underestimating one's enemy was always a bad thing.

.   .   .

Leia went through the second exercise routine of the day, but kept it light. She might need to move in a hurry, and she wanted to be flexible and warmed up but not exhausted.

Things were about to happen.

36

The sludge was a greenish black, thick, oily, and it stank worse than anything Luke had ever smelled before. Dregs of the dregs, the silty goop was liquid, or at least fluid, and it flowed around their feet, sloshing sometimes deeper than their ankles.

Luke was very glad he had calf-length boots with his new clothes.

The tunnel in which they walked was as big as Vidkun had promised. It was lighted from a row of somewhat dim overhead glowsticks but bright enough to see as much as they wanted.

Something ahead of them chittered, and there came a pair of splashes, as if somebody had dropped a couple of head-size stones into the inky liquid.

Chewie, in the lead, muttered something. He sounded quite agitated. He stopped moving.

Lando, right behind him and just ahead of Luke and Vidkun, said, "I heard it. It's not my fault you didn't want to wear boots. Go on, it's more afraid of you than you are of it."

Behind them, bringing up the rear, Dash said, "Yeah, better watch yourself, Chewbacca! I hear that sewer serpents *love* Wookiee toes!"

Chewie's reply to that was short, sharp, and probably obscene.

Lando said, "Fine, forget the life debt you owe Han. Let the bad guys keep Leia because you're afraid of a toothless little slitherette."

Chewie growled, but started moving again.

Vidkun said, "What's with the Wook?"

"He doesn't like little swimming or running things," Luke said. "He *really* doesn't like 'em."

Vidkun shrugged. "A few hundred more meters," he said. He was apparently unaffected by their slog through the foul flow sloshing against their legs.

"Hey!" Dash said. "Look out!"

Luke spun, pulled his lightsaber from his belt, and thumbed the weapon's control on—

Just in time to see a large bloodshot eye pop up on a fleshy stalk attached to something slithering through the murky effluvium toward him. He also caught sight of Dash's fast draw. A dianoga!

"Don't shoot!" Luke ordered. With that, he dropped into a crouch and swung the lightsaber.

The dianoga tried to duck, but it was too slow. The shimmering beam of hard light sliced through the stalk, and the eye tumbled into the sludge. The wounded creature began to thrash wildly, heaving large and muscular coils of its body every which way.

Luke stepped in closer and brought the blade down. Hit the dianoga's body a solid blow and chopped it in half.

The cut pieces continued thrashing, but the spasms quickly subsided.

Dash spun his blaster around his finger and dropped it back into his holster. "Nice move, kid."

"I've seen these things before," Luke said. "Last time I ran into one was in a trash compactor. It nearly got me."

Chewie harned his agreement.

"You spend a lot of time in places like this?" Dash said.

"Not if I can help it."

The five of them continued to wade through the mire.

"Just ahead, there," Vidkun said.

They stopped. There were two large, round holes in the wall, covered with finger-thick metal mesh gates. The holes were angled down slightly. More sludge ran from the smaller tubes in a shallow stream to join the slow-moving slurry in the large pipe.

Lando said, "Okay, Vidkun, let's see if those codes you have work."

The engineer moved forward, did something to the locking mechanisms with a plastic card. The gates swung open. He grinned at them. "See? Just like I told you. We want the one on the right."

Chewie started to climb into the new tunnel. It was a little short for him, but the others should have no trouble walking upright in it.

Chewie slipped, nearly fell, managed to catch himself. He had to put one hand into the goo to do it, and when he pulled that hand out, it was as dark as the stuff that covered it. He shook his hand violently.

Chewie was *not* happy.

"Careful," Vidkun said. "It's a little slippery in places."

Chewie turned slowly to stare at Vidkun. Lucky for the engineer that Wookiee eyes weren't lasers; otherwise, Vidkun would have been burned into a crispy black lump where he stood.

Lando chuckled. "Yeah, be careful, you big clumsy —yow!"

Lando skidded and sat down in the sludge. He came

up fast, but not fast enough to keep his backside from being soaked.

Chewie laughed so hard Luke thought he might fall again.

Luke fought his own grin. It served Lando right, but he didn't want to be next, so he kept quiet. Things had a way of happening if you tempted fate.

"You should have worn old clothes," Dash put in.

"Hey, Rendar, I don't *have* any old clothes."

"You do now. I don't think you'll ever get 'em clean enough to wear in public. They'd drum you right out of the Elite Stormtroopers smelling like that."

"Shut up," Lando said.

They moved into the drain and climbed the slight incline very carefully.

"Coming on the zap field," Vidkun said. "Lemme run the deactivator."

Everybody stopped while the engineer fiddled with the controls on a small black box he pulled from his belt.

Just ahead of them the air shimmered. There was a brief flash of purplish light.

"Should be okay now," Vidkun said.

"Fine, you go first," Lando said.

The engineer glared at him but moved to the front. When he'd walked a few more meters without turning into crispy fried Vidkun, they followed him.

You'd think that after a while you'd get used to the smell, Luke thought. But it seemed to be constantly shifting, going from bad to worse, bringing forth stinks he'd never imagined.

It was going to take a real hot and real long shower to wash the stench off.

Where they walked, the sludge reflected the pale glowstick light onto the walls of the tunnel in eerie, rippling waves. The smallest sounds were magnified and echoed, lapping back at them from the hard duracrete walls.

"Not far now," the engineer said.

"Good," Lando, Luke, and Dash all said together. Chewie said something, too, and Luke didn't need a translator to figure out he was in agreement. Better to face Xizor's guards than endure this guck much longer.

"There," Vidkun whispered. "There is the entrance to the building. It leads into the recycler in the sub-subbasement. There won't be any guards inside the recycler itself, but there will probably be some in the adjoining flow chamber. Here's the key to the rat-grate." He handed a plastic card to Lando. "See you."

He turned to leave.

Dash stepped in front of him. "Where do you think you're going?"

"Hey, I'm done. I got you to the building, I got you the floor plans for the place, that was the deal."

"Well, I guess you have us there," Dash said. "That was the deal, all right. But see, there's been a little change in our itinerary."

Vidkun looked alarmed.

"Easy, we aren't going to blast you or anything. We'd just like you to come along until we get to a place where you can safely . . . wait for us."

Vidkun wasn't having any of it. "No offense or anything, but what if you get killed? I might be waiting a long time!"

"I guess you'll have to take that chance," Lando said. "It's not that we don't trust you. It's just that we don't trust you. Besides, it'll be a lot nicer inside." He waved at the gurgling black flow.

"I don't mind the runoff," Vidkun said. "I'm in it all the time."

"Nevertheless, we insist," Lando said. He patted his blaster.

Vidkun shrugged. "Well. Okay. Since you put it that way . . ."

And before anybody could react, he pulled a small

blaster of his own from his coverall and started shooting wildly.

Luke hadn't seen it coming. The guy didn't seem to
be the type. As a result, Luke was slow to clear his
lightsaber.

The first shot seared past, a clean miss.

The second shot hit Dash; Luke heard him grunt.
Move, Luke!

The engineer didn't get off a third shot because Dash
snapped his blaster up and put a bolt right between the
man's eyes.

Vidkun went down with a gooey splash that sprayed
black onto the tunnel walls. He slid a little way down
the gentle slope on his back, turned slightly, then
stopped.

A wisp of smoke rose from the ragged hole in his
forehead.

"Dash?"

"I'm okay. Just scorched me a little."

He turned and showed the burn along his left hip.
The bolt had sliced a clean line of Dash's coverall away
and raised a large blister. It wasn't even bleeding.

"Don't get any of this crud on you," Lando said,
waving at the sewage. "Probably wouldn't do you any
good."

"Where'd he get the blaster?" Luke said, replacing
his lightsaber.

"Must have had it all along," Lando said. "What
I'm wondering is, why'd he do it? We weren't going to
hurt him."

"Guy like that, he figures he sold out, why shouldn't
we?" Dash said.

Luke opened the first aid kit he'd brought and offered Dash a surgical dressing. Dash slapped the patch
on over his hip, pressed the seal, and relaxed a little as
the topical painkiller in the bandage coated the wound.
He moved to look down at Vidkun. "I stand cor-

rected," he said. "I guess we *were* going to blast you. But it wasn't our idea."

"Let's hope the guards didn't hear the shooting," Lando said.

"Yeah." Luke looked around, took a deep breath. "Ready?"

They were.

37

"Uh-oh," Luke whispered.

Crouched behind him in the recycler, Lando also whispered, "I do *not* need to hear that." A beat. "What?"

Even a whisper seemed loud in the chamber. More of the foul, murky fluid pooled around their ankles. A converter inset into the circular walls hummed and made yet more of the sewage, trickling it down an open drain.

"Guards," Luke said.

"So?"

"There are six of them."

"Six? To guard a sewage plant?"

Dash added his whisper: "So what? That's only one and a half each. How long does it take for you to pull a trigger, Calrissian?"

"Listen, pal, don't worry about how long I—"

"Shhh!" Luke said. He peered through the half-fogged cover plate on the recycler's door again. True,

there were six men only a few meters away; then again,
four of them sat at a table, playing cards, blast rifles
stacked against the wall. Two others stood near the
cardplayers, watching and apparently offering advice,
but they had their weapons slung over their shoulders.
Dash was right. If they moved fast, they could cover
the guards before they had a chance to unship their
rifles; they could disarm them, tie them up, and be on
their way with nobody the wiser. The trick was to do it
before one of the guards got his comlink out to call for
help.

Luke moved away from the cover plate and
crouched in the mire with the others. "Okay, here's the
deal. Dash, you pop the hatch; I'll go first; Chewie is
behind me, then Lando. You come last."

"Whoa, why that order?" Dash whispered. "And
who put you in charge?"

"I can stop a bolt with my lightsaber if one of the
guards is some kind of quick-draw expert. Chewie is
pretty impressive with his bowcaster; they'll pay more
attention to him than you or Lando. Plus he's a better
shot if it comes to that."

"Not a better shot than I am. And it'd be a lot easier
just to jump out and mow 'em all down," Dash said.
"We hit 'em fast and hard, they're history."

"That's the difference between us and the Empire,"
Luke said. "They wouldn't hesitate to do it that way.
We don't shoot unless we have to."

"Fine. Get us all killed being a nice guy."

Luke shook his head. A Jedi had to know how to be
active if the situation required it, but a Jedi was also
supposed to avoid violence whenever he could possibly
do so. "Warrior" and "killer" did not mean the same
thing.

"Okay. Ready?" Luke held the lightsaber down low
so the glow wouldn't give them away and clicked it on.
He took a couple of deep breaths.

"On three. One . . . two . . . *three*!"

Dash shoved the hatch open—

Luke leaped out, brought his lightsaber up into a ready stance—

"Nobody move!" he yelled—

Chewie jumped out behind him—

—the Wookiee's wet feet slid on the floor as if he were wearing ice skates, and he fell flat on his back—

Lando tried to leap over Chewie but tripped on the fallen Wookiee and sprawled facedown—

The startled guards leaped up and went for their weapons—

Oh, *man*!

Leia was sitting on the bed, when all of a sudden she felt a hot jolt of fear.

What—?

They might be stuck in a lousy assignment, but the guards weren't slow. The two standing unslung their blast rifles and swung them up, fired—

Luke blocked the first bolt, shifted in the Force, blocked the second—

Dash dived over Lando and Chewie, shoulder-rolled once, stretched out prone, fired once, twice, three times—

The two standing guards went down, but another one spun away from the wall, blast rifle spewing—

Chewie sat up, and the bowcaster spoke—

The third guard went down, but the fourth one shot at them—

Luke barely blocked a beam that vibrated his hands and arms hard, but the reflected bolt hit one of the overhead lamps and shattered it; the room went dimmer—

Dash's blaster spat hard light again and again; Chewie's bowcaster thrummed—

The guards were all down now, save one, but he didn't have a gun, he was yelling—

Yelling into a *comlink*—

Lando shot the last guard and he dropped; the comlink flew from his hand and rolled to a stop next to Luke's boots.

From the comlink came a tinny voice: "Thix? What is going on down there? Thix? Come in, sector one-one-three-eight, come in—"

Chewie came to his feet. The Wookiee shrugged and looked embarrassed.

Luke shook his head. Stomped down on the squawking comlink with his boot heel and smashed it.

"So much for sneaking in quietly," Lando said.

Xizor was paying the cultural minister his monthly bribe when Guri stepped into the room. The Dark Prince made polite noises and dismissed the minister.

When the man was gone, he said, "What?"

"A problem in the sub-subbasement."

"What kind of problem?"

She shrugged. "We don't know. That area is still not wired for surveillance and the guards are not answering."

"Another communication failure," he said. That happened a lot down where the pipes and conduits and heavy durasteel beams were thick, some kind of com wave interference the engineers had not been able to resolve. Dead spots, they called them. "It's either a com glitch—or Skywalker is faster and smarter than we thought. Have the drain sensors picked up any armies marching in under the building?"

"No."

"Good. If it is Skywalker, he's probably alone, or perhaps the Wookiee is with him. Send a unit to check it out."

"Two squads are already on the way," she said.

"Good. Send in the Moff on your way out. There is nothing to worry about."

There really wasn't anything to be worried about, he told himself. One *boy* wasn't going to get past his security, no matter how lucky he was.

Luke and the others ran. So far, the floor plan they'd memorized was accurate, but it was too big to have learned it all, and there was a chance they might blunder into a dead end if they weren't careful. Still, speed was the most important thing now; the place was alerted. They'd have to risk it—they couldn't afford to take the guided tour.

Chewie knew where Leia was, and he was in the lead.

The quartet came around a sharp corner in a wide corridor and nearly ran into four more guards.

Everybody who had a blaster started shooting.

From the comlink on Luke's belt, Threepio's strident and excited voice suddenly began calling: "Master Luke, Master Luke!"

Luke blocked an incoming blaster beam. He yelled at the comlink but left it on his belt: "We're busy here, Threepio!"

"But Master Luke, there are men coming toward the ship! Men with guns!"

Great. Just what he needed.

Luke deflected another beam, leaped forward, and found himself within reach of the man who'd shot at him. He whipped the lightsaber down, and the hand holding the blaster dropped to the floor. Luke spun and thrust a side kick at the guard, hit him squarely on the nose, and knocked him flat.

The other guards were all down as well. Luke pointed the way the guards had just come. "That way —it ought to be clear!"

As they ran, he pulled his comlink from his belt.
"Threepio?"

"Oh, dear, oh, dear!"

"Threepio!"

"Master Luke. Oh, what shall we do?"

"Take the ship out of there, now! Just like we talked
about. Artoo knows the systems; you can operate the
controls. Call me back when you're in the air. Keep it
suborbital and under the stratospheric security scanners, you got that?"

"Yes, Master Luke!"

"Go!"

Leia felt something in the air. A sense of impending . . . *something* she couldn't quite touch.

Luke. Luke was here.

She began to gather the parts of her disguise.

"We've lost contact with the second unit of guards,"
Guri told Xizor.

"Same area?"

"No. Four levels up."

Hmm. That was well above the normal area of com
problems in the castle. And an unlikely coincidence.

"Put security on full alert."

"Already done," she said.

Could it be Skywalker? Had he somehow gotten
into the castle without being detected? Or was it someone else?

"Cancel my appointments. Go and fetch Princess
Leia. Bring her to my strong room."

Chewie led them up another eight or ten floors before they ran into another group of guards. The exchange of blaster fire was fast, the air full of crackling

energy, yelling men, the smell of burned wall and ozone.

Dash was right about one thing: He could shoot. He nailed three guards with three shots—*zap, zap, zap!*—as fast as anybody Luke had ever seen. Luke himself deflected or blocked the bolts that came his way, the ricochets adding to the general confusion. Chewie and Lando pounded away with their weapons. The guards were not bad, but they weren't desperate. They were shooting for pay; Luke and his friends were shooting for their lives. The last guard standing turned and ran. Chewie spiked him and he did a belly flop onto the floor and skidded two meters before veering into a side wall and thumping to a halt.

"Go, go, go!"

Leia felt somebody approaching her room. Intuition, she guessed, but she trusted it. She grabbed one of the chairs and slid it next to the door. Stood on the back of it, balanced carefully against the wall, the heavy bounty hunter's helmet clutched tightly in her hands.

The door opened, and Guri stepped into the room. She was fast, but Leia had already started moving. Before Guri could turn, Leia hammered the back of her head with the helmet. It was a powerful blow and would have knocked a human woman unconscious. As it was, the impact was enough to off-balance the droid, and she stumbled forward.

That was enough for Leia to leap from the chair and scoot out of the room into the hall. She slapped the door control—

Guri recovered and was on the way back, when the door shut. Leia jammed the lock mechanism closed—

The door shook from Guri's impact.

The next hit splintered the heavy plastic, spiderwebbed it with tiny cracks. It wasn't going to hold her long, Leia knew.

She turned and ran.

Chewie led them up a stairwell a dozen levels above where they'd entered the castle.

"Master Luke? We have successfully left the building."

Threepio.

Luke pulled his comlink so he wouldn't have to yell at it. "Where are you?"

"Somewhere in the sky, Master Luke, I—what? Oh, be quiet, I'm flying it correctly, it—ah! Ahh!"

"Threepio?"

There was a moment of silence. Then a crunching noise. "I saw it, you blithering ash can! If you hadn't distracted me I would have turned in time."

"Threepio, what is going on?"

Luke heard Artoo whistling frantically in the background.

"Shut up, you twit! It was *not* my fault!"

"Threepio?"

The droid said, "What? Where? *Oh, no!*"

There came a sound like breaking glass.

"Threepio!"

"I'm sorry, Master Luke. Thanks to Artoo's woefully inadequate instructions, we've accidentally destroyed an advertising billboard and a broadcasting tower. No, I don't think we hit that hover van, we just brushed it. Yes, it was *too* your fault! If you hadn't been jabbering at me like an overheated *teakettle*, I would have—"

"Threepio, stop talking to Artoo and tell me what is going on."

"We are flying somewhat low to the ground because Artoo said we should, but I do think we should climb a bit higher. No, I don't care how much astronavigation you know, *I* am flying the ship now. Just give me the directions."

"All right. Listen. Bring the *Falcon* to the coordinates I told you. Hurry. And gain enough altitude so you don't hit anything."

"You see? I *told* you we were too low, but no, no one can tell *you* anything, *you* know it all—"

"Threepio!"

"Yes, Master Luke. We are on the way. No, I don't think we should go that way, that building is much too tall, we should go this way, oh, *look out*!"

Luke had to break the connection then. There was a door just ahead of them, a heavy fireproof door, and it was locked.

Lando leveled his blaster at it, but Luke stopped him. "Don't. It's magnetically shielded. That will bounce off and maybe hit one of us."

"How are we supposed to get through it, then?"

"Stand back. Let's see if it will stop a lightsaber."

He lit the blade.

The door would not stop a lightsaber.

They went through and continued to climb.

Guri burst into Xizor's strong room. He blinked at her. "What?"

"She got away. She was waiting when I got there. She struck me from behind. I am undamaged but it gave her enough time to slip out."

"Blast!" Xizor could not control his outburst. This was not good. This was his castle, and things were getting out of control. Had he underestimated Skywalker? Apparently so. Time to correct that.

He moved to a desk, opened a sliding panel. Removed from the hidden compartment a sleek and high-powered blaster.

"All right. Let's go find her. And whoever is causing these problems."

.   .   .

"Hold up a second," Lando said.

"What? Why?"

Lando pointed at a junction box inset into the wall. "This is a security breaker."

"So?"

"Move to that side."

Everybody did. Lando fired a blaster bolt into the simple lock mechanism, swung the thin plate open. "The surveillance holocams and sensors are routed through these fiber-optic cables." He waved his blaster at several finger-thick translucent white wires.

"How do you know that?"

"Trust me. I have some experience with such things." With that, he blasted the cables. Smoke and sparks spewed from the wall, made a short-lived fountain of yellow and orange before it shorted out. The acrid stink of burned plastic filled the corridor.

"Now they won't be able to see us, at least on this level. If we take out all of these we find, they'll go blind."

Chewie yelled something. Luke turned. More guards, and they weren't blind, although they shot as if they were. Good thing, too.

"This way!" Luke yelled.

Firing behind them, the four of them ran, blaster bolts stabbing after them.

They rounded another corner, zigzagged through a side corridor, and sprinted toward a door at the end of the hall. Heard somebody pounding toward the other side, saw the door start to slide back. Dash and Lando brought their guns up—

"No!" Luke yelled. "Don't shoot!"

The door opened wide to reveal—

"Leia!"

Luke grinned, and she returned it. He ran to her. They embraced.

"Took you long enough," she said. She looked closer at them, wrinkled her nose. "Gah, what have you been swimming in? You smell like that stuff Lando tried to feed us. And you look like it, too."

"The ship broke down," Luke said. "So we had to take a shortcut through the sewer."

Both of them glanced at Lando.

"It was not my fault about the ship," Lando said. "It was Han's modification!"

"Never mind. Let's get out of here."

Now five, they ran.

"Master Luke?"

"What is it now, Threepio?"

"We appear to have caught the attention of a robotic police vessel. It seems to be following us."

"Well, lose it."

"How, Master Luke?"

"Fly like Han does."

As she ran next to him, Leia's eyes went wide. "You're letting the *droids* fly the ship? Are you crazy?"

"They're doing all right. Just a few jitters, that's all. They're really doing quite well."

"No, shut up, Artoo!" Threepio said. "You heard what Master Luke said. I'll just loop around, whoa—yaahh!"

Artoo's whistles and squeals sounded even more frantic.

"Master Luke! Help! Help!"

"Threepio, what are you doing?"

Artoo's whistles sounded like a recording played at ultrahigh speed.

"I'm *trying* to turn it right side up! Be quiet. Ahh!"

"Sounds as if they are upside down," Lando said.

" 'Doing all right,' you said," Leia said. "I can't believe you let them fly the ship."

"Threepio, do what Artoo tells you! Artoo, show him how to pull out of the loop!"

There came another exchange of squeals and nervous chatter over the comlink.

"Ah, that's better. We seem to have lost the pursuer, Master Luke. I believe it smashed into that walkway we flew under while we were upside down."

"I can't believe you let the droids fly the—"

Luke glared at her. "Will you stop saying that?" He looked back at the comlink. "All right, you two, get to the coordinates like I said. And be more careful."

"We're doing quite well now, Master Luke. Don't worry."

Luke stared up at the ceiling and sighed.

38

"I'll sound the general alarm—" Guri said.

"*No!* How would that look? The head of Black Sun allows his security to be breached? Tell the perimeter guards to watch their backs—whoever got in had better not get out."

Guri nodded and spoke into her comlink.

They hurried down the corridor past the room from which Leia had escaped. There was a surveillance nexus, a substation not far ahead, where they could access the feed and see holograms of the holocam input. They would stop there and spot the intruders, who were inside the camnet once they ascended from the basement.

They arrived at the node. Guri tapped commands into an old-fashioned keypad. An image of Xizor's personal logo appeared in the air. She tapped in her security ID code, changed the reader from pad to vox access. "Display level fifteen, anybody not wearing an employee uniform."

The image broke into a million tiny dots, swirled like water going down a drain, then went blank.

Xizor frowned. Tapped his forehead with the blaster he held.

"Where is the image?" Guri asked the computer.

"Holocam and sensor feed on level fifteen are currently nonoperational."

"Display level sixteen."

Again, the image stayed blank.

"Display level seventeen."

The same.

"Display level eighteen."

The air swirled, and a multiple scan of empty hallways and rooms blinked into ghostly images.

"They are on seventeen," Xizor said.

Guri looked at him.

He waved the blaster at the images. "They're blowing out the breakers so we won't see them. If they'd gotten to eighteen yet, that floor would also be gone. Come on."

"We don't know how many of them there are," Guri said. "We've lost at least a dozen guards. It is too dangerous for you to go there."

"I will be the judge of what is too dangerous," he said. "And since we know it is Skywalker, this is where it ends. I will dispatch him *personally*!"

He would *not* be embarrassed in his own castle.

"So what . . . is . . . the plan?" Leia said, breathless.

"We get out of here," Luke said. "Get to the *Falcon* and get offworld as fast as we can." As if to head off her much-repeated amazement, he said, "Threepio and Artoo can do it."

She shook her head.

Chewie said something, and Leia guessed that the

Wookiee wasn't too pleased with their new pilots, either.

"Listen," Lando said, "if we don't get out of here, it doesn't matter who is flying what. Come on."

Leia nodded. Lando had a good grasp of the situation.

Dash said, "The man is right."

Luke said, "Nobody will think we're stupid enough to go up. They'll look for us to try and leave at ground level."

Lando laughed. "Yeah, that's the problem with our opposition—they keep thinking nobody could possibly be as stupid as we are. Fools 'em every time."

Leia shook her head again. She now carried a blaster somebody had taken from one of the fallen guards along the way, and that made her feel a little better. Not much better, but a little. She'd seen enough of Xizor to realize that if they couldn't escape, it would be better if he didn't take them alive. Beneath that charming facade lurked a monster, and she had no intention of falling into his hands again.

Xizor and Guri stepped into the turbolift. "Level twenty," Xizor ordered. "We'll wait for them there."

The turbolift dropped, gave him a moment of free fall that fluttered in his belly like a trapped bird trying to escape. Despite the anger he felt at being invaded, there was a sense of excitement about all this. It wasn't very often he got to dispatch people with his own hands. He was certain that the castle-breakers included Luke Skywalker. For daring to get this far, he would take particular pleasure in killing the boy.

He took a deep breath, exhaled part of it, fought for control. It was not seemly to allow his emotions such free play. Then again, there was no one here but Guri and his staff. He didn't care what she thought, and his guards were going to be replaced to a man after this was over. Failure of one was, as far as Xizor was concerned, failure of all. And those other than foot soldiers —the supervisors—would find their dismissals particularly painful.

The turbolift slowed. His weight seemed to increase as the floor of the lift pressed harder against the soles of his boots.

"Level twenty," the turbolift announced.

The door slid wide.

Xizor raised the blaster to point at the ceiling next to his right ear in a ready-carry position. He spent a few hours a week practicing at his personal firing range. He was an excellent shot.

Guri bore no weapon; though she also excelled at marksmanship, she seldom needed to use a blaster.

They stepped out into the corridor.

"Level twenty," Dash said. "Stairs end here, we'll have to zip in and find another set."

"How many levels are in this place?"

"As I recall, a hundred and two aboveground."

"Oh, man," Lando said. "And we have to go all the way to the roof?"

"No, there's a landing pad extending out from level fifty," Luke said.

"That's nothing. Another thirty flights, we won't even be breathing hard," Dash said.

"I can barely breathe now," Lando said.

"You're getting old, Calrissian."

"Yeah, and I'd like to get a lot *older*, too."

"There should be another set of stairs across the hall and down about sixty meters," Luke said. "Let's move."

They moved.

.   .   .

Xizor saw them first because Guri was opening a side door looking to see if they were already here and hiding. Five of them, Leia included. The Wookiee was there—he should have expected him to come back for her—and three men. One of them was dark-skinned; that would be the gambler. Another one was not somebody he recognized, and the third was Skywalker.

The Dark Prince smiled. Turned sideways, lowered his blaster, and extended it one-handed, his free hand on his opposite hip, just as if he were shooting targets in a sanctioned competition. Lined his sights up on Skywalker's left eye, let out half his breath, held it, squeezed the trigger gently . . .

Luke spotted the tall alien just as he brought his blaster to bear.

Uh-oh. Looked like the guy had spent a lot of time at the range.

He jerked his lightsaber from his belt, flicked it on, and let the Force claim him—

The deadly lance of energy rocketed at Luke—

His lightsaber came across, an inward move, and stopped as if by its own volition in front of his face, blocking the view from his left eye—

He felt the impact as the energy of his blade deflected the energy of the incoming bolt. It would have hit him right in the eye—

The alien fired again—

Again the lightsaber moved, directed by the Force. Another beam splashed harmlessly against the handmade Jedi weapon and bounced back and down, hit the floor, and burned through—

Xizor frowned. How could he *do* that? He couldn't be that fast!

He fired again—

Guri leaped out into the corridor. She held a chair, a heavy metal thing with casters on the bottom. She hurled it down the hallway as if it weighed no more than a pebble—

"Look out!" Luke yelled.

A chair pinwheeled at him. He couldn't use his saber to cut it down, and risk another bolt from the shooter—

Chewie stepped forward, level with Luke, brought his bowcaster up, fired—

The chair exploded into shrapnel and sprayed them with a prickly hail—

Leia saw Xizor and Guri in front of them. She snapped her borrowed blaster up and fired. Saw immediately that she was too high, tried to lower her sights—

Xizor realized two things: He was outgunned, and Skywalker could stop his fire. He was more startled than afraid, but he knew he had to get out of the hall fast. "Move!" he yelled at Guri.

She stepped in front of him and blocked him from the five down the hall as he stepped into the empty room from where she'd gotten the chair. A second later she joined him.

"That's an interesting trick he does with that lightsaber," Xizor observed.

"He *is* related to Vader," she said. "Shall I call the guards now?"

He sighed. "Call them."

She was already speaking into her comlink.

· · ·

"That was Xizor!" Leia yelled.

"Good. Let's get him!" Luke yelled back.

"I don't think so," Lando said. "Look!"

A dozen guards rounded the far end of the corridor and started shooting.

"In there!" Dash yelled.

There was a door to their left. Chewie opened it by smashing through it. Leia followed him, Lando and Dash behind her. Luke went last, blocking and batting aside beams that zipped at them like angry hornets.

Inside the room, some kind of office, they looked at each other.

"Now what?" Leia said.

Blaster bolts continued to whiz past the destroyed doorway.

Lando looked at Luke, who nodded. "Well," Lando said, "it's time for desperate measures." He reached into the small backpack he wore and came out with a round, silvery ball about the size of a man's fist. There were some controls, a finger-wide slot around the ball's equator and what looked like some kind of electronic diode on the top and in the slot.

Leia looked at the shiny ball, then at Luke. He nodded at Dash.

More blaster bolts sizzled past. They apparently hadn't noticed out there yet nobody was shooting back.

Dash took the ball from Lando. "It's a thermal detonator," he said. "Lando's got three of them. They run on a timer or a deadman's switch. Flip that switch right there, press that button in and hold it. If you let go without disarming the deadman's switch first, it goes off."

"And does what, exactly?"

"Makes a small thermonuclear fusion reaction."

"A small thermonuclear fusion reaction," she said.

"Yeah, just enough to vaporize a good-size chunk of whatever is next to it."

"I see. That includes us if it goes off in here, right?"

"Right. But we're betting your friend the leader of Black Sun won't want us to trigger it while he's around, not to mention what it would do to his castle."

She nodded. "Let me see it."

Dash's eyes went wide. Luke nodded at him.

Leia took the device, examined it. "And if you don't use the deadman's switch?"

"It runs on a timer. The default setting is five minutes. If you lock it in, here, once the timer starts, nobody can turn it off."

"Got it." She hefted the metal ball, then tucked it inside the bounty hunter's helmet hooked to her belt.

The males all looked at each other. Luke said, "Uh, Leia . . ."

"You said you had more of them, right? I want to hang on to this one. It might come in handy."

Luke shrugged. "Okay. We bought it with your money anyhow."

The blaster bolts outside the doorway stopped.

"I guess we'd better have a little talk with Xizor," Luke said.

Lando handed him another of the thermal detonators. Luke touched the controls. The device started making a beeping sound. Tiny lights winked on and off.

Luke took a deep breath.

Xizor moved out into the hall behind the dozen or so guards who moved toward an open door across from where he and Guri had ducked.

He heard a small noise, a repetitive beep. What was that?

Skywalker stepped out into the hall. The guards pointed their blasters, but the boy didn't have his lightsaber in hand. Instead, he held some kind of small device—

Xizor had not always been an armchair commander.

He had paid his dues in head-knocking and strongarm work, and he knew a bomb when he saw one.

"Don't shoot!" he yelled. "Lower your weapons!"

The guards looked at him as if he had gone mad, but they obeyed.

"Good idea," Luke said.

The other intruders and Leia moved out into the hall behind Skywalker.

The beep was suddenly very loud in the silence. Tiny lights blinked on the device.

"You know what this is?" Skywalker said.

"I have a pretty good idea," Xizor said.

"It's rigged with a deadman's switch," Luke said. "If I let it go . . ."

There was no need to finish that sentence.

"What do you want?"

"To leave. My friends and I."

"If you release the bomb, you'll die. So will your friends." He glanced at Leia. That would be such a waste.

The boy shrugged. "Like it stands, we're dead anyway. We have nothing to lose. How about you? You ready to give all this up?" He waved at the building around them. "This is a Class-A thermal detonator, you know what that means?"

Some of the guards knew, to judge from the sudden intakes of breath and muttered curses.

"I think you're bluffing."

"Only one way to find out. Your move."

Xizor thought about it. If the boy wasn't bluffing and somebody shot him, a Class-A TD would take out several floors of this building in a heartbeat. With that many of the support girders erased, the eighty-odd stories above would collapse. The structure might topple like a logged tree, to smash into the streets below. Or it might telescope straight down and flatten whatever base remained. Either way, the castle would be a total loss—as would anybody trapped inside it.

He could build another castle. But if the bomb went off this close, he wouldn't be around to do that. Was he willing to risk all he had worked for, his very life itself, that Skywalker was not suicidal? He was Vader's relative, wasn't he? Vader wouldn't bluff. And these Alliance types had demonstrated over and over again how brave they were against overwhelming odds.

No. He could not take the chance.

"All right. Leave. Nobody will stop you."

Alive, he would be able to chase them down. Dead, well, dead was dead.

Four of them edged past the guards, who nearly fell over themselves trying to get out of the way, as if a few meters would make any difference. Fools.

Skywalker stood facing him alone.

Xizor watched the others walk away. Maybe Guri could move fast enough to grab the thing before it exploded—

Where *was* Guri?

Maybe he could try a bluff, Xizor thought. To Skywalker, he said, "You've caused me a great deal of trouble."

"That's too bad," the boy said. "You had it coming."

"I could still shoot you."

"You could try." He still held the lightsaber. He flicked it on, held it loosely in one hand.

"I could shoot one of the others. Your friend the Wookiee. Or the princess."

"We'd all be vapor before he hit the floor. You included."

It was a standoff, and Skywalker knew it.

Xizor looked around. Suddenly the four stopped. The dark man reached into his pack and produced another shining ball.

Xizor smirked, said, "What's the point of that? You can't blow us up any more with two of those."

The dark man grinned. There was a garbage chute

next to him, and he opened it. It led to the recycling bins in the sub-subbasement. He flipped a control on the device. It started beeping and flashing—

Xizor had an awful premonition. He yelled, "No!"

But the man tossed the bomb into the chute.

"You have five minutes to leave the building," the dark man said. "If I were you I'd get moving."

Xizor spun, faced his guards. "Get to the turbolifts, get to the basement, and find that device! Get it out of here!"

But he was wasting his time. The guards panicked. They broke and ran, yelling frantically. They nearly knocked him over.

By the time he'd recovered, Skywalker and Leia and the others had gone, and the guards were hurrying to do the same.

Blast!

In five minutes, Xizor's castle was going to be destroyed.

Xizor ran, too. He had a private express turbolift. If he hurried, he'd have plenty of time to get to his personal ship and get clear.

His emotions raged uncontrolled. A cold fire cooked his reason into deadly anger. He would get his ship and he would follow them—to the end of the whole galaxy if he had to.

Then they were going to pay for this with their lives.

39

They took the lift and told it to hurry. Less than a minute later, they were on level fifty. During the trip, Luke shut the thermal detonator off and gave it back to Lando. It wasn't likely Xizor would have much luck getting guards to chase them now. Anybody with half a working brain would be heading for the nearest exit, especially given the alarms blaring so loud it was hard to think. Probably one of the outgoing guards had tripped the warning hooter.

They should have plenty of time to make their own escape—

If Threepio and Artoo had gotten there.

If not, they weren't going to have long to regret it.

The doors opened, and as they exited, twenty or thirty very excited people jammed in past them, stuffed the lift so full there was no room left. Those people who couldn't make it cursed or screamed or cried, moved to the next turbolift door, and pounded on the call button.

"Must be quitting time," Dash observed.

"They have four whole minutes," Lando said, his voice dry. "Better hurry."

"That's cold," Luke said.

"They should have thought about that when they decided to go to work for Black Sun," Lando said. "It's a high-risk operation, being a crook."

"The landing pad ought to be that way," Dash said. "Come on."

There didn't seem to be many people left in the hall. As they watched, another turbolift arrived, and what room there was—it was already half full of people, presumably from floors higher up—was quickly taken. When the doors closed, the five of them appeared to be alone.

They hurried in the direction Dash remembered was the right one.

Fifty meters down the hall, Luke heard something. He reached out with the Force, couldn't find anything. He waved the others on. "Go ahead, I'll be right there!"

They did as he said.

He pulled his lightsaber, flicked it on—

"Behold the Jedi Knight," a woman said. "The man of legend."

He turned. The woman called Guri stood there. A droid. Lando had described her in great detail on the way here.

"You have caused my master much misfortune," she said. "You should die for that."

Luke aimed the sword point at her. She didn't seem to be carrying any kind of weapon that he could see, but Lando had told him how fast she was. And how strong.

"But you have that blade and I am unarmed," she said. She held her hands away from her sides, empty palms facing him.

He had maybe three minutes. The smart thing to do

would be to cut her down and get moving. Or at least herd her out of the way using his sword and head for the rendezvous with—he hoped—the *Falcon*.

But—why start doing the smart thing now?

He clicked the lightsaber off, rehooked it to his belt, made sure it was securely fastened. "What do you want?"

"A test," she said. "My master pits himself against the deadliest opponents he can find. There is no man who is my equal in hand-to-hand combat. Except perhaps, if the stories are true, a Jedi Knight."

"This building is going to blow to pieces in three minutes," he said. "And you want to play games?"

"It won't take that long. Are you afraid to die, Skywalker?"

Yes, of course he was—

But then, in a moment, he realized that he really wasn't.

The Force was with him. Whatever happened, happened.

She leaped at him—

She was impossibly fast. On his own, he'd never have dodged, but he was permeated with the Force.

He stepped to his right and kicked at her as she flew past. Hit her on the hip and knocked her sideways, but not off her feet.

"Good," she said.

Glad she thought so. She was supernaturally fast, and it was only by holding to the Force that he could begin to match her.

She circled, looked for an opening—

"Luke—!"

Leia's scream distracted him. He flicked his gaze toward the sound of her voice, saw her and the others turn to look at him—

It was enough for Guri. She took a long, sliding step and punched—

Luke backpedaled, but even so, her fist hit him in the belly hard.

"Ooooff!"

She followed up with an elbow, but he dived away, rolled and turned, came up with his hands lifted as she darted after him—

He lost contact with the Force. He was on his own—

She slapped him next to the ear and he went down, dazed.

If he didn't do something fast, she was going to kill him!

The Force. Let it work for you, Luke.

Luke heard Ben's voice calling as if from a great distance, echoing across time and space. Yes. He managed a breath as Guri raised her hand, formed now into a blade instead of a fist, a grin of triumph lighting her features—

When he blew out his air, he blew his fear out with it.

He had to trust the Force *completely*—

Guri slowed, as if she were suddenly mired in thickened time. He saw her hand descending, saw it moving to smash him, but it was so incredibly slow, why, he could easily just roll aside and stand, before she ever reached him . . .

He did so. He felt as if he were moving at normal speed, though there was a crackling feeling to his motion, a sound like a strong wind whistling about his ears.

He came up, pivoted, thrust his open palm against the descending chop, shoved it aside. He used his left leg, a sweep that caught Guri behind the right ankle. Her feet left the floor, still moving in slow motion, and she fell, floated down, hit flat on her back . . .

Time speeded up.

Leia's yell still echoed down the corridor.

Guri hit the floor. He had never heard anybody fall

that hard; it was a thump that shook him where he stood.

It stunned her.

Luke pulled his lightsaber, ignited it. This droid was deadly, too dangerous to remain in existence. He lifted the blade.

Lying on her back, stunned, she managed to smile. "You won fairly," she said. "Go ahead."

She would have finished you.

Time stalled again, stretched like plastic melting in a hot fire . . .

Luke lowered the blade. Shut it off. "Come with us. We can have you reprogrammed."

She sat up. "No. If they can find a way around my brainblock, if somehow my memory is downloaded, it will be fatal for me—and my master. We have much to answer for. Better to kill me now."

"It's not your fault," he said. "You didn't program yourself."

"I am what I am, Jedi. I don't think there can be any salvation for me."

"Luke! Come on!"

He shook his head. "There's been enough killing," he said. "I'm not adding to it today." He nodded at her once, turned and ran.

Leia watched Luke click his lightsaber off, say something to the downed Guri, then turn and jog toward them.

She had lost track of the time, but it had to be getting close.

The five of them made it outside to the landing pad. There was no sign of the *Millennium Falcon*.

Xizor's personal ship, the *Virago*, was on the top level. Since it was always kept fueled and ready to go, it needed no preparation. He reached the ship. With the sounds of the emergency warning system braying over and over, he was somewhat surprised to see the ship guards still in place, albeit they were very nervous.

"The building is going to blow up," he said, as if talking about the weather. "Take one of the airspeeders and get away. You have two minutes to get clear."

The guards bowed and hurried away. Perhaps the failure of one was not the failure of all. These two guards would keep their jobs when this was done, maybe even get promoted. So rare to find loyalty these days.

He hurried onto the *Virago* and closed the hatch. It would take a minute to bring all the systems online. Thirty seconds later he would be five kilometers away —the *Virago* was one of the fastest ships on the planet.

He settled into the control seat, waved his hand over the computer sensors, and watched the screens light up. He would fly to his skyhook. He had his own navy stationed in and around the space station, several corvettes, a few frigates, hundreds of rebuilt surplus fighters. He assumed those responsible for destroying his castle had a ship standing by to rescue them.

By the time that ship made it into orbit, his navy would be waiting.

"All systems go," the *Virago*'s computer said.

Good. He reached for the lift controls. More than a minute left.

He paused for a second, looked through the viewscreen at his castle. It was too bad about its destruction. He had spent many good years here, and he would miss it. But he would rebuild, a bigger, better, more majestic place.

Until he could take over the Emperor's castle.

He touched the lift controls. The *Virago* rose smoothly from the pad and away into the bright sunshine.

He was a few hundred meters away, clear enough to

be safe, when he saw a beat-up Corellian freighter coming at him. The ship seemed to be out of control; it corkscrewed on its horizontal axis, pitched and yawed.

Xizor cursed, hit his emergency boosters, and turned. The *Virago* jagged to port, then jumped as if kicked by a giant boot.

The incoming ship barely missed him.

What kind of idiot was in control of that vessel?

It didn't matter. He was safe. For a moment, he wondered what had happened to Guri. Another loss.

Well. Life was difficult at times. The trick was to survive—and once again, the Dark Prince had done so. Survive, then make your enemies regret that you did.

Dash saw it first. "Mother of Madness!" he yelled, pointing.

Luke looked up and saw the *Millennium Falcon* coming in.

Coming in too fast and spinning like a demented toy gyroscope.

As they watched, the wobbly ship straightened; at least it stopped twirling, but it was still coming in too fast—

"Duck!" Lando hollered.

The five of them dropped flat.

The ship almost did a touch-and-go. It pulled up no more than a meter from the pad's deck and veered to starboard. The wind of its passage tugged at them.

Luke glanced up in the backwash just as the *Falcon*'s port edge hit a Doppler sensor array and shattered it, spraying pieces every which way.

"Threepio, I'm gonna kill you!" Lando roared.

Luke came up with the others and watched the ship circle around. He pulled his comlink. "Threepio, cut your drives! Bring it on the repulsors only! And hurry!"

"I'm trying, Master Luke. The controls are somewhat sensitive."

The ship hopped upward a hundred meters as if hurled from a sling.

Artoo was going to blow a circuit, he was whistling so fast and so loud.

The *Falcon* lurched, canted sideways, and fell. Righted itself just before it would have plowed into the roof, bounced upward on an invisible column of air.

Finally the ship lost speed. Seemed to float like a falling leaf on a gentle breeze, then stopped and hovered in place fifty meters above them.

Luke glanced around. Fifty meters, five thousand meters, it was too far away. They had less than a minute left.

"Bring it down, you fool droid!" Lando yelled.

"Too bad Leebo isn't at the controls," Dash said. "He's a pretty good pilot."

"While you're wishing, wish that *we* were at the controls," Leia said.

Standing next to the exit were what looked like two sets of folded wings. Abruptly Luke realized what they were: paragliders. Slip a set of those on and you could sail down to a shorter building's top, or kilometers away to the street. If the ship didn't get here in the next few seconds, he was going to strap Leia into one of those and throw her off the building. The other paraglider would have four passengers, one of them a Wookiee. They'd be way too heavy, but there was a chance it might work—he'd learned while fighting the walkers on Hoth that he could slow a fall considerably using the Force, and Master Yoda had taught him more—

"Here she comes!" Dash said.

The *Falcon* drifted down toward them. They backed up. The ship hovered over the landing pad two meters up, then dropped like a stone. The landing struts groaned but held. The belly hatch's ramp yawned wide.

"Go, go, go!" Luke yelled.

Chewie grabbed Leia, picked her up, and ran. Dash and Lando were right behind, and Luke followed.

By the time Luke made it into the ship, the ramp was already closing.

Luke followed the others toward the cockpit.

They had maybe thirty seconds left . . .

Dash got to the cockpit first, Lando and Luke right behind him.

"Move!" Dash yelled at Threepio.

"I'm moving, I'm moving!"

Dash shoved Threepio and slid into the seat. His hands danced over the controls.

Threepio fell into a heap against the copilot's seat. Artoo whistled frantically.

"You don't need to be so rude, Master Dash—"

There came a deep rumble from underneath them. The *Falcon* shook.

"Come on, Dash!" Lando yelled.

Luke looked through the screen, and even though they were in grave danger, he noticed something:

One of the sets of paragliders was gone.

The ship lurched, tilted, started to slide . . .

. . . lifted . . .

"Go, go!"

The *Millennium Falcon* spun away. As it did, Luke saw the building shake and the landing pad fall away, then drop straight down, like a tower of sand with the base kicked out. Smoke rose; a terrible screech like a giant nail being pulled from wet wood came with the smoke. Blasts of fire erupted skyward. Giant electrical conduits sprayed multicolored sparks. Things exploded and hurled shrapnel at them. The ship rocked under the impacts—

Dash hit the thrusters, and the *Falcon* leaped upward—

Below, the castle of Xizor, Underlord of Black Sun, collapsed into a heap of flaming, smoking ruin.

For once, even Lando didn't have a funny remark.

Leia joined the others in the crowded cockpit.

"Let's get out of here," Luke said. "Nothing fancy, just run as fast as we can."

"I hear you," Dash said.

Threepio got up from where he had fallen. "I thought I flew rather well," he said.

Everybody turned to stare at the droid.

"But I don't think I would like to do it again anytime soon," he hurried to add.

Luke shook his head, smiled, and started to chuckle.

It was an unstoppable release of nervous tension. In a few seconds, they were all laughing except Threepio and Artoo.

"What is so funny?" Threepio asked, indignant.

That set them off again. They'd made it. They were safe.

Well, almost. But at least the hard part should be over.

40

Xizor was angry and, save for the death of his family, could not recall ever having been more so. His castle was gone, his valuables, much of his massive information base, all destroyed in an instant. Artifacts and records that could not be replaced because they had no duplicates anywhere else. Blackmail files, personal projects, the most central secrets of Black Sun since he had taken over, gone—just like that. It would take years to recover, and should something happen to him, his successor would never know much of what was missing because he would never know it had ever *existed*. He wouldn't even know who had been responsible—all of the files on Skywalker and the princess had been in his personal computer, and it and its backups were slag.

Whatever anger he felt, it was no longer in his voice as Xizor called ahead to his skyhook. He had figured out that the small Corellian freighter that had nearly smashed into him as he leaped away from his castle was the same one his people had been searching for.

The same one that had come to rescue Skywalker and Leia and their friends.

Perhaps it had failed in that mission. Given the way things had been going of late, likely that was not so. Best to be sure.

Being the head of a shipping concern had some advantages when it came to describing ships: "There is a dilemma-saucer-style Corellian freighter leaving the planet shortly," he told the commander of his navy over the comm. "It is a YT-Thirteen Hundred, a little over twenty-five meters long, a hundred-ton capacity. Locate it and destroy it. If you can disable it and capture the crew and passengers, that would also be acceptable.

"If, however, it gets past, you and anybody else I consider responsible will be fertilizer before the next sunrise—are we perfectly clear on that?"

"Clear, my prince."

"Good." He reached for the comm switch to shut off the transmission. "I've got you now, Skywalker."

"I beg your pardon, Highness."

"What? Nothing. Never mind."

He flipped the switch and killed the transmission. Probably should not have mentioned Skywalker's name that way, but it didn't matter. The opchan was scrambled. It did not matter. He was so close to finishing this now.

He looked at the console's timer. He should be at the skyhook shortly.

"My lord Vader, you asked to see anything regarding this name," the officer said.

Vader stared at the man. Took the printout flimsy from him and scanned it.

"Where did this originate?"

"An encoded transmission from the ship *Virago,* my

lord, en route to the skyhook *Falleen's Fist* in high orbit. The ship is registered to—"

"I know who it is registered to," Vader said. He crumpled the thin plastic hardcopy sheet in his hand.

And though the attending officer could not see it, Darth Vader smiled, ignoring the pain it caused.

"Prepare my shuttle," he said.

He had warned Xizor to stay away from Luke. The criminal had chosen to ignore that order.

That was a grievous error.

As much as it was possible, Vader was delighted. They had played Xizor's game long enough. Now they would play his.

Dash said, "Take over, would you, Luke?"

"Sure." Luke, already in the copilot's seat, took the controls. "Where are you going?"

"Nowhere. I just need to whistle up my steed."

"What?"

Dash pulled a small black rectangular box from his belt. "Long-range shielded single-channel comlink. Time to have Leebo lift and put my ship into orbit. We can rendezvous; I can borrow one of your suits—this bucket still has vac-suits, doesn't it?—and get back to a real ship instead of this rickety crate."

Luke smiled. "I guess we can do that."

"After that, you go your way, I'll go mine. I figure the cleanup bill for that building down there ought to go a long way to balancing my account with the Empire."

"You really ought to consider signing on with the Alliance," Luke said. "You're a good man and we could use you."

"Thanks, Luke, but I don't think so. I'm not much of a joiner."

He tapped the command button on his specialized

comlink. "Hey, Leebo, you rust bucket, get your gears meshing and meet me at the following coordinates."

"My master is not in at the moment. Who is calling, please?"

"Very funny," Dash said. He looked at Luke. "Never buy a droid programmed by a failed comedian."

Xizor's landing at the skyhook was uneventful. His navy had already deployed. Since they had all the proper clearances, the Imperial Navy didn't bother them.

Xizor strode to his command center, a deck surrounded by transparisteel plate that allowed him an almost 360-degree unimpeded view of space around the skyhook.

He had the comm to his commander opened. A holoproj of the man appeared. "Yes, my prince?"

"Have you deployed your vessels, Commander?"

"Yes, Highness. Our sensors have been set to detect any ship matching the criteria you gave me. If it comes this way, we will spot it."

"Good. Keep me informed."

The image vanished, and Xizor stared out into the blackness of space. He had heard the buzz of conversation when he arrived. The rumor had reached here fast, though no one dared speak directly to him about the disaster below. Well. No matter. He had survived worse.

He would survive this; survive it and somehow turn it into a victory.

"Thanks for the ride," Dash said over the comm.

The *Outrider* hung just off the *Millennium Falcon*'s port bow in a matching orbit. If you had a good arm, you could hit it with a rock, even in full gravity. Dash had jetted across the short gap, complaining all the while about how bad the borrowed suit smelled.

"Want to race to the jump spot?" Luke said. He now sat at the controls, taking a turn piloting. Lando sat next to him, Leia stood behind them.

Dash laughed. "You want a parsec head start?"

"No, I—"

A hard green beam of light flashed between the two ships. The sighting ray of a big ship's cannon—you couldn't see the laser itself in vacuum, of course, but it followed the ionized marker you *could* see precisely.

Somebody was shooting at them.

"Uh-oh, looks like we got company."

More laser and charged-particle bolts blinked, none really close. Well, no closer than a couple of meters—

Luke punched it. The *Falcon* jumped like a startled hopperoo.

Lando said, "We've got an unmarked corvette coming in at two-seventy! And four fighters at three-five-nine! Those aren't Imperial ships! Who are these guys?"

"Who cares?" Luke said. "We've got to move! Chewie, the guns!"

"You heard the man, furball," Leia said. "You want dorsal or ventral?"

Chewie harned. He and Leia disappeared.

"Good luck, Dash!" Luke yelled.

"You, too, Luke."

Luke pointed the *Falcon* into the deep and ran. The ship rocked as a beam found the shields and splashed from them.

They needed to get clear of this system, fast, and make the jump to hyperspace.

"Prince Xizor, we have located the Corellian freighter," came the commander's voice from the holoproj.

"And . . . ?"

"We are engaging it now. It should be destroyed momentarily."

Xizor nodded. "Don't be too sure, Commander. They seem to be extremely lucky."

"They'll need more than luck, my prince. We have them completely surrounded. They'll need a miracle."

Xizor nodded again.

"There is a wall between us and where we need to go," Luke said.

"So find another way," Lando said. "You want me to fly her?"

"No."

A beam hit them, slapped them crooked. The shields held.

Lando yelled into the comlink. "I thought you two were supposed to be shooting back!"

Both Chewie and Leia yelled at him, but Luke was too busy flying to pay attention to what they said. He put the *Falcon* into a power climb and turned the move into a half twist at the top of the arc, heading back the way they'd come.

"Chewie wants to know how he's supposed to hit anything with you looping like that," Lando said.

"How can he miss? We're surrounded! He should hit something no matter where he shoots!"

A black shape zipped past them. The *Outrider,* cannons blazing.

Ahead of the *Falcon* a fighter exploded.

Lando said, "See how it's done, Chewie?"

Chewie yelled something back at Lando.

"Have you stopped the ship yet, Commander?"

"Not yet, Highness. They are, ah, quite skilled. And there are two ships returning our fire. We don't have a transponder signal on the other one, but it is heavily armed."

"If my navy can't defeat two ships it certainly needs another commander," Xizor said.

"We will defeat them. Our net is closing. They are running out of room."

The attacking ships had formed a loose hemisphere in space. There were an awful lot of civilian freighter and passenger ships going to and coming from the planet, and it was all Luke could do to avoid hitting one of them as he dodged the fighters buzzing them. The civilians tried to get out of the way, which made things worse. And sooner or later, the Imperial Navy was going to wake up and probably add to the confusion. Why they hadn't already made Luke wonder.

As he watched, one of the aggressors fired at the *Falcon*. The cannon's beam struck one of those passenger ships, punched a hole through a power converter, and caused a bright flash as the unit shorted out. Lot of damage, probably nobody hurt.

"Lousy shots," Lando said. "Don't care who they hit."

Luke nodded. He had thought they might weave in and out of the thick traffic and avoid being blasted, but it seemed Lando was right: The bad guys didn't care who got fried.

The attackers had them boxed. There didn't seem to be any way out. Too bad he couldn't get to his X-wing —though one more ship probably wouldn't be much help.

Things looked bad. Really bad . . .

One of the attacking fighters came straight at them, cannons winking hot plasma eyes—

The attacker exploded. The *Falcon* blew through the cloud of debris. It pattered like hard rain against the shields.

"Good shot!" Luke yelled. "Who got it, was that you, Leia?"

"Not me," her voice came back. "I've got plenty to worry about coming in from my side. Must have been Chewie."

Chewie said something.

Lando said, "Chewie says he didn't get it, either."

Luke blinked. Then who did?

Over the comm: "Hey, Luke! Okay if we join your party?"

"Wedge! What are you doing here?"

"Waiting for you. Dash's droid sent us a distress signal. Sorry it took so long to get here."

Another of the unmarked attackers blossomed into a fireball.

"Well, just don't let it happen again," Luke said. He grinned. Now that Rogue Squadron was here, the odds were a little better.

He swung the *Falcon* into a wide turn.

"There seems to be a slight problem, my prince," the commander said.

Xizor, watching the flashes of weapons and exploding ships from his deck, frowned. "So I noticed. Why are your ships blowing up, Commander?"

"A squadron of X-wing fighters has joined the fray. No more than a dozen of them. It will merely . . . delay the inevitable."

"Are you certain, Commander?"

"We still outnumber them twenty to one, Highness. And our frigates are standing by in case they get past the corvettes and fighters. They cannot escape."

"Hope that you are right, Commander."

Luke did a belly-twisting power dive at almost a ninety-degree angle to their path. A trio of fighters stayed with him, firing all the while. He was glad to see the Rogues on the one hand; on the other hand, they were losing the fight. With all the civilian traffic around, the wheelworlds and skyhooks, the power sats, the communications switching platforms and who knew what else, the space around Coruscant was anything but pure vacuum.

The comm hummed with conversations:

"I got 'em, Luke," Wedge said.

"No, let me," Dash said.

Another attacker blew up off the port side.

"That one was mine," Leia said. "You figured out who these guys are?"

"Not yet," Luke said.

"Bet you a credit they're Xizor's."

Luke and Lando exchanged glances. Of course, that made sense.

Not that it made any *difference*—

"Two coming in at one-fifty!" Lando yelled.

Luke punched it. The *Millennium Falcon* rocketed away in a steep turn.

"What are you *doing* up there?" Leia yelled.

"Giving you a perfect setup shot," Luke yelled back.

Vader stalked the bridge of the *Executor*.

"How long before we can get around the planet?" he asked.

"A few minutes, my lord," the nervous commander answered.

"As soon as we come within range, establish communications with the skyhook *Falleen's Fist*. I will speak with Prince Xizor."

"Of course, my lord."

.   .   .

"I think we got problems, buddy," Dash said. His voice was calm over the comm, but it was also resigned.

Luke nodded. "Wedge?"

"I'm afraid he's right, Luke. These guys are only so-so pilots, but there are a lot of 'em. I figure we're still outnumbered fifteen to one, and there are a couple of frigates who are just sitting there waiting. We don't have room to run, don't have room to maneuver. They're closing in and they don't care if they kill civilian ships, either."

"Yeah," Luke said. He took a deep breath. "Well, I guess all we can do is take as many of them with us as we can. Unless anybody wants to surrender?"

Both Dash and Wedge laughed.

"That's what I thought. May the Force be with you."

Luke flew as he had never flown before. He weaved, rolled, stalled, dived, threw power turns that came close to blacking them all out. He was giving it his best and he had the Force helping him, but they were losing.

It would only be a matter of time.

"Prince Xizor, we are starting to pick them off. Three of the X-wings have been destroyed or disabled. Our net is closing in. It will be only a matter of time."

Xizor nodded. Finally.

"Coming within range, Lord Vader."

"Good. Deploy your fighters."

Leia tracked the incoming fighter, fired, missed, swiveled in the gun seat. The fighter streaked past.

Well. There was another right behind it, and more behind that one. She lined up, fired, saw the lances of energy rake the attacker, saw part of a wing shatter and spew away, saw the wounded fighter spin out of control. There were hundreds of the blasted things, and counting Dash and the *Falcon,* they were down to what? nine, ten ships?

It looked as if Xizor was going to win after all.

Luke saw the TIE fighters screaming toward them. A dozen, at least.

Lando said, "Uh-oh."

"Yeah, I wondered what was keeping them." Luke looked at Lando. "Listen, thanks for everything, Lando. You've been a good friend."

"I don't want to hear that kind of talk. I still *am* a good friend."

Luke nodded, turned back to look at the TIE fighters. There was nowhere to go; space was thick with ships; it was like trying to fly through a hailstorm without being hit. He took a deep breath—

Saw the TIEs flash past. Watched them take out two of the unmarked attackers.

"Huh?" Lando said.

"Luke," came Leia's voice over the comlink, "I just saw—"

"I know, I know. What's going on?"

Xizor heard the panic in his commander's voice: "Highness, we're being attacked by the Imperial Navy!"

Next to him, a communications tech waved frantically.

Xizor fixed the man with a baleful stare. "This better be good, your life hangs in the balance."

"It—It's Lord Vader. He wants to speak to you."

Vader! He should have known!

"Put him on."

Vader's image swirled into being in front of him. Xizor went on the offensive immediately: "Lord Vader! Why is the Navy attacking my ships?"

There was a pause; then Vader said, "Because the ships, under your orders, are engaging in criminal activity."

"Nonsense! My ships are trying to stop a Rebel traitor who destroyed my castle!"

There came another pause. "You have two standard minutes to recall your vessels," Vader said. "And to offer yourself into my custody."

The coldness at Xizor's core blossomed uncontrolled into an angry heat. He tried to keep his voice calm. "I will not. I will take this up with the Emperor."

"The Emperor is not here. *I* speak for the Empire, Xizor."

"*Prince* Xizor."

"You may keep the title—for another two minutes."

Xizor forced a confident smile. "What are you going to do, Vader? Destroy my skyhook? You wouldn't dare. The Emperor—"

"I warned you to stay away from Skywalker. Recall your ships and surrender into my custody or pay the consequences. I will risk the Emperor's displeasure." He paused. "However, *you* will not be there to see it, this time."

Xizor felt a surge of fear as the image of Vader turned ghostly and vanished. Would he do it? Would he fire on the skyhook?

He had less than two minutes before he found out. He had better decide what he was going to do.

Fast.

"Luke, look out!" Lando yelled.

"I see him!"

Luke put the *Falcon* into a steep climb, but there were more ships looming at that angle, and he peeled off to starboard. The vacuum was filled with energy flashes, debris of destroyed fighters, more ships than he'd ever seen in such a small space. The area looked like a nest of angry mermyns.

But—while the TIE fighters occasionally fired on the X-wings, they seemed to be targeting the unmarked attackers. Xizor's ships. Why? "They're on the same side, aren't they?"

Luke didn't realize he'd spoken this aloud until Lando said, "Thank your lucky stars for small favors. If they're shooting at each other, they aren't shooting at *us*! Look out!"

Luke zagged, missed the incoming fighter by centimeters.

He felt a familiar disturbance in the Force then. *Vader?*

No time to worry about that, either. Luke put his questions aside for later—if there was a later for them —and concentrated on flying the *Falcon*.

The commander of Xizor's navy put in a frantic call to his master. Vader listened to the decoded communication over the speaker system.

"My prince, we are being destroyed by the attackers! We are outnumbered and being slaughtered! I need permission to offer our surrender! Highness?"

Vader watched the chronometer, enjoyed the time melting away. Not much left for the Dark Prince now.

Seven seconds . . . six seconds . . . five . . .

The terrified commander kept babbling: "Prince Xizor, please respond! We must surrender or we will be blown to pieces! Please!"

. . . four seconds left . . . three seconds . . .

"Highness, I—" The commander's transmission ended abruptly. One of the Imperial fighters must have gotten him.

. . . two . . . one—

"Commander, destroy the skyhook."

One did not stay in command of Darth Vader's ship by questioning orders. "Yes, my lord."

Darth Vader took a deep breath, painful as it was to do so, and let it out slowly. Smiled, unseen.

Goodbye, Xizor. And good riddance.

As it happened, the *Millennium Falcon* was facing it when the skyhook exploded.

Luke saw the giant Star Destroyer's powerful beam strobe, saw it pierce the skyhook. The planetoid shattered, blew apart, went nova, became a small star that burned brightly for an instant before it faded, leaving millions of glowing pieces behind.

It was a spectacular sight, for all its violence. It reminded Luke of the explosion that had destroyed the Death Star.

"Oh, man," Lando said softly. "They must have made somebody real mad."

Luke shook his head, didn't speak.

Dash said, "Heads up, boys. Follow me."

Luke blinked. "Huh?"

"Somebody just opened us an escape hatch."

"Are you crazy? We can't fly through that wreckage!"

"We don't have a choice. There are ships everywhere. What's the matter, kid? Don't think you can do it?"

"If you can, my *droid* can. Go." Luke understood what Dash meant. It would be tricky, dangerous, but the space around the destroyed skyhook was relatively clear—the debris was expanding outward. If they could avoid being holed by the stuff on the way there, it was their best chance.

"Yeeeehaww!" somebody in Rogue Squadron yelled.

Luke laughed. He knew just how they felt.

They headed for the debris, and it looked as if it was going to be just fine. The good guys had triumphed!

"*Look out, Dash!*" Lando yelled.

Luke could hardly spare a glance, but he did. Just in time to see a block of shattered skyhook the size of a resiplex zero in on the *Outrider*.

"Dash!" Luke yelled. It was too close to avoid—

There was an actinic flare of light too bright to look at. Luke turned away, saw Lando throw one arm up to block the glare.

When the light faded, the *Outrider* had vanished.

"Oh, man," Lando said. "He—he's . . . gone."

Just like that.

The sweet taste of triumph went bitter in Luke's mouth.

There wasn't time to worry about it now. "Brace yourselves! This is going to be rough!"

The debris flashed around them, impacts waiting at every turn. He was sorry about Dash—the man had turned out to be okay after all—but he didn't want to end up a pile of flaming rubble. He let the Force take him and flew.

The secret Alliance base was light-years away from Coruscant and they had barely made it—but they *had* made it.

Luke stood with Leia, Lando, and Chewie, with Threepio and Artoo behind them. The building was, like so many of the Alliance structures, a big, cheap prefab unit. It did boast a large transparisteel that faced out from the surface of the asteroid into the blackness of space. Luke stared through the thick transparisteel into the depths of the galaxy.

"So, if Xizor was on that skyhook like our intelligence reports say, I would guess that would put a stop to Black Sun bounty hunters looking to kill you," Lando said.

"There's still Vader," Leia said.

Luke looked at her, shook his head. "I don't think Vader wants me dead. Yet, anyway. I'll deal with him when the time comes."

They looked up to see Wedge approaching. "Got a message for you, Luke," Wedge said, "from the Bothans. It was for Dash, but, well . . ." He trailed off. "Um. Anyway, that missile Dash supposedly missed during that fracas off Kothlis? Turns out he didn't miss."

"What?" Luke blinked at Wedge.

"Thing was one of the Empire's new diamond-boron-armored jobs. Nothing he had to throw at it could have stopped it. The Bothans wanted him to know."

Luke felt a lump of liquid air form in his belly. Oh, man. Dash hadn't screwed up, but now he would never know. How awful, to get taken out before you could learn that you *hadn't* been responsible for the loss of your comrades. And worse was the knowledge that Luke had felt just a little bit glad—not for the deaths, but to see the braggart Dash taken down a notch.

Oh, *man.*

"What are you going to do now?" Wedge said.

"We're going to get Han," Luke said. "If he isn't on Tatooine yet, he soon will be."

"Going to dance into the Hutt's guarded palace and get him? Just like that?" Wedge said.

"I have a plan," Luke said.

He turned and looked at the stars. Maybe he wasn't a Master yet, but he had learned a lot.

He was a Jedi Knight, and that was enough for now.

Epilogue

In the Emperor's most private sanctum, Darth Vader knelt before his master. He believed he had reason to be worried.

"You defied my orders, Lord Vader."

"Yes, my master. But I hope I have not failed you."

"Get up."

Vader stood.

The Emperor favored Vader with a dark smile. "I am not unaware that Xizor served his own ends and that you were shrewd to have uncovered his plot. I knew about it, of course."

Vader did not speak.

"Are we certain he is dead?"

"I do not see how he could have survived. I watched his skyhook blown to bits."

"Just as well. Black Sun is useful, but it is also like a chirru: Cut off its head and another will appear to replace it." He cackled, amused at his own simile.

"Perhaps the next leader will be equally dangerous," Vader said.

"No leader of Black Sun could ever be a match for the power of the dark side."

"But what of the plot to ensnare the Rebel leaders?"

"The new Death Star will draw them in, and this time, you and I will be there to finish this Rebellion."

Vader wanted to shake his head. As always, the Emperor was one step ahead of him.

"Young Skywalker will be there, too. I have seen it."

Vader sighed.

"It is all proceeding exactly as I have foreseen it, Lord Vader."

He smiled again, and Vader felt a chill touch him. Truly there was no one in the galaxy who had control of the dark side as did the Emperor. It was a weakness in Vader that he could feel that fear. Some part of Anakin Skywalker still existed in him, despite all he had done. He would have to eliminate it or it would eventually be his undoing.

In Ben's house on Tatooine, Luke took a deep breath and reached for calmness. They didn't expect that Jabba would be interested in the proposal, given what they had learned about how nasty he was, but that was not the point. Lando had a way in, as did Chewie and Leia, and this should get Threepio and Artoo into the palace. If the Hutt was willing to negotiate, it would save a lot of trouble, but none of them really expected it. Jabba was, according to all they'd learned, extremely mean-spirited, and he didn't need the money. Too bad.

Oh, well. They'd just have to do things the hard way. What else was new?

"Okay, Artoo, start recording."

Artoo bleeped.

"Greetings, Exalted One. Allow me to introduce myself. I am Luke Skywalker, Jedi Knight and friend to

Captain Solo. I know that you are powerful, mighty
Jabba, and that your anger with Solo must be equally
powerful. I seek an audience with Your Greatness to
bargain for Solo's life."

That ought to be servile enough, though if what
they'd heard was true, Jabba would probably start
laughing about now. Luke paused for a moment,
caught his breath, went on:

"With your wisdom, I'm sure that we can work
out an arrangement which will be mutually beneficial
and enable us to avoid any unpleasant confronta-
tion."

Small chance of that. But he pressed on:

"As a token of my goodwill, I present to you a gift—
these two droids."

Luke fought the grin that threatened him: No doubt
whatsoever that Threepio would be stunned to hear
this when the recording was played. Luke had considered telling him but thought it would be better if he
didn't know. He got rattled so easily. Besides,
Threepio's surprise would help convince Jabba.

"Both are hardworking and will serve you well,"
Luke finished.

He glanced at Artoo, raised an eyebrow, and the little droid shut his recorder off.

Leia, standing behind Artoo, shook her head. "You
think that will do it?"

Luke shrugged. "I hope so. Only one way to find
out."

She moved closer, touched his arm.

Luke said, "Hey, after all we just went through,
rescuing one beat-up old pirate ought to be easy,
right?"

She smiled. "Right."

He returned her smile. His emotions were mixed. He
didn't know how she really felt, about him or about
that beat-up old pirate, but he knew how he felt about

both of them. Whatever happened, he had to do the right thing; that was just how things were. And the right thing here was simple, if not easy.

Hang on, Han.

We're coming for you.

ABOUT THE AUTHOR

STEVE PERRY is the author of dozens of science fiction and fantasy novels, the most recent of which is *Spindoc,* and numerous teleplays for a variety of series. He lives in Oregon with his wife, who publishes a small monthly newspaper.

The World of
STAR WARS Novels

In May 1991, *Star Wars* caused a sensation in the publishing industry with the Bantam Spectra release of Timothy Zahn's novel *Heir to the Empire*. For the first time, Lucasfilm Ltd. had authorized new novels that *continued* the famous story told in George Lucas's three block-buster motion pictures: *Star Wars*, *The Empire Strikes Back*, and *Return of the Jedi*. Reader reaction was immediate and tumultuous: *Heir* reached #1 on the *New York Times* bestseller list and demonstrated that *Star Wars* lovers were eager for exciting new stories set in this universe, written by leading science fiction authors who shared their passion. Since then, each Bantam *Star Wars* novel has been an instant national bestseller.

Lucasfilm and Bantam decided that future novels in the series would be interconnected: that is, events in one novel would have consequences in the others. You might say that each Bantam *Star Wars* novel, enjoyable on its own, is also part of a much larger tale.

Here is a special look at Bantam's *Star Wars* books, along with excerpts from the more recent novels. Each one is available now wherever Bantam Books are sold.

SHADOWS OF THE EMPIRE
by Steve Perry
Setting: Between *The Empire Strikes Back* and *Return of the Jedi*

Here is a very special STAR WARS story dealing with Black Sun, a galaxy-spanning criminal organization that is masterminded by one of the most interesting villains in the STAR WARS universe: Xizor, dark prince of the Falleen. Xizor's chief rival for the favor of Emperor Palpatine is none other than Darth Vader himself—alive and well, and a major character in this story, since it is set during the events of the STAR WARS film trilogy.

In the opening prologue, we revisit a familiar scene from The Empire Strikes Back, *and are introduced to our marvelous new bad guy:*

He looks like a walking corpse, Xizor thought. *Like a mummified body dead a thousand years. Amazing he is still alive, much less the most powerful man in the galaxy. He isn't even that old; it is more as if something is slowly eating him.*

Xizor stood four meters away from the Emperor, watching as the man who had long ago been Senator Palpatine moved to stand in the holocam field. He imagined he could smell the decay in the Emperor's worn body. Likely that was just some trick of the recycled air, run through dozens of filters to ensure that there was no chance of any poison gas being introduced into it. Filtered the life out of it, perhaps, giving it that dead smell.

The viewer on the other end of the holo-link would see a close-up of the Emperor's head and shoulders, of an age-ravaged face shrouded in the cowl of his dark zeyd-cloth robe. The man on the other end of the transmission, light-years away, would not see Xizor, though Xizor would be able to see him. It was a measure of the Emperor's trust that Xizor was allowed to be here while the conversation took place.

The man on the other end of the transmission—if he could still be called that—

The air swirled inside the Imperial chamber in front of the Emperor, coalesced, and blossomed into the image of a figure down on one knee. A caped humanoid biped dressed in jet black, face hidden under a full helmet and breathing mask:

Darth Vader.

Vader spoke: "What is thy bidding, my master?"

If Xizor could have hurled a power bolt through time and space to strike Vader dead, he would have done it without blinking. Wishful thinking: Vader was too powerful to attack directly.

"There is a great disturbance in the Force," the Emperor said.

"I have felt it," Vader said.

"We have a new enemy. Luke Skywalker."

Skywalker? That had been Vader's name, a long time ago. Who was this person with the same name, someone so powerful as to be worth a conversation between the Emperor and his most loathsome creation? More importantly, why had Xizor's agents not uncovered this before now? Xizor's ire was instant—but cold. No sign of his surprise or anger would show on his imperturbable features. The Falleen did not allow their emotions to burst forth as did many of the inferior species; no, the Falleen ancestry was not fur but scales, not mammalian but reptilian. Not wild but coolly calculating. Such was much better. Much safer.

"Yes, my master," Vader continued.

"He could destroy us," the Emperor said.

Xizor's attention was riveted upon the Emperor and the holographic image of Vader kneeling on the deck of a ship far away. Here was interesting news indeed. Something the Emperor perceived as a danger to himself? Something the Emperor feared?

"He's just a boy," Vader said. "Obi-Wan can no longer help him."

Obi-Wan. That name Xizor knew. He was among the last of the Jedi Knights, a general. But he'd been dead for decades, hadn't he?

Apparently Xizor's information was wrong if Obi-Wan had been helping someone who was still a boy. His agents were going to be sorry.

Even as Xizor took in the distant image of Vader and the nearness of the Emperor, even as he was aware of the luxury of the Emperor's private and protected chamber at the core of the giant pyramidal palace, he was also able to make a mental note to himself: Somebody's head would roll for the failure to make him aware of all this. Knowledge was power; lack of knowledge was weakness. This was something he could not permit.

The Emperor continued. "The Force is strong with him. The son of Skywalker must not become a Jedi."

Son of Skywalker?

Vader's son! Amazing!

"If he could be turned he would become a powerful ally," Vader said.

There was something in Vader's voice when he said this, something Xizor could not quite put his finger on. Longing? Worry?

Hope?

"Yes . . . yes. He would be a great asset," the Emperor said. "Can it be done?"

There was the briefest of pauses. "He will join us or die, master."

Xizor felt the smile, though he did not allow it to show any more than he had allowed his anger play. Ah. Vader wanted Skywalker alive, *that* was what had been in his tone. Yes, he had said that the boy would join them or die, but this latter part was obviously meant only to placate the Emperor. Vader had no intention of killing Skywalker, his own son; that was obvious to one as skilled in reading voices as was Xizor. He had not gotten to be the Dark Prince, Underlord of Black Sun, the largest criminal organization in the galaxy, merely on his formidable good looks. Xizor didn't truly understand the Force that sustained the Emperor and made him and Vader so powerful, save to know that it certainly worked somehow. But he did know that it was something the extinct Jedi had supposedly mastered. And now, apparently, this new player had tapped into it. Vader wanted Skywalker alive, had practically promised the Emperor that he would deliver him alive—and converted.

This was most interesting.

Most interesting indeed.

The Emperor finished his communication and turned back to face him. "Now, where were we, Prince Xizor?"

The Dark Prince smiled. He would attend to the business at hand, but he would not forget the name of Luke Skywalker.

THE TRUCE AT BAKURA by Kathy Tyers
Setting: Immediately after *Return of the Jedi*

The day after his climactic battle with Emperor Palpatine and the sacrifice of his father, Darth Vader, who died saving his life, Luke Skywalker helps recover an Imperial drone ship bearing a startling message intended for the Emperor. It is a distress signal from the far-off Imperial outpost of Bakura, which is under attack by an alien invasion force, the Ssi-ruuk. Leia sees a rescue mission as an opportunity to achieve a diplomatic victory for the Rebel Alliance, even if it means fighting alongside former Imperials. But Luke receives a vision from Obi-Wan Kenobi revealing that the stakes are even higher: the invasion at Bakura threatens everything the Rebels have won at such great cost.

STAR WARS: X-WING
by Michael A. Stackpole
ROGUE SQUADRON
WEDGE'S GAMBLE
THE KRYTOS TRAP
THE BACTA WAR
Setting: Three years after *Return of the Jedi*

Inspired by X-wing, the bestselling computer game from LucasArts Entertainment Co., this exciting series chronicles the further adventures of the most feared and fearless fighting force in the galaxy. A new generation of X-wing pilots, led by Commander Wedge Antilles, is combating the remnants of the Empire still left after the events of the STAR WARS movies. Here are novels full of explosive space action, nonstop adventure, and the special brand of wonder known as STAR WARS.

In this very early scene, young Corellian pilot Corran Horn faces a tough challenge fast enough to get his heart pounding—and this is only a simulation! [P.S.: "Whistler" is Corran's R2 astromech droid]:

The Corellian brought his proton torpedo targeting program up and locked on to the TIE. It tried to break the lock, but turbolaser fire from the *Korolev* boxed it in. Corran's heads-up display went red and he triggered the torpedo. "Scratch one eyeball."

The missile shot straight in at the fighter, but the pilot broke hard to port and away, causing the missile to overshoot the target. *Nice flying!* Corran brought his X-wing over and started down to loop in behind the TIE, but as he did so, the TIE vanished from his forward screen and reappeared in his aft arc. Yanking the stick hard to the right and pulling it back, Corran wrestled the X-wing up and to starboard, then inverted and rolled out to the left.

A laser shot jolted a tremor through the simulator's couch. *Lucky thing I had all shields aft!* Corran reinforced them with energy from his lasers, then evened them out fore and aft. Jinking the fighter right and left, he avoided laser shots coming in from behind, but they all came in far closer than he liked.

He knew Jace had been in the bomber, and Jace was the only pilot in the unit who could have stayed with him. *Except for our leader.* Corran smiled broadly. *Coming to see how good I really am, Commander Antilles? Let me give you a clinic.* "Make sure you're in there solid, Whistler, because we're going for a little ride."

Corran refused to let the R2's moan slow him down. A snap-roll brought the X-wing up on its port wing. Pulling back on the stick yanked the fighter's nose up away from the original line of flight. The TIE stayed with him, then tightened up on the arc to close distance. Corran then rolled another ninety degrees and continued the turn into a dive. Throttling back, Corran hung in the dive for three seconds, then hauled back hard on the stick and cruised up into the TIE fighter's aft.

The X-wing's laser fire missed wide to the right as the TIE cut to the left. Corran kicked his speed up to full and broke with the TIE. He let the X-wing rise above the plane of the break, then put the fighter through a twisting roll that ate up enough time to bring him again into the TIE's rear. The TIE snapped to the right and Corran looped out left.

He watched the tracking display as the distance between them grew to be a kilometer and a half, then slowed. *Fine, you want to go nose to nose? I've got shields and you don't.* If Commander Antilles wanted to commit virtual suicide, Corran was happy to oblige him. He tugged the stick back to his sternum and rolled out in an inversion loop. *Coming at you!*

The two starfighters closed swiftly. Corran centered his foe in the crosshairs and waited for a dead shot. Without shields the TIE fighter would die with one burst, and Corran wanted the kill to be clean. His HUD flicked green as the TIE juked in and out of the center, then locked green as they closed.

The TIE started firing at maximum range and scored hits. At that distance the lasers did no real damage against the shields, prompting Corran to wonder why Wedge was wasting the energy. Then, as the HUD's green color started to flicker, realization dawned. *The bright bursts on the shields are a distraction to my targeting! I better kill him now!*

Corran tightened down on the trigger button, sending red laser needles stabbing out at the closing TIE fighter. He couldn't tell if he had hit anything. Lights flashed in the cockpit and Whistler started screeching furiously. Corran's main monitor went black, his shields were down, and his weapons controls were dead.

The pilot looked left and right. "Where is he, Whistler?"

The monitor in front of him flickered to life and a diagnostic report began to scroll by. Bloodred bordered the damage reports. "Scanners, out; lasers, out; shields, out; engine, out! I'm a wallowing Hutt just hanging here in space."

THE COURTSHIP OF PRINCESS LEIA
by Dave Wolverton
Setting: Four years after *Return of the Jedi*

One of the most interesting developments in Bantam's Star Wars *novels is that in their storyline, Han Solo and Princess Leia start a family. This tale reveals how the couple originally got together. Wishing to strengthen the fledgling New Republic by bringing in powerful allies, Leia opens talks with the Hapes consortium of more than sixty worlds. But the consortium is ruled by the Queen Mother, who, to Han's dismay, wants Leia to marry her son, Prince Isolder. Before this action-packed story is over, Luke will join forces with Isolder against a group of Force-trained "witches" and face a deadly foe.*

HEIR TO THE EMPIRE
DARK FORCE RISING
THE LAST COMMAND
by Timothy Zahn
Setting: Five years after *Return of the Jedi*

This #1 bestselling trilogy introduces two legendary forces of evil into the Star Wars *literary pantheon. Grand Admiral Thrawn has taken control of the Imperial fleet in the years since the destruction of the Death Star, and the mysterious Joruus C'baoth is a fearsome Jedi Master who has been seduced by the dark side. Han and Leia have now been married for about a year, and as the story begins, she is pregnant with twins. Thrawn's plan is to crush the Rebellion and resurrect the Empire's New Order with C'baoth's help—and in return, the Dark Master will get Han and Leia's Jedi children to mold as he wishes. For as readers of this magnificent trilogy will see, Luke Skywalker is not the last of the old Jedi. He is the first of the new.*

The Jedi Academy Trilogy:
JEDI SEARCH
DARK APPRENTICE
CHAMPIONS OF THE FORCE
by Kevin J. Anderson
Setting: Seven years after *Return of the Jedi*

In order to assure the continuation of the Jedi Knights, Luke Skywalker has decided to start a training facility: a Jedi Academy. He will gather Force-sensitive students who show potential as prospective Jedi and serve as their mentor, as Jedi Masters Obi-Wan Kenobi and Yoda did for him. Han and Leia's twins are now toddlers, and there is a third Jedi child: the infant Anakin, named after Luke and Leia's father. In this trilogy, we discover the existence of a powerful Imperial doomsday weapon, the horrifying Sun Crusher—which will soon become the centerpiece of a titanic struggle between Luke Skywalker and his most brilliant Jedi Academy student, who is delving dangerously into the dark side.

CHILDREN OF THE JEDI
by Barbara Hambly
Setting: Eight years after *Return of the Jedi*

The Star Wars *characters face a menace from the glory days of the Empire when a thirty-year-old automated Imperial Dreadnaught comes to life and begins its grim mission: to gather forces and annihilate a long-forgotten stronghold of Jedi children. When Luke is whisked onboard, he begins to communicate with the brave Jedi Knight who paralyzed the ship decades ago, and gave her life in the process. Now she is part of the vessel, existing in its artificial intelligence core, and guiding Luke through one of the most unusual adventures he has ever had.*

In this scene, Luke discovers that an evil presence is gathering, one that will force him to join the battle:

Like See-Threepio, Nichos Marr sat in the outer room of the suite to which Cray had been assigned, in the power-down mode that was the droid equivalent of rest. Like Threepio, at the sound of Luke's almost noiseless tread he turned his head, aware of his presence.

"Luke?" Cray had equipped him with the most sensitive vocal modulators, and the word was calibrated to a whisper no louder than the rustle of the blueleaves massed outside the windows. He rose, and crossed to where Luke stood, the dull silver of his arms and shoulders a phantom gleam in the stray flickers of light. "What is it?"

"I don't know." They retreated to the small dining area where Luke had earlier probed his mind, and Luke stretched up to pin back a corner of the lamp-sheath, letting a slim triangle of butter-colored light fall on the purple of the vulwood tabletop. "A dream. A premonition, maybe." It was on his lips to ask, *Do you dream?* but he remembered the ghastly, imageless darkness in Nichos's mind, and didn't. He wasn't sure if his pupil was aware of the difference from his human perception and knowledge, aware of just exactly what he'd lost when his consciousness, his self, had been transferred.

In the morning Luke excused himself from the expedition Tomla El had organized with Nichos and Cray to the Falls of Dessiar, one of the places on Ithor most renowned for its beauty and peace. When they left he sought out Umwaw Moolis, and the tall herd leader listened gravely to his less than logical request and promised to put matters in train to fulfill it. Then Luke descended to the House of the Healers, where Drub McKumb lay, sedated far beyond pain but with all the perceptions of agony and nightmare still howling in his mind.

"Kill you!" He heaved himself at the restraints, blue eyes glaring furiously as he groped and scrabbled at Luke with his clawed hands. "It's all poison! I see you! I see the dark light all around you! You're him! You're him!" His back bent like a bow; the sound of his shrieking was like something being ground out of him by an infernal mangle.

Luke had been through the darkest places of the universe and of his own mind, had done and experienced greater evil than perhaps any man had known on the road the Force had dragged him . . . Still, it was hard not to turn away.

"We even tried yarrock on him last night," explained the Healer in charge, a slightly built Ithorian beautifully tabby-striped green and yellow under her simple tabard of purple linen. "But apparently the earlier doses that brought him enough lucidity to reach here from his point of origin oversensitized his system. We'll try again in four or five days."

Luke gazed down into the contorted, grimacing face.

"As you can see," the Healer said, "the internal perception of pain and fear is slowly lessening. It's down to ninety-three percent of what it was when he was first brought in. Not much, I know, but something."

"Him! *Him! HIM!*" Foam spattered the old man's stained gray beard.

Who?

"I wouldn't advise attempting any kind of mindlink until it's at least down to fifty percent, Master Skywalker."

"No," said Luke softly.

Kill you all. And, *They are gathering* . . .

"Do you have recordings of everything he's said?"

"Oh, yes." The big coppery eyes blinked assent. "The transcript is available through the monitor cubicle down the hall. We could make nothing of them. Perhaps they will mean something to you."

They didn't. Luke listened to them all, the incoherent groans and screams, the chewed fragments of words that could be only guessed at, and now and again the clear disjointed cries: "Solo! Solo! Can you hear me? Children . . . Evil . . . Gathering here . . . Kill you all!"

DARKSABER by Kevin J. Anderson
Setting: Immediately thereafter

Not long after Children of the Jedi, *Luke and Han learn that evil Hutts are building a reconstruction of the original Death Star—and that the Empire is still alive, in the form of Daala, who has joined forces with Pellaeon, former second in command to the feared Grand Admiral Thrawn. In this early scene, Luke has returned to the home of Obi-Wan Kenobi on Tatooine to try and consult a long-gone mentor:*

He stood anxious and alone, feeling like a prodigal son outside the ramshackle, collapsed hut that had once been the home of Obi-Wan Kenobi.

Luke swallowed and stepped forward, his footsteps crunching in the silence. He had not been here in many years. The door had fallen off its hinges; part of the clay front wall had fallen in. Boulders and crumbled adobe jammed the entrance. A pair of small, screeching desert rodents snapped at him and fled for cover; Luke ignored them.

Gingerly, he ducked low and stepped into the home of his first mentor.

Luke stood in the middle of the room breathing deeply, turning around, trying to sense the presence he desperately needed to see. This was the place where Obi-Wan Kenobi had told Luke of the Force. Here, the old man had first given Luke his lightsaber and hinted at the truth about his father, "from a certain point of view," dispelling the diversionary story that Uncle Owen had told, at the same time planting seeds of his own deceptions.

"Ben," he said and closed his eyes, calling out with his mind as well as his voice. He tried to penetrate the invisible walls of the Force and reach to the luminous being of Obi-Wan Kenobi who had visited him numerous times, before saying he could never speak with Luke again.

"Ben, I need you," Luke said. Circumstances had changed. He could think of no other way past the obstacles he faced. Obi-Wan had to answer. It wouldn't take long, but it could give him the key he needed with all his heart.

Luke paused and listened and sensed—

But felt nothing. If he could not summon Obi-Wan's spirit here in the empty dwelling where the old man had lived in exile for so many years, Luke didn't believe he could find his former teacher ever again.

He echoed the words Leia had used more than a decade earlier, beseeching him, "Help me, Obi-Wan Kenobi," Luke whispered, "you're my only hope."

THE CRYSTAL STAR
by Vonda N. McIntyre
Setting: Ten years after *Return of the Jedi*

Leia's three children have been kidnapped. That horrible fact is made worse by Leia's realization that she can no longer sense her children through the Force! While she, Artoo-Detoo, and Chewbacca trail the kidnappers, Luke and Han discover a planet that is suffering strange quantum effects from a nearby star. Slowly freezing into a perfect crystal and disrupting the Force, the star is blunting Luke's power and crippling the Millennium Falcon. *These strands converge in an apocalyptic threat not only to the fate of the New Republic, but to the universe itself.*

The Black Fleet Crisis
BEFORE THE STORM
SHIELD OF LIES
TYRANT'S TEST
by Michael P. Kube-McDowell
Setting: Twelve years after *Return of the Jedi*

Long after setting up the hard-won New Republic, yesterday's Rebels have become today's administrators and diplomats. But the peace is not to last for long. A restless Luke must journey to his mother's homeworld in a desperate quest to find her people; Lando seizes a mysterious spacecraft with unimaginable weapons of destruction; and waiting in the wings is an horrific battle fleet under the control of a ruthless leader bent on a genocidal war.

Here is an opening scene from Before the Storm:

In the pristine silence of space, the Fifth Battle Group of the New Republic Defense Fleet blossomed over the planet Bessimir like a beautiful, deadly flower.

The formation of capital ships sprang into view with startling suddenness, trailing fire-white wakes of twisted space and bristling with weapons. Angular Star Destroyers guarded fat-hulled fleet carriers, while the assault cruisers, their mirror finishes gleaming, took the point.

A halo of smaller ships appeared at the same time. The fighters among them quickly deployed in a spherical defensive screen. As the Star Destroyers firmed up their formation, their flight decks quickly spawned scores of additional fighters.

At the same time, the carriers and cruisers began to disgorge the bombers, transports, and gunboats they had ferried to the battle. There was no reason to risk the loss of one fully loaded—a lesson the Republic had learned in pain. At Orinda, the commander of the fleet carrier *Endurance* had kept his pilots waiting in the launch bays, to protect the smaller craft from Imperial fire as long as possible. They were still there when *Endurance* took the brunt of a Super Star Destroyer attack and vanished in a ball of metal fire.

Before long more than two hundred warships, large and small, were bearing down on Bessimir and its twin moons. But the terrible, restless power of the armada could be heard and felt only by the ships' crews. The silence of the approach was broken only on the fleet comm channels, which had crackled to life in the first moments with encoded bursts of noise and cryptic ship-to-ship chatter.

At the center of the formation of great vessels was the flagship of the Fifth Battle Group, the fleet carrier *Intrepid*. She was so new from the yards at Hakassi that her corridors still reeked of sealing compound and cleaning solvent. Her huge realspace thruster engines still sang with the high-pitched squeal that the engine crews called "the baby's cry."

It would take more than a year for the mingled scents of the crew to displace the chemical smells from the first impressions of visitors. But after a hundred more hours under way, her engines' vibrations would drop two octaves, to the reassuring thrum of a seasoned thruster bank.

On *Intrepid*'s bridge, a tall Dornean in general's uniform paced along an arc of command stations equipped with large monitors. His eye-folds were swollen and fanned by an unconscious Dornean defensive reflex, and his leathery face was flushed purple by concern. Before the deployment was even a minute old, Etahn A'baht's first command had been bloodied.

The fleet tender *Ahazi* had overshot its jump, coming out of hyperspace too close to Bessimir and too late for its crew to recover from the error. Etahn A'baht watched the bright flare of light in the upper atmosphere from *Intrepid*'s forward viewstation, knowing that it meant six young men were dead.

THE NEW REBELLION
by Kristine Kathryn Rusch
Setting: Thirteen years after *Return of the Jedi*

Victorious though the New Republic may be, there is still no end to the threats to its continuing existence—this novel explores the price of keeping the peace. First, somewhere in the galaxy, millions suddenly perish in a blinding instant of pain. Then, as Leia prepares to address the Senate on Coruscant, a horrifying event changes the governmental equation in a flash.

Here is that latter calamity, in an early scene from The New Rebellion:

An explosion rocked the Chamber, flinging Leia into the air. She flew backward and slammed onto a desk, her entire body shuddering with the power of her hit. Blood and shrapnel rained around her. Smoke and dust rose, filling the room with a grainy darkness. She could hear nothing. With a shaking hand, she touched the side of her face. Warmth stained her cheeks and her earlobes. The ringing would start soon. The explosion was loud enough to affect her eardrums.

Emergency glow panels seared the gloom. She could feel rather than hear pieces of the crystal ceiling fall to the ground. A guard had landed beside her, his head tilted at an unnatural angle. She grabbed his blaster. She had to get out. She wasn't certain if the attack had come from within or from without. Wherever it had come from, she had to make certain no other bombs would go off.

The force of the explosion had affected her balance. She crawled over bodies, some still moving, as she made her way to the stairs. The slightest movement made her dizzy and nauseous, but she ignored the feelings. She had to.

A face loomed before hers. Streaked with dirt and blood, helmet askew, she recognized him as one of the guards who had been with her since Alderaan. *Your Highness*, he mouthed, and she couldn't read the rest. She shook her head at him, gasping at the increased dizziness, and kept going.

Finally she reached the stairs. She used the remains of a desk to get to her feet. Her gown was soaked in blood, sticky, and clinging to her legs. She held the blaster in front of her, wishing that she could hear. If she could hear, she could defend herself.

A hand reached out of the rubble beside her. She whirled, faced it, watched as Meido pulled himself out. His slender features were covered with dirt, but he appeared unharmed. He saw her blaster and cringed. She nodded once to acknowledge him, and kept moving. The guard was flanking her.

More rubble dropped from the ceiling. She crouched, hands over her head to protect herself. Small pebbles pelted her, and the floor shivered as large chunks of tile fell. Dust rose, choking her. She coughed, feeling it, but not able to hear it. Within an instant, the Hall had gone from a place of ceremonial comfort to a place of death.

The image of the death's-head mask rose in front of her again, this time from memory. She had known this was going to happen. Somewhere, from some part of her Force-sensitive brain, she had seen this. Luke said that Jedi were sometimes able to see the future. But she had never completed her training. She wasn't a Jedi.

But she was close enough.

The Corellian Trilogy:
AMBUSH AT CORELLIA
ASSAULT AT SELONIA
SHOWDOWN AT CENTERPOINT
by Roger MacBride Allen
Setting: Fourteen years after *Return of the Jedi*

This trilogy takes us to Corellia, Han Solo's homeworld, which Han has not visited in quite some time. A trade summit brings Han, Leia, and the children—now developing their own clear personalities and instinctively learning more about their innate skills in the Force—into the middle of a situation that most closely resembles a burning fuse. The Corellian system is on the brink of civil war, there are New Republic intelligence agents on a mysterious mission which even Han does not understand, and worst of all, a fanatical rebel leader has his hands on a superweapon of unimaginable power—and just wait until you find out who that leader is!

Here is an early scene from Ambush *that gives you a wonderful look at the growing Solo children (the twins are Jacen and Jaina, and their little brother is Anakin):*

Anakin plugged the board into the innards of the droid and pressed a button. The droid's black, boxy body shuddered awake, it drew in its wheels to stand up a bit taller, its status lights lit, and it made a sort of triple beep. "That's good," he said, and pushed the button again. The droid's status lights went out, and its body slumped down again. Anakin picked up the next piece, a motivation actuator. He frowned at it as he turned it over in his hands. He shook his head. "That's *not* good," he announced.

"What's not good?" Jaina asked.

"This thing," Anakin said, handing her the actuator. "Can't you *tell*? The insides part is all melty."

Jaina and Jacen exchanged a look. "The outside looks okay," Jaina said, giving the part to her brother. "How can he tell what the *inside* of it looks like? It's sealed shut when they make it."

Anakin, still sitting on the floor, took the device from his brother and frowned at it again. He turned it over and over in his hands, and then held it over his head and looked at it as if he were holding it up to the light. "There," he said, pointing a chubby finger at one point on the unmarked surface. "In there is the bad part." He rearranged himself to sit cross-legged, put the actuator in his lap, and put his right index finger over the "bad" part. "Fix," he said. "Fix." The dark brown outer case of the actuator seemed to glow for a second with an odd blue-red light, but then the glow sputtered out and Anakin pulled his finger away quickly and stuck it in his mouth, as if he had burned it on something.

"Better now?" Jaina asked.

"*Some* better," Anakin said, pulling his finger out of his mouth. "Not *all* better." He took the actuator in his hand and stood up. He opened the access panel on the broken droid and plugged in the actuator. He closed the door and looked expectantly at his older brother and sister.

"Done?" Jaina asked.

"Done," Anakin agreed. "But *I'm* not going to push the button." He backed well away from the droid, sat down on the floor, and folded his arms.

Jacen looked at his sister.

"Not me," she said. "This was your idea."

Jacen stepped forward to the droid, reached out to push the power button from as far away as he could, and then stepped hurriedly back.

Once again, the droid shuddered awake, rattling a bit this time as it did so. It pulled its wheels in, lit its panel lights, and made the same triple beep. But then its holocam eye viewlens wobbled back and forth, and its panel lights dimmed and flared. It rolled backward just a bit, and then recovered itself.

"Good morning, young mistress and masters," it said. "How may I surge you?"

Well, one word wrong, but so what? Jacen grinned and clapped his hands and rubbed them together eagerly. "Good day, droid," he said. They had done it! But what to ask for first? "First tidy up this room," he said. A simple task, and one that ought to serve as a good test of what this droid could do.

Suddenly the droid's overhead access door blew off and there was a flash of light from its interior. A thin plume of smoke drifted out of the droid. Its panel lights flared again, and then the work arm sagged downward. The droid's body, softened by heat, sagged in on itself and drooped to the floor. The floor and walls and ceiling of the playroom were supposed to be fireproof, but nonetheless the floor under the droid darkened a bit, and the ceiling turned black. The ventilators kicked on high automatically, and drew the smoke out of the room. After a moment they shut themselves off, and the room was silent.

The three children stood, every bit as frozen to the spot as the droid was, absolutely stunned. It was Anakin who recovered first. He walked cautiously toward the droid and looked at it carefully, being sure not to get too close or touch it. "*Really* melty now," he announced, and then wandered off to the other side of the room to play with his blocks.

The twins looked at the droid, and then at each other.

"We're dead," Jacen announced, surveying the wreckage.

STAR WARS®

THE FORCE IS WITH YOU

whenever you open a *Star Wars* novel from Bantam Spectra Books!

The dazzling original trilogy written by Timothy Zahn

___29612-4	HEIR TO THE EMPIRE	$5.99/$6.99 Canada
___56071-9	DARK FORCE RISING	$5.99/$6.99
___56492-7	THE LAST COMMAND	$5.99/$6.99

The New York Times *bestselling Jedi Academy trilogy by Kevin J. Anderson*

___29798-8	JEDI SEARCH	$5.99/$6.99
___29799-6	DARK APPRENTICE	$5.99/$7.50
___29802-X	CHAMPIONS OF THE FORCE	$5.99/$7.99

The bestselling Corellian trilogy by Roger MacBride Allen

___29803-8	AMBUSH AT CORELLIA	$5.99/$7.99
___29805-4	ASSAULT AT SELONIA	$5.99/$7.99
___29806-2	SHOWDOWN AT CENTERPOINT	$5.99/$7.99

The breathtaking X-wing series by Michael A. Stackpole

___56801-9	ROGUE SQUADRON	$5.99/$7.99
___56802-7	WEDGE'S GAMBLE	$5.99/$7.99
___56803-5	THE KRYTOS TRAP	$5.99/$7.99
___56804-3	THE BACTA WAR	$5.99/$7.99

The thrilling Black Fleet Crisis trilogy by Michael P. Kube-McDowell

___57273-3	BEFORE THE STORM	$5.99/$7.99
___57277-6	SHIELD OF LIES	$5.99/$7.99
___57275-X	TYRANT'S TEST	$5.99/$7.99

Please send me the books I have checked above. I am enclosing $____ (add $2.50 to cover postage and handling). Send check or money order, no cash or C.O.D.'s, please.

Name _____

Address _____

City/State/Zip _____

Send order to: Bantam Books, Dept. SF 11, 2451 S. Wolf Rd., Des Plaines, IL 60018.
Allow four to six weeks for delivery.

Prices and availability subject to change without notice.   SF 11 4/97

®, ™, and © 1997 Lucasfilm Ltd. All rights reserved. Used under authorization.

STAR WARS®

THE FORCE IS WITH YOU

whenever you open a *Star Wars* novel from Bantam Spectra Books!

The latest hardcover Star Wars *adventure:*

___10093-9 THE NEW REBELLION
Kristine Kathryn Rusch $22.95/$27.95

The action-packed paperback collection

___56872-8 THE TRUCE AT BAKURA, Kathy Tyers $5.99/$7.50
___56937-6 THE COURTSHIP OF PRINCESS LEIA
Dave Wolverton $5.99/$7.50
___57174-5 THE CRYSTAL STAR, Vonda N. McIntyre $5.99/$7.99
___57293-8 CHILDREN OF THE JEDI, Barbara Hambly $5.99/$7.99
___57611-9 DARKSABER, Kevin J. Anderson $5.99/$7.99
___57413-2 SHADOWS OF THE EMPIRE, Steve Perry $5.99/$7.99

The first original Star Wars *anthologies,*
edited by Kevin J. Anderson

___56468-4 TALES FROM THE MOS EISLEY CANTINA $5.99/$7.99
___56815-9 TALES FROM JABBA'S PALACE $5.99/$7.99
___56816-7 TALES OF THE BOUNTY HUNTERS $5.99/$7.99

And the lavish gift book, with illustrations by
Ralph McQuarrie and text by Kevin J. Anderson

___09302-9 THE ILLUSTRATED STAR WARS UNIVERSE $35.00/$50.00

Look for all of these exciting Star Wars *novels, now available wherever*
Bantam Spectra Books are sold, or use this page for ordering.

Please send me the books I have checked above. I am enclosing $_____ (add $2.50 to cover postage and handling). Send check or money order, no cash or C.O.D.'s, please.

Name _____

Address _____

City/State/Zip _____

Send order to: Bantam Books, Dept. SF 11, 2451 S. Wolf Rd., Des Plaines, IL 60018.
Allow four to six weeks for delivery.

Prices and availability subject to change without notice.   SF 11 4/97

®, ™, and © 1997 Lucasfilm Ltd. All rights reserved. Used under authorization.